LEABHARLANN CHONTAE ROSCOMAIN

C C

This book should be returned not later than the last date shown below. It may be renewed if not requested by another borrower.

Books are on loan for 14 days from the date of issue.

DATE DUE	DATE DUE	DATE DUE	DATE DUE
27. APR 05.	29. NOV 06.		
01. JUN 05.	24. APR 08.		
17. JUL 05	12. NOV 09.		
13 OCT	17. JUN 10.		
26. AUG 05.			
12. NOV.			

SRH

5

The Pride of Palomar

OTHER SAGEBRUSH LARGE PRINT WESTERNS BY
PETER B. KYNE

The Enchanted Hill
The Valley of the Giants

The Pride of Palomar

PETER B. KYNE

Sagebrush
Large Print Westerns

Published in Large Print 2004 by ISIS Publishing Ltd,
7 Centremead, Osney Mead,
Oxford OX2 0ES, United Kingdom
by arrangement with
Golden West Literary Agency

The moral right of the author has been asserted

British Library Cataloguing in Publication Data
Kyne, Peter B.
The pride of Palomar. – Large print ed. –
(Sagebrush western series)
1. Western stories
2. Large type books
I. Title
813.5′2 [F]

ISBN 0–7531–7111–2 (hb)

Printed and bound by
Antony Rowe, Chippenham, United Kingdom

DEDICATION

FRANK L. MULGREW, ESQ.
 THE BOHEMIAN CLUB
  SAN FRANCISCO, CALIFORNIA

DEAR FRIEND MUL.—

I have at last finished writing *"The Pride of Palomar."* It isn't at all what I wanted it to be; it isn't at all what I planned it to be, but it does contain something of what you and I both feel, something of what you wanted me to put into it. Indeed, I shall always wish to think that it contains just a few faint little echoes of the spirit of that old California that was fast vanishing when I first disturbed the quiet of the Mission Dolores with infantile shrieks—when you first gazed upon the redwood-studded hills of Sonoma County.

You adventured with me in my quest for local color for "The Valley of the Giants," in Northern California; you performed a similar service in Southern California last summer and unearthed for me more local color, more touches of tender sentiment than I could use. Therefore, "The Pride of Palomar" is peculiarly your book.

On a day a year ago, when the story was still so vague I could scarcely find words in which to sketch for you an outline of the novel I purposed writing, you said: "It will be a good story. I'm sold on it already!" To you the *hacienda* of a Rancho Palomar will always bring delightful recollections of the gracious hospitality of Señor Cave Coutts, sitting at the head of that table hewed in the forties. Little did Señor Coutts realize that he, the last of the dons in San Diego County, was to furnish copy for my novel; that his pride of ancestry, both American and Castilian, his love for his ancestral *hacienda* at the Rancho Guajome, and his old-fashioned garden with the great Bougainvillea in flower, were the ingredients necessary to the production of what I trust will be a book with a mission.

When we call again at the Moreno *hacienda* on the Rio San Luis Rey, Carolina will not be there to metamorphose her home into a restaurant and serve us *gallina con arroz, tortillas* and *frijoles refritos.* But if she should be, she will not answer, when asked the amount of the score: "What you will, *señor*" Ah, no, Mul. Scoundrels devoid of romance will have discovered her, and she will have opened an inn with a Jap cook and the tariff will be *dos pesos y media;* there will be a strange waiter and he will scowl at us and expect a large tip. And Stephen Crane's brother, the genial judge, will have made his fortune in the mine on the hill, and there will be no more California wine as a first aid to digestion.

I had intended to paint the picture that will remain longest in your memory—the dim candlelight in the whitewashed chapel at the Indian Reservation at Pala, during Benediction of the Blessed Sacrament—the young Indian Madonna, with her naked baby lying in her lap, while she sang:

> "Come, Holy Ghost, creator blest,
> And in my heart take up thy rest."

But the picture was crowded out in the makeup. There was too much to write about, and I was always overset!

I saw and felt, with you, and regarded it as more poignantly pathetic, the tragedy of that little handful of San Luisanos, herded away in the heart of those barren hills to make way for the white man. And now the white man is almost gone and Father Dominic's Angelus, ringing from Mission San Luis Rey, falls upon the dull ear of a Japanese farmer, usurping that sweet valley, hallowed by sentiment, by historical association, by the lives and loves and ashes of the men and women who carved California from the wilderness.

I have given to this book the labor of love. I know it isn't literature, Mul, but I have joyed in writing it and it has, at least, the merit of sincerity. It is an expression of faith and for all its faults and imperfections, I think you will find, tucked away in it somewhere, a modicum of merit. I have tried to limn something, however vague, of the beauty of the land we saw through boyish eyes before the real estate agent had profaned it.

You were born with a great love, a great reverence for beauty. That must be because you were born in Sonoma County in the light of God's smile. Each spring in California the dogwood blossoms are, for you, a creamier white, the buckeye blossoms more numerous and fragrant, the hills a trifle greener and the old order, the old places, the old friends a little dearer.

Wherefore, with much appreciation of your aid in its creation and of your unfaltering friendship and affection, I dedicate "The Pride of Palomar" to you.

Faithfully,
PETER B. KYNE
SAN FRANCISCO
JUNE 9, 1921.

Acknowledgment is made of the indebtedness of the author for much of the material used in this book to Mr. Montaville Flowers, author of "The Japanese Conquest of American Opinion."

P. B. K.

The Pride of Palomar

I

FOR THE FIRST TIME IN SIXTY YEARS, Pablo Artelan, the majordomo of the Rancho Palomar, was troubled of soul at the approach of winter. Old Don Miguel Farrel had observed signs of mental travail in Pablo for a month past, and was at a loss to account for them. He knew Pablo possessed one extra pair of overalls, brand-new, two pairs of boots which young Don Miguel had bequeathed him when the Great White Father at Washington had summoned the boy to the war in April of 1917, three chambray shirts in an excellent state of repair, half of a fat steer jerked, a full bag of Bayo beans, and a string of red chili peppers pendant from the rafters of an adobe shack which Pablo and his wife, Carolina, occupied rent free. Certainly (thought old Don Miguel) life could hold no problems for one of Pablo's race thus pleasantly situated.

Coming upon Pablo this morning, as the latter sat in his favorite seat under the catalpa tree just outside the wall of the ancient adobe compound, where he could command a view of the white wagon road winding down the valley of the San Gregorio, Don Miguel decided to question his ancient retainer.

"My good Pablo," he queried, "what has come over, thee of late? Thou art of a mien as sorrowful as that of a sick steer. Can it be that thy stomach refuses longer to digest thy food? Come; permit me to examine thy teeth. Yes, by my soul; therein lies the secret. Thou hast a toothache and decline to complain, thinking that, by thy silence, I shall be saved a dentist's bill." But Pablo shook his head in negation "Come!" roared old Don

1

Miguel. "Open thy mouth!"

Pablo rose creakily and opened a mouth in which not a tooth was missing. Old Don Miguel made a most minute examination, but failed to discover the slightest evidence of deterioration.

"Blood of the devil!" he cried, disgusted beyond measure. "Out with thy secret! It has annoyed me for a month."

"The ache is not in my teeth, Don Miguel. It is here." And Pablo laid a swarthy hand upon his torso. "There is a sadness in my heart, Don Miguel. Two years has Don Mike been with the soldiers. Is it not time that he returned to us?"

Don Miguel's aristocratic old face softened.

"So that is what disturbs thee, my Pablo?"

Pablo nodded miserably, seated himself, and resumed his task of fashioning the hondo of a new rawhide riata.

"It is a very dry year," he complained. "Never before have I seen December arrive ere the grass in the San Gregorio was green with the October rains. Everything is burned; the streams and the springs have dried up, and for a month I have listened to hear the quail call on the hillside yonder. But I listen in vain. The quail have moved to another range."

"Well, what of it, Pablo?"

"How our beloved Don Mike enjoyed the quail shooting in the fall! Should he return now to the Palomar, there will be no quail to shoot." He wagged his gray head sorrowfully. "Don Mike will think that, with the years, laziness and ingratitude have descended upon old Pablo. Truly, Satan afflicts me." And he cursed with great depth of feeling—in English.

"Yes, poor boy," old Don Miguel agreed; "he will miss more than the quail shooting when he returns—if

2

he should return. They sent him to Siberia to fight the Bolsheviki."

"What sort of country is this where Don Mike slays our enemy?" Pablo queried.

"It is always winter there, Pablo. It is inhabited by a wild race of men with much whiskers."

"Ah, our poor Don Mike! And he a child of the sun!"

"He but does his duty," old Don Miguel replied proudly. "He adds to the fame of an illustrious family, noted throughout the centuries for the gallantry of its warriors."

"A small comfort, Don Miguel, if our Don Mike comes not again to those that love him."

"Pray for him," the old Don suggested piously.

Fell a silence. Then,

"Don Miguel, yonder comes one over the trail from El Toro."

Don Miguel gazed across the valley to the crest of the hills. There, against the skyline, a solitary horseman showed. Pablo cupped his hands over his eyes and gazed long and steadily.

"It is Tony Moreno," he said, while the man was still a mile distant. "I know that scuffling cripple of a horse he rides."

Don Miguel seated himself on the bench beside Pablo and awaited the arrival of the horseman. As he drew nearer, the Don saw that Pablo was right.

"Now, what news does that vagabond bear?" he muttered. "Assuredly he brings a telegram; otherwise the devil himself could not induce that lazy wastrel to ride twenty miles."

"Of a truth you are right, Don Miguel. Tony Moreno is the only man in El Toro who is forever out of a job, and the agent of the telegraph company calls upon him always to deliver messages of importance."

With the Don, he awaited, with vague apprehension, the arrival of Tony Moreno. As the latter pulled his sweating horse up before them, they rose and gazed upon him questioningly. Tony Moreno, on his part, doffed his shabby sombrero with his right hand and murmured courteously,

"*Buenas tardes,* Don Miguel."

Pablo he ignored. With his left hand, he caught a yellow envelope as it fell from under the hat.

"Goodafternoon, Moreno." Don Miguel returned his salutation with a gravity he felt incumbent upon one of his station to assume when addressing a social inferior. "You bring me a telegram?" He spoke in English, for the sole purpose of indicating to the messenger that the gulf between them could not be spanned by the bridge of their mother tongue. He suspected Tony Moreno very strongly of having stolen a yearling from him many years ago.

Tony Moreno remembered his manners, and dismounted before handing Don Miguel the telegram.

"The delivery charges?" Don Miguel queried courteously.

"Nothing, Don Miguel." Moreno's voice was strangely subdued. "It is a pleasure to serve you, *señor.*"

"You are very kind." And Don Miguel thrust the telegram, unopened, into his pocket. "However," he continued, "it will please me, Moreno, if you accept this slight token of my appreciation." And he handed the messenger a five dollar bill. The don was a proud man, and disliked being under obligation to the Tony Morenos of this world. Tony protested, but the don stood his ground, silently insistent, and, in the end, the other pouched the bill, and rode away. Don Miguel

4

seated himself once more beside his retainer and drew forth the telegram.

"It must be evil news," he murmured, with the shade of a tremor in his musical voice; "otherwise, that fellow could not have felt so much pity for me that it moved him to decline a gratuity."

"Read, Don Miguel!" Pablo croaked. "Read!"

Don Miguel read. Then he carefully folded the telegram and replaced it in the envelope; as deliberately, he returned the envelope to his pocket. Suddenly his hands gripped the bench, and he trembled violently.

"Don Mike is dead?" old Pablo queried softly. He possessed all the acute intuition of a primitive people.

Don Miguel did not reply; so presently Pablo turned his head and gazed up into the master's face. Then he knew—his fingers trembled slightly as he returned to work on the hondo, and, for a long time, no sound broke the silence save the song of an oriole in the catalpa tree.

Suddenly, the sound for which old Pablo had waited so long burst forth from the sage-clad hillside. It was a cock quail calling, and, to the majordomo, it seemed to say: "Don Mike! Come home! Don Mike! Come home!"

"Ah, little truant, who has told you that you are safe?" Pablo cried in agony. "For Don Mike shall not come home—no, no—never any more!"

His Indian stoicism broke at last; he clasped his hands and fell to his knees beside the bench, sobbing aloud.

Don Miguel regarded him not, and when Pablo's babbling became incoherent, the aged master of Palomar controlled his twitching hands sufficiently to roll and light a cigarette. Then he reread the telegram.

Yes; it was true. It was from Washington, and signed by the adjutant general; it informed Don Miguel José

Farrel, with regret, that his son, First Sergeant Miguel José Maria Federico Noriaga Farrel, Number 765,438, had been killed in action in Siberia on the fourth instant.

"At least," the old don murmured, "he died like a gentleman. Had he returned to the Rancho Palomar, he could not have continued to live like one. Oh, my son, my son!"

He rose blindly and groped his way along the wall until he came to the inset gate leading into the patio; like a stricken animal retreating to its lair, he sought the privacy of his old-fashioned garden, where none might intrude upon his grief.

II

FIRST SERGEANT MICHAEL JOSEPH FARREL entered the orderly room and saluted his captain, who sat, with his chair tilted back, staring mournfully at the opposite wall.

"I have to report, sir, that I have personally delivered the battery records, correctly sorted, labeled, and securely crated, to the demobilization office. The typewriter, field desk, and stationery have been turned in, and here are the receipts."

The captain tucked the receipts in his blouse pocket.

"Well, Sergeant, I dare say that marks the completion of your duties—all but the last formation." He glanced at his wristwatch. "Fall in the battery and call the roll. By that time, I will have organized my farewell speech to the men. Hope I can deliver it without making a fool of myself."

"Very well, sir."

The first sergeant stepped out of the orderly room and

blew three long blasts on his whistle—his signal to the battery to "fall in." The men came out of the demobilization shacks with alacrity and formed within a minute; without command, they "dressed" to the right and straightened the line. Farrel stepped to the right of it, glanced down the long row of silent, eager men, and commanded,

"Front!"

Nearly two hundred heads described a quarter circle.

Farrel stepped lithely down the long front to the geometrical center of the formation, made a right-face, walked six paces, executed an about-face, and announced complainingly:

"Well, I've barked at you for eighteen months—and finally you made it snappy. On the last day of your service, you manage to fall in within the time limit and dress the line perfectly. I congratulate you." Covert grins greeted his ironical sally. He continued: "I'm going to say good-by to those of you who think there are worse tops in the service than I. To those who did not take kindly to my methods, I have no apologies to offer. I gave everybody a square deal, and for the information of some half dozen Hotspurs who have vowed to give me the beating of my life the day we should be demobilized, I take pleasure in announcing that I will be the first man to be discharged, that there is a nice clear space between these two demobilization shacks and the ground is not too hard, that there will be no guards to interfere, and if any man with the right to call himself 'Mister' desires to air his grievance, he can make his engagement now, and I shall be at his service at the hour stipulated. Does anybody make me an offer?" He stood there, balanced nicely on the balls of his feet, cool, alert, glancing interestedly up and down the battery front. "What?" he bantered, "nobody bids? Well, I'm glad of that. I part friends with everybody. Call rolls!"

The section chiefs called the rolls of their sections and reported them present. Farrel stepped to the door of the orderly room.

"The men are waiting for the captain," he reported.

"Sergeant Farrel," that bedeviled individual replied frantically, "I can't do it. You'll have to do it for me."

"Yes, sir; I understand."

Farrel returned to the battery, brought them to attention, and said:

"The skipper wants to say good-by, men, but he isn't up to the job. He's afraid to tackle it; so he has asked me to wish you light duty, heavy pay, and double rations in civil life. He has asked me to say to you that he loves you all and will not soon forget such soldiers as you have proved yourselves to be."

"Three for the Skipper! Give him three and a tiger!" somebody pleaded, and the cheers were given with a hearty generosity which even the most disgruntled organization can develop on the day of demobilization.

The skipper came to the door of the orderly room.

"Good-by, good luck, and God bless you, lads!" he shouted, and fled with the discharges under his arm, while the battery "counted off," and, in command of Farrel (the lieutenants had already been demobilized), marched to the pay tables. As they emerged from the paymaster's shack, they scattered singly, in little groups, back to the demobilization shacks. Presently, bearing straw suitcases, "tin" helmets, and gas masks (these latter articles presented to them by a paternal government as souvenirs of their service), they drifted out through the Presidio gate, where the world

8

swallowed them.

Although he had been the first man in the battery to receive his discharge, Farrel was the last man to leave the Presidio. He waited until the captain, having distributed the discharges, came out of the pay-office and repaired again to his deserted orderly room; whereupon the former first sergeant followed him.

"I hesitate to obtrude, sir," he announced, as he entered the room, "but whether the captain likes it or not, he'll have to say good-by to me. I have attended to everything I can think of, sir; so, unless the captain has some further use for me, I shall be jogging along."

"Farrel," the captain declared, "if I had ever had a doubt as to why I made you top cutter of B battery, that last remark of yours would have dissipated it. Please do not be in a hurry. Sit down and mourn with me for a little while."

"Well, I'll sit down with you, sir, but I'll be hanged if I'll be mournful. I'm too happy in the knowledge that I'm going home."

"Where is your home, sergeant?"

"In San Marcos County, in the southern part of the state. After two years of Siberia and four days of this San Francisco fog, I'm fed up on low temperatures, and, by the holy poker, I want to go home. It isn't much of a home—just a quaint, old, crumbling adobe ruin, but it's home, and it's mine. Yes, sir; I'm going home and sleep in the bed my great-great-grandfather was born in."

"If I had a bed that old, I'd fumigate it," the captain declared. Like all regular army officers, he was a very devil of a fellow for sanitation. "Do you worship your ancestors, Farrel?"

"Well, come to think of it, I have rather a reverence for 'the ashes of my fathers and the temples of my

9

gods.' "

"So have the Chinese. Among Americans, however, I thought all that sort of thing was confined to the descendants of the Pilgrim Fathers."

"If I had an ancestor who had been a Pilgrim Father," Farrel declared, "I'd locate his grave and build a garbage incinerator on it."

"What's your grouch against the Pilgrim Fathers?"

"They let their religion get on top of them, and they took all the joy out of life. My Catalonian ancestors, on the other hand, while taking their religion seriously, never permitted it to interfere with a *fiesta*. They were what might be called 'regular fellows.' "

"Your Catalonian ancestors? Why, I thought you were black Irish, Farrel?"

"The first of my line that I know anything about was a lieutenant in the force that marched overland from Mexico to California under command of Don Gaspar de Portola. Don Gaspar was accompanied by Fray Junipero Serra. They carried a sword and a cross respectively, and arrived in San Diego on July first, 1769. So, you see, I'm a real Californian."

"You mean Spanish-Californian."

"Well, hardly in the sense that most people use that term, sir. We have never intermarried with Mexican or Indian, and until my grandfather Farrel arrived at the ranch and refused to go away until my grandmother Noriaga went with him, we were purebred Spanish blonds. My grandmother had red hair, brown eyes, and a skin as white as an old bleached-linen napkin. Grandfather Farrel is the fellow to whom I am indebted for my saddle-colored complexion."

"Siberia has bleached you considerably. I should say you're an ordinary brunet now."

10

Farrel removed his overseas cap and ran long fingers through his hair.

"If I had a strain of Indian in me, sir," he explained, "my hair would be straight, thick, coarse, and blue-black. You will observe that it is wavy, a medium crop, of average fineness, and jet black."

The captain laughed at his frankness.

"Very well, Farrel; I'll admit you're clean-strain white. But tell me: How much of you is Latin and how much Farrel?"

It was Farrel's turn to chuckle now.

"Seriously, I cannot answer that question. My grandmother, as I have stated, was purebred Castilian or Catalonian, for I suppose they mixed. The original Michael Joseph Farrel (I am the third of the name) was Tipperary Irish, and could trace his ancestry back to the fairies—to hear him tell it. But one can never be quite certain how much Spanish there is in an Irishman from the west, so I have always started with the premise that the result of that marriage—my father—was three-fifths Latin. Father married a Galvez, who was half Scotch; so I suppose I'm an American."

"I should like to see you on your native heath, Farrel. Does your dad still wear a conical crowned sombrero, bell-shaped trousers, bolero jacket, and all that sort of thing?"

"No, sir. The original Mike insisted upon wearing regular trousers and hats. He had all of the prejudices of his race, and regarded folks who did things differently from him as inferior people. He was a lieutenant on a British sloop of war that was wrecked on the coast of San Marcos County in the early 'Forties. All hands were drowned, with the exception of my grandfather, who was a very contrary man. He swam ashore and strolled

11

up to the hacienda of the Rancho Palomar, arriving just before luncheon. What with a twenty mile hike in the sun, he was dry by the time he arrived, and in his uniform, although somewhat bedraggled, he looked gay enough to make a hit with my great-grandfather Noriaga, who invited him to luncheon and begged him to stay a while. Michael Joseph liked the place; so he stayed. You see, there were thousands of horses on the ranch and, like all sailors, he had equestrian ambitions."

"Great snakes! It must have been a sizable place."

"It was. The original Mexican grant was twenty leagues square."

"I take it, then, that the estate has dwindled in size."

"Oh, yes, certainly. My great-grandfather Noriaga, Michael Joseph I, and Michael Joseph II shot craps with it, and bet it on horse races, and gave it away for wedding doweries, and, in general, did their little best to put the Farrel posterity out in the mesquite with the last of the Mission Indians."

"How much of this principality have you left?"

"I do not know. When I enlisted, we had a hundred thousand acres of the finest valley and rolling grazing land in California and the hacienda that was built in 1782. But I've been gone two years, and haven't heard from home for five months."

"Mortgaged?"

"Of course. The Farrels never worked while money could be raised at ten percent. Neither did the Noriagas. You might as well attempt to yoke an elk and teach him how to haul a cart."

"Oh, nonsense, Farrel! You're the hardest working man I have ever known."

Farrel smiled boyishly.

"That was in Siberia, and I had to hustle to keep

12

warm. But I know I'll not be home six months before that delicious *mañana* spirit will settle over me again, like mildew on old boots."

The captain shook his head.

"Any man who can see so clearly the economic faults of his race and nevertheless sympathize with them is not one to be lulled to the ruin that has overtaken practically all of the old native California families. That strain of Celt and Gael in you will triumph over the easygoing Latin."

"Well, perhaps. And two years in the army has helped tremendously to eradicate an inherited tendency toward procrastination."

"I shall like to think that I had something to do with that," the officer answered. "What are your plans?"

"Well, sir, this hungry world must be fed by the United States for the next ten years, and I have an idea that the Rancho Palomar can pull itself out of the hole with beef cattle. My father has always raised short-legged, longhorned scrubs, descendants of the old Mexican breeds, and there is no money in that sort of stock. If I can induce him to turn the ranch over to me, I'll try to raise sufficient money to buy a couple of car-loads of purebred Hereford bulls and grade up that scrub stock; in four or five years I'll have steers that will weigh eighteen hundred to two thousand pounds on the hoof, instead of the little eight-hundred-pounders that have swindled us for a hundred years."

"How many head of cattle can you run on your ranch?"

"About ten thousand—one to every ten acres. If I could develop water for irrigation in the San Gregorio valley, I could raise alfalfa and lot feed a couple of thousand more."

"What is the ranch worth?"

"About eight per acre is the average price of good cattle range nowadays. With plenty of water for irrigation, the valley land would be worth five hundred dollars an acre. It's as rich as cream, and will grow anything—with water."

"Well, I hope your dad takes a back seat and gives you a free hand, Farrel. I think you'll make good with half a chance."

"I feel that way also," Farrel replied seriously.

"Are you going south tonight?"

"Oh, no. Indeed not! I don't want to go home in the dark, sir." The captain was puzzled. "Because I love my California, and I haven't seen her for two years," Farrel replied, to the other's unspoken query. "It's been so foggy since we landed in San Francisco I've had a hard job making my way round the Presidio. But if I take the eight o'clock train tomorrow morning, I'll run out of the fog belt in forty-five minutes and be in the sunshine for the remainder of the journey. Yes, by Jupiter—and for the remainder of my life!"

"You want to feast your eyes on the countryside, eh?"

"I do. It's April, and I want to see the Salinas valley with its oaks; I want to see the benchlands with the grapevines just budding; I want to see some bald-faced cows clinging to the Santa Barbara hillsides, and I want to meet some fellow on the train who speaks the language of my tribe."

"Farrel, you're all Irish. You're romantic and poetical, and you feel the call of kind to kind. That's distinctly a Celtic trait."

"*Quién sabe?* But I have a great yearning to speak Spanish with somebody. It's my mother tongue."

"There must be another reason," the captain bantered

14

him. "Sure there isn't a girl somewhere along the right of way and you are fearful, if you take the night train, that the porter may fail to waken you in time to wave to her as you go by her station?"

Farrel shook his head.

"There's another reason, but that isn't it. Captain, haven't you been visualizing every little detail of your homecoming?"

"You forget, Farrel, that I'm a regular army man, and we poor devils get accustomed to being uprooted. I've learned not to build castles in Spain, and I never believe I'm going to get a leave until the old man hands me the order. Even then, I'm always fearful of an order recalling it."

"You're missing a lot of happiness, sir. Why, I really believe I've had more fun out of the anticipation of my homecoming than I may get out of the realization. I've planned every detail for months, and, if anything slips, I'm liable to sit right down and bawl like a kid."

"Let's listen to your plan of operations, Farrel," the captain suggested. "I'll never have one myself, in all probability, but I'm child enough to want to listen to yours."

"Well, in the first place, I haven't communicated with my father since landing here. He doesn't know I'm back in California, and I do not want him to know until I drop in on him."

"And your mother, Farrel?"

"Died when I was a little chap. No brothers or sisters. Well, if I had written him or wired him when I first arrived, he would have had a week of the most damnable suspense, because, owing to the uncertainty of the exact date of our demobilization, I could not have informed him of the exact time of my arrival home.

15

Consequently, he'd have had old Carolina, our cook, dishing up nightly fearful quantities of the sort of grub I was raised on. And that would be wasteful. Also, he'd sit under the catalpa tree outside the western wall of the hacienda and never take his eyes off the highway from El Toro or the trail from Sespe. And every night after the sun had set and I'd failed to show up, he'd go to bed heavyhearted. Suspense is hard on an old man, sir."

"On young men, too. Go on."

"Well, I'll drop off the train tomorrow afternoon about four o'clock at a lonely little flag station called Sespe. After the train leaves Sespe, it runs southwest for almost twenty miles to the coast and turns south to El Toro. Nearly everybody enters the San Gregorio from El Toro, but, via the shortcut trail from Sespe, I can hike it home in three hours and arrive absolutely unannounced and unheralded.

"Now, as I pop up over the mile-high ridge back of Sespe, I'll be looking down on the San Gregorio while the last of the sunlight still lingers there. You see, sir, I'm only looking at an old picture I've always loved. Tucked away down in the heart of the valley, there is an old ruin of a mission—the Mission de la Madre Dolorosa—the Mother of Sorrows. The light will be shining on its dirty white walls and red-tiled roof, and I'll sit me down in the shade of a manzanita bush and wait, because that's my valley and I know what's coming.

"Exactly at six o'clock, I shall see a figure come out on the roof of the mission and stand in front of the old gallows frame on which hang eight chimes that were carried in on mules from the City of Mexico when Junipero Serra planted the cross of Catholicism at San Diego, in 1769. That distant figure will be Brother

16

Flavio, of the Franciscan Order, and the old boy is going to ramp up and down in front of those chimes with a hammer and give me a concert. He'll bang out 'Adeste Fideles' and 'Gloria in Excelsis.' That's a cinch, because he's a creature of habit. Occasionally he plays 'Lead, Kindly Light' and 'Ave Maria'!"

Farrel paused, a faint smile of amusement fringing his handsome mouth. He rolled and lighted a cigarette and continued:

"My father wrote me that old Brother Flavio, after a terrible battle with his own conscience and at the risk of being hove out of the valley by his indignant superior, Father Dominic, was practicing 'Hail, The Conquering Hero Comes!' against the day of my homecoming. I wrote father to tell Brother Flavio to cut that out and substitute 'In the Good Old Summertime' if he wanted to make a hit with me. Awfully good old hunks, Brother Flavio! He knows I like those old chimes, and, when I'm home, he most certainly bangs them so the melody will carry clear up to the Palomar."

The captain was gazing with increasing amazement upon his former first sergeant. After eighteen months, he had discovered a man he had not known heretofore.

"And after the 'Angelus'—what?" he demanded.

Farrel's smug little smile of complacency had broadened.

"Well, sir, when Brother Flavio pegs out, I'll get up and run down to the Mission, where Father Dominic, Father Andreas, Brother Flavio, Brother Anthony, and Brother Benedict will all extend a welcome and muss me up, and we'll all talk at once and get nowhere with the conversation for the first five minutes. Brother Anthony is just a little bit—ah—nutty, but harmless. He'll want to know how many men I've killed, and I'll

17

tell him two hundred and nineteen. He has a leaning toward odd numbers, as tending more toward exactitude. Right away, he'll go into the chapel and pray for their souls, and while he's at this pious exercise, Father Dominic will dig up a bottle of old wine that's too good for a nut like Brother Anthony, and we'll sit on a bench in the mission garden in the shade of the largest bougainvillea in the world and tuck away the wine. Between tucks, Father Dominic will inquire casually into the state of my soul, and the information thus elicited will scandalize the old saint. The only way I can square myself is to go into the chapel with them and give thanks for my escape from the Bolsheviki.

"By that time, it will be a quarter of seven and dark, so Father Dominic will crank up a prehistoric little automobile my father gave him in order that he might spread himself over San Marcos County on Sundays and say two masses. I have a notion that the task of keeping that old car in running order has upset Brother Anthony's mental balance. He used to be a blacksmith's helper in El Toro in his youth, and therefore is supposed to be a mechanic in his old age."

"Then the old padre drives you home, eh?" the captain suggested.

"He does. Providentially, it is now the cool of the evening. The San Gregorio is warm enough, for all practical purposes, even on a day in April, and, knowing this, I am grateful to myself for timing my arrival after the heat of the day. Father Dominic is grateful also. The old man wears thin sandals, and on hot days be suffers continuous martyrdom from the heat of that little motor. He is always begging Satan to fly away with that hot-foot accelerator.

"Well, arrived home, I greet my father alone in the

patio, Father Dominic, meanwhile, sits outside in his flivver and permits the motor to roar, just to let my father know he's there, although not for money enough to restore his mission would he butt in on us at that moment.

"Well, my father will not be able to hear a word I say until Padre Dominic shuts off his motor; so my father will yell at him and ask him what the devil he's doing out there and to come in, and be quick about it, or he'll throw his share of the dinner to the hogs. We always dine at seven; so we'll be in time for dinner. But before we go in to dinner, my dad will ring the bell in the compound, and the help will report. Amid loud cries of wonder and delight, I shall be welcomed by a mess of mixed breeds of assorted sexes, and old Pablo, the majordomo, will be ordered to pass out some wine to celebrate my arrival. It's against the law to give wine to an Indian, but then, as my father always remarks on such occasions: 'To hell with the law! They're my Indians, and there are damned few of them left.'

"Padre Dominic, my father, and I will, in all probability, get just a little bit jingled at dinner. After dinner, we'll sit on the porch flanking the patio and smoke cigars, and I'll smell the lemon verbena and heliotrope and other old-fashioned flowers modern gardeners have forgotten how to grow. About midnight, Father Dominic's brain will have cleared, and he will be fit to be trusted with his accursed automobile; so he will snort home in the moonlight, and my father will then carefully lock the patio gate with a nine inch key. Not that anybody ever steals anything in our country, except a cow once in a while—and cows never range in our patio—but just because we're hellbenders for conforming to custom. When I was a boy, Pablo

19

Artelan, our majordomo, always slept athwart that gate, like an old watchdog. I give you my word I've climbed that patio wall a hundred times and dropped down on Pablo's stomach without wakening him. And, for a quarter of a century, to my personal knowledge, that patio gate has supported itself on a hinge and a half. Oh, we're a wonderful institution, we Farrels!"

"What did you say this Pablo was?"

"He used to be a majordomo. That is, he was the foreman of the ranch when we needed a foreman, We haven't needed Pablo for a long time, but it doesn't cost much to keep him on the payroll, except when his relatives come to visit him and stay a couple of weeks."

"And your father feeds them?"

"Certainly. Also, he houses them, It can't be helped. It's an old custom."

"How long has Pablo been a pensioner?"

"From birth. He's mostly Indian, and all the work he ever did never hurt him. But, then, he was never paid very much. He was born on the ranch and has never been more than twenty miles from it. And his wife is our cook. She has relatives, too."

The captain burst out laughing.

"But surely this Pablo has some use," he suggested.

"Well he feeds the dogs, and in order to season his *frijoles* with the salt of honest labor, he saddles my father's horse and leads him round to the house every morning. Throughout the remainder of the day, he sits outside the wall and, by following the sun, he manages to remain in the shade. He watches the road to proclaim the arrival of visitors, smokes cigarettes, and delivers caustic criticisms on the younger generation when he can get anybody to listen to him,"

"How old is your father, Farrel?"

"Seventy-eight."

"And he rides a horse!"

"He does worse than that." Farrel laughed. "He rides a horse that would police you, sir. On his seventieth birthday, at a rodeo, he won first prize for roping and hogtying a steer."

"I'd like to meet that father of yours, Farrel."

"You'd like him. Any time you want to spend a furlough on the Palomar, we'll make you mighty welcome. Better come in the fall for the quail shooting." He glanced at his wristwatch and sighed. "Well. suppose I'd do well to be toddling along. Is the captain going to remain in the service?"

The captain nodded.

"My people are hellbenders on conforming to custom, also," he added. "We've all been field artillery-men."

"I believe I thanked you for a favor you did me once, but to prove I meant what I said, I'm going to send you a horse, sir. He is a chestnut with silver points, five years old, sixteen hands high, sound as a Liberty Bond, and bred in the purple. He is beautifully reined, game, full of ginger, but gentle and sensible. He'll weigh ten hundred in condition, and he's as active as a cat. You can win with him at any horse show and at the head of a battery. *Dios!* He is every inch a *caballero!*"

"Sergeant, you're much too kind. Really—"

"The things we have been through together, sir—all that we have been to each other—never can happen again. You will add greatly to my happiness if you will accept this animal as a souvenir of our very pleasant association."

"Oh, son, this is too much! You're giving me your own private mount. You love him. He loves you. Doubtless he'll know you the minute you enter the

21

pasture."

Farrel's fine white teeth flashed in a brilliant smile.

"I do not desire to have the captain mounted on an inferior horse. We have many other good horses on the Palomar. This one's name is Panchito; I will express him to you some day this week."

"Farrel, you quite overwhelm me. A thousand thanks! I'll treasure Panchito for your sake as well as his own."

The soldier extended his hand, and the captain grasped it.

"Good-by, Sergeant. Pleasant green fields!"

"Good-by, sir. Dry camps and quick promotion."

The descendant of a conquistador picked up his straw suitcase, his helmet, and gas mask. At the door, he stood to attention and saluted. The captain leaped to his feet and returned this salutation of warriors; the door opened and closed, and the officer stood staring at the space so lately occupied by the man who, for eighteen months, had been his right hand.

"Strange man!" he muttered. "I didn't know they bred his kind any more. Why, he's a feudal baron!"

III

THERE WERE THREE PEOPLE in the observation car when Michael Joseph Farrel boarded it a few minutes before eight o'clock the following morning. Of the three, one was a girl, and, as Farrel entered, carrying the souvenirs of his service—a helmet and gas mask—she glanced at him with the interest which the average civilian manifests in any soldier obviously just released from service and homeward bound. Farrel's glance met hers for an instant with equal interest; then he turned to stow

22

his impedimenta in the brass rack over his seat. He was granted an equally swift but more direct appraisal of her as he walked down the observation car to the rear platform, where he selected a chair in a corner that offered him sanctuary from the cold, fog-laden breeze, lighted a cigar, and surrendered himself to contemplating, in his mind's eye, the joys of homecoming.

He had the platform to himself until after the train had passed Palo Alto, when others joined him. The first to emerge on the platform was a Japanese. Farrel favored him with a cool, contemptuous scrutiny, for he was a Californian and did not hold the members of this race in a tithe of the esteem he accorded other Orientals. This Japanese was rather shorter and thinner than the majority of his race. He wore large, round tortoiseshell spectacles, and clothes that proclaimed the attention of the very best tailors; a gold-band ring, set with one blue-white diamond and two exquisite sapphires, adorned the pudgy finger of his right hand. Farrel judged that his gray beaver hat must have cost at least fifty dollars.

"We ought to have Jim Crow cars for these cock-sure sons of Nippon," the ex-soldier growled to himself. "We'll come to it yet if something isn't done about them. They breed so fast they'll have us crowded into back seats in another decade."

He had had some unpleasant clashes with Japanese troops in Siberia, and the memory of their studied insolence was all the more poignant because it had gone unchallenged. He observed, now, that the Japanese passenger had permitted the screen door to slam in the face of the man following him; with a very definite appreciation of the good things of life, he had instantly selected the chair in the corner opposite Farrel, where he

23

could smoke his cigar free from the wind. Following the Japanese came an American, as distinctive of his class as the Japanese was of his. In point of age, this man was about fifty years old—a large man strikingly handsome and of impressive personality. He courteously held the door open to permit the passage of the girl whom Farrel had noticed when he first entered the car.

To Farrel, at least, a surprising incident now occurred. There were eight vacant seats on the platform, and the girl's glance swept them all; he fancied it rested longest upon the chair beside him. Then, with the faintest possible little *moue* of disapproval, she seated herself beside the Japanese. The other man took the seat in front of the girl, half turned, and entered into conversation with the Jap.

Farrel studied the trio with interest, decided that they were traveling together, and that the man in the gray tweeds was the father of the girl. She bore a striking resemblance to him and had inherited his handsome features a thousandfold, albeit her eyes were different, being large, brown, and wide apart; from them beamed a sweetness, a benignancy, and tenderness that, to the impressionable Farrel, bespoke mental as well as physical beauty. She was gowned, gloved, and hatted with rich simplicity.

"I think that white man is from the East," Farrel concluded, although why that impression came to him, he would have been at a loss to explain. Perhaps it was because he appeared to associate on terms of social equality with a Japanese whose boorishness, coupled with an evident desire to agree with everything the white man said, proclaimed him anything but a consular representative or a visiting merchant.

Presently the girl's brown eyes were turned casually

24

in Farrel's direction, seemingly without interest. Instantly he rose, fixed her with a comprehending look, nodded almost imperceptibly toward the chair he was vacating, and returned to his seat inside the car. Her fine brows lifted a trifle; her slight inclination of the head was robbed of the chill of brevity by a fleeting smile of gratitude, not so much for the sacrifice of his seat in her favor as for the fine courtesy which had moved him to proffer it without making of his action an excuse to sit beside her and attempt an acquaintance.

From his exile, Farrel observed with satisfaction how quickly the girl excused herself to her companions and crossed over to the seat vacated in her favor.

At the first call for luncheon, he entered the diner and was given a seat at a small table. The seat opposite him was unoccupied, and when the girl entered the diner alone and was shown to this vacant seat, Farrel thrilled pleasurably.

"Three long, loud ones for you, young lady!" he soliloquized. "You didn't care to eat at the same table with the brown beggar; so you came to luncheon alone."

As their glances met, (here was in Farrel's black eyes no hint of recognition, for he possessed in full measure all of the modesty and timidity of the most modest and timid race, on earth where women are concerned—the Irish—tempered with the exquisite courtesy of that race for whom courtesy and gallantry toward woman are a tradition—the Spanish of that all but extinct Californian caste known as the *gente*.

It pleased Farrel to pretend careful study of the menu. Although his preferences in food were simple, he was extraordinarily hungry and knew exactly what he wanted. For long months he had dreamed of a porterhouse steak smothered in mushrooms, and now,

25

finding that appetizing viand listed on the menu, he ordered it without giving mature deliberation to the possible consequences of his act. For the past two months he had been forced to avoid, when dining alone, meats served in such a manner as to necessitate firm and skilful manipulation of a knife—and when the waiter served his steak, he discovered, to his embarrassment, that it was not particularly tender nor was his knife even reasonably sharp. Consequently, following an unsatisfactory assault, he laid the knife aside and cast an anxious glance toward the kitchen, into which his waiter had disappeared; while awaiting the aid of this functionary, he hid his right hand under the table and gently massaged the back of it at a point where a vivid red scar showed.

He was aware that the girl was watching him, and, with the fascination peculiar to such a situation, he could not forbear a quick glance at her. Interest and concern showed in the brown eyes, and she smiled frankly, as she said:

"I very much fear, Mr. Ex-First Sergeant, that your steak constitutes an order you are unable to execute. Perhaps you will not mind if I carve it for you."

"Please do not bother about me!" he exclaimed. "The waiter will be here presently. You are very kind, but—"

"Oh, I'm quite an expert in the gentle art of mothering military men. I commanded a hotcake and doughnut brigade in France." She reached across the little table and possessed herself of his plate.

"I'll bet my last copeck you had good discipline, too," he declared admiringly. He could imagine the number of daring devils from whose amorous advances even a hot cake queen was not immune.

"The recipe was absurdly simple: No discipline, no

hot cakes. And there were always a sufficient number of good fellows around to squelch anybody who tried to interfere with my efficiency. By the way, I observed how hungrily you were looking out the window this morning. Quite a change from Siberia, isn't it?"

"How did you know I'd soldiered in Siberia?"

"You said you'd bet your last copeck."

"You should have served in Intelligence."

"You are blessed with a fair amount of intuition yourself."

"Oh, I knew you didn't want to sit near that Jap. Can't bear the race myself."

She nodded approvingly.

"Waiter's still out in the kitchen," she reminded him. "Now, old soldier, aren't you glad I took pity on you? Your steak would have been cold before he got round to you, and I imagine you've had sufficient cold rations to do you quite a while."

"It was sweet of you to come to my rescue. I'm not exactly crippled, though I haven't used my hand for more than two months, and the muscles are slightly atrophied. The knife slips because I cannot close my hand tightly. But I'll be all right in another month."

"What happened to it?"

"Saber-thrust. Wouldn't have amounted to much if the Bolshevik who did the thrusting had had a clean saber. Blood poisoning set in, but our battalion surgeon got to work on it in time to save me from being permanently crippled."

" 'Saber-thrust?' They got that close to you?"

He nodded.

"Troop of Semenoff's bandits in a little two-by-four fight out on the trans-Siberian railroad. Guess they wanted the trainload of rations we were guarding. My

27

captain killed the fellow who stuck me and accounted for four others who tried to finish me."

"Captains think a great deal of good first sergeants," she suggested. "And you got a wound-chevron out of it. I suppose, like every soldier, you wanted one, provided it didn't cost too much."

"Oh, yes. And I got mine rather cheap. The battalion surgeon fixed it so I didn't have to go to the hospital. Never missed a day of duty."

She handed him his plate with the steak cut into bits.

"It was nice of you to surrender your cozy seat to me this morning, Sergeant." She buttered a piece of bread for him and added, "But very much nicer the way you did it."

" 'Cast thy bread upon the waters,' " he quoted, and grinned brazenly. "Nevertheless, if I were in civvies, you'd have permitted the waiter to cut my steak."

"Oh, of course we veterans must stand together, Sergeant."

"I find it pleasanter sitting together. By the way, may I ask the identity of the Nipponese person with your father?"

"How do you know he is my father?" she parried.

"I do not know. I merely thought he looked quite worthy of the honor."

"While away with the rough, bad soldiers, you did not forget how to make graceful speeches," she complimented him. "The object of your pardonable curiosity is a Mr. Okada, the potato baron of California. He was formerly prime minister to the potato king of the San Joaquin, but revolted and became a pretender to the throne. While the king lives, however, Okada is merely a baron, although in a few years he will probably control the potato market absolutely."

28

He thumped the table lightly with his maimed hand.

"I knew he was just a coolie dressed up."

She reached for an olive.

"Go as far as you like, native son. He's no friend of mine."

"Well, in that case, I'll spare his life," he countered boldly. "And I've always wanted to kill a Japanese potato baron. Do you not think it would be patriotic of me to immolate myself and reduce the cost of spuds?"

"I never eat them. They're very fattening. Now, if you really wish to be a humanitarian, why not search out the Japanese garlic king?"

"I dare not. His demise would place me in bad odor."

She laughed merrily. Evidently she was finding him amusing company. She looked him over appraisingly and queried bluntly,

"Were you educated abroad?"

"I was not. I'm a product of a one room schoolhouse perched on a bare hill down in San Marcos County."

"But you speak like a college man."

"I am. I'm a graduate of the University of California Agricultural College, at Davis. I'm a sharp on purebred beef cattle, purebred swine, and irrigation. I know why hens decline to lay when eggs are worth eighty cents a dozen, and why young turkeys are so blamed hard to raise in the fall. My grandfather and my father were educated at Trinity College, Dublin, and were sharps on Latin and Greek, but I never figured the dead languages as much of an aid to a man doomed from birth to view cows from the hurricane-deck of a horse."

"But you have such a funny little clipped accent."

He opened his great black eyes in feigned astonishment.

"Oh, didn't you know?" he whispered.

"Know what?"

"Unfortunate young woman!" he murmured to his water glass. "No wonder she sits in public with that pudgy son of a chrysanthemum, when she isn't even able to recognize a greaser at a glance. Oh, Lord!"

"You're not a greaser," she challenged.

"No?" he bantered. "You ought to see me squatting under an avocado tree, singing the 'Spanish Cavalier' to a guitar accompaniment. Listen: I'll prove it without the accompaniment." And he hummed softly:

> "The Spanish cavalier,
> Went out to rope a steer,
> Along with his paper cigar-o,
> *'Car-ramba!'* says he.
> *'Mañana* you will be
> *Mucho bueno carne por mio!'* "

Her brown eyes danced.

"That doesn't prove anything except that you're an incorrigible Celt. When you stooped down to kiss the stone at Blarney Castle, you lost your balance and fell in the well. And you've dripped blarney ever since."

"Oh, not that bad, really! I'm a very serious person ordinarily. That little forget-me-not of language is a heritage of my childhood. Mother taught me to pray in Spanish, and I learned that language first. Later, my grandfather taught me to swear in English with an Irish accent, and I've been fearfully balled up ever since. It's very inconvenient."

"Be serious, soldier, or I shall not cut your meat for you at dinner."

"Excuse me. I forgot I was addressing a hot cake queen. But please do not threaten me, because I'm out

30

of the army just twenty-four hours, and I'm independent and I may resent it. I can order spoon-victuals, you know."

"You aren't really Spanish?"

"Not really. Mostly. I'd fight a wild bull this minute for a single red-chilli pepper. I eat them raw."

"And you're going home to your ranch now?"

"*Si.* And I'll not take advantage of any stopover privileges on the way, either. Remember the fellow in the song who kept on proclaiming that he had to go back— that he must go back—that he would go back—to that dear old Chicago town? Well, that poor exile had only just commenced to think that he ought to begin feeling the urge to go home. And when you consider that the unfortunate man hailed from Chicago, while I—" He blew a kiss out the window and hummed:

"I love you, California.
You're the greatest state of all—"

"Oh dear! You native sons are all alike. Congenital advertisers, every one."

"Well, isn't it beautiful? Isn't it wonderful?" He was serious now.

"One-half of your state is worthless mountain country—"

"He-country—and beautiful!" he interrupted.

"The other half is desert."

"Ever see the Mojave in the late afternoon from the top of the Tejon Pass?" he challenged. "The wild, barbaric beauty of it? And with water it would be a garden spot."

"Of course your valleys are wonderful."

"*Gracias, señorita.*"

31

"But the bare brown hills in summertime—and the ghost rivers of the South! I do not think they are beautiful."

"They grow on one," he assured her earnestly. "You wait and see. I wish you could ride over the hills back of Sespe with me this afternoon, and see the San Gregorio valley in her new spring gown. Ah, how my heart yearns for the San Gregorio!"

To her amazement, she detected a mistiness in his eyes, and her generous heart warmed to him.

"How profoundly happy you are!" she commented.

" 'Happy'? I should tell a man! I'm as happy as a cock valley quail with a large family and no Coyotes in sight. Wow! This steak is good."

"Not very, I think. It's tough."

"I have good teeth."

She permitted him to eat in silence for several minutes, and when he had disposed of the steak, she asked,

"You live in the San Gregorio valley?"

He nodded.

"We have a ranch there also," she volunteered "Father acquired it recently."

"From whom did he acquire it?"

"I do not know the man's name, but the ranch is one of those old Mexican grants. It has a Spanish name. I'll try to remember it." She knitted her delicate brows. "It's Pal-something or other."

"Is it the Palomares grant?" he suggested.

"I think it is. I know the former owner is dead, and my father acquired the ranch by foreclosure of mortgage on the estate."

"Then it's the Palomares grant. My father wrote in his last letter that old man Gonzales had died and that a suit

32

to foreclose the mortgage had been entered against the estate. The eastern edge of that grant laps over the lower end of the San Gregorio. Is your father a banker?"

"He controls the First National Bank of El Toro."

"That settles the identity of the ranch. Gonzales was mortgaged to the First National." He smiled a trifle foolishly. "You gave me a bad ten seconds," he explained. "I thought you meant my father's ranch at first."

"Horrible!" She favored him with a delightful little grimace of sympathy. "Just think of coming home and finding yourself homeless!"

"I think such a condition would make me wish that Russian had been given time to finish what he started. By the way, I knew all of the stockholders in the First National Bank, of El Toro. Your father is a newcomer. He must have bought out old Dan Hayes' interest." She nodded affirmatively. "Am I at liberty to be inquisitive—just a little bit?" he queried.

"That depends, Sergeant. Ask your question, and if I feel at liberty to answer it, I shall."

"Is that Japanese, Okada, a member of your party?"

"Yes; he is traveling with us. He has a land deal on with my father."

"Ah!"

She glanced across at him with new interest.

"There was resentment in that last observation of yours," she challenged.

"In common with all other Californians with manhood enough to resent imposition, I resent all Japanese."

"Is it true, then, that there is a real Japanese problem out here?"

"Why, I thought everybody knew that," he replied, a

33

trifle reproachfully. "As the outpost of Occidental civilization, we've been battling Oriental aggression for forty years."

"I had thought this agitation largely the mouthings of professional agitators—a part of the labor leaders' plan to pose as the watchdogs of the rights of the California laboring man."

"That is sheer buncombe carefully fostered by a very efficient corps of Japanese propagandists. The resentment against the Japanese invasion of California is not confined to any class, but is a very vital issue with every white citizen of the state who has reached the age of reason and regardless of whether he was born in California or Timbuctoo. Look!"

He pointed to a huge signboard fronting a bend in the highway that ran close to the railroad track and parallel with it:

NO MORE JAPS WANTED HERE

"This is entirely an agricultural section," he explained. "There are no labor unions here. But," he added bitterly, "you could throw a stone in the air and be moderately safe on the small end of a bet that the stone would land on a Jap farmer."

"Do the white farmers think that sign will frighten them away?"

"No; of course not. That sign is merely a polite intimation to white men who may contemplate selling or leasing their lands to Japs that the organized sentiment of this community is against such a course. The lower standards of living of the Oriental enable him to pay much higher prices for land than a white man can."

"But," she persisted, "these aliens have a legal right

34

to own and lease land in this state, have they not?"

"Unfortunately, through the treachery of white lawyers, they have devised means to comply with the letter of a law denying them the right to own land, while evading the spirit of that law. Corporations with white dummy directors—purchases by alien Japs in the names of their infants in arms who happen to have been born in this country—" he shrugged.

"Then you should amend your laws."

He looked at her with the faintest hint of cool belligerence in his fine dark eyes.

"Every time we Californians try to enact a law calculated to keep our state a white man's country, you Easterners, who know nothing of our problem, and are too infernally lazy to read up on it, permit yourselves to be stampeded by that hoary shibboleth of strained diplomatic relations with the Mikado's government. Pressure is brought to bear on us from the seat of the national government; the President sends us a message to proceed cautiously, and our loyalty to the sisterhood of states is used as a club to beat our brains out. Once, when we were all primed to settle this issue decisively, the immortal Theodore Roosevelt—our two-fisted, nonbluffable President at that time—made us call off our dogs. Later, when again we began to squirm under our burden, the Secretary of State, pacific William J. Bryan, hurried out to our state capital, held up both pious hands, and cried: 'Oh, no! Really, you mustn't! We insist that you consider the other members of the family. Withhold this radical legislation until we can settle this row amicably.' Well, we were dutiful sons. We tried out the gentleman's agreement imposed on us in 1907, but when, in 1913, we knew it for a failure, we passed our Alien Land Bill, which hampered but did not prevent, although we knew from experience that the class of Japs who have a stranglehold on California are not gentlemen but coolies, and never respect an agreement they can break if, in the breaking, they are financially benefited.'"

"Well," the girl queried, a little subdued by his vehemence, "how has that law worked out?"

"Fine—for the Japs. The Japanese population of California has doubled in five years; the area of fertile lands under their domination has increased a thousand-fold, until eighty-five percent of the vegetables raised in this state are controlled by Japs. They are not a dull people, and they know how to make that control yield rich dividends—at the expense of the white race. That man Okada is called the 'potato baron' because presently he will actually control the potato crop of central California—and that is where most of the potatoes of this state are raised. Which reminds me that I started to ask you a question about him. Do you happen to know if he is contemplating expanding his enterprise to include a section of southern California?"

"I suppose I ought not discuss my father's business affairs with a stranger," she replied, "but since be is making no secret of them, I dare say I do not violate his confidence when I tell you that he has a deal on with Mr. Okada to colonize the San Gregorio valley in San Marcos County."

The look of a thousand devils leaped into Farrel's eyes. The storm of passion that swept him was truly Latin in its terrible intensity. He glared at the girl with a malevolence that terrified her.

"My valley!" he managed to murmur presently. "My beautiful San Gregorio! Japs! Japs!"

"I hadn't the faintest idea that information would

36

upset you so," the girl protested, "Please forgive me."

"I—I come from the San Gregorio," he cried passionately. "I love every rock and cactus and rattlesnake in it. *Válgame Dios!*" And the maimed right hand twisted and clutched as, subconsciously, he strove to clench his fist. "Ah, who was the coward—who was the traitor that betrayed us for a handful of silver?"

"Yes; I believe there *is* a great deal of the Latin about you," she said demurely. "If I had a temper as volcanic as yours, I would never, never go armed."

"I could kill with my naked hands the white man who betrays his community to a Jap. *Madre de Dios,* how I hate them!"

"Well, wait until your trusty right hand is healed before you try garroting anybody," she suggested dryly. "Suppose you cool off, Mr. Pepper-pot, and tell me more about this terrible menace?"

"You are interested—really?"

"I could be made to listen without interrupting you, if you could bring yourself to cease glaring at me with those terrible *chile con carne* eyes. I can almost see myself at my own funeral. Please remember that I have nothing whatsoever to do with my father's business affairs."

"Your father looks like a human being, and if he realized the economic crime he is fostering—"

"Easy, soldier! You're discussing my father, whereas I desire to discuss the Yellow Peril. To begin, are you prejudiced against a citizen of Japan just because he's a Jap?"

"I will be frank. I do not like the race. To a white man, there is nothing lovable about a Jap, nothing that would lead, except in isolated cases, to a warm friendship between members of our race and theirs. And

I dare say the individual Jap has as instinctive a dislike for us as we have for him."

"Well then, how about John Chinaman?"

His face brightened.

"Oh, a Chinaman is different. He's a regular fellow. You can have a great deal of respect and downright admiration for a Chinaman, even of the coolie class."

"Nevertheless, the Chinese are excluded from California."

He nodded.

"But not because of strong racial prejudice. The Chinese, like any other Oriental, are not assimilable; also, like the Jap and the Hindu, they are smart enough to know a good thing when they see it—and California looks good to everybody. John Chinaman would overrun us if we permitted it, but since he is a mighty decent sort and realizes the sanity of our contention that he is not assimilable with us, or we with him, he admits the wisdom and justice of our slogan: 'California for white men.' There was no protest from Peking when we passed the Exclusion Act. Now, however, when we endeavor to exclude Japanese, Tokio throws a fit. But if we can muster enough courage among our state legislators to pass a law that will absolutely divorce the Japanese coolie from California 'and, we can cope with him in other lines of trade."

She had listened earnestly to his argument. delivered with all the earnestness of which he was capable.

"Why is he not assimilable?" she asked.

"Would you marry the potato baron?" he demanded bluntly.

"Certainly not!" she answered.

"He has gobs of money. Is that not a point worthy of consideration?"

"Not with me. It never could be."

"Perhaps you have gobs of money also."

"If I were a scrubwoman and starving, I wouldn't consider a proposal of marriage from that Jap sufficiently long to reject it."

"Then you have answered your own question," he reminded her triumphantly. "The purity of our race—aye, the purity of the Japanese race—forbids intermarriage; hence we are confronted with the intolerable prospect of sharing our wonderful state with an alien race that must forever remain alien—in thought, language, morals, religion, patriotism, and standards of living. They will dominate us, because they are a dominant people; they will shoulder us aside, control us, dictate to us, and we shall disappear from this beautiful land as surely and as swiftly as did the Mission Indian, While the South has its negro problem—and a sorry problem it is—we Californians have had an infinitely more dangerous problem thrust upon us. We've got to shake them off, We've *got* to!"

"I'll speak to my father. I do not think he understands—that he fully realizes—"

"Ah! Thank you so much. Your father is rich is he not?"

"I think he possesses more money than he will ever need," she replied soberly.

"Please try to make him see that the big American, thing to do would be to colonize his land in the San Gregorio for white men and take a lesser profit. Really, I do not relish the idea of Japanese neighbors."

"You live there, then?"

He nodded.

"Hope to die there, too. You leave the train at El Toro, I suppose?"

"My father has telegraphed mother to have the car meet us there. We shall motor out to the ranch. And are you alighting at El Toro also?"

"No. I plan to pile off at Sespe, away up the lines and take a short cut via a cattle trail over the hills. I'll hike it."

She hesitated slightly. Then:

"I'm sure father would be very happy to give you a lift out from El Toro, Sergeant. We shall have oodles of room."

"Thank you. You are very kind. But the fact is," he went on to explain, "nobody knows I'm coming home, and I have a childish desire to sneak in the back way and surprise them. Were I to appear in El Toro, I'd have to shake hands with everybody in town and relate a history of my exploits and—"

"I understand perfectly. You just want to get home, don't you?" And she bent upon him a smile of complete understanding—a smile all-compelling, maternal. "But did you say you'd hike it in from Sespe? Why not hire a horse?"

"I'd like to have a horse, and if I cared to ask for one, I could borrow one. But I'll hike it instead. It will be easy in light marching order."

"Speaking of horses," she said abruptly. "Do you know a horse in the San Gregorio named Panchito?"

"A very dark chestnut with silver mane and tail, five-gaited, and as stylish as a lady?"

"The very same."

"I should say I do know that horse! What about him?"

"My father is going to buy him for me."

This was news, and Farrel's manner indicated as much.

"Where did you see Panchito?" he demanded.

40

"An Indian named Pablo rode him into El Tore to be shod one day while we were living at the hotel there. He's perfectly adorable."

"Pablo? Hardly. I know the old rascal."

"Be serious. Panchito—I was passing the blacksmith's shop, and I simply had to step in and admire him."

"That tickled old Pablo to death—of course."

"It did. He put Panchito through all of his tricks for me, and, after the horse was shod, he permitted me to ride the dear for half an hour. Pablo was *so* kind! He waited until I could run back to the hotel and change into my riding habit."

"Did you try to give Pablo some money—say, about five dollars?" he demanded, smilingly.

"Yes." Her eyes betrayed wonder.

"He declined it with profuse thanks, didn't he?"

"You're the queerest man I've ever met. Pablo did refuse it. How did you know?"

"I know Pablo. He wouldn't take money from a lady. It's against the code of the Rancho Palomar, and if his boss ever heard that he had fractured that code, he'd skin him alive."

"Not Pablo's boss. Pablo told me his Don Mike, as he calls him, was killed by the bewhiskered devils in a cold country the name of which he had heard but could not remember. He meant Siberia."

Farrel sat up suddenly.

"What's that?" he cried sharply, "He told you Don Mike had been killed?"

"Yes—poor fellow! Pablo said Don Mike's father had had a telegram from the War Department."

Farrel's first impulse was to curse the War Department—in Spanish, so she would not understand.

41

His second was to laugh, and his third to burst into tears. How his father had suffered! Then he remembered that tonight, he, the said Don Mike, was to have the proud privilege of returning from Valhalla, of bringing the light of joy back to the faded eyes of old Don Miguel, and in the swift contemplation of the drama and the comedy impending, he stood staring at her father stupidly. Pablo would doubtless believe he was a ghost returned to haunt old scenes; the majordomo would make the sign of the cross and start running, never pausing till he would reach the Mission of the Mother of Sorrows, there to pour forth his unbelievable tale to Father Dominic. Whereupon Father Dominic would spring into his prehistoric automobile and come up to investigate. Great jumped up Jehoshaphat! What a climax to two years of soldiering!

"Wha—what—why—do you mean to tell me poor old Mike Farrel has lost the number of his mess?" he blurted, "Great snakes! That news breaks me all up in business."

"You knew him well, then?"

" 'Knew him?' Why, I ate with him, slept with him, rode with him, went to school with him. Know him? I should tell a man! We even soldiered together in Siberia; but, strange to say, I hadn't heard of his death."

"Judging by all the nice things I heard about him in El Toro, his death was a genuine loss to his section of the country. Everybody appears to have known him and loved him."

"One has to die before his virtues are apparent to some people," Farrel murmured philosophically. "And now that Don Mike Farrel is dead, you hope to acquire Panchito, eh?"

"I'll be brokenhearted if I cannot."

42

"He'll cost you a lot of money."

"He's worth a lot of money."

He gazed at her very solemnly.

"I am aware that what I am about to say is but poor return for your sweet courtesy, but I feel that you might as well begin now to abandon all hope of ever owning Panchito."

"Why?"

"I—I hate to tell you this, but the fact is—I'm going to acquire him."

She shook her head and smiled at him—the superior smile of one quite conscious of her strength.

"He is to be sold at public auction," she informed him. "And the man who outbids me for that horse will have to mortgage his ranch and borrow money on his Liberty Bonds."

"We shall see that which we shall see," he returned, enigmatically. "Waiter, bring me my check, please."

While the waiter was counting out the change from a twenty dollar bill, Farrel resumed his conversation with the girl.

"Do you plan to remain in the San Gregorio very long?"

"All summer, I think."

He rose from his chair and bowed to her with an Old World courtliness.

"Once more I thank you for your kindness to me, *señorita*," he said. "It is a debt that I shall always remember—and rejoice because I can never repay it. I dare say we shall meet again in the very near future, and when we do, I am going to arrange matters so that I may have the honor of being properly introduced." He pocketed his change. "Until some day in the San Gregorio, then," he finished, *"adios!"*

Despite his smile, her woman's intuition told her that something more poignant than the threatened Japanese invasion of the San Gregorio valley that had cast a shadow over his sunny soul. She concluded it must have been the news of the death of his childhood chum., the beloved Don Mike.

"What a wonderful fellow Don Mike must have been!" she mused. 'White men sing his praises, and Indians and mixed breeds cry them. No wonder this ex-soldier plans to outbid me for Panchito. He attaches a sentimental value to the horse because of his love for poor Don Mike. I wonder if I ought to bid against him under the circumstances. Poor dear! He wants his buddy's horse so badly. He's really very nice—so old-fashioned and sincere And he's dread fully goodlooking."

"Nature was over-generous with that young lady," Farrel decided, as he made his way up to the smoking car, "As a usual thing, she seldom dispenses brains with beauty—and this girl has both. I wonder who she can be. Well, she's too late for Panchito. She may have any other horse on the ranch, but—" He glanced down at the angry red scar on the back of his right hand and remembered. What s charger was Panchito for a battery commander!

IV

FARREL REMAINED IN THE SMOKING CAR throughout the rest of his journey, for he feared the possibility of a renewal of acquaintance with his quondam companion of the dining car should he return to the observation platform. He did not wish to meet her as a discharged

44

soldier, homeward bound—the sort of stray dog every man, woman, and child feels free to enter into conversation with and question regarding his battles, wounds, and post office address. When he met that girl again, he wanted to meet her as Don Miguel José Farrel, of Palomar. He was not so unintelligent as to fail to realize that in his own country he was a personage, and he had sufficient self-esteem to desire her to realize it also. He had a feeling that, should they meet frequently in the future, they would become very good friends. Also, he looked forward with quiet amusement to the explanations that would ensue when the supposedly dead should return to life.

During their brief conversation, she had given him much food for thought—so much, in fact, that presently he forgot about her entirely. His mind was occupied with the problem that confronts practically all discharged soldiers—that of readjustment, not to the life of pre-war days, but to one newer, better, more ambitious and efficient. Farrel realized that a continuation of his *dolce-far-niente* life on the Rancho Palomar under the careless, generous, and rather shiftless administration of his father was not for him. Indeed, the threatened invasion of the San Gregorio by Japanese rendered imperative an immediate decision to that effect. He was the first of an ancient lineage who had even dreamed of progress; he *had* progressed, and he could never, by any possibility, afford to retrograde.

The Farrels had never challenged competition. They had been content to make their broad acres pay a sum sufficient to meet operating expenses and the interest charges on the ancient mortgage, meanwhile supporting themselves in all the ease and comfort of their class by nibbling at their principal. Just how far his ancestors had

45

nibbled, the last of the Farrels was not fully informed, but he was young and optimistic, and believed that, with proper management and the application of modern ranching principles, he would succeed, by the time he was fifty, in saving this principality intact for those who might come after him, for it was not a part of his life plan to die childless—now that the war was over and he out of it practically with a whole skin. This aspect of his future he considered as the train rolled into the Southland. He was twenty-eight years old, and he had never been in love, although, since his twenty-first birthday, his father and Don Juan Sepulvida, of the Rancho Carpajo, had planned a merger of their involved estates through the simple medium of a merger of their families. Anita Sepulvida was a beauty that any man might be proud of; her blood was of the purest and best, but, with a certain curious hardheadedness (the faint strain of Scotch in him, in all likelihood), Don Mike had declined to please the oldsters by paying court to her.

"There's sufficient of the *mañana* spirit in our tribe now., even with the Celtic admixture," he had declared forcibly. "I believe that like begets like in the human family as well as in the animal kingdom, and we know from experience that it never fails there. An infusion of pep is what our family needs, and I'll be hanged if I relish the job of rehabilitating two decayed estates for a posterity that I know could no more compete with the Anglo-Saxon race than did their ancestors."

Whereat, old Don Miguel, who possessed a large measure of the Celtic instinct for domination, had informed Don Mike that the latter was too infernally particular. By the blood of the devil, his son's statement indicated a certain priggishness, which he, Don Miguel, could not deplore too greatly.

"You taught me pride of race," his son reminded him. "I merely desire to improve our race by judicious selection when I mate. And, of course, I'll have to love the woman I marry. And I do not love Anita Sepulvida."

"She loves you," the old don had declared bluntly.

"Then she's playing in hard luck. Believe me, father, I'm no prig, but I do realize the necessity for grafting a little gringo hustle to our family tree. Consider the supergrandson you will have if you leave me to follow my own desires in this matter. In him will be blended the courtliness and chivalry of Spain, the imagery and romance and belligerency of the Irish, the thrift and caution of the Scotch, and the go-get-him-boy, knock-down-and-drag-out spirit of our own Uncle Sam. Why, that's a combination you cannot improve upon!"

"I wish I could fall in love with some fine girl, marry her, and give my father optical assurance, before he passes on, that the Farrel tribe is not, like the mule, without pride of ancestry or hope of posterity," he mused; "but I'll be shot if I'll ever permit myself to fall in love with the sort of woman I want until I know I have something more tangible than love and kisses to offer her. About all I own in this world is this old uniform and Panchito—and I'm getting home just in time to prevent my father from selling him at auction for the benefit of my estate. And since I'm going to chuck this uniform tomorrow and give Panchito away the day after—by the gods of War, that girl gave me a fright when she was trying to remember the name of old man Gonzales's ranch! If it had been the Palomar instead of the Palomares! I might be able to stand the sight of Japs on the Palomares end of the San Gregorio, but on the Palomar—"

At four o'clock, when the train whistled for Sespe, he

47

hurried back to the observation car to procure his baggage preparatory to alighting from the train. The girl sat in the seat opposite his, and she looked up at him now with friendly eyes.

"Would you care to leave your things in the car and entrust them to father's man?" she queried. "We would be glad to take them in the motor as far as the mission. My father suggested it," she added.

"Your father's a brick. I shall be happy to accept, thank you. Just tell the chauffeur to leave them off in front of the mission and I'll pick them up when I come over the trail from Sespe. I can make far better time over the hills without this suitcase, light as it is."

"You're exceedingly welcome, Sergeant. And, by the way, I have decided not to contest your right to Panchito. It wouldn't be sporty of me to outbid you for your dead buddy's horse."

His heart leaped.

"I think you're tremendously sweet," he declared bluntly. "As matters stand, we happen to have a half brother of Panchito up on the ranch—or, at least, we did have when I enlisted. He's coming four, and he ought to be a beauty. I'll break him for you myself. However," he added, with a deprecatory grin, "I—I realize you're not the sort of girl who accepts gifts from strangers; so, if you have a nickel on you, I'll sell you this horse, sight unseen. If he's gone, I'll give the nickel back."

"You are quite right," she replied, with an arch smile. "I could not possibly accept a gift from a stranger Neither could I buy a horse from a stranger—no; not even at the ridiculous price of five cents."

"Perhaps if I introduced myself—have I your permission to be that bold?"

"Well," she replied, still with that bright, friendly,

48

understanding smile, "that might make a difference."

"I do not deserve such consideration. Consequently, for your gentle forbearance, you shall be accorded a unique privilege—that of meeting a dead soldier. I am Miguel José Farrel, better known as 'Don Mike,' of the Rancho Palomar, and I own Panchito. To quote the language of Mark Twain, 'the report of my death has been grossly exaggerated,' as is the case of several thousand other soldiers in this man's army." He chuckled as he saw a look of amazement replace the sweet smile. "And you are Miss—" he queried.

She did not answer. She could only stare at him, and in that look he thought he noted signs of perturbation. While he had talked, the train had slid to a momentary halt for the flag station, and while he waited now for her name, the train began creeping out of Sespe.

"All right," he laughed. "You can tell me your name when we meet again. I must run for it. Good-by." He hurried through the screen door to the platform, stepped over the brass railing, and clung there a moment, looking back into the car at her before dropping lightly to the ground between the tracks.

"Now what the devil is the meaning of that?" he mused, as he stood there watching the train. "There were tears in her eyes."

He crossed the tracks, climbed a fence, and after traversing a small piece of bottom land, entered a trail through the chaparral, and started his upward climb to the crest of the range that hid the San Gregorio. Suddenly he paused.

Had the girl's unfamiliarity with Spanish names caused her to confuse Palomar with Palomares? And why was Panchito to be sold at auction? Was it like his father to sacrifice his son's horse to any fellow with the

49

money to buy him? No! No! Rather would he sell his own mount and retain Panchito for the sake of the son he mourned as dead. The Palomares end of the San Gregorio was too infertile to interest an experienced agriculturist like Okada; there wasn't sufficient acreage to make a colonization scheme worth while. On the contrary, fifty thousand acres of the Rancho Palomar lay in the heart of the valley and immediately contiguous to the floodwaters at the head of the ghost river for which the valley was named.

Don Mike, of Palomar, leaned against the bole of a scrub oak and closed his eyes in sudden pain. Presently, he roused himself and went his way with uncertain step, for, from time to time, tears blinded him. And the last of the sunlight had faded from the San Gregorio before he topped the crest of its western boundary; the melody of Brother Flavio's angelus had ceased an hour previous, and over the mountains to the east a full moon stood in a cloudless sky, flooding the silent valley with its silver light, and pricking out in bold relief the gray-white walls of the Mission de la Madre Dolorosa, crumbling souvenir of a day that was done.

He ran down the long hill, and came presently to the mission. In the grass beside the white road, he searched for his straw suitcase, his gas mask, and the helmet, but failing to find them, he concluded the girl had neglected to remind her father's chauffeur to throw them off in front of the mission, as promised So he passed along the front of the ancient pile and let himself in through a wooden door in the high adobe wall that surrounded the churchyard immediately adjacent to the mission. With the assurance of one who treads familiar ground, he strode rapidly up a weed grown path to a spot where a tall black granite monument, proclaimed that here rested the clay of one superior to his peon and Indian neighbors. And this was so, for the shaft marked the grave of the original Michael Joseph Farrel, the adventurer the sea had cast up on the shore of San Marcos County.

Immediately to the left of this monument, Don Mike saw a grave that had not been there when he left the Palomar. At the head of it stood a tile taken from the ruin of the mission roof, and on this brown tile some one had printed in rude lettering with white paint:

Falleció
Don Miguel José Señoriaga Farrel
Nacio, Junio 3, 1841
Muerto, Deciembre 29, 1919.

The last scion of that ancient house knelt in the mold of his father's grave and made the sign off the cross.

V

THE TEARS WHICH Don Mike Farrel had descried in the eyes of his acquaintance on the train were, as he came to realize when he climbed the steep cattle trail from Sespe, the tribute of a gentle heart moved to quick and uncontrollable sympathy. Following their conversation in the diningcar, the girl—her name was Kay Parker—bad continued her luncheon, her mind busy with thoughts of this strange homebound ex-soldier who had so signally challenged her attention. "There's breeding back of that man," the girl mused. "He's only a rancher's son from the San Gregorio; where did he acquire his drawing room manners?"

She decided, presently, that they were not drawing room manners. They were too easy and graceful and natural to have been acquired. He must have been born with them. There was something old-fashioned 'bout him—as if part of him dwelt in the past century. He appeared to be quite certain of himself, yet there was not even a hint of ego in his cosmos. His eyes were wonderful—and passionless, like a boy's. Yes; there was a great deal of the little boy about him, for all his years, his wounds, and his adventures. Kay thought him charming, yet he did not appear to be aware of his charm, and this fact increased her attraction to him. It pleased her that he had preferred to discuss the Japanese menace rather than his own exploits, and had been human enough to fly in a rage when told of her father's plans with the potato baron. Nevertheless, he had himself under control, for he had smothered his rage as quickly as he had permitted it to flare up.

"Curious man!" the girl concluded. "However—he's a man, and when we meet again, I'm going to investigate thoroughly and see what else he has in his head."

Upon further reflection, she reminded herself that he hadn't disclosed, in anything he had said, the fact that his head contained thoughts or information of more than ordinary value. He had merely created that impression. Even his discussion of the Japanese problem had been cursory, and, as she mentally back-tracked on their conversation, the only striking remark of his which she recalled was his whimsical assurance that he knew why young turkeys are hard to raise in the fall. She smiled to herself.

"Well, Kay, did you find him pleasant company?"

She looked up and discovered her father slipping into

the chair so lately vacated by the object of her thoughts.

" 'Lo, pop! You mean the ex-soldier?" He nodded. "Queerest man I've ever met, But he *is* pleasant company."

"I thought so. Tell me, daughter: What you were smiling about just now."

"He said he knew why young turkeys are hard to raise in the fall."

"Why are they?"

"I don't know, dear. He didn't tell me. Can you?"

"The problem is quite beyond me, Kay." He unfolded his napkin. "Splendid loking young chap, that! Struck me he ought to have more in his head than frivolous talk about the difficulty of rearing young turkeys."

"I think he has a great deal more in his head than that. In fact, I do not understand why he should have mentioned young turkeys at all, because he's a cattleman. And he comes from the San Gregorio valley."

"Indeed! What's his name?"

"He didn't tell me. But he knows all about the ranch you took over from the Gonzales estate."

"But I didn't foreclose on that. It was the Farrel estate."

"He called it something else—the Palomares rancho, I think."

"Gonzales owns the Palomares rancho, but the Palomar rancho belonged to old Don Miguel Farrel."

"Was he the father of the boy they call 'Don Mike'—he who was killed in Siberia?"

"The same."

"Why did you have to foreclose on his ranch, father?"

"Well, the interest had been unpaid for two years and the old man was getting pretty feeble; so, after the boy

53

was killed, I realized that was the end of the Farrel dynasty and that the mortgage would never be paid. Consequently, in self-protection, I foreclosed. Of course, under the law, Don Miguel had a year's grace in which to redeem the property, and during that year I couldn't take possession without first proving that he was committing waste upon it. However, the old man died of a broken heart a few months after receiving news of his son's death, and, in the protection of my interest, I was forced to petition the court to grant me permission to enter into possession. It was my duty to protect the equity of the heirs, if any."

"Are there any heirs?"

"None that we have been able to discover."

The girl thoughtfully traced a pattern on the tablecloth with the tine of her fork.

"How will it be possible for you to acquire that horse, Panchito, for me, dearest?" she queried presently.

"I have a deficiency judgment against the Rancho Palomar," he explained. "Consequently, upon the expiration of the redemption period of one year, I shall levy an attachment against the Farrel estate. All the property will be sold at public auction by the sheriff to satisfy my deficiency judgment, and I shall, of course bid in this horse."

"I have decided I do not want him, father," she informed him half sadly. "The ex-soldier is an old boyhood chum of the younger Farrel who was killed, and he wants the horse."

He glanced at her with an expression of shrewd suspicion.

"As you desire, honey," he replied.

"But I want you to see to it that nobody else outbids him for the horse," she continued, earnestly. "If some

54

one should run the price up beyond the limits of his purse, of course I want you to outbid that someone, but what I do not desire you to do is to run the price up on him yourself. He wants the horse out of sentiment, and it isn't nice to force a wounded exserviceman to pay a high price for his sentiment."

"Oh, I understand now," her father assured her. "Very well, little daughter; I have my orders and will obey them."

"Precious old darling!" she whispered, gratefully, and pursed her adorable lips to indicate to him that he might consider himself kissed. His stern eyes softened in a glance of father love supreme.

"Whose little girl are you?" he whispered, and, to that ancient query of parenthood, she gave the reply of childhood:

"Daddy's."

"Just for that, I'll offer the soldier a tremendous profit on Panchito. We'll see what his sentiment is worth."

"Bet you a new hat, angel-face, you haven't money enough to buy him," Kay challenged.

"Considering the cost of your hats, I'd be giving you rather long odds, Kay. You say this young man comes from the San Gregorio valley?"

"So he informed me."

"Well, there isn't a young man in the San Gregorio who doesn't need a couple of thousand dollars far worse than he needs a horse. I'll take your bet, Peaches. Of course you mentioned to him the fact that you wanted this horse?"

"Yes. And he said I couldn't have him—that he was going to acquire him."

"Perhaps he was merely jesting with you."

"No; he meant it."

"I believe," he said, smiling, "that it is most unusual of young men to show such selfish disregard of your expressed desires."

"Flatterer! I like him all the more for it. He's a man with some backbone."

"So I noticed. He wears the ribbon of the Congressional Medal of Honor. Evidently he is given to exceeding the speedlimit. Did he tell you how he won that pale-blue ribbon with the little white stars sprinkled on it?"

"He did not. Such men never discuss those things."

"Well, they raise fighting men in the San Gregorio, at any rate," her father continued. "Two Medal of Honor men came out of it. Old Don Miguel Farrel's boy was awarded one posthumously. I was in El Toro the day the commanding general of the Western Department came down from San Francisco and pinned the medal on old Don Miguel's breast. The old fellow rode in on his son's horse, and when the little ceremony was over, he mounted and rode back to the ranch alone. Not a tear, not a quiver. He looked as regal as the American eagle—and as proud. Looking at that old don, one could readily imagine the sort of son he had bred. The only trouble with the Farrels," he added, critically, "was that they and work never got acquainted. If these old Californians would consent to imbibe a few lessons in industry and economy from their Japanese neighbors, their wonderful state would be supporting thirty million people a hundred years from now."

"I wonder how many of that mythical thirty millions would be Japs?" she queried, innocently.

"That is a problem with which we will not have to concern ourselves, Kay, because we shall not be here."

"Some day, popsy-wops, that soldier will drop in at

56

our ranch and lock horns with you on the Japanese question."

"When he does," Parker replied, good-naturedly, "I shall make a star-spangled monkey out of him. I'm loaded for these Californians. I've investigated their arguments, and they will not hold water, I tell you. I'll knock out the contentions of your unknown knight like tenpins in a bowling alley. See if I don't."

"He's nobody's fool, dad."

"Quite so. He knows why young turkeys are hard to raise in the fall?"

She bent upon him a radiant smile of the utmost good humor.

"Score one for the unknown knight," she bantered. "That is more than we know. And turkey was sixty cents a pound last Thanksgiving! Curious information from our viewpoint, perhaps, but profitable."

He chuckled over his salad.

"You're hopelessly won to the opposition," he declared. "Leave your check for me, and I'll pay it. And if your unknown knight returns to the observation car, ask him about those confounded turkeys."

VI

BUT THE UNKNOWN KNIGHT HAD NOT RETURNED to the observation car until the long train was sliding into Sespe, and Kay had no time to satisfy her thirst for information anent young turkeys. With unexpected garrulity, he had introduced himself; with the receipt of this information, she had been rendered speechless, first with surprise, and then with distress as her alert mind swiftly encompassed the pitiful awakening that was coming to this joyous homecomer. Before she could master her emotions, be was disappearing over the brass rail at the end of the observation car; even as he waved her a debonair farewell, she caught the look of surprise and puzzlement in his black eyes. Wherefore, she knew the quick tears had betrayed her.

"Oh, you poor fellow!" she whispered to herself, as she dabbed at her eyes with a wisp of a lace handkerchief. "What a tragedy!"

What a tragedy, indeed!

She had never been in the San Gregorio, and today was to mark her first visit to the Rancho Palomar, although her father and mother and the servants had been occupying the Farrel hacienda for the past two months. Of the beauty of that valley, of the charm of that ancient seat, she had heard much from her parents if they could be so enthusiastic about it in two short months, how tremendously attached to it must be this cheerful Don Mike, who had been born and raised there, who was familiar with every foot of it, and doubtless cherished every tradition connected with it. He had imagination, and in imaginative people wounds drive deep and are hard to heal; he loved this land of his, not with the passive loyalty of the average American citizen, but with the strange, passionate intensity of the native Californian for his state. She had met many Californians, and, in this one particular, they had all been alike. No matter how far they had wandered from the Golden West, no matter how long or how pleasant had been their exile, they yearned, with a great yearning, for that intangible something that all Californians feel but can never explain—which is found nowhere save in this land of romance and plenty, of hearty good will, of life lived without too great effort,

58

and wherein the desire to play gives birth to that large and kindly tolerance that is the unfailing sweetener of all human association.

And Don Mike was hurrying home to a grave in the valley, to a home no longer his, to the shock of finding strangers ensconced in the seat of his prideful ancestors, to the prospect of seeing the rich acres that should have been his giving sustenance to an alien race, while he must turn to a brutal world for his daily bread earned by the sweat of his brow.

Curiously enough, in that moment, without having given very much thought to the subject, she decided that she must help him bear it. In a vague way, she felt that she must see him and talk with him before he should come in contact with her father and mother. She wanted to explain matters, hoping that he would understand that she, at least, was one of the interlopers who were not hostile to him.

For she did, indeed, feel like an interloper now. But, at the same time, she realized, despite her small knowledge of the law, that, until the expiration of the redemption period, the equity of Don Mike in the property was unassailable. With that unpleasant sense of having intruded came the realization that tonight the Parker family would occupy the position of uninvited and unwelcome guests. It was not a comfortable thought.

Fortunately, the potato baron and her father were up in the smoker; hence, by the time the train paused at El Toro, Kay had composed herself sufficiently to face her father again without betraying to him any hint of the mental disturbance of the past forty minutes. She directed the porter in the disposition of Don Mike's scant impedimenta, and watched to see that the Parker chauffeur carried it from the station platform over to the waiting automobile. As he was lashing their hand-baggage on the running board, she said,

"William, how long will it take you to get out to the ranch?"

"Twenty miles, miss, over a narrow dirt road, and some of it winds among hills. I ought to do it handily in an hour without taking any chances."

"Take a few chances," she ordered, in a voice meant for his ear alone. "I'm in a hurry."

"Forty-five minutes, miss," he answered, in the same confidential tone.

Kay sat in the front seat with William, while her father and Okada occupied the tonneau. Within a few minutes, they were clear of the town and rolling swiftly across a three mile-wide mesa. Then they entered a long, narrow canyon, which they traversed for several miles, climbed a six percent grade to the crest of a ridge, rolled down into another canon, climbed another ridge, and from the summit gazed down on the San Gregorio in all the glory of her new April gown. Kay gasped with the shock of such loveliness, and laid a detaining hand on the chauffeur's arm. Instantly he stopped the car.

"I always get a kick out of the view from here, miss," he informed her. "Can you beat it? You can't!"

The girl sat with parted lips.

"This—this is the California he loves," she thought.

She closed her eyes to keep back the tears, and the car rolled gently down the grade into the valley. From the tonneau she could catch snatches of the conversation between her father and the potato baron; they were discussing the agricultural possibilities of the valley, and she realized, with a little twinge of outrage, that its wonderful pastoral beauty had been quite lost on them.

As they swept past the mission, Kay deliberately refrained from ordering William to toss Don Mike's baggage off in front of the old pile, for she knew now whither the latter was bound. She would save him that added burden. Three miles from the mission, the road swung up a gentle grade between two long rows of ancient and neglected palms. The dead, withered fronds of a decade still clung to the corrugated trunks. In the adjoining oaks vast flocks of crows perched and cawed raucously. This avenue of palms presently debouched onto a little mesa, oak-studded and covered with lush grass, which gave it a pretty, parklike effect. In the center of this mesa stood the hacienda of the Rancho Palomar.

Like all adobe dwellings of its class, it was not now, nor had it ever been, architecturally beautiful. It was low, with a plain hip roof covered with ancient red tiles, many of which were missing. When the house had first been built, it had been treated to a coat of excellent plaster over the adobe, and this plaster had never been renewed. With the attrition of time and the elements, it had worn away in spots, through which the brown adobe bricks showed, like the bones in a decaying corpse. The main building faced down the valley; from each end out, an ell extended to form a patio in the rear, while a seven-foot adobe wall, topped with short tile, connected with the ell and formed a parallelogram.

"The old ruin doesn't look very impressive from the front, Kay," her father explained, as he helped her out of the car, "but that wall hides an old-fashioned garden that will delight you. A porch runs all round the inside of the house, and every door opens on the patio, That long adobe barracks over yonder used to house the help. In the old days, a small army of peons was maintained

61

here. The small adobe house back there in the trees houses the majordomo—that old rascal, Pablo."

"He is still here, dad?"

"Yes—and as belligerent as old billy owl. He pretends to look after the stock. I ordered him off the ranch last week; but do you think he'd go? Not much. He went inside his shack, sorted out a rifle, came outside, sat down, and fondled the weapon all day long. Ever since then he has carried it, mounted or afoot. So I haven't bothered him. He's a bad old Indian, and when I secure final title to the ranch, I'll have the sheriff of the county come out and remove him."

"But how does he live, dear?"

"How does any Indian live? He killed a steer last week, jerked half of it, and sold the other half for some beans and flour. It wasn't his steer and it wasn't mine. It belonged to the Farrel estate, and, since there is nobody to lodge a complaint against him, I suppose he'll kill another steer when his rations run low. This way, daughter. Right through the hole in the wall."

They passed through a big inset gate in the adobe wall, into the patio. At once the scent of lemon and orange blossoms, mingled with the more delicate aroma of flowers, assailed them. Kay stood, entranced, gazing upon the hodgepodge of color; she had the feeling of having stepped out of one world into another.

Her father stood watching her.

"Wonderful old place, isn't it, Kay?" he suggested. "The garden has been neglected, but I'm going to clean it out."

"Do not touch it," she commanded, almost sharply. "I want it the way it is."

"You little tyrant!" he replied good-naturedly. " You run me ragged and make me like it."

From a rocker on the porch at the eastern end of the patio Kay's mother rose and called to them, and the girl darted away to greet her. Mrs. Parker folded the girl to a somewhat ample bosom and kissed her lovingly on her ripe red lips; to her husband she presented a cheek that showed to advantage the artistry of a member of that tribe of genii who strive so valiantly to hold in check the ravages of age. At fifty, Kay's mother was still a handsome woman; her carriage, her dress, and a certain repressed vivacity indicated that she had mastered the art of growing old gracefully.

"Well, kitten," she said, a trifle louder and shriller than one seemed to expect of her, "are you going to remain with us a little while, or will next week see you scampering away again?"

"I'll stay all summer, fussbudget. I'm going to paint the San Gregorio while it's on exhibition, and then this old house and the garden. Oh, mother dear, I'm in love with it! It's wonderful!"

The potato baron had followed Parker and his daughter into the patio, and stood now, showing all of his teeth in an amiable smile. Parker suddenly remembered his guest.

"My dear," he addressed his wife, "I have brought a guest with me. This is Mr. Okada, of whom I wrote you."

Okada bowed low—as low as the rules of Japanese etiquette prescribe, which is to say that he bent himself almost double. At the same time, he lifted his hat. Then he bowed again twice, and, with a pleasing smile proffered his hand. Mrs. Parker took it and shook it with hearty good will.

"You are very welcome, Mr. Okada," she shrilled. "Murray," she added, turning to the butler, who was approaching with Okada's suitcase, "show the gentleman to the room with the big bed in it. Dinner will be ready at six, Mr. Okada. Please do not bother to dress for dinner. We're quite informal here."

"Sank you very much," he replied, with an unpleasant whistling intake of breath; with another profound bow to the ladies, he turned and followed Murray to his room.

"Well, John," Mrs. Parker demanded, as the Japanese disappeared, "your little playmate's quite like a mechanical toy. For heaven's sake, where did you pal up with him?"

"That's the potato baron of the San Joaquin valley, Kate," he informed her. "I'm trying to interest him in a colonization scheme for his countrymen. A thousand Japs in the San Gregorio can raise enough garden truck to feed the city of Los Angeles—and they will pay a whooping price for good land with water on it. So I brought him along for a preliminary survey of the deal."

"He's very polite, but I imagine he's not very brilliant company," his wife averred frankly. "When you wired me you were bringing a guest, I did hope you'd bring some jolly young jackanapes to amuse Kay and me."

She sighed and settled back in her comfortable rocking chair, while Kay, guided by a maid, proceeded to her room. A recent job of calcimining had transformed the room from a dirty grayish white to a soft shade of pink; the old-fashioned furniture had been "done over," and glowed dully in the fading light. Kay threw open the small square-hinged window, gazed through the iron bars sunk in the thick walls, and she found herself looking down the valley, more beautiful than ever now in the rapidly fading light.

"I'll have to wait outside for him," she thought. "It

will be dark when he gets here."

She washed and changed into a dainty little dinner dress, after which she went on a tour of exploration of the hacienda. Her first port of call was the kitchen.

"Nishi," she informed the cook, "a gentleman will arrive shortly after the family has finished dinner. Keep his dinner in the oven. Murray will serve it to him in his room, I think."

She passed out through the kitchen, and found herself in the rear of the hacienda. A hundred yards distant, she saw Pablo Artelan squatting on his heels beside the portal of his humble residence, his back against the wall. She crossed over to him, smiling as she came.

"How do you do, Pablo ?" she said. "Have you forgotten me? I'm the girl to whom you were kind enough to give a ride on Panchito one day in El Toro."

The glowering glance of suspicion and resentment faded slowly from old Pablo's swarthy countenance. He scrambled to his feet and swept the ground with his old straw sombrero.

"I am at the service of the *señorita,*" he replied gravely.

"Thank you, Pablo. I just wanted to tell you that you need not carry that rifle any more. I shall see to it that you are not removed from the ranch."

He stared at her with stolid interest.

"*Muchas gracias, señorita,*" he mumbled. Then, remembering she did not understand Spanish, he resumed in English: "I am an old man, mees. Since my two boss he's die, pretty soon Pablo die, too. For what use eet is for live now I don' tell you. Those ol' man who speak me leave theese rancho—he is your father, no?"

"Yes, Pablo. And he isn't such a terrible man, once

65

you get acquainted with him."

"I don' like," Pablo muttered frankly. "He have eye like lookin' glass. Mebbeso for you, mees, eet is different, but for Pablo Artelan—" he shrugged. "Eef Don Mike is here, nobody can talk to me like dose ol' man, your father, he speak to me." And he wagged his head sorrowfully.

Kay came close to him.

"Listen, Pablo: I have a secret for you. You must not tell anybody. Don Mike is not dead."

He raised his old head with languid interest and nodded comprehension.

"My wife, Carolina, she tell me same thing all time. She say: '*Pablo mio,* somebody make beeg mistake. Don Mike come home pretty queeck, you see. Nobody can keel Don Mike. Nobody have that mean the deesposition for keel the boy.' But I don' theenk Don Mike come back to El Palomar."

"Carolina is right, Pablo. Somebody did make a big mistake. He was wounded in the hand, but not killed. I saw him today, Pablo, on the train."

"You see Don Mike? You see heem with the eye?"

"Yes. And he spoke to me with the tongue. He will arrive here in an hour."

Pablo was on his knees before her, groping for her hand. Finding it, he carried it to his lips. Then, leaping to his feet with an alacrity that belied his years, he yelled:

"Carolina! Come queeck, *Pronto! Aquí,* Carolina."

"Si, Pablo mio."

Carolina appeared in the doorway and was literally deluged with a stream of Spanish. She stood there, hands clasped on her tremendous bosom, staring unbelievingly at the bearer of these tidings of great joy, the while tears cascaded down her flat, homely face. With a snap of his fingers, Pablo dismissed her; then he darted into the house and emerged with his rifle. A cockerel, with the carelessness of youth, had selected for his roost the limb of an adjacent oak and was still gazing about him instead of secreting his head under his wing, as cockerels should at sunset. Pablo neatly shot his head off, seized the fluttering carcass, and started plucking out the feathers with neatness and despatch.

"Don Mike, he's like *gallina con arroz espagñol,*" he explained. "What you call chick-een with rice Spanish," he interpreted. "Eet mus' not be that Don Mike come home and Carolina have not cook for heem the grub he like. *Carramba!*"

"But he cannot possibly eat a chicken before—I mean, it's too soon. Don Mike will not eat that chicken before the animalheat is out of it."

"You don' know Don Mike, mees. W'en dat boy he's hongry, he don' speak so many questions."

"But I've told our cook to save dinner for him."

"Your cook! *Señorita,* I don' like make fun for you, but I guess you don' know my wife Carolina, she have been cook for Don Miguel and Don Mike since long time before he's beeg like little kitten. Don Mike, he don' understan' those gringo grub."

"Listen, Pablo: There is no time to cook Don Mike a Spanish dinner. He must eat gringo grub tonight. Tell me, Pablo: Which room did Don Mike sleep in when he was home?"

"The room in front the house—the beeg room with the beeg black bed. Carolina!" He threw the half plucked chicken at the old cook, wiped his hands on his overalls, and started for the hacienda. "I go for make the bed for Don Mike," he explained, and started running.

Kay followed breathlessly, but he reached the patio before her, scuttled along the porch with surprising speed, and darted into the room. Immediately the girl heard his voice raised angrily.

"Hullo! What you been do in my boss's room? *Madre de Dios!* You theenk I let one Chinaman—no, one Jap—sleep in the bed of Don Victoriano Noriaga. No! *Vamos!*"

There was a slight scuffle, and the potato baron came hurtling through the door, propelled on the boot of the aged but exceedingly vigorous Pablo. Evidently the Jap had been taken by surprise. He rolled off the porch into a flower bed, recovered himself, and flew at Pablo with the ferocity of a bulldog. To the credit of his race, be it said that it does not subscribe to the philosophy of turning the other cheek.

But Pablo was a peon. From somewhere on his person, he produced a dirk and slashed vigorously. Okada evaded the blow, and gave ground.

"*Quidado!*" Pablo roared, and charged; whereupon the potato baron, evidently impressed with the wisdom of the ancient adage that discretion is the better part of valor, fled before him. Pablo followed, opened the patio gate, and, with his long dirk, motioned the Jap to disappear through it. "The hired man, he don' sleep in the bed of the *gente,*" he declared. "The barn is too good for one Jap. *Santa Maria!* For why I don' keel you, I don' know."

"Pablo!"

The majordomo turned.

"Yes, mees lady."

"Mr. Okada is our guest. I command you to leave him alone. Mr. Okada, I apologize to you for Pablo's impetuosity. He is not a servant of ours, but a retainer of the former owner. Pablo, will you please attend to your own business?" Kay was angry now, and Pablo realized it.

"Don Mike's beesiness, she is my beesiness, too, *señorita,*" he growled.

"Yes; I zink so," Okada declared. "I zink I go 'nother room."

"Murray will prepare one for you, Mr. Okada. I'm so sorry this has happened. Indeed I am!"

Pablo hooted.

"You sorry, mees? Wait until my Don Mike he's come home and find thees fellow in hees house."

He closed the gate, returned to the room, and made a critical inspection of the apartment. Kay could see him wagging his grizzled head approvingly as she came to the door and looked in.

"Where those fellow *El Mono,* he put my boss's clothes?" Pablo demanded.

" '*El Mono?*' Whom do you mean, Pablo?"

"*El Mono*—the monkey. He wear long tail to the coat; all the time he look like mebbeso somebody in the house she's goin' die pretty queeck."

"Oh, you mean Murray, the butler."

Pablo was too ludicrous, and Kay sat down on the edge of the porch and laughed until she wept. Then, as Pablo still stood truculently in the doorway, waiting an answer to his query, she called to Murray, who had rushed to the aid of the potato baron, and asked him if he had found any clothing in the room, and, if so, what he had done with it.

"I spotted and pressed them all, Miss Kay, and hung them in the clothes-press of the room next door."

"I go get," growled Pablo, and did so; whereupon the artful Murray took advantage of his absence to dart over to the royal chamber and remove the potato baron's effects.

"I don't like that blackamoor, Miss Kay," *El Mono* confided to the girl. "I feel assured he is a desperate vagabond to whom murder and pillage are mere pastimes. Please order him out of the garden. He pays no attention to me whatsoever."

"Leave him severely alone," Kay advised. "I will find a way to handle him."

Pablo returned presently, with two suits of clothing, a soft white-linen shirt, a black necktie, a pair of low cut brown shoes, and a pair of brown socks. These articles he laid out on the bed. Then he made another trip to the other room, and returned bearing an armful of framed portraits of the entire Noriaga and Farrel dynasty, which he proceeded to hang in a row on the wall at the foot of the bed. Lastly, be removed a rather fancy spread from the bed and substituted therefor an ancient silk crazy quilt that had been made by Don Mike's grandmother. Things were now as they used to be, and Pablo was satisfied.

When he came out, Kay had gone in to dinner; so he returned to his own *casa* and squatted against the wall, with his glance fixed upon the point in the palm avenue where it dipped over the edge of the mesa.

VII

AT SEVEN O'CLOCK, dinner being over, Kay excused herself to the family and Mr. Okada, passed out through the patio gate, and sought a bench which she had noticed under a catalpa tree outside the wall. From this seat, she, like Pablo, could observe anybody coming up the palm-lined avenue. A young moon was rising over the hills, and by its light Kay knew she could detect Don Mike while he was yet some distance from the house.

At seven-thirty, he had not appeared, and she grew impatient and strolled round to the other side of the hacienda. Before Pablo's *casa,* she saw the red end of a cigarette; so she knew that Pablo also watched.

"I *must* see him first," she decided. "Pablo's heart is right toward Don Mike, but resentful toward us. I do not want him to pass that resentment on to his master."

She turned back round the hacienda again, crossed down over the lip of the mesa at right angles to the avenue, and picked her way through the oaks. When she was satisfied that Pablo could not see her, she made her way back to the avenue, emerging at the point where it connected with the wagon road down the valley. Just off the avenue, a live oak had fallen, and Kay sat down on the trunk of it to watch and wait.

Presently she saw him coming, and her heart fluttered in fear at the meeting. She, who had for months marked the brisk tread of military men, sensed now the drag, the slow cadence of his approach; wherefore she realized that he knew! In the knowledge that she would not have to break the news to him, a sense of comfort stole over her.

As he came closer, she saw that he walked with his chin on his breast; when he reached the gate at the end of the avenue, he did not see it and bumped into it. *"Dios mio!"* she heard him mutter. *"Dios! Dios! Dios!"* The last word ended in tragic crescendo; he leaned on the gate, and there, in the white silence, the last of the Farrels stood gazing up the avenue as if he feared to enter.

Kay sat on the oak trunk, staring at him, fascinated by

the tragic tableau.

Suddenly, from the hacienda, a hound gave tongue-along, bell-like baying, with a timbre in it that never creeps into a hound's voice until he has struck a warm scent. Another hound took up the cry—and still another. Don Mike started.

"That's Nip!" Kay heard him murmur, as the first hound sounded. "Now, Mollie! Come now, Nailer! Where's Hunter? Hunter's dead! You've scented me!"

Across the mesa, the pack came bellowing, scattering the wet leaves among the oaks as they took the short cut to the returning master. Into the avenue they swept; the leader leaped for the top of the gate, poised there an instant, and fell over into Don Mike's arms. The others followed, overwhelming him. They licked his hands; they soiled him with their reaching paws, the while their cries of welcome testified to their delight. Presently, one grew jealous of the other in the mad scramble for his caressing hand, and Nip bit Mollie, who retaliated by biting Nailer, who promptly bit Nip, thus completing the vicious circle. In an instant, they were battling each other.

"Stop it!" Don Mike commanded. "Break!"

They "broke" at his command, and, forgetting their animosities, began running in circles, in a hopeless effort to express their happiness. Suddenly, as if by common impulse, they appeared to remember a neglected duty, and fled noisily whence they had come.

"Ah, only my dogs to welcome me!" Kay heard Don Mike murmur. And then the stubborn tears came and blinded him, so he did not see her white figure step out into the avenue and come swiftly toward him. The first he knew of her presence was when her hand touched his glistening black head bent on his arms over the top rail of the gate.

"No, no, Don Mike," he heard a sweet voice protesting; "somebody else cares, too. We wouldn't be human if we didn't. Please—please try not to feel so badly about it."

He raised his haggard face.

"Ah, yes—you!" he cried. "You—you've been waiting here—for me?"

"Yes. I wanted to tell you—to explain before you got to the house. We didn't know, you see—and the notice was so terribly short; but we'll go in the morning. I've saved dinner for you, Don Mike—and your old room is ready for you. Oh, you don't know how sorry I am for you, you poor man!"

He hid his face again.

"Don't—please!" he cried, in a choked voice. Can't stand sympathy—tonight—from you!"

She laid a hand on his shoulder.

"Come, come; you must buck up, old soldier," she assured him. "You'll have to meet Pablo and Carolina very soon."

"I'm so alone and desperate," he muttered, through clenched teeth. "You can't—realize what this means—to me. My father was an old man—he had—accomplished his years—and I weep for him, because I loved—him. But oh, my home—this—dear land—"

He choked, and, in that moment, she forgot that this man was a stranger to her. She only knew that he had been stricken, that he was helpless, that he lacked the greatest boon of the desolate—a breast upon which he might weep. Gently she lifted the black head and drew it down on her shoulder; her arm went round his neck and patted his cheek, and his full heart was emptied.

There was so much of the little boy about him!

73

VIII

THE FIERCE GUST OF EMOTION which swept Don Mike Farrel was of brief duration. He was too sane, too courageous to permit his grief to overwhelm him completely; he had the usual masculine horror of an exhibition of weakness, and although the girl's sweet sympathy and genuine womanly tenderness had caught him unawares, he was, nevertheless, not insensible of the incongruity of a grown man weeping like a child on the shoulder of a young woman—and a strange young woman at that. With a supreme effort of will, he regained control of himself as swiftly as he had lost it, and began fumbling for a handkerchief.

"Here," she murmured; "use mine." She reached up and, with her dainty wisp of handkerchief, wiped his wet cheeks exactly as if he had been a child.

He caught the hand that wielded the handkerchief and kissed it gratefully, reverently.

"God bless your dear, kind heart!" he murmured. "I had thought nobody could possibly care—that much. So few people—have any interest in the—unhappiness of others." He essayed a twisted smile. "I'm not usually this weak," he continued, apologetically. "I never knew until tonight that I could be such a lubberly big baby, but, then, I wasn't set for this blow. This afternoon, life executed an about face for me—and the dogs got me started after I'd promised myself—" He choked again on the last word.

She patted his shoulder in comradely fashion.

"Buck up, Don Mike!" she pleaded. "Tears from such men as you are signs of strength, not weakness. And remember—life has a habit of obeying commanding

74

men. It may execute another about face for you."

"I've lost everything that made life livable," he protested.

"Ah! No, no! You must not say that. Think of that cheerful warrior who, in defeat, remarked, 'All is lost save honor.' " And she touched the pale-blue star sprinkled ribbon on his left breast.

He smiled again the twisted smile.

"That doesn't amount to a row of pins in civil life." Something of that sense of bitter disillusionment, of blasted idealism, which is the immediate aftermath of war, had crept into his voice. "The only thrill I ever got out of its possession was in the service. My colonel was never content merely with returning my salute. He always uncovered to me. That ribbon will have little weight with your father, I fear, when I ask him to set aside the foreclosure, grant me a new mortgage, and give me a fighting chance to retain the thing I love." And his outflung arm indicated the silent, moonlit valley.

"Perhaps," she replied, soberly. "He is a business man. Nevertheless, it might not be a bad idea if you were to defer the crossing of your bridges until you come to them." She unlatched the gate and swung it open for him to pass through.

He hesitated.

"I didn't intend to enter the house tonight," he explained. "I merely wanted to see Pablo and have a talk with him. My sudden appearance on the scene might, perhaps, prove very embarrassing to your family."

"I dare say. But that cannot be helped. Your right of entrance and occupancy cannot be questioned. Until the period of redemption expires, I think nobody will dispute your authority as master here."

"I had forgotten that phase of the situation. Thank you." he passed through the gate and closed it for her. Then he stepped to the side of the road, wet his handkerchief in a pool of clean rainwater, and mopped his eyes. "I'll have to abandon the luxury of tears,"' he declared, grimly. "They make one's eyes burn. By the way, I do not know your name."

"I am Kay Parker."

" 'Kay' for what?"

"Kathleen."

He nodded approvingly.

"You neglected to leave my dunnage at the mission, Miss Parker."

"After you told me who you were, I realized you would sleep at the ranch tonight, so I kept your things in the car. They are in your old room now."

"Thank you for an additional act of kindness and thoughtfulness." He adjusted his overseas cap, snugged his blouse down over his hips, flipped from it the wet sand deposited there by the paws of the hound-pack, and said, "Let's go."

Where the avenue debouched into the ranch yard, Pablo and Carolina awaited them. The old majordomo was wrapped in aboriginal dignity. His Indian blood bade him greet Don Mike as casually as if the latter had merely been sojourning in El Toro the past two years, but the faint strain of Spanish in him dictated a different course as Don Mike stepped briskly up to him with outstretched hand and greeted him affectionately in Spanish. Off came the weather-stained old sombrero, flung to the ground beside him, as Pablo dropped on his knees, seized his master's hand, and bowed his head over it.

76

"Don Miguel," he said, "my life is yours."

"I know it, you blessed old scalawag!" Don Mike replied in English, and ruffled the grizzled old bead before passing on to the expectant Carolina, who folded him tightly in her arms and wept soundlessly when he kissed her leathery cheek. While he was murmuring words of comfort to her, Pablo got up on his feet and recovered his hat.

"You see," he said to Kay, in a confidential tone, "Don Miguel José Maria Federico Noriaga Farrel loves us. Never no woman those boy kees since hees mother die twenty year before. So Carolina have the great honor like me. Yes!"

"Oh, but you haven't seen him kiss his sweetheart," Kay bantered the old man—and then blushed, in the guilty knowledge that her badinage had really been inspired by a sudden desire to learn whether Don Mike had a sweetheart or not. Pablo promptly and profanely disillusioned her.

"Those boy, he don' have some sweethearts, mees lady. He's pretty parteecular." He paused a moment and looked her in the face meaningly. "Those girls in thees country—pah! Hee's pretty parteecular, those boy."

His childish arrogance and consuming pride in his master stirred the girl's sense of humor.

"I think your Don Mike is *too* particular," she whispered. "Personally, I wouldn't marry him on a bet."

His slightly bloodshot eyes flickered with rage.

"You never get a chance," he assured her. "Those boy is of the *gente.* An' we don' call heem 'Don Mike' now. Before, yes; but now he is 'Don Miguel,' like hees father. Same, too, like hees gran'father."

Throughout this colloquy, Carolina had been busy exculpating herself from possible blame due to her failure to have prepared for the prodigal the sort of food she knew he preferred.

Farrel had quite a task pacifying her. At length he succeeded in gently dismissing both servants, and followed Kay toward the patio.

The girl entered first, and discovered that her family and their guest were not on the veranda, whereat she turned and gave her hand to Farrel.

"The butler will bring you some dinner to your room. We breakfast at eight-thirty. Good night."

"Thank you," he replied. "I shall be deeper in your debt if you will explain to your father and mother my apparent lack of courtesy in failing to call upon them this evening."

He held her hand for a moment. Then he bowed, gracefully and with studied courtesy, cap in hand, and waited until she had turned to leave him before he, in turn, betook himself to his room.

IX

IT WAS AS HE HAD LEFT IT. He smiled sadly as he noted his civilian clothes laid out on the bed. However, he would not wear them tonight. A little later, while he was hanging them in the clothes-press, a propitiatory cough sounded at the door. Turning, he beheld the strangest sight ever seen on the Rancho Palomar—a butler, bearing a tray covered with a napkin.

"Good evening," quoth Don Miguel civilly. "Set it down on the little table yonder, please. May I inquire why you bear the tray on your left hand and carry a pistol in your right?"

"Your servant, the man Pablo, has threatened my life,

sir, if I dared bear your dinner to you, sir. He met me a moment ago and demanded that I surrender the tray to him, sir. Instead, I returned to the kitchen, possessed myself of this pistol, and defied him, sir."

"I apologize for Pablo, and will see to it that he does not disturb you again—er—"

"Murray, sir."

"Thank you, Murray."

The butler was about to advance into the room and set the tray on the table as directed, when an unexpected *contretemps* occurred. A swarthy hand followed by a chambray-clad arm was thrust in the door, and the pistol snatched out of Murray's hand before the latter even knew what was about to transpire. Pablo Artelan stepped into the room.

"*Vamos!* Go!" he ordered, curtly, and relieved the astonished butler of the tray. Murray glanced at Don Miguel.

"Perhaps you'd better go," Don Miguel suggested, weakly. "Pablo is a trifle jealous of the job of waiting on me. We'll iron everything out in the morning. Good night, Murray."

"*Buenas noches, mono mio,*" Pablo grunted.

"I have a slight knowledge of the Spanish tongue, sir," Murray protested. "This blackamoor has insulted me, sir. Just now he said, in effect, 'Good night, monkey mine.' Earlier in the evening, he attempted to murder Mr. Parker's guest, Mr. Okada."

"It's a pity he didn't succeed," Don Miguel replied, and drew a dollar from his pocket. "You are very kind, Murray, but hereafter I shall not require your attendance. Pablo, give Murray his pistol."

Pablo returned the weapon.

"She ees one of those leetle lady-pistols, Don Miguel.

79

She can't kill somebody if she try," he declared, contemptuously. Murray pouched the dollar gratefully and beat a hurried retreat.

From under his denim jumper, Pablo brought forth a pint of claret.

"When the damned proheebeetion she's come, you father hee's sell fifty cow and buy plenty booze," he explained. He broke off into Spanish. "This wine, we stored in the old bakery, and your father entrusted me with the key. It is true. Although it is not lawful to permit one of my blood to have charge of wines and liquors, nevertheless, your sainted father reposed great confidence in me. Since his death, I have not touched one drop, although I was beset with temptation, seeing that if we did not drink it, others would. But Carolina would have none of it, and, as you know, your father, who is now, beyond doubt, an archangel, was greatly opposed to any man who drank alone. How often have I heard him declare that such fellows were not of the *gente!* And Carolina always refused to believe that you were dead. As a result, the years will be many before that wine is finished."

"My good Pablo, your great faith deserves a great reward. It is my wish that, tonight, you and Carolina shall drink one pint each to my health. Have you given some of this wine to the Parkers?"

Pablo shook his bead vigorously.

"That fellow, *El Mono,* was desirous of serving some to his master, and demanded of me the key, which I refused. Later, Señor Parker made the same demand. Him I refused also. This made him angry, and he ordered me to depart from El Palomar. Naturally, I told him to go to the devil. Don Miguel, this gringo grub appears to be better than I had imagined."

80

Farrel had little appetite for food, but, to please Pablo, be drank the soup and toyed with a piece of toast and a glass of wine while the majordomo related to him the events which had taken place at El Palomar since that never-to-be-forgotten day when Tony Moreno had ridden in with the telegram from Washington.

"Your beloved father—may the smile of Jesus warm him!—said nothing when he read this accursed message, Don Miguel. For three days, he tasted no food; throughout the days he sat beside me on the bench under the catalpa tree, gazing down into the San Gregorio as if he watched for you to ride up the road. He shed no tears—at least, not in the presence of his servants—but he was possessed of a great trembling. At the end of the third day, I rode to the mission and informed Father Dominic. Ah, Don Miguel, my heart was afflicted tenfold worse than before to see that holy man weep for you. When he had wept a space, he ordered Father Andréas to say a high mass for the repose of your soul, while he came up to the hacienda to remind your father of the comforts of religion. Whereat, for the first time since that vagabond Moreno came with his evil tidings, your father smiled. 'Good Father Dominic,' said he, 'I have need of the comfort of your presence and your friendship, but I would not blot out with thoughts of religion the memory of the honor that has come upon my house. God has been good to me. To me has been given the privilege of siring a man, and I shall not affront him with requests for further favors. Tomorrow, in El Toro, a general will pin on my breast the medal for gallantry that belongs to my dead son. As for this trembling, it is but a palsy that comes to many men of my age.'"

"He had a slight touch of it before I left," Don Miguel

reminded Pablo.

"The following day," Pablo continued, "I assisted him to dress, and was overjoyed to observe that the trembling had abated by half. By his direction, I saddled Panchito with the black carved leather saddle, and he mounted with my aid and rode to El Toro. I followed on the black mare. At El Toro, in the plaza, in the presence of all the people, a great general shook your father's hand and pinned upon his breast the medal that belongs to you. It was a proud moment for all of us. Then we rode back to the San Gregorio. At the mission, your father dismounted and went into the chapel to pray for your soul. For two hours, I waited before entering to seek him. I found him kneeling with his great body spread out over the *prie-dieu* where the heads of your house have prayed since the Mission de la Madre Dolorosa was built. His brain was alive, but one side of him was dead, and he smiled with his eyes. We carried him home in Father Dominic's automobile, and, two weeks later, he died in sanctity. The *gente* of San Marcos County attended his funeral.

"In February came Señor Parker, with great assurance, and endeavored to take possession. He showed me a paper, but what do I know of papers? I showed him your rifle, and he departed, to return with Don Nicolás Sandoval, the sheriff, who explained matters to me and warned me to avoid violence. I have dwelt here since in sorrow and perplexity, and because I have ridden the fences and watched over the stock, there has been no great effort made to disturb me. They have a cook—a Japanese, and two Japanese women servants. Also, this evening, Señor Parker brought with him as a guest another Japanese, whom he treats with as much consideration as if the fellow were your sainted father. I

82

do not understand such people. This Japanese visitor was given this room, but this honor I denied him."

"My father's business affairs are greatly tangled, Pablo. I shall have quite a task to place them in order," Don Miguel informed him, sadly.

"If it is permitted an old servant to appear curious, Don Miguel, how long must we submit to the presence of these strangers?"

"For the present, Pablo, I am the master here; therefore, these people are my guests. It has never been the custom with my people to be discourteous to guests."

"I shall try to remember that," Pablo replied, bitterly. "Forgive me, Don Miguel, for forgetting it. Perhaps I have not played well my part as the representative of my master during his absence."

"Do not distress yourself further in the matter, Pablo. What food have we at the ranch? Is there sufficient with which to enable Carolina to serve breakfast?"

"To serve it where, Don Miguel?"

"Where but in my home?"

"Blood of the devil!" Pablo slapped his thigh and grinned in the knowledge that the last of the Farrels, having come home, had decided to waste no time in assuming his natural position as the master of the Rancho Palomar. "We have oranges," he began, enumerating each course of the forthcoming meal on his tobacco-stained fingers. "Then there is flour in my possession for biscuits, and, two weeks ago, I robbed a bee tree; so we have honey. Our coffee is not of the best, but it is coffee. And we have eggs."

"Any butter, sugar, and cream?"

"Alas, no, Don Miguel!"

"Saddle a horse at once, go down to the mission, and

83

borrow some from Father Dominic. If he has none, ride over to the Gonzales rancho and get it. Bacon, also, if they have it. Tell Carolina I will have breakfast for five at half after eight."

"But this Japanese cook of Señor Parker's, Don Miguel?"

"I am not in a mood to be troubled by trifles tonight, Pablo."

"I understand, Don Miguel. The matter may safely be entrusted to me." He picked up the tray. "Sweet rest to you, sir, and may our Saviour grant a quick healing to your bruised heart. Good night."

"Good night, Pablo." Farrel rose and laid his hand on the old retainer's shoulder. "I never bothered to tell you this before, Pablo, but I want you to know that I do appreciate you and Carolina tremendously. You've stuck to me and mine, and you'll always have a home with me."

"Child," Pablo queried, huskily, "must we leave the rancho?"

"I'm afraid we must, Pablo. I shall know more about our plans after I have talked with Señor Parker."

X

THAT NIGHT, MIGUEL FARREL did not sleep in the great bed of his ancestors. Instead, he lay beneath his grandmother's silk crazy quilt and suffered. The shock incident to the discovery of the desperate straits to which he had been reduced had, seemingly, deprived him of the power to think coherently. Along toward daylight, however, what with sheer nervous exhaustion, he fell into a troubled doze from which he was awakened at seven o'clock by the entrance of Pablo, with a pitcher of hot water for his shaving.

"Carolina will serve breakfast, Don Miguel," he announced. "The Japanese cook tried to throw her out of the kitchen; so I have locked him up in the room where of old I was wont to place vaqueros who desired to settle their quarrels without interference."

"How about food, Pablo?"

"Unfortunately, Father Dominic had neither sugar nor cream. It appears such things are looked upon at the mission as luxuries, and the padres have taken the vow of poverty. He could furnish nothing save half a ham, which is of Brother Flavio's curing, and very excellent. I have tasted it before. I was forced to ride to the Gonzales rancho for the cream and sugar this morning, and have but a few moments ago returned."

Having deposited the pitcher of hot water, Pablo retired and, for several minutes, Miguel Farrel lay abed, gazing at the row of portraits of Noriagas and Farrels. His heart was heavy enough still, but the first benumbing shock of his grief and desperation had passed, and his natural courage and common sense were rapidly coming to his aid. He told himself that, with the dawning of the new day, he would no longer afford the luxury of self-pity, of vain repining for the past. He had to be up and doing, for a man's-sized task now confronted him. He had approximately seven months in which to rehabilitate an estate which his forebears had been three generations in dissipating, and the Gaelic and Celtic blood in him challenged defeat even in the very moment when, for all he knew to the contrary, his worldly assets consisted of approximately sixty dollars, the bonus given him by the government when parting with his services.

"I'll not give up without a battle," he told his ancestors aloud. "You've all contributed to my heavy load, but while the pack-straps hold and I can stand and see, I'll carry it. I'll fight this man Parker up to the moment he hands the county recorder the commissioner's deed and the Rancho Palomar has slipped out of my hands forever. But I'll fight fair. That splendid girl—ah, pooh! Why am I thinking of her?"

Disgusted with himself for having entertained, for a fleeting instant, a slight sentimental consideration for the daughter of his enemy—for as such he now regarded this man who planned to colonize the San Gregorio with Japanese farmers—he got out of bed and under the cold shower bath he had installed in the adjoining room years before. It, together with the tub bath formerly used by his father, was the only plumbing in the hacienda, and Farrel was just a little bit proud of it. He shaved, donned clean linen and an old dressing gown, and from his closet brought forth a pair of old tan riding-boots, still in an excellent state of repair. From his army-kit he produced a boot-brush and a can of tan polish, and fell to work, finding in the accustomed task some slight surcease from his troubles.

His boots polished to his satisfaction, he selected from the stock of old civilian clothing a respectable riding suit of English whip cord, inspected it carefully for spots, and, finding none, donned it. A clean starched chambray shirt, set off by a black silk Windsor tie, completed his attire, with the exception of a soft, wide, flat-brimmed gray-beaver hat, and stamped him as that which he had once been but was no longer—a California rancher of taste and means somewhat beyond the average.

It was twenty-five minutes past eight when he

concluded his leisurely toilet; so he stepped out of his room, passed round two sides of the porched patio, and entered the dining room. The long dining-table, hewed by band from fir logs by the first of the Noriagas, had its rough defects of manufacture mercifully hidden by a snow-white cloth, and he noted with satisfaction that places had been set for five persons. He hung his hat on a wall peg and waited with his glance on the door.

Promptly at eight-thirty, Carolina, smiling, happy, resplendent in a clean starched calico dress of variegated colors, stepped outside the door and rang vigorously a dinner bell that had called three generations of Noriagas and an equal number of generations of Farrels to their meals. As its musical notes echoed through the dewy patio, Murray, the butler, appeared from the kitchen. At sight of Farrel, he halted, puzzled, but recognized in him almost instantly the soldier who had so mysteriously appeared at the house the night before. *El Mono* was red of face and obviously controlling with difficulty a cosmic cataclysm.

"Sir," he announced, respectfully, "that Indian of yours has announced that he will shoot me if I attempt to serve breakfast."

Farrel grinned wanly.

"In that event, Murray," he replied, "if I were you, I should not attempt to serve breakfast. You might be interested to know that I am now master here and that, for the present, my own servants will minister to the appetites of my guests. Thank you for your desire to serve, but, for the present, you will not be needed here. If you will kindly step into the kitchen, Carolina will later serve breakfast to you and the maids."

"I'm quite certain I've never heard of anything so

extraordinary," Murray murmured. "Mrs. Parker is not accustomed to being summoned to breakfast with a bell."

"Indeed? I'm glad you mentioned that, Murray. Perhaps you would be good enough to oblige me by announcing breakfast to Mr. and Mrs. Parker, Miss Parker, and their guest, Mr. Okada."

"Thank you, sir," Murray murmured, and departed on his errand.

The first to respond to the summons was Kay. She was resplendent in a stunning wash dress and, evidently, was not prepared for the sight of Farrel standing with his back to the black adobe fireplace. She paused abruptly and stared at him frankly. He bowed.

"Good morning, Miss Parker. I trust that, despite the excitement of the early part of the night, you have enjoyed a very good rest."

"Good morning, Don Miguel. Yes; I managed rather well with my sleep, all things considered."

"You mustn't call me 'Don Miguel,' " he reminded her, with a faint smile. "I am only Don Miguel to the Indians and *pelados* and a few of my father's old Spanish friends who are sticklers for etiquette. My father was one of the last dons in San Marcos County, and the title fitted him because he belonged to the generation of dons. If you call me 'Don Miguel,' I shall feel a little bit alien."

"Well, I agree with you, Mr. Farrel. You are too young and modern for such an antiquated title. I like 'Don Mike' better."

"There is no further need for that distinguishing appellation," he reminded her, "since my father's death."

She looked at him for several seconds and said:

88

"I'm glad to see you've gotten a firm grip on yourself so soon. That will make it ever so much nicer for everybody concerned. Mother and father are fearfully embarrassed."

"I shall endeavor to relieve them of their embarrassment the instant I meet them."

"Here they come now," Kay warned, and glanced at him appealingly.

Her mother entered first, followed by the potato baron, with Parker bringing up the rear. Mrs. Parker's handsome face was suffused with confusion, and, from the hesitant manner in which she entered, Farrel realized she was facing an ordeal.

"Mother, this is Mr. Miguel Farrel," Kay announced.

"You are welcome to my poor house, Mrs. Parker," Farrel informed her, gravely, as he crossed the room and bent over her hand for a moment, releasing it to grasp the reluctant hand of her husband. "A double welcome, sir," he said, addressing Kay's father, who mumbled something in reply and introduced him to the potato baron, who bowed ceremoniously.

"Won't you please be seated?" Farrel pleaded. He gently steered Kay's mother to the seat on his right, and tucked her chair in under her, while Parker performed a similar service for his daughter. With the assurance of one whose right to do was unquestioned, Farrel took his seat at the head of the table and reached for the little silver call bell beside his plate, while Parker took an unaccustomed seat opposite the potato baron.

"Considering the distressing circumstances under which I arrived," Farrel observed, addressing himself to Mrs. Parker, and then, with a glance, including the rest of the company, "I find myself rather happy in the possession of unexpected company. The situation is delightfully unique—don't you think so, Mrs. Parker?"

"It isn't the least bit delightful, Mr. Farrel," the lady declared frankly and forcibly; "but it's dear of you to be so nice about it."

Mr. Parker's momentary embarrassment had passed, and with the feeling that his silence was a trifle disconcerting, he rallied to meet Miguel Farrel's attempt at gaiety.

"Well, Mr. Farrel, we find ourselves in a unique position, as you say. Kay informs me, however, that you are conversant with the circumstances that have conspired to make us your guests."

"Pray do not mention it. Under the peculiar conditions existing, I quite realize that you followed the only logical and sensible course."

Mrs. Parker heaved a small sigh of relief and gazed upon Farrel with new interest. He returned her gaze with one faintly quizzical, whereat, emboldened, she demanded,

"Well, what do you think of us for a jolly little band of usurpers, Mr. Farrel?"

"Why, I think I'm going to like you all very much if you'll give me half a chance."

"I'd give you almost anything rather than be kicked out of this house," she replied, in her somewhat loud, high-pitched voice. "I love it, and I think it's almost sinful on your part to have bobbed up so unexpectedly."

"Mother!" Kay cried reproachfully.

"Tut, tut, Kay, dear! When an obnoxious heir is reported dead, he should have the decency to stay dead, although, now that our particular nuisance is here, alive and well, I suppose we ought to let bygones be bygones and be nice to him—provided, of course, he continues to be nice to us. Are you inclined to declare war, Mr.

Farrel?"

"Not until every diplomatic course has been tried and found wanting," he replied.

Carolina entered, bearing five portions of sliced oranges.

"O Lord, forgive us our trespasses as we forgive those who trespass against us," Mrs. Parker cried. "Where is Murray?"

Farrel glanced down at his oranges and grinned.

"I'm afraid I excused Murray," he confessed.

Mrs. Parker burst into shrill laughter.

"John," she demanded of her husband, "what do you think of this young man?"

"Pick up the marbles, Mr. Farrel," Parker replied, with poorly assumed good humor. "You win."

"I think this is a jolly adventure," Kay struck in, quick to note the advantage of her outspoken mother's course. "Here you have been more than two months, mother, regarding yourself as the mistress of the Rancho Palomar, retinting rooms, putting in modern plumbing, and cluttering up the place with a butler and maids, when—presto!—overnight a stranger walks in and says kindly, 'Welcome to my poor house!' After which, he appropriates pa's place at the head of the table, rings in his own cook and waitress, forces his own food on us, and makes us like it. Young man, I greatly fear we're going to grow fond of you."

"You had planned to spend the summer here, had you not, Mrs. Parker?"

"Yes. John Parker, have you *any* idea what's going to become of us?"

"We'll go to Santa Barbara and take rooms at a hotel there for the present," he informed her.

"I loathe hotels," she protested.

"I think I informed you, Mrs. Parker, that you are welcome to my poor house," Farrel reminded her. "I shall be happy to have you remain here until I go away. After that, of course, you can continue to stay on without any invitation from me."

Parker spoke up.

"My dear Mr. Farrel, that is charming of you! Indeed, from all that we have heard of you, it is exactly the course we might expect you to take. Nevertheless, we shall not accept of your kindness. Now that you are here, I see no reason why I should impose the presence of my family and myself upon your hospitality, even if the court has given me the right to enter upon this property. I am confident you are competent to manage the ranch until I am eliminated or come into final possession."

"John, don't he a nut," his wife implored him. "We'll stay here. Yes, we shall, John. Mr. Farrel has asked us in good faith. You weren't trying to be polite just to put us at our ease, were you?" she demanded, turning to Farrel.

"Certainly not, Mrs. Parker. Of course, I shall do my level best to acquire the legal right to dispossess you before Mr. Parker acquires a similar right to dispossess me, but, in the interim, I announce an armistice. All those in favor of the motion will signify by saying 'Aye.' "

"Aye!" cried Kay, and "Aye!" shrilled her mother.

"No!" roared her husband.

"Excess of sound has no weight with me, Mr. Parker," their host announced. "The 'ayes' have it, and it is so ordered. I will now submit a platform for the approval of the delegates. Having established myself as host and won recognition as such, the following rules and regulations will govern the convention."

"Hear! Hear!" cried Mrs. Parker, and tapped the table with her spoon.

"The rapid ringing of a bell will be the signal for meals."

"Approved!" cried Kay.

"Second the motion!" shrilled her mother.

"My cook, Carolina, is queen of the kitchen, and Spanish cuisine will prevail. When you weary of it, serve notice, and your Japanese cook will be permitted to vary the monotony."

"Great!" Mrs. Parker almost yelled. "Right as a fox!"

"Murray shall serve meals, and—"

Pablo appeared in the door leading to the kitchen and spoke to Farrel in Spanish.

"Pardon, folks. Pablo has a telegram for me. Bring it here, Pablo."

The master of Palomar excused himself to his guests long enough to read the telegram, and then continued the announcement of his platform.

"My old battery commander, to whom I had promised Panchito, wires me that, for his sins, he has been made a major and ordered to the Army of Occupation on the Rhine. Therefore, he cannot use Panchito, and forbids me to express the horse to him. Consequently, Miss Parker, Panchito is *almost* yours. Consider him your property while you remain my guest."

"You darling Don Miguel Farrel!"

"Exuberant, my dear," her curious mother remarked, dryly, "but, on the whole, the point is well taken." She turned to Farrel. "How about some sort of nag for mother?"

"You may ride my father's horse, if that animal is still on the ranch, Mrs. Parker. He's a beautiful single-footer." He addressed Parker. "We used to have a big gray gelding that you'd enjoy riding, sir. I'll look him up for you after breakfast."

"Thank you, Mr. Farrel," Parker replied, flushing slightly, "I've been riding him already."

"Fine! He needed exercising. I have a brown mare for Mr. Okada, and you are all invited out to the corral after luncheon to see me bust Panchito's wild young brother for my own use."

"Oh, splendid!" Kay cried, enthusiastically.

"The day starts more auspiciously than I had hoped," her mother declared. "I really believe the Rancho Palomar is going to develop into a regular place with you around, Mr. Farrel."

XI

I AM CONVINCED," said Miguel Farrel, as he followed his guests out of the dining room onto the veranda, "that the Parkers' invasion of my home is something in the nature of a mixed misfortune. I begin to feel that my cloud has a silver lining."

"Of all the young men I have ever met, you can say the nicest things," Mrs. Parker declared. "I don't think you mean that last remark the least bit, but still I'm silly enough to like to hear you say it. Do sit down here awhile, Mr. Farrel, and tell us all about yourself and family."

"At the risk of appearing discourteous, Mrs. Parker, I shall have to ask you to excuse me this morning. I have a living to make. It is now a quarter past nine, and I should have been on the job at seven."

"But you only got home from the army last night," Kay pleaded. "You owe yourself a little rest, do you

94

not?"

"Not a minute. I must not owe anything I cannot afford. I have approximately seven months in which to raise approximately a quarter of a million dollars. Since I am without assets, I have no credit; consequently, I must work for that money. From today I am Little Mike, the Hustler."

"What's your program, Mr. Farrel?" Parker inquired, with interest.

"I should be grateful for an interview with you, sir, if you can spare the time. Later, I shall ride out over the ranch and make an inventory of the stock. Tomorrow, I shall go in to El Toro, see my father's attorney, ascertain if father left a will, and, if so, whom he named as executor. If he died intestate, I shall petition for letters of administration."

"Come, Kay, dear," Mrs. Parker announced; "heavy businessman stuff! I can't bear it! Will you take a walk with us, Mr. Okada?"

"Very much pleased," the potato baron replied, and flashed his fine teeth in a fatuous grin.

Farrel smiled his thanks as the good lady moved off with her convoy. Parker indicated a chair and proffered a cigar.

"Now then, Mr. Farrel, I am quite at your service."

Miguel Farrel lighted his cigar and thoughtfully tossed the burnt match into a bed of pansies. Evidently, he was formulating his queries.

"What was the exact sum for which the mortgage on this ranch was foreclosed, Mr. Parker?"

"Two hundred and eighty-three thousand, nine-hundred and forty-one dollars, and eight cents, Mr, Farrel."

"A sizable wad. Mortgage covered the entire ranch?"

95

Parker nodded.

"When you secured control of the First National Bank of El Toro, you found that old mortgage carried in its list of assets. You also discovered that it had been renewed several times, each time for a larger sum, from which you deduced that the prospects for the ultimate payment of the mortgage were nebulous and distant. Your hypothesis was correct. The Farrels never did today a task that could be deferred until tomorrow. Well, you went out and looked over the security for that mortgage. You found it to be ample—about three to one, as a very conservative appraisal. You discovered that all of the stockholders in the First National were old friends of my father and extremely reluctant to foreclose on him. As a newcomer, you preferred not to antagonize your associates by forcing the issue upon them, so you waited until the annual election of stockholders, when you elected your own Board of Directors. Then this Board of Directors sold you the mortgage, and you promptly foreclosed it. The shock of this unexpected move was a severe one on my father; the erroneous report of my death killed him, and here you are, where you have every legal right in the world to be. We were never entitled to pity, never entitled to the half-century of courtesy and consideration we received from the bank. We met the fate that is bound to overtake impractical dreamers and non-hustlers in this generation. The Mission Indian disappeared before the onslaught of the earlier Californians, and the old-time Californians have had to take a back seat before the onslaught of the Go-get-'em boys from the Middle West and the East. Presently they, too, will disappear before the hordes of Japanese that are invading our state. Perhaps that is progress—the survival of the fittest,

96

Quién sabe?"

He paused and smoked contemplatively. Parker cast a sidelong glance of curiosity at him, but said nothing, by his silence giving assent to all that the younger man had said.

"I suppose you wanted the Rancho Palomar," Miguel Farrel suggested, presently. "I dare say your purchase of this mortgage was not the mere outgrowth of an altruistic desire to relieve the First National Bank of El Toro of an annoyance and a burden."

"I think I admire your direct way of speaking, even if I hardly relish it," Parker answered, good-humoredly. "Yes; I wanted the ranch. I realized I could do things with it that nobody else in this county could do or would even think of doing."

"Perhaps you are right. For the sake of argument, I will admit that you are right. Now then, to business. This ranch is worth a million dollars, and at the close of the exemption period your claim against it will probably amount to approximately three hundred thousand dollars, principal and interest. If I can induce somebody to loan me three hundred thousand dollars wherewith to redeem this property, I can get the ranch back."

"Naturally."

"Not much use getting it back, however, unless I can raise another hundred thousand to restock it with purebred or good grade Herefords and purchase modern equipment to operate it." Parker nodded approvingly. "Otherwise," Farrel continued, "the interest would eat me alive, and in a few years I'd be back where I started."

"Do you think you can borrow four hundred thousand dollars in San Marcos County, Mr. Farrel?"

"No, sir. No private loan of that magnitude can be

97

floated in this country. You control the only bank in the county that can even consider it—and you'll not consider it."

"Hardly."

"Added to which handicap, I have no additional security to offer in the shape of previous reputation for ability and industry. I am the last of a long line of indolent, carefree spendthrifts."

"Yes; that is unfortunately true," Parker assented, gravely.

"Oh, not so unfortunate as it is embarrassing and inconvenient. We have always enjoyed life to the fullest, and, for that, only a fool would have regret. Would you be willing to file a satisfaction of that old mortgage and give me a new loan for five years for the amount now due on the property? I could induce one of the big packing companies to stake me to the cattle. All I would have to provide would be the range, and satisfy them that I am honest and know my business. And I can do that. Such an arrangement would give me time to negotiate a sale of part of the ranch and pay up your mortgage."

"I am afraid that my present plans preclude consideration of that suggestion," the banker replied, kindly, but none the less forcibly.

"I didn't think you would, but I thought I'd ask. As a general rule, it pays to try anything once where a fellow is in as desperate case as I am. My only hope, then, is that I may be able to sell the Farrel equity in the ranch prior to the twenty-second day of November."

"That would seem to be your best course, Mr. Farrel."

"When does the redemption period expire?"

Parker squirmed slightly.

"That is a difficult question to answer, Mr. Farrel. It

seems your father was something of a lawyer—"

"Yes; he graduated in law. Why, nobody ever knew, for he never had the slightest intention of practicing it. I believe it must have been because my grandfather, Michael Joseph I, had an idea that, since his son was a gentleman, he ought to have a college degree and the right to follow some genteel profession in case of disaster."

"Your father evidently kept abreast of the law," Parker laughed. "Before entering suit for foreclosure, I notified him by registered mail that the mortgage would not be renewed and made formal demand upon him for payment in full. When he received the notice from the El Toro postmaster to call for that registered letter, he must have suspected its contents, for he immediately deeded the ranch to you and then called for the registered letter."

Farrel began to chuckle.

"Good old dad!" he cried. "Put over a dirty Irish trick on you to gain time!"

"He did. I do not blame him for it. I would have done the same thing myself under the same circumstances." And Parker had the grace to join in the laugh. "When I filed suit for foreclosure," he continued, "he appeared in court and testified that the property belonged to his son, who was in the military service, in consequence of which the suit for foreclosure could not be pressed until after said son's discharge from the service."

"All praise to the power of the wartime moratoriums," Farrel declared. "I suppose you reentered the suit as soon as the report of my death reached you."

Parker chuckled.

"I did, Mr. Farrel, and secured a judgment. Then I took possession."

"Aren't you the picture of bad luck? Just when everything is shaping up beautifully for you, I appear in the flesh as exhibit A in the contention that your second judgment will now have to be set aside, because, at the time it was entered, it conflicted with the provisions of that blessed moratorium." Don Miguel smiled mirthlessly.

"There's luck in odd numbers," Parker retorted, dryly. "The next time I shall make that judgment stick."

"Well, at any rate, all these false starts help me out wonderfully," Don Miguel reminded him. "As matters stand this morning, the mortgage hasn't been foreclosed at all; consequently, you are really and truly my guests and doubly welcome to my poor house." He rose and stretched himself, gazing down the while at Parker, who regarded him quizzically. "Thank you for the interview, Mr. Parker. I imagine we've had our first and last business discussion. When you are ready to enter your third suit for foreclosure, I'll drop round to your attorney's office, accept service of the summons, appear in court, and confess judgment." Fell a silence. Then, "Do you enjoy the study of people, sir?" Don Miguel demanded, apropos of nothing.

"Not particularly, Mr. Farrel. Of course, I try to know the man I'm doing business with, and I study him accordingly, but that is all."

"I have not made myself explicit," his host replied. "The racial impulses which I observed cropping out in my father—first Irish, then Spanish—and a similar observance of the mixed impulses of the peons of this country, all of whom are Indian, with a faint admixture of Spanish blood—always interested me. I agree with Pope that 'the proper study of mankind is man.' I find it most interesting."

"For instance?" Parker queried. He had a feeling that in any conversation other than business which he might indulge in with this young man he would speedily find himself, as it were, in deep water close to the shore.

"I was thinking of my father. In looking through his effects last night, I came across indubitable evidence of his Celtic blood. Following the futile pursuit of an enemy for a quarter of a century, he died and left the unfinished job to me. Had he been all Spanish, he would have wearied of the pursuit a decade ago."

"I think every race has some definite characteristics necessary to the unity of that race," Parker replied, with interest. "Hate makes the Irish cohesive; pride or arrogance prevents the sun from setting on British territory; a passionate devotion to the soil has solidified the French republic in all its wars, while a blind submission to an overlord made Germany invincible in peace and terrible in war."

"I wonder what spiritual binder holds the people of the United States together, Mr. Parker?" Don Miguel queried naively.

"Love of country, devotion to the ideals of liberty and democracy," Parker replied promptly, just as his daughter joined them.

Farrel rose and surrendered to her his chair, then seated himself on the edge of the porch with his legs dangling over into a flower bed. His face was grave, but in his black eyes there lurked the glint of polite contempt.

"Did you hear the question and the answer, Miss Parker?" he queried.

She nodded brightly.

"Do you agree with your father's premise?" he pursued.

"Yes, I do, Don Mike."

"I do not. The mucilage in our body politic is the press agent, the advertising specialist, and astute propagandist. I wonder if you know that, when we declared war against Germany, the reason was *not* to make the world safe for democracy, for there are only two real reasons why wars are fought. One is greed and the other self-protection. Thank God, we have never been greedy or jealous of the prosperity of a neighbor. National aggrandizement is not one of our ambitions."

Kay stared at him in frank amazement.

"Then you mean that we entered the late war purely as a protective measure?"

"That's why I enlisted. As an American citizen, I was unutterably weary of having our hand crowded and our elbow joggled. I saw very clearly that, unless we interfered, Germany was going to dominate the world, which would make it very uncomfortable and expensive for us. I repeat that for the protection of our comfort and our bankroll we declared war, and anybody who tells you otherwise isn't doing his own thinking, he isn't honest with himself, and he's the sort of citizen who is letting the country go to the dogs because he refuses to take an intelligent interest in its affairs."

"What a perfectly amazing speech from an ex soldier!" Kay protested.

He smiled his sad, prescient smile.

"Soldiers deal with events, not theories. They learn to call a spade a spade, Miss Parker. I repeat: It wasn't a war to make the world safe for democracy. That phrase was just a slogan in a business campaign—the selling of stock in a military enterprise to apathetic Americans. We had to fight or be overrun; when we realized that, we fought. Are not the present antics of the Supreme

Council in Paris sufficient proof that saving democracy was just another shibboleth? Is not a ghastly war to be followed by a ghastly peace? The press agents and orators popularized the war with the unthinking and the hesitant, which is proof enough to me that we lack national unity and a definite national policy. We're a lot of sublimated jackasses, sacrificing our country to ideals that are worn at elbow and down at heel. 'Other times, other customs.' But we go calmly and stupidly onward, hugging our foolish shibboleths to our hearts, hiding behind them, refusing to do today that which we can put off until tomorrow. That is truly an Anglo-Saxon trait. In matters of secondary importance, we yield a ready acquiescence which emboldens our enemies to insist upon acquiescence in matters of primary importance. And quite frequently they succeed. I tell you the Anglo-Saxon peoples are the only ones under heaven that possess a national conscience, and because they possess it, they are generous enough to assume that other races are similarly endowed."

"I believe," Parker stuck in, as Don Miguel ceased from his passionate denunciation, "that all this is leading quite naturally to a discussion of Japanese emigration."

"I admit that the sight of Mr. Okada over in the corner of the patio, examining with interest the only sweet lime tree in North America, inspired my out burst," Farrel answered smilingly.

"You speak of our national shibboleths, Don Mike Farrel," Kay reminded him. "If you please, what might they be?"

"You will recognize them instantly, Miss Parker. Let us start with our Declaration of Independence 'All men are created equal.' Ah, if the framers of that great document had only written, 'All men are created theoretically equal!' For all men are not morally, intellectually, or commercially equal: For instance, Pablo is equal with me before the law, although I hazard the guess that if he and I should commit a murder, Pablo would be hanged and I would be sentenced to life imprisonment; eventually, I might be pardoned or paroled. Are you willing to admit that Pablo Artelan is not my equal?" he challenged suddenly.

"Certainly!" Kay and her father both cried in unison.

"Very well. Is Mr. Okada my equal?"

"He is Pablo's superior," Parker felt impelled to declare.

"He is not your equal," Kay declared firmly. "Dad, you're begging the question."

"Well, no," he assented, "Not from the Anglo-Saxon point of view. He is, however, from the point of view of his own nationals."

"Two parallel lines continued into infinity will never meet, Mr. Parker. I am a believer in Asia for Asiatics, and, in Japan, I am willing to accord a Jap equality with me. In my own country, however, I would deny him citizenship, by any right whatsoever, even by birth, I would deny him the right to lease or own land for agricultural or other purposes, although I would accord him office and warehouse space to carry on legitimate commerce. The Jap does that for us and no more, despite his assertions to the contrary. I would deny the right of emigration to this country of all Japanese, with certain exceptions necessary to friendly intercourse between the two countries; I would deny him the privilege of economic competition and marriage with our women. When a member of the great Nordic race fuses with a member of a pigmented race, both parties

104

to the union violate a natural law. Pablo is a splendid example of mongrelization."

"You are forgetting the shibboleths," Kay ventured to remind him.

"No; I am merely explaining their detrimental effect upon our development. The Japanese are an exceedingly clever and resourceful race. Brilliant psychologists and astute diplomatists, they have taken advantage of our pet shibboleth to the effect that all men are equal. Unfortunately, we propounded this monstrous and half-baked ideal to the world, and a sense of national vanity discourages us from repudiating it, although we really ought to. And as I remarked before, we possess an alert national conscience in international affairs, while the Jap possesses none except in certain instances where it is obvious that honesty is the best policy. I think I am justified, however, in stating that, upon the whole, Japan has no national conscience in international affairs. Her brutal exploitation of China and her merciless and bloody conquest of Korea impel that point of view from an Anglo-Saxon. When, therefore, the Tokyo government says, in effect, to us: 'For one hundred and forty-four years you have proclaimed to the world that all men are equal. Very well. Accept us. We are a world power. We are on a basis of equality with you,' and we lack the courage to repudiate this pernicious principle, we have tacitly admitted their equality. That is, the country in general has, because it knows nothing of the Japanese race—at least not enough for moderately practical understanding of the biological and economic issues involved. Indeed, for a long time, we Californians dwelt in the same fool's paradise as the remainder of the states. Finally, members of the Japanese race became so numerous and aggressive here that we couldn't help noticing them. Then we began to study them, and now, what we have learned amazes and frightens us, and we want the sister states to know all that we have learned, in order that they may cooperate with us. But, still, the Jap has us *tiron* in other ways."

"Has us what?" Parker interrupted.

"*Tiron*. Spanish slang. I mean he has us where the hair is short; we're hobbled."

"How?" Kay demanded.

His bright smile was triumphant.

"By shibboleths, of course. My friends, we're a race of sentimental idiots, and the Japanese know this and capitalize it. We have promulgated other fool shibboleths which we are too proud or too stupid to repudiate. 'America, the refuge for all the oppressed of the earth!' Ever hear that perfectly damnable shibboleth shouted by a Fourth of July orator? 'America, the hope of the world!' What kind of hope? Hope of freedom, social and political equality, equality of opportunity? Nonsense! Hope of more money, shorter hours, and license misnamed liberty; and when that hope has been fulfilled, back they go to the countries that denied them all that we give. How many of them feel, when they land at Ellis Island, that the ground whereon they tread is holy, sanctified by the blood and tears of a handful of great, brave souls who really had an ideal and died for it. Mighty few of the cattle realize what that hope is, even in the second generation."

"I fear," quoth Parker, "that your army experience has embittered you."

"On the contrary, it has broadened and developed me. It has been a liberal education, and it has strengthened my love for my country."

"Continue with the shibboleths. Don Mike," Kay

pleaded. Her big, brown eyes were alert with interest now.

"Well, when Israel Zangwill coined that phrase: 'The Melting Pot,' the title to his play caught the popular fancy of a shibboleth-crazy nation, and provided pap for the fanciful, for the theorists, for the nabby idealists and doctrinaires. If I melt lead and iron and copper and silver and gold in the same pot, I get a bastard metal, do I not? It is not, as a fused product, worth a tinker's hoot. Why, even Zangwill is not an advocate of the melting pot. He is a Jew, proud of it, and extremely solicitous for the welfare of the Jewish race. He is a Zionist—a leader of the movement to crowd the Arabs out of Palestine and repopulate that country with Jews. He feels that the Jews have an ancient and indisputable right to Palestine, although, parenthetically speaking, I do not believe that any smart Jew who ever escaped from Palestine wants to go back. I wouldn't swap the Rancho Palomar for the whole country."

Kay and her father laughed at his earnest yet whimsical tirade Don Miguel continued:

"Then we have that asinine chatter about 'America, the land of fair play.' In theory—yes, In actual practice—not always. You didn't accumulate your present assets, Mr. Parker, without taking an occasional chance on sidetracking equity when you thought you could beat the case. But the Jap reminds us of our reputation for fair play, and smilingly asks us if we are going to prejudice that reputation by discriminating unjustly against him?"

"It appears," the girl suggested. "that all these ancient national brags come home, like curses, to roost."

"Indeed they do, Miss Parker! But to get on with our shibboleths. We hear a great deal of twaddle about the

107

law of the survival of the fittest. I'm willing to abide by such a natural law, provided the competition is confined to mine own people—and I'm one of those chaps, who, to date, has failed to survive. But I cannot see any common sense in opening the lists to Orientals. We Californians know we cannot win in competition with them." He paused and glanced at Kay. "Does all this harangue bore you, Miss Parker?"

"Not at all. Are there any more shibboleths?"

"I haven't begun to enumerate them. Take, for instance, that old pacifist gag, that Utopian dream that is crystallized in the words: 'The road to universal peace.' All the long years when we were not bothered by wars or rumors of wars, other nations were whittling each other to pieces. And these agonized neighbors, longing, with a great longing, for world peace, looked to the United States as the only logical country in which a great cure-all for wars might reasonably be expected to germinate. So their propagandists came to our shores and started societies looking toward the establishment of brotherly love, and thus was born the shibboleth of universal peace, with Uncle Sam heading the parade like an old bellmare in a pack train. What these peace patriots want is peace at any price, although they do not advertise the fact. We proclaim to the world that we are a Christian nation. *Ergo,* we must avoid trouble. The avoidance of trouble is the policy of procrastinators, the vacillating, and the weak. For one cannot avoid real trouble. It supply will not be avoided; consequently, it might as well be met and settled for all time."

"But surely," Parker remarked, "California should subordinate herself to the wishes of the majority."

"Yes, she should," he admitted doggedly, "and she has in the the past. I think that was before California herself really knew that Oriental emigration was not solely a California problem but a national problem of the utmost importance. Indeed, it is international. Of course, in view of the fact that we Californians are already on the firing line, necessarily it follows that we must make some noise and, incidentally, glean some real first hand knowledge of this so-called problem. I think that when our fellow citizens know what we are fighting, they will sympathize with us and promptly dedicate the United States to the unfaltering principle that ours is a white man's country, that the heritage we have won from the wilderness shall be held inviolate for Nordic posterity and none other."

"Nevertheless, despite your prejudice against the race, you are bound to admire the Japanese—their manners, thrift, industry, and cleanliness." Parker was employing one of the old stock protests, and Don Miguel knew it.

"I do not admire their manners, but I do admire their thrift, industry, and cleanliness. Their manners are abominable. Their excessive courtesy is neither instinctive nor genuine; it is camouflage for a ruthless, greedy, selfish, calculating nature. I have met many Japanese, but never one with nobility or generosity of soul. They are disciples of the principles of expediency. If a mutual agreement works out to their satisfaction, well and good. If it does not, they present a humble and saddened mien. 'So sorry. I zink you no understand me. I don't mean zat.' And their peculiar Oriental psychology leads them to believe they can get away with that sort of thing with the straight thinking Anglo-Saxon. They have no code of sportsmanship; they are irritable and quarrelsome, and their contractual relations are incompatible with those of the Anglo-Saxon. They are not truthful. Individually and collectively, they are past masters of evasion and deceit, and therefore they are the greatest diplomatists in the world, I verily believe. They are wonderfully shrewd, and they have sense enough to keep their heads when other men are losing theirs. They are patient: they plan craftily and execute carefully and ruthlessly. Would you care to graft their idea of industry on the white race, Mr. Parker?"

"I would," Parker declared, firmly. "It is getting to be the fashion nowadays for white men to do as little work as possible, and half do that."

"I would not care to see my wife or my mother or my sister laboring twelve to sixteen hours a day as Japanese force their women to labor, I would not care to contemplate the future mothers of our race drawn from the ranks of twisted, stunted, broken-down, and prematurely aged women. Did you ever see a bent Japanese girl of twenty waddling in from a day of labor in a field? To emulate Japanese industry, with its peonage, its horrible, unsanitary factory conditions, its hopelessness, would be to thrust woman's hard won sphere in modern civilization back to where it stood at the dawn of the Christian era. Do you know, Miss Parker, that love never enters into consideration when a Japanese contemplates marriage? His sole purpose in acquiring a mate is to beget children, to scatter the seed of Yamato over the world, for that is a religious duty. A Jap never kisses his wife or shows her any evidences of affection. She is a chattel, and if anybody should, by chance, discover him kissing his wife, he would be frightfully mortified."

"What of their religious views, Don Mike?"

"If Japan can be said to have an official religion, it is

Shintoism, not Buddhism, as so many Occidental people believe. Shintoism is ancestor worship, and ascribes divinity to the emperor. They believe he is a direct descendant of the sun-god, Yamato."

"Why, they're a heathen nation!" Kay's tones were indicative of amazement.

Farrel smiled his tolerant smile.

"I believe, Miss Parker, that any people who will get down on all fours to worship the picture of their emperor and, at this period of the world's progress, ascribe to a mere human being the attributes of divinity, are certainly deficient in common sense, if not in civilization. However, for the purpose of insuring the realization of the Japanese national aspirations, Shintoism is a need vital to the race. Without it, they could never agree among themselves for they are naturally quarrelsome, suspicious and irritable. However, by subordinating everything to the state via this religious channel, there has been developed a national unity that has never existed with any other race. The power of cohesion of this people is marvelous, and will enable it, in days to come, to accomplish much for the race. For that reason alone, our very lack of cohesion renders the aspirations of Japan comparatively easy of fulfillment unless we wake up and attend to business."

"How do you know all this, Mr. Farrel?" Parker demanded incredulously.

"I have read translations from editorials in Japanese newspapers both in Japan and California; I have read translations of the speeches of eminent Japanese statesmen; I have read translations from Japanese official or semi-official magazines, and I have read translations from patriotic Japanese novels. I know what

111

I am talking about. The Japanese race holds firmly to the belief that it is the greatest race on the face of the globe, that its religion, Shintoism, is the one true faith, that it behooves it to carry this faith to the benighted of other lands and, if said benighted do not readily accept Shintoism, to force its blessings upon them willy-nilly. They believe that they know what is good for the world; they believe that the resources of the world were put here to be exploited by the people of the world, regardless of color, creed, or geographical limitation. They feel that they have as much right in North America as we have, and they purpose overrunning us and making our country Japanese territory. And it was your purpose to aid in the consummation of this monstrous ambition," he charged bluntly.

"At least," Parker defended, "they are a more wholesome people than southern Europeans. And they are not Mongolians."

Farrel's eyebrows arched.

"You have been reading Japanese propaganda," he replied. "Of course they are Mongolians. Everybody who has reached the age of reason knows that. One does not have to be a biologist to know that they are Mongolians. Indeed, the only people who deny it are the Japanese, and they do not believe it. As for southern Europeans, have you not observed that nearly all of them possess brachycephalic skulls, indicating the influence upon them of Mongolian invasions thousands of years ago and supplying, perhaps, a very substantial argument that, if we find the faintly Mongoloid type of emigrant repugnant to us, we can never expect to assimilate the purebred Mongol."

"What do you mean, 'brachycephalic'?" Parker queried, uneasily.

"They belong to the race of round heads. Didn't you know that ethnologists grub round in ancient cemeteries and tombs and trace the evolution and wanderings of tribes of men by the skulls they find there?"

"I did not."

Kay commenced to giggle at her father's confusion The latter had suddenly, as she realized, made the surprising discovery that in this calm son of the San Gregorio he bad stumbled upon a student, to attempt to break a conversational lance with whom must end in disaster. His daughter's mirth brought him to a realization of the sorry figure he would present in argument.

"Well, my dear, what are you laughing at?" he demanded, a trifle austerely.

"I'm laughing at you. You told me yesterday you were loaded for these Californians and could flatten their anti-Japanese arguments in a jiffy."

"Perhaps I am loaded still. Remember, Kay, Mr. Farrel has done all of the talking and we have been attentive listeners. Wait until I have had my innings."

"By the way, Mr. Parker," Farrel asked, "who loaded you up with pro-Japanese arguments?"

Parker flushed and was plainly ill at ease. Farrel turned to Kay.

"I do not know yet where you folks came from, but I'll make a bet that I can guess—in one guess."

"What will you bet, my erudite friend?" the girl bantered.

"I'll bet you Panchito against a box of fifty of the kind of cigars your father smokes,"

"Taken. Where do we hail from, Don Mike?"

"From New York city."

"Dad, send Mr. Farrel a box of cigars."

113

"Now, I'll make you another bet. I'll stake Panchito against another box of the same cigars that your father is a member of the Japan Society, of New York city."

"Send Mr. Farrel another box of cigars, popsy-wops. Don Mike, how *did* you guess it?"

"Oh, all the real plutocrats in New York have been sold memberships in that instrument of propaganda by the wily sons of Nippon. The Japan Society is supposed to be a vehicle for establishing friendlier commercial and social relations between the United States and Japan. The society gives wonderful banquets and yammers away about the Brotherhood of Man and sends out pro-Japanese propaganda. Really, it's a wonderful institution, Miss Parker. The millionaire white men of New York finance the society, and the Japs run it. It was some shrewd Japanese member of the Japan Society who sent you to Okada on this land deal, was it not, Mr. Parker?"

"You're too good a guesser for comfort," the latter parried, "I'm going to write some letters. I'm motoring in to El Toro this afternoon, and I'll want to mail them."

" 'Sufficient unto the day is the evil thereof,' " Don Miguel assured him lightly, "Whenever you feel the urge for further information about yourself and your Japanese friends, I am at your service I expect to prove to you in about three lessons that you have unwittingly permitted yourself to develop into a very poor citizen, even if you did load up with Liberty Bonds and deliver four minute speeches during all of the loan drives."

"Oh, I'm as good as the average American, despite what you say," retorted the banker, good-naturedly, as be left them.

The master of Palomar gazed after the retreating figure of his guest. In his glance there was curiosity,

114

pain, and resignation. He continued to stare at the door through which Parker had disappeared, until roused from his reverie by Kay's voice.

"The average American doesn't impress you greatly, does he, Don Mike?"

"Oh, I'm not one of that supercilious breed of Americans which toadies to an alleged European culture by finding fault with his own people," he hastened to assure her. "What distresses me is the knowledge that we are a very moral nation, that we have never subjugated weaker peoples, that we have never coveted our neighbor's goods, that we can outthink and outwork and outgame and outinvent every nation under heaven, and yet haven't brains enough to do our own thinking in world affairs. It is discouraging to contemplate the smug complacency, whether it be due to ignorance or apathy, which permits aliens to reside in our midst and set up agencies for our destruction and their benefit. If I— Why, you're in riding costume, aren't you?"

"You will never be popular with women if you do not mend your ways," she informed him, with a little grimace of disapproval. "Do you not know that women loathe non-observing men?"

"So do I. Stodgy devils! Sooner or later, the fool killer gets them all. Please do not judge me today, Miss Parker. Perhaps, after a while, I may be more discerning. By Jupiter, those very becoming riding togs will create no end of comment among the natives!"

"You said Panchito was to be mine while I am your guest, Don Mike."

"I meant it."

"I do not relish the easy manner in which you risk parting with him. The idea of betting that wonder horse against a box of filthy cigars!"

115

"Oh, I wasn't risking him," he retorted, dryly, "However, before you ride Panchito, I'll put him through his paces. He hasn't been ridden for three or four months, I dare say, and when he feels particularly good, he carries on just a little."

"If he's sober-minded, may I ride him today?"

"We shall quarrel if you insist upon treating yourself as company. My home and all I possess are here for your happiness. If your mother and father do not object—"

"My father doesn't bother himself opposing my wishes, and mother—by the way, you've made a perfectly tremendous hit with mother. She told me I could go riding with you."

He blushed boyishly at this vote of confidence. Kay noted the blush, and liked him all the better for it.

"Very well," he answered. "We'll ride down to the mission first. I must pay my respects to my friends there—didn't bother to look in on them last night, you know. Then we will ride over to the Sepulvida ranch for luncheon. I want you to know Anita Sepulvida. She's a very lovely girl and a good pal of mine. You'll like her."

"Let's go," she suggested, "while mother is still convoying Mr. Okada. He is still interested in that sweet lime tree. By the way," she continued, as they rose and walked down the porch together, "I have never heard of a sweet lime before."

"It's the only one of its kind in this country, Miss Parker, and it is very old. Just before it came into bearing for the first time, my grandmother, while walking along the porch with a pan of sugar in her hands, stubbed her toe and fell off the porch, spilling her pan of sugar at the base of the tree. The result of this accident is noticeable in the fruit to this very day."

She glanced up at him suspiciously, but not even the shadow of a smile hovered on his grave features. He opened the rear gate for her and they passed out into the compound.

"That open fireplace in the adobe wall under the shed yonder was where the cowboys used to sit and dry themselves after a rainy day on the range," he informed her. "In fact, this compound was reserved for the help. Here they held their bailies in the old days."

"What is that little building yonder—that lean-to against the main adobe wall?" Kay demanded.

"That was the settlement room. You must know that the possessors of dark blood seldom settle a dispute by argument, Miss Parker, In days gone by, whenever a couple of peons quarreled (and they quarreled frequently), the majordomo, or foreman of the ranch, would cause these men to be stripped naked and placed in this room to settle their row with nature's weapons. When honor was satisfied, the victor came to this grating and announced it. Not infrequently, peons have emerged from this room minus an ear or a nose, but, as a general thing, this method of settlement was to be preferred to knife or pistol."

Farrel tossed an empty box against the door and invited the girl to climb up on it and peer into the room. She did so. Instantly a ferocious yell resounded from the semidarkness within.

"Good gracious! Is that a ghost?" Kay cried, and leaped to the ground.

"No; confound it!" Farrel growled. "It's your Japanese cook. Pablo locked him in there this morning, in order that Carolina might have a clear field for her culinary art. Pablo!"

His cry brought an answering hail from Pablo, over at

117

the barn, and presently the old majordomo entered the compound. Farrel spoke sternly to him in Spanish, and, with a shrug of indifference, Pablo unlocked the door of the settlement room and the Japanese cook bounded out. He was inarticulate with frenzy, and disappeared through the gate of the compound with an alacrity comparable only to that of a tin-canned dog.

"I knew he had been placed here temporarily," Don Miguel confessed, "but I did think Pablo would have sense enough to let him out when breakfast was over. I'm sorry."

"I'm not. I think that incident is the funniest I have ever seen," the girl laughed. "Poor outraged fellow!"

"Well, if you think it's funny, so do I. Any sorrow I felt at your cook's incarceration was due to my apprehension as to your feelings, not his."

"What a fearful rage he is in, Don Mike!"

"Oh, well, he can help himself to the fruit of our famous lime tree and get sweet again. Pablo, you russet scoundrel, no more rough stuff if you know what's good for you. Where is Panchito?"

"I leave those horse loose in the pasture," Pablo replied, a whit abashed. "I like for see if those horse he got some brains like before you go ride heem. For long time Panchito don' hear hees boss call heem. Mebbeso he forget—no?"

"We shall see, Pablo."

XII

THEY WALKED OUT TO THE BARN. In a little green field, in the oak-studded valley below, a dozen horses were feeding. Farrel whistled shrilly. Instantly, one of the horses raised his head and listened. Again Farrel whistled, and a neigh answered him as Panchito broke from the herd and came galloping up the slope. When his master whistled again, the gallop developed into a furious burst of speed; whereat Farrel slipped inside the barn and shut the door, while round and round the barn Panchito galloped, seeking the lost master.

Suddenly Don Miguel emerged and, with little affectionate nickerings, the beautiful animal trotted up to him, ran his head over the master's shoulder, and rubbed his sleek cheek against the man's. Farrel nuzzled him and rubbed him lovingly between the ears before producing a lump of sugar. Upon command, Panchito squatted on his hind quarters like a dog and held his head out stiffly. Upon his nose Farrel balanced the lump of sugar, backed away, and stood in front of him. The horse did not move. Suddenly Farrel snapped his fingers. With a gentle toss of his head, Panchito threw the lump of sugar in the air and made a futile snap at it as it came down. Then he rose, picked the lump up carefully, and, holding it between his lips, advanced and proffered his master a bite.

"Oh, you eat it yourself!" Farrel cried, and reached for the horse's unkempt mane. With the ease of long practice, he swung aboard the horse and, at the touch of his heels, Panchito bounded away. Far down the mesa he raced, Farrel guiding him with his knees; then back and over the six-foot corral fence with something of the airy freedom of a bird. In the corral, Farrel slid off, ran with the galloping animal for fifty feet, grasping his mane, and sprang completely over him, ran fifty feet more and sprang back, as nimbly as a monkey. Panchito was galloping easily, steadily, now, at a trained gait, like a circus horse, so Farrel sat sideways on him and discarded his boots, after which he stood erect on the smooth, glossy back and rode him, first on one foot, then on the other. Next he sat down on the animal again and clapped his hands.

"Panchito, my boots!" he ordered. But Panchito only pinned his ears and shook his head. "You see," Farrel called to Kay, "he is a gentleman, and declines to perform a menial service. But I shall force him. Panchito, you rebel, pick up my boots and hand them to me."

For answer, Panchito threw his hind end aloft half a dozen times, and Kay's silvery laugh echoed through the corral as Farrel, appearing to lose his seat, slid forward on the horse's withers and clung with arms and legs round Panchito's neck, simulating terror. Thereupon, Panchito stood up on his hind legs, and Farrel, making futile clutchings at the horse's mane, slid helplessly back over his mount's glossy rump and sat down rather solidly in the dust of the corral.

"Bravo!" the girl cried. "Why, he's a circus horse!"

"I've schooled him a little for trick riding at rodeos, Miss Parker. We've carried off many a prize, and when I dress in the motley of a clown and pretend to ride him rough and do that silly slide, most people enjoy it."

Farrel got up, recovered his boots, and put them on.

"He'll do, the old humorist," he announced, as he joined her. "He hasn't forgotten anything, and wasn't he

120

glad to see me again? You use an English saddle, I dare say, and ride with a short stirrup?"

Panchito dutifully followed like a dog at heel to the tackroom, where Farrel saddled him and carefully fitted the bridle with the snaffle-bit. Following a commanding slap on the fore leg, the intelligent animal knelt for Kay to mount him, after which, Farrel adjusted the stirrup leathers for her.

In the meantime, Pablo was saddling a splendid, big dappled-gray gelding.

"One of the best roping horses in California, and very fast for half a mile. He's half thoroughbred," Farrel explained. "He was my father's mount." He caressed the gray's head. "Do you miss him, Bob, old-timer?" he queried.

Kay observed her companion's saddle. It was of black, hand carved leather, with sterling silver trimmings and long *tapaderas*—a saddle to thrill every drop of the Castilian blood that flowed in the veins of its owner. The bridle was of finely plaited rawhide, with fancy sliding knots, a silver Spanish bit, and single reins of silver link chain and plaited rawhide. At the pommel hung coiled a well-worn rawhide riata.

When the gray was saddled, Farrel did not mount, but came to Kay and handed her the horsehair leading rope.

"If you will be good enough to take the horses round in front," he suggested, "I'll go back to the kennels and loose the hounds. On our way over to the Sepulvida rancho, we're liable to put up a panther or a coyote, and if we can get our quarry out into the open, we'll have a glorious chase. I've run coyotes and panthers down with Panchito and roped them. A panther isn't to be sneezed at," he continued, apologetically. "The state pays a bounty of thirty dollars for a panther pelt, and then gives

121

you back the pelt."

Five minutes later, when he came round the north corner of the old hacienda, his hounds frisking before him, he met Kay riding to meet him on Panchito, but the gray gelding was not in sight. The girl was excited.

"Where is my mount, Miss Parker?" he demanded.

"Just as I rode up in front, a man came out of the patio, and started that automobile hurriedly. He had scarcely gotten it turned round when one of his front tires blew out. This seemed to infuriate him and frighten him. He considered a minute or two, then suddenly ran over to me, snatched the leading rope out of my hand, mounted, and fled down the avenue at top speed."

" 'The wicked flee when no man pursueth'," the master of Palomar replied, quietly, and stepped over to the automobile for an examination of the license "Ah, my father's ancient enemy!" he exclaimed, "André Loustalot has been calling on your father, and has just learned that I am living. I think I comprehend his reason for borrowing my horse and dusting out of here so precipitately."

"There he goes now!" Kay cried, as the gray burst from the shelter of the palms in the avenue and entered the long open stretch of white road leading down the San Gregorio.

Don Mike's movements were as casual as if the theft of a horse in broad daylight was an everyday occurrence.

"Unfortunately for that stupid fellow, he borrowed the wrong horse," he announced, gravely. "The sole result of his action will be to delay our ride until tomorrow. I'm sorry, but it now becomes necessary for me to ask you for Panchito."

She slid silently to the ground. Swiftly but calmly he

122

readjusted the stirrups; then he faced the girl.

"Want to see some fun?" he demanded.

"Why—yes," she replied, breathlessly.

"You're a good little sport. Take your father's car and follow me. Please bring Pablo with you, and tell him I said he was to bring his rifle. If Loustalot gets me, he is to follow on Panchito and get Loustalot. Thank you, Miss Parker."

He swung lightly into the unaccustomed flat saddle and, disdaining to follow the road, cut straight across country, Panchito taking the fences easily, the hounds belling lustily as they strung out behind him. Kay did not wait to follow his flight, but calling for William to get out the car, she ran round to the barn and delivered Farrel's message to Pablo, who grunted his comprehension and started for his cabin at a surprising rate of speed for an old man. Five minutes after Farrel had left the Rancho Palomar, Kay and Pablo were roaring down the valley in pursuit.

Half a mile beyond the mission they came upon Don Mike and his father's enemy. In the first mile, the latter had ridden the gray out; spent, gasping, the gallant animal was proceeding at a leg-weary, lumbering gallop when Miguel Farrel, following on Panchito at half that gallant animal's speed, came up with Loustalot. Straight at the big gray he drove, "hazing" him off the road and stopping him abruptly, At the same time, he leaped from Panchito full on top of Loustalot, and bore the latter crashing to the ground.

The chase was over. Half-stunned, the enemy of Don Miguel José Farrel II lay flat on his back, blinking up at Don Miguel Farrel III as the latter's knees pressed the Loustalot breast, the while his fingers clasped the hairy Loustalot throat in a grip that was a promise of death if

123

the latter struggled.

As Kay drew up in the car and, white-faced and wondering, gazed at the unwonted spectacle, Miguel Farrel released his captive and stood erect.

"So sorry to have made a brawl in your presence, Miss Parker, but he would have ruined our old Bob horse if I hadn't overtaken him." He turned to the man on the ground. "Get up, Loustalot!" The latter staggered to his feet. "Pablo," Farrel continued, "take this man back to the ranch and lock him up in your private calaboose. See that he does not escape, and permit no one to speak with him,"

From the gray's saddle he took a short piece of rope, such as vaqueros use to tie the legs of an animal when they have roped and thrown it.

"Mount!" he commanded. Loustalot climbed wearily aboard the spent gray, and held his hands behind him with Farrel bound them securely. Pablo thereupon mounted Panchito, took the gray's leading rope, and started back to the ranch.

"How white your face is!" Farrel murmured, deprecatingly, as be came to the side of the car. "So sorry our ride has been spoiled." He glanced at his wristwatch. "Only ten o'clock," he continued. "I wonder if you'd be gracious enough to motor me in to El Toro. Your father plans to use the car after luncheon, but we will be back by twelve-thirty."

"Certainly. Delighted!" the girl replied, in rather a small, frightened voice.

"Thank you." He considered a moment. "I think it no less than fair to warn you, Miss Parker, that my trip has to do with a scheme that may deprive your father of his opportunity to acquire the Rancho Palomar at one-third of its value. I think the scheme may be at least partially

124

successful, but if I am to succeed at all, I'll have to act promptly."

She held out her hand to him.

"My father plays fair, Don Mike. I hope you win."

And she unlatched the door of the tonneau and motioned him to enter.

XIII

THE RETURN OF PABLO ARTELAN to the hacienda with his employer's prisoner was a silent and dignified one up to the moment they reached the entrance to the palm avenue. Here the prisoner, apparently having gathered together his scattered wits, turned in the saddle and addressed his guard.

"Artelan," he said, in Spanish, "if you will permit me to go, I will give you five thousand dollars."

"If you are worth five thousand dollars to me," the imperturbable Pablo replied, calmly, "how much more are you worth to Don Miguel Farrel?"

"Ten thousand! You will be wealthy."

"What need have I for wealth, Loustalot? Does not Don Miguel provide all things necessary for a happy existence?"

"I will give you twelve thousand. Do not be a fool, Artelan. Come; be sensible and listen to reason."

"Silence, animal! Is not the blood of my brother on your head? One word—"

"Fifteen thousand, Artelan. Quick. There is little time to—"

Pablo rode up beside him and quite deliberately smote the man heavily across the mouth with the back of his hand.

"There will be no more talk of money," he commanded, tersely.

John Parker had finished writing his letters and was standing, with his wife and the potato baron, in front of the hacienda when Pablo and his prisoner rode into the yard. Thin rivulets of blood were trickling from the Basque's nose and lips; his face was ashen with rage and apprehension.

"Why, Loustalot, what has happened?" Parker cried, and stepped out to intercept the gray gelding, but Pablo, riding behind, struck the gray on the flank, and the animal bounded forward. But Parker was not to be denied. He, too, leaped, seized the reins, and brought the animal to a halt. Pablo glared at him balefully; then, remembering that this man was no longer an interloper, but an honored guest of the house of Farrel, he removed his sombrero and bowed courteously.

"Señor Parker," he explained, "thees man, Loustalot, have made the beeg meestake to steal thees horse from Don Miguel Farrel. For long time since Don Miguel he's beeg like leetle baby, thees Basque he cannot set the foot on the Rancho Palomar, but today, because he theenk Don Miguel don' leeve, theese fellow have the beeg idea she's all right for come to theese rancho. Well, he come." Here Pablo shrugged. "I think mebbeso you tell theese Loustalot Don Miguel have come back. *Car-ramba!* He is scared like hell. Queeck, like rabbeet, he run for those automobile, but those automobile she have one leak in the wheel. *Señor,* thees is the judgment of God. Myself, I theenk the speerit of Don Miguel's father have put the nail where thees fellow can peeck heem up. Well, when hee's nothing for do, hee's got for do sometheeng, eh? *Mira!* If Don Miguel catch thees coyote on the Rancho Palomar, hee's cut off hees tail

126

like that"—and Pablo snapped his tobacco-stained fingers. "Queeck! Hees got for do something for make the vamose. The Señorita Parker, she rides Panchito and holds the gray horse for Don Miguel, who has gone for get the dogs. Thees animal, Loustalot, hee's go crazy with the fear, so he grab thees gray horse from the Señorita Parker and hee's ride away fast like the devil just when Don Miguel arrive with the hounds. Then Don Miguel, hee's take Panchito and go get thees man."

"But where are Don Miguel and Miss Parker now?"

"Mees Parker, she take the automobile; the *señorita* and Don Miguel go to El Toro. Me, I come back with thees Basque for put heem in the calaboose."

"But, Pablo, you cannot confine this man without a warrant."

Pablo, too polite to argue with a guest, merely bowed and smiled deprecatingly.

"My boss, hee's tell me put thees fellow in the calaboose. If trouble come from thees—well, Don Miguel have the fault, not Pablo Artelan. If the *señor* please for let go the gray horse—no?"

"Farrel has gone to El Toro to attach my bank account and my sheep," the Basque explained in a whisper, leaning low over the gray's neck. "His father had an old judgment against me. When I thought young Farrel dead, I dared do business—in my own name— understand? Now, if he collects, you've lost the Rancho Palomar—help me, for God's sake, Parker!"

Parker's hand fell away from the reins.

"I have no sympathy for you, Loustalot," he replied. coldly. "If you have stolen this horse, you must pay the penalty. I shall not help you. This is no affair of mine." And he stepped aside and waved Loustalot back into Pablo's possession, who thanked him politely and rode

127

away round the hacienda wall. Three minutes later, Loustalot, his hands unbound, was safe under lock and key in the settlement room, and Pablo, rifle in lap, sat on a box outside the door and rolled a brown-paper cigarette.

Throughout the preceding colloquy, Mrs. Parker had said nothing. When Pablo and his prisoner had disappeared, she asked her husband:

"What did that man say to you? He spoke in such a low tone I couldn't hear him."

Parker, without hesitation, related to her, in the presence of Okada, the astonishing news which Loustalot had given him.

"Good!" the lady declared, emphatically. "I hope that delightful Don Mike collects every penny."

"Very poor business, I zink," Mr. Okada opined, thoughtfully.

"At any rate," Parker observed, "our host isn't letting the grass grow under his feet. I wonder if he'll attach Loustalot's automobile. It's new, and worth about eight thousand dollars. Well, we shall see what we shall see."

"I zink I take little walk. 'Scuse me, please," said Okada, and bowed to Parker and his wife. He gave both the impression that he had been an unwilling witness to an unhappy and distressing incident and wished to efface himself from the scene. Mrs. Parker excused him with a brief and somewhat wintry smile, and the little Oriental started strolling down the palm-lined avenue. No sooner had the gate closed behind them, however, than he hastened back to Loustalot's car, and at the end of ten minutes of furious labor had succeeded in exchanging the deflated tire for one of the inflated spare tires at the rear of the car. This matter attended to, he strolled over to the ranch blacksmith shop and searched

128

through it until he found that which he sought—a long, heavy pair of bolt clippers such as stockmen use for dehorning young cattle. Armed with this tool, he slipped quietly round to the rear of Pablo's "calaboose," and went to work noiselessly on the small iron-grilled window of the settlement room.

The bars were an inch in diameter and too thick to be cut with the bolt clippers, but Okada did not despair. With the tool he grasped the adobe window ledge and bit deeply into it. Piece after piece of the ancient adobe came away, until presently the bases of the iron bars lay exposed; whereupon Okada seized them, one by one, in his hands and bent them upward. and outward, backward and forward, until he was enabled to remove them altogether. Then he stole quietly back to the blacksmith shop, restored the bolt clippers, went to the Basque's automobile, and waited.

Presently, Loustalot appeared warily round the corner. A glance at his automobile showed that the flat tire had been shifted; whereupon he nodded his thanks to the Japanese, who stared impassively while the Basque climbed into his car, threw out his low gear, let go his brakes, and coasted silently out of the yard and into the avenue. The hacienda screened him from Pablo's view as the latter, all unconscious of what was happening, dozed before the door of the empty settlement room. Once over the lip of the mesa, Loustalot started his car and sped down the San Gregorio as fast as he dared drive.

XIV

FOLLOWING HIS ILLUMINATING INTERVIEW with Pablo and Loustalot, John Parker returned to a chair on the porch patio, lighted a fresh cigar, and gave himself up to contemplating the tangle in his hitherto well laid plans. An orderly and methodical man always, it annoyed him greatly to discover this morning that a diabolical circumstance over which he had no control and which he had not remotely taken into consideration should have arisen to embarrass and distress him and, perchance, plunge him into litigation. Mrs. Parker, having possessed herself of some fancy work, took a seat beside him, and, for the space of several minutes, stitched on, her thoughts, like her husband's, evidently bent upon the affairs of Miguel Farrel.

"Who is this gory creature Pablo just brought in?" she demanded, finally.

"His name is André Loustalot, Kate, and he is a sheepman from the San Carpojo country—a Basque, I believe. He hasn't a particularly good reputation in San Marcos County, but he's one of the biggest sheepmen in the state and a heavy depositor in the bank at El Toro. He was one of the reasons that moved me to buy the Farrel mortgage from the bank."

"Explain the reason, John."

"Well, I figured that eventually I would have to foreclose on old Don Miguel Farrel, and it would re-quire approximately two years after that before my irrigation system would be completed and the valley lands ready for colonization. I was tolerably certain I would never restock the range with cattle, and I knew

Loustalot would buy several thousand young sheep and run them on the Palomar, provided I leased the grazing privilege to him for two years at a reasonable figure. I was here, under authority of a court order, to conserve the estate from waste, and my attorney assured me that, under that order, I had authority to use my own judgment in the administration of the estate, following the order of foreclosure. Now young Farrel shows up alive, and that will nullify my suit for foreclosure. It also nullifies my lease to Loustalot."

"I'm quite certain that fiery Don Mike will never consent to the lease, John," his wife remarked.

"If he declines to approve the lease, I shall be quite embarrassed I fear, Kate. You see, dear, Loustalot bought about fifteen thousand sheep to pasture on the Palomar, and now he's going to find himself in the unenviable position of having the sheep but no pasture. He'll probably sue me to recover his loss, if any."

"It's too bad you didn't wait ten days before signing that lease, John."

"Yes," he replied, a trifle testily. "But we all were convinced that young Farrel had been killed in Siberia."

"But you hadn't completed your title to this ranch, John?"

"You wouldn't murder a man who was going to commit suicide, would you? The ranch was as good as mine. If I had waited to make absolutely certain Farrel was dead, the wait might have cost me fifty thousand dollars. I rented the ranch at fifty cents per acre."

"One hundred thousand acres, more or less, for two years, at fifty cents per acre per annum. So, instead of making fifty thousand you've lost that sum," his wife mused aloud.

"I've lost one hundred thousand," he corrected. "A

131

one year lease is not desirable; Loustalot was my sole client, and I've lost him for good."

"Why despair, John? I've a notion that if you give Don Mike fifty thousand dollars to confirm Loustalot in the lease, he will forget his enmity and agree to the lease. That would, at least, prevent a lawsuit."

Parker's face brightened.

"I might do that," he assented. "The title will remain in Farrel's name for another year, and I have always believed that half a loaf was better than none at all. If young Farrel subscribes to the same sentiments, all may yet go nicely."

"Fifty thousand dollars would be rather a neat sum to save out of the wreck," she observed, sagely. "He seems quite a reasonable young man."

"I like him," Parker declared. "I like him ever so much."

"So do I, John. He's an old-fashioned gentleman."

"He's a he man—the sort of chap I'd like to see Kay married to some day."

Mrs. Parker looked searchingly at her husband.

"He told Kay he was half greaser, John. Would you care to have our little daughter married to that sort of man?"

"How like a woman! You always take the personal viewpoint. I said I'd like to see Kay married to a he man *like* Miguel Farrel. And Farrel is not half greaser. A greaser is, I take it, a sort of mongrel—Indian and Spanish. Farrel is clean-strain Caucasian, Kate. He's a white man—inside and out."

"His financial situation renders him impossible, of course."

"Naturally."

"I wish it were otherwise, Johnny. Perhaps, if you were

132

a little easy with him—if you gave him a chance—"

"Kate, I'd always be afraid of his easygoing Latin blood. If I should put him on his feet, he would, in all probability, stand still. He might even walk a little, but I doubt me if he'd ever do a Marathon."

"John, you're wrong," Mrs. Parker affirmed, with conviction. "That young man will go far. What would you do if Kay should fall in love with him?"

"I'm sure I do not know, Kate. What would you do?"

"I do not know, John. Nevertheless, it is interesting to contemplate the situation. If he should win this ranch back from you, he could have her with my blessing."

"Likewise with mine. That would put him right up in the go-getter class, which is the class I want to see Kay marry into. But he will not win back this ranch, Kate."

"How do you know he will not?"

"Because I'm going to do everything in my power to keep him from redeeming it—and I'm neither a mental nor a financial cripple."

"Where did the potato baron go?" Mrs. Parker queried, suddenly changing the conversation.

"Down into the valley, I imagine, to look over the land."

"His presence here is not agreeable to Mr. Farrel, John. I think you might manage to indicate to Mr. Okada that now, Mr. Farrel having returned so unexpectedly, your land deal must necessarily be delayed for a year, and consequently, further negotiations at this time are impossible."

"Yes; I think I had better give him a strong hint to go away. It irritates Farrel to have him in the house, although he'd never admit it to us."

"I wonder, John, if it irritates him to have us in the house?"

133

"I wanted to leave today, but when he invited us to stay, you wouldn't permit me to consider leaving," he reminded her.

"But, John, his manner was so hearty and earnest we had to accept. Really, I think we might have hurt his feelings if we had declined."

"Kay seemed happy to stay."

"That is another reason for accepting his invitation. I know she'll enjoy it so here."

"I wouldn't be at all surprised," Parker replied, dryly. "She has helped herself to the car and driver in order to aid Farrel at my expense."

His humorous wife smiled covertly. Parker smoked contemplatively for a quarter of an hour. Then,

"Here comes the smiling son of Nippon, John," Mrs. Parker remarked.

The potato baron entered the secluded patio and sat down beside them on the porch. With a preliminary whistling intake of breath, he remarked that it was a beautiful day and then proceeded, without delay, to discuss the subject closest to his heart—the fertile stretches of the San Gregorio valley.

Parker squirmed a trifle uneasily.

"As I explained to you this morning, Mr. Okada," he began, "our deal has become a trifle complicated by reason of the wholly unexpected return of Mr. Miguel Farrel."

"Very great misfortune," Okada sympathized. "Very great disappointment."

Mrs. Parker favored him with a look of violent dislike and departed abruptly, much to Okada's relief. Immediately he drew his chair close to Parker's.

"You zink Mr. Farrel perhaps can raise in one year the money to redeem property?" he demanded.

"I haven't the slightest information as to his money raising ability, other than the information given me by that man Pablo has just locked up. If, as Loustalot informed me, Farrel has a judgment against him, he is extremely liable to raise a hundred thousand or more today, what with funds in bank and about fifteen thousand sheep."

"I zink Farrel not very lucky today wiz sheep, Mr. Parker."

"Well, whether he's lucky or not, he has our deal blocked for one year. I can do nothing now until title to this ranch is actually vested in me. I am morally certain Farrel will never redeem the property, but—well, you realize my predicament, Mr. Okada. Our deal is definitely hung up for one year."

"Very great disappointment!" Okada replied sadly. "Next year, I zink California legislature make new law so Japanese people have very much difficulty to buy land. Attorneys for Japanese Association of California very much frightened because they know Japanese treaty rights not affected by such law. If my people can buy this valley before that law comes to make trouble for Japanese people, I zink very much better for everybody."

"But, my dear Mr. Okada, I cannot make a move until Miguel Farrel fails to redeem the property at the expiration of the redemption period, one year hence."

"Perhaps that sheepman kill Mr. Farrel," Okada suggested, hopefully. "I hoping, for sake of Japanese people, that sheepman very bad luck for Mr. Farrel."

"Well, I wouldn't care to have him for an enemy. However, I dare say Farrel knows the man well enough and will protect himself accordingly. By the way, Farrel is violently opposed to Japanese colonization of the San

135

Gregorio."

"You zink he have prejudice against Japanese people?"

"I know it, Mr. Okada, and, for that reason, and the further reason that our deal is now definitely hung up for a year, I suggest that you return to El Toro with me this afternoon. I am no longer master here, but I shall be delighted to have you as my guest at the hotel in El Toro while you are making your investigations of the property. I wish to avoid the possibility of embarrassment to you, to Mr. Farrel, and to my family. I am sure you understand our position, Mr. Okada."

The potato baron nodded, scowling slightly.

XV

AT A POINT WHERE THE ROAD, having left the valley and climbed a grade to a mesa that gave almost an airplane view of the San Gregorio, Miguel Farrel looked back long and earnestly. For the first time since entering the car, at Kay Parker's invitation, he spoke.

"It's worth it," he announced, with conviction, "worth a fight to a finish with whatever weapons come to hand. If I—By the holy poker! Sheep! Sheep on the Rancho Palomar! Thousands of them. Look! Over yonder!"

"How beautiful they look against those green and purple and gold hillsides!" the girl exclaimed.

"Usually a sheep is not beautiful to a cowman," he reminded her. "However, if those sheep belong to Loustalot, they constitute the fairest sight mine eyes have gazed upon to date."

"And who might he be?"

"That shaggy thief I manhandled a few minutes ago.

136

He's a sheepman from the San Carpojo, and for a quarter of a century he has not dared set foot on the Palomar. Your father, thinking I was dead and that the ranch would never be redeemed after foreclosure of the mortgage, leased the grazing privilege to Loustalot. I do not blame him. I do not think we have more than five hundred head of cattle on the ranch, and it would be a shame to waste that fine green feed." Suddenly the sad and somber mien induced by his recent grief fled his countenance. He turned to her eagerly. "Miss Parker, if I have any luck worth while today, I think I may win back my ranch."

"I wish you could win it back, Don Mike. I think we all wish it."

"I hope you all do." He laughed joyously. "My dear Miss Parker, this is the open season on terrible practical jokes. I'm no judge of sheep in bulk, but there must be not less than ten thousand over on that hillside, and if the title to them is vested in André Loustalot today, it will be vested in me about a month from now. I shall attach them; they will be sold at public auction by the sheriff to satisfy in part my father's old judgment against Loustalot, and I shall bid them in—cheap. Nobody in San Marcos County will bid against me, for I can outbid everybody and acquire the sheep without having to put up a cent of capital. Oh, my dear, thoughtful, vengeful old dad! Dying, he assigned that judgment to me and had it recorded. I came across it in his effects last night."

"What are sheep worth, Don Mike?"

"I haven't the slightest idea, but I should say that, by next fall, those sheep should be worth not less than six dollars a head, including the wool clip. They will begin to lamb in February, and by the time your father

137

dispossesses me a year hence, the increase will amount to considerable. That flock of sheep should be worth about one hundred thousand dollars by the time I have to leave the Palomar, and I *know* I'm going to collect at least fifty thousand dollars in cash in addition."

He drew from his vest pocket a check for that sum, signed by André Loustalot and drawn in favor of John Parker, Trustee.

"How did you come by that check?" Kay demanded. "It belongs to my father, so, if you do not mind, Mr. Farrel, I shall retain it and deliver it to my father." Quite deliberately, she folded the check and thrust it into her handbag. There was a bright spot of color in each cheek as she faced him, awaiting his explanation. He favored her with a Latin shrug.

"Your father will not accept the check, Miss Parker. Loustalot came to the hacienda this morning for the sole purpose of handing him this check, but your father refused to accept it on the plea that the lease he had entered into with Loustalot for the grazing privilege of the ranch was now null and void."

"How do you know all this? You were not present."

"No; I was not present, Miss Parker, but—this check is present; those sheep are present; André Loustalot was present, then absent, and is now present again. I deduce the facts in the case. The information that I was alive and somewhere around the hacienda gave Loustalot the fright of his unwashed existence; that's why he appropriated that gray horse and fled so precipitately when he discovered his automobile had a flat tire. The scoundrel feared to take time to shift wheels."

"Why ?"

"He had the promise of a Farrel that a great misfortune would overtake him if he ever set foot on the

138

Rancho Palomar. And he knows the tribe of Farrel."

"But how did you secure possession of that check, Don Mike?"

"Miss Parker, when a hard-boiled, unconvicted murderer and grass thief borrows my horse without my permission, and I ride that sort of man down, upset him, sit on him, and choke him, the instincts of my ancestors, the custom of the country, common sense, and my late military training all indicate to me that I should frisk him for deadly weapons. I did that. Well, I found this check when I frisked Loustalot back yonder. And—if a poor bankrupt like myself may be permitted to claim a right, you are not so well entitled to that check as I am. At least, I claim it by right of discovery."

"It is worthless until my father endorses it, Don Mike."

"His clear, bold chirography will not add a mite to its value, Miss Parker. Checks by André Loustalot on the First National Bank of El Toro aren't going to be honored for some little time. Why? I'll tell you. Because Little Mike the Hustler is going to attach his bank account this bright April morning."

She laughed happily.

"You haven't wasted much time in vain regret, have you?" she teased him. "When you start hustling for a living, you're a man what hustles, aren't you?"

" 'Eternal vigilance is the price of liberty,' " he quoted. "Those sheep weren't visible to us from the floor of the valley; so I take it I was not visible to Loustalot's shepherds from the top of those hills when I redeemed my father's promise to their employer. They'd never suspect the identity of either of us, I dare say. Well, Pablo will hold him *incomunicado* until I've completed my investigations."

"Why are you incarcerating him in your private bastile, Don Mike?"

"Well, I never thought to profane my private bastile with that fellow, but I have to keep him somewhere while I'm looking up his assets."

"But he may sue you for false imprisonment, kidnapping, or—or something."

"Yes; and I imagine he'd get a judgment against me. But what good would that do him? I haven't any assets."

"But you're going to acquire some rather soon, are you not?"

"I'll give all my money to my friend, Father Dominic, to do with as he sees fit. He'll see fit to loan it all back to me."

"But can you hide ten thousand sheep?"

"If that fellow tries to levy on my sheep, I'll about murder him," Farrel declared. "But we're crossing our bridges before we come to them."

"So we are, Don Mike. Tell me all about this ancient feud with André Loustalot."

"Certainly. Twenty-five-odd years ago, this county was pestered by a gang of petty cow thieves. They'd run lots of from ten to twenty fat steers off the range at a time, slaughter them in El Toro, and bury the hides to conceal the identity of the animals—the brands, you understand. The meat they would peddle to butchers in towns along the railroad line. The ringleader owned a slaughterhouse in El Toro, and, for a long time, nobody suspected him—the cattle were driven in at night. Well, my father grew weary of this form of old-fashioned profiteering, and it seemed to him that the sheriff of San Marcos County was too great a simpleton to do anything about it. So my father stood for the office as an independent candidate and was elected on a platform which read, 'No steers taken off this ranch without permission in writing from the owner.' Within six months, dad had half a dozen of our prominent citizens in San Quentin Penitentiary; then he resigned the office to his chief deputy, Don Nicolás Sandoval, who has held it ever since.

"Now, during that political campaign, which was a warm and bitter one, André Loustalot permitted himself the privilege of libeling my father. He declared in a public address to a gathering of voters in the San Carpojo valley that my father was a crook, the real leader of the rustlers, and merely seeking the office of sheriff in order to protect the cow thieves. When the campaign ended, my father swore to a warrant charging Loustalot with criminal libel and sued him for one hundred thousand dollars damages. A San Marcos County jury awarded my father a judgment in the sum prayed for. Loustalot appealed the case to the Supreme Court, but inasmuch as there wasn't the slightest doubt of his guilt, the higher court affirmed the decision of the Superior Court.

"Loustalot was a poor man in those days. He was foreman of a sheep outfit, with an interest in the increase of the flock, and inasmuch as these Basques seldom reduce their deals to writing, the sheriff could never satisfy himself that Loustalot had any assets in the shape of sheep. At any rate, the Basque and his employer and all of his Basque friends denied that Loustalot had any assets.

"For twenty-five years, my father has, whenever the statute of limitations threatened to kill this judgment, revived it by having Loustalot up on an order of court to be questioned regarding his ability to meet the

141

judgment; every once in a while my father would sue out a new writ of execution, which would be returned unsatisfied by the sheriff. Six months ago, my father had the judgment revived by due legal process, and, for some reason best known to himself, assigned it to me and had the assignment recorded. Of course, when I was reported killed in Siberia, Loustalot's attorneys naturally informed him that my judgment had died with me unless I had left a will in favor of my father. But when my father died intestate and there were no known heirs, Loustalot doubtless felt that at last the curse had been lifted and probably began doing business in his own name. He's a thrifty fellow and, I dare say, he made a great deal of money on sheep during the war. I hope he has. That old judgment has been accumulating interest at seven percent for more than a quarter of a century, and in this state I believe the interest is compounded."

"But why did Loustalot hate your father so?" the girl queried.

"We had good fences on our ranch, but somehow those fences always needed repairing whenever André Loustalot's flock wandered over from the San Carpojo. In this state, one cannot recover for trespass unless one keeps one's fences in repair—and Loustalot used to trespass on our range quite frequently and then blame his cussedness on our fences. Of course, he broke our fences to let his sheep in to water at our water holes, which was very annoying to us, because sheep befoul a range and destroy it; they eat down to the very grassroots, and cattle will not drink at a waterhole patronized by sheep. Well, our patience was exhausted at last; so my father told Pablo to put out saltpeter at all of our water holes. Saltpeter is not harmful to cattle but

142

it is death to sheep, and the only way we could keep Loustalot off our range without resorting to firearms was to make his visits unprofitable. They were. That made Loustalot hate us, and one day, over in the Agua Caliente basin, when Pablo and his riders found Loustalot and his sheep there, they rushed about five hundred of his sheep over a rocky bench and dropped them a sheer two hundred feet into a canyon. That started some shooting, and Pablo's brother and my first cousin, Juan Galvez, were killed. Loustalot, wounded, escaped on the pack mule belonging to his sheep outfit, and after that he and my father didn't speak."

Kay turned in her seat and looked at Farrel curiously.

"If you were not so desperately situated financially," she wanted to know, "would you continue to pursue this man?"

He smiled grimly.

"Certainly. My father's honor, the blood of my kinsman, and the blood of a faithful servant call for justice, however long delayed. Also, the honor of my state demands it now. I am prepared to make any sacrifice, even of my life, and grasp eagerly at all legal means—to prevent your father putting through this monstrous deal with Okada."

She was troubled of soul.

"Of course," she pleaded presently, "you'll play the game with dad as fairly as he plays it with you."

"I shall play the game with him as fairly as he plays it with this land to which he owes allegiance," he corrected her sternly.

XVI

IT WAS ELEVEN O'CLOCK when the car rolled down the main street of El Toro. From the sidewalk, sundry citizens, of diverse shades of color and conditions of servitude, observing Miguel Farrel, halted abruptly and stared as if seeing a ghost. Don Mike wanted to shout to them glad words of greeting, of affectionate badinage, after the fashion of that easygoing and democratic community, but he feared to make the girl at his side conspicuous; so he contented himself by uncovering gravely to the women and waving debonairly to the men. This constituting ocular evidence that he was not a ghost or a man who bore a striking physical resemblance to one they mourned as dead, the men so saluted returned his greeting.

The few who had recognized him as he entered the town, quickly, by their cries of greeting, roused the loungers and idle conversationalists along the sidewalks further down the street. There was a rush to shop doors, a craning of necks, excited inquiries in Spanish and English; more shouts of greeting. A gaunt, hawk-faced elderly man, with Castilian features, rode up on a bay horse, showed a sheriff's badge to William, the chauffeur, and informed him he was arrested for speeding. Then he pressed his horse close enough to extend a hand to Farrel."

"Miguel, my boy," he said in English, out of deference to the girl in the car, "this is a very great—a very unexpected joy. We have grieved for you, my friend."

His faint clipped accent, the tears in his eyes, told

144

Kay that this man was one of Don Miguel's own people. Farrel clasped the proffered hand and replied to him in Spanish; then, remembering his manners, he presented the horseman as Don Nicolás Sandoval, sheriff of the county. Don Nicolás bent low over his horse's neck, his wide gray hat clasped to his gallant heart.

"You will forgive the emotion of a foolish old man, Miss Parker," he said, "but we of San Marcos County love this boy."

Other friends now came running; in a few minutes perhaps a hundred men, boys, and women had surrounded the car, struggling to get closer, vying with each other to greet the hero of the San Gregorio. They babbled compliments and jocularities at him; they cheered him lustily; with homely bucolic wit they jeered his army record because they were so proud of it, and finally they began a concerted cry of: "Speech! Speech! Speech!"

Don Mike stood up in the tonneau and removed his hat. Instantly silence settled over the crowd, and Kay thought that she had never seen a more perfect tribute of respect paid anyone. He spoke to them briefly, with a depth of sentiment only possible in a descendant of two of the most sentimental races on earth; but he was not maudlin. When he had concluded his remarks, he repeated them in Spanish for the benefit of those who had never learned English very well or at all.

And now, although Kay did not understand a word of what he said, she realized that in his mother tongue he was infinitely more tender, more touching, more dramatic than he could possibly be in English, for his audience wagged approving heads now and paid him the tribute of many a furtive tear.

Don Nicolás Sandoval rode his horse through the

145

crowd presently and opened a path for the car.

"I'm afraid this has been a trifle embarrassing for you, Miss Parker," Farrel remarked, as they proceeded down the street. "I shall not recognize any more of them. I've greeted them all in general, and some day next week I'll come to town and greet them in detail. They were all glad I came back, though, weren't they?" he added, with a boy's eagerness. "Lord, but I was glad to see them!"

"I can hardly believe you are the same man I saw manhandling your enemy an hour ago," she declared.

"Oh," he replied, with a careless shrug, "fighting and loving are the only two worthwhile things in life. Park in front of the courthouse, William, please."

He excused himself to Kay and ran lightly up the steps. Fifteen minutes later, he returned.

"I have a writ of execution," he declared. "Now to find the sheriff and have him serve it."

They located Don Nicolás Sandoval at the post office, one leg cocked over the pommel of his saddle, and the El Toro *Sentinel* spread on his knee.

"Father's old business with the Basque, Don Nicolás," Farrel informed him. "He has money deposited in his own name in the First National Bank of El Toro."

"I have grown old hunting that fellow's assets, Miguel, my boy," quoth Don Nicolás. "If I can levy on a healthy bank account, I shall feel that my life has not been lived in vain."

He folded his newspaper, uncoiled his leg from the pommel, and started up the street at the dignified fast walk he had taught his mount. Farrel returned to the car and, with Kay, arrived before the portals of the bank a few minutes in advance of the sheriff, just in time to see

146

André Loustalot leap from his automobile, dash up the broad stone steps, and fairly hurl himself into the bank.

"I don't know whether I ought to permit him to withdraw his money and have Don Nicolás attach it on his person or not. Perhaps that would be dangerous," Miguel remarked. He stepped calmly out of the car, assisted Kay to alight, and, with equal deliberation, entered the bank with the girl.

"Now for some fun," he whispered. "Behold the meanest man in America—myself!"

Loustalot was at the customers' desk writing a check to cash for his entire balance in bank. Farrel permitted him to complete the drawing of the check, watched the Basque almost trot toward the paying-teller's window, and as swiftly trotted after him.

"All—everything!" Loustalot panted, and reached over the shoulders of two customers in line ahead of him. But Don Miguel Farrel's arm was stretched forth also; his long brown fingers closed over the check and snatched it from the Basque's hand as he murmured soothingly:

"You will have to await your turn, Loustalot. For your bad manners, I shall destroy this check." And he tore the signature off and crumpled the little slip of paper into a ball, which he flipped into Loustalot's brutal face.

The Basque stood staring at him, inarticulate with fury; Don Mike faced his enemy with a bantering, prescient little smile. Then, with a great sigh that was in reality a sob, Loustalot abandoned his primal impulse to hurl himself upon Farrel and attempt to throttle; instead, he ran back to the customers' desk and started scribbling another check. Thereupon, the impish Farrel removed the ink, and when Loustalot moved to another

147

inkwell, Farrel's hand closed over that. Helpless and desperate, Loustalot suddenly began to weep; uttering peculiar mewing cries, he clutched at Farrel with the fury of a gorilla. Don Mike merely dodged round the desk, and continued to dodge until out of the tail of his eye, he saw the sheriff enter the bank and stop at the cashier's desk. Loustalot, blinded with tears of rage, failed to see Don Nicolás; he had vision only for Don Mike, whom he was still pursuing round the customers' desk.

The instant Don Nicolás served his writ of attachment, the cashier left his desk, walked round in back of the various tellers' cages, and handed the writ to the paying teller; whereupon Farrel, pretending to be frightened, ran out of the bank. Instantly, Loustalot wrote his check and rushed again to the paying-teller's window.

"Too late, Mr. Loustalot. Your account has been attached," that functionary informed him.

Meanwhile, Don Nicolás had joined his friend on the sidewalk.

"Here is his automobile, Don Nicolás," Farrel said, "I think we had better take it away from him."

Don Nicolás climbed calmly into the driver's seat, filled out a blank notice of attachment under that certain duly authorized writ which his old friend's son had handed him, and waited until Loustalot came dejectedly down the bank steps to the side of the car; whereupon Don Nicolás served him with the fatal document stepped on the starter, and departed for the county garage, where the car would be stored until sold at auction.

"Who let you out of my calaboose, Loustalot?" Don Mike queried amiably.

"That high-toned Jap friend of Parker's," the Basque replied, with malicious enjoyment.

"I'm glad it wasn't Mr. Parker. Well, you stayed there long enough to serve my purpose. By the way, your sheep are trespassing again."

"They aren't my sheep."

"Well, if you'll read that document, you'll see that all the sheep on the Rancho Palomar at this date are attached, whether they belong to you or not. Now, a word of warning to you, Loustalot: Do not come on the Rancho Palomar for any purpose whatsoever. Understand?"

Loustalot's glance met his unflinchingly for fully ten seconds, and, in that glance, Kay thought she detected something tigerish.

"Home, William," she ordered the driver, and they departed from El Toro, leaving André Loustalot standing on the sidewalk staring balefully after them.

They were halfway home before Don Mike came out of the reverie into which that glance of Loustalot's had, apparently, plunged him.

"Some day very soon," he said, "I shall have to kill that man or be killed. And I'm sorry my guest, Mr. Okada, felt it incumbent upon himself to interfere. If, between them, they have hurt Pablo, I shall certainly reduce the extremely erroneous Japanese census records in California by one."

XVII

JOHN PARKER AND HIS WIFE, with the unsuspecting Okada, were lingering over a late luncheon when Kay and Don Mike entered the dining room.

"Well, you bold Spanish cavalier, what do you mean by running away with my little girl?" Mrs. Parker demanded.

Before Farrel could reply, Kay answered for him.

"We've had quite a wild and woolly Western adventure, mother dear. Have you seen Pablo since we left together?"

"I have," the lady replied. "He had Monsieur Loustalot in charge, and related to us the details of the adventure up to the moment you and Mr. Farrel left him with the prisoner while you two continued on to El Toro. What happened in El Toro?"

"Don Mike succeeded in attaching Loustalot's bank account," Kay informed the company. "The loot will probably amount to something over fifty thousand dollars."

"I should say that isn't a half-bad stipend to draw for your first half-day pursuit of the nimble cartwheel of commerce," Parker suggested.

Mrs. Parker pursed her lips comically.

"The boy is clever, John. I knew it the moment I met him this morning. Felicitations, Don Miguel. John intends to strip you down to your birthday suit—fairly, of course—so keep up the good work, and everything may still turn out right for you. I'll cheer for you, at any rate."

"Thank you, dear Mrs. Parker." Don Miguel slipped

150

into his seat at the head of the table. "I have also attached Loustalot's new automobile."

"You Shylock! What else?" Mrs. Parker demanded eagerly.

"About ten thousand sheep, more or less. I attached these on suspicion, although the burden of proving that Loustalot owns them will be upon me. However, he concluded, with a bright glance at Parker, "I believe that can readily be accomplished—with your aid."

"I shall be the poorest witness in the world, Mr. Farrel."

"Well, I shall see to it, Mr. Parker, that you are given an opportunity to tell the judge of the Superior Court in El Toro why Loustalot called on you this morning, why a great band of sheep is trespassing on the Rancho Palomar, why Loustalot drew a check in your favor for fifty thousand dollars, why you declined to take it, what you said to Loustalot this morning to cause him to steal one of my horses in his anxiety to get off the ranch, why your attorneys drew up a certain lease of the grazing privilege to Loustalot, and why the deal fell through."

Parker flushed.

"Can you produce that fifty-thousand dollar check? I happen to know it has not been cashed."

"No, I cannot, Mr. Parker."

Kay opened her purse and tossed the check across to her father.

"It was drawn in your favor, dad," she informed him; "so I concluded it was your property, and when Mr. Farrel came by it—ah, illegally—and showed it to me, I retained it."

"Good girl! Mr. Farrel, have you any objection to my returning this check?"

"Not the slightest. It has served its purpose. However,

you will have to wait until you meet Loustalot somewhere outside the boundaries of the Rancho Palomar, sir. I had comforted myself with the thought that he was safe under lock and key here, but, to my vast surprise, I met him in the bank at El Toro making futile efforts to withdraw his cash before I could attach the account. The confounded ingrate informs me that Mr. Okada turned him loose."

There was no mistaking the disapproval in the glance which Parker turned upon Okada.

"Is this true, Mr. Okada?"

"It is not true," Okada replied promptly. "I know nozzing about. Nozzing."

"Well, Pablo thinks it is true, Mr. Okada." Don Miguel's voice was unruffled, his manner almost benignant. "The old man is outside, and absolutely brokenhearted. His honor appears to be quite gone. I imagine," Don Mike continued, with a fleeting and whimsical glance at the potato baron, "that he has evolved some primitive plan for making his honor whole again. Direct methods always did appeal to Pablo."

"Mr. Farrel," John Parker began, "I regret this incident more than I can say. I give you my word of honor I had nothing to do with it directly or indirectly—"

"John, for goodness' sake, old dear, give Mr. Farrel credit for some common sense. He knows very well you wouldn't break bread with him and then betray him. Don't you, Mr. Farrel?" Mrs. Parker pleaded.

"Of course, Mr. Parker's assurance is wholly unnecessary, Mrs. Parker."

"Mr. Okada is leaving this afternoon," Parker hastened to assure him.

"Mr. Okada shows commendable prudence." Don

152

Mike's tones were exceedingly dry.

Okada rose and bowed his squinch owl bow.

"I very sorry," he sputtered. "I zink that man Pablo one big liar. 'Scuse, please; I go."

"If he hadn't called Pablo a liar," Don Mike murmured plaintively, "I should have permitted him to march out with the honors of war. As the matter stands now, however, I invite all of you to listen attentively. In a few minutes you're going to hear something that will remind you of the distant whine of a sawmill. After all, Pablo is a poor old fellow who lives a singularly humdrum existence."

"Ah, yes; let the poor fellow have his simple little pleasures," Mrs. Parker pleaded. " 'All work and no play'—you know, Don Miguel."

"My dear," Parker answered testily, "there are occasions when your sense of humor is positively oppressive."

"Very well, John; I'll be serious." His wife turned to Farrel. "Mr. Farrel," she continued, "while you were away, I had a very bright idea. You are much too few in the family for such a large house, and it occurred to me that you might care to lease the Palomar hacienda to us for a year. I'm so weary of hotels and equally weary of a town house, with its social obligations and the insolence of servants—particularly cooks. John needs a year here, and we would so like to remain if it could be arranged. Your cook, Carolina, is not the sort that leaves one's employ in the middle of a dinner party."

"Would five hundred dollars a month for the house and the use of Carolina and three saddle horses interest you, Mr. Farrel? From our conversation of this morning, I judge you have abandoned hope of redeeming the property, and during the year of the redemption period, six thousand dollars might—ah—er—"

"Well, it would be better than a poke in the eye with a sharp stick," Don Miguel replied genially. "I need the money; so I accept—but with certain reservations. I like Carolina's cooking, too; I have a couple of hundred head of cattle to look after, and I'd like to reserve one room, my place at this table, and my position as master of Palomar. Of course, I'm not so optimistic as to think you folks would accept of my hospitality for a year, so I suggest that you become what our British cousins call 'paying guests,' albeit I had never expected to fall low enough to make such a dastardly proposition. Really, it abases me. It's never been done before in this house."

"I declare you're the most comfortable young man to have around that I have ever known. Isn't he, Kay?" Mrs. Parker declared.

"I think you're very kind," the girl assured him. "And I think it will be very delightful to be paying guests to such a host, Don Mike Farrel."

"Then it's settled," Parker announced, much relieved.

"And let us here highly resolve that we shall always be good friends and dwell together in peace," Kay suggested.

"I made that resolve when you met me at the gate last night, Miss Parker. Hark! Methinks I hear a young riot. Well, we cannot possibly have any interest in it, and, besides, we're talking business now. Mr. Parker, there isn't the slightest hope of my *earning* sufficient money to pay the mortgage you hold against this ranch of mine, so I have resolved to *gamble* for it whenever and wherever I can. You have agreed to pay me six thousand dollars, in return for which I guarantee to feed you and your family and servants well, and house you comfortably and furnish three saddle horses, with

154

saddles and bridles, for a period of one year. Understand?"

"Understood."

Don Miguel Farrel took two dice out of his pocket and cuddled them in his palm.

"I'll roll you the bones, one flop, twelve thousand dollars or nothing, sir," he challenged.

"But if I win—"

"You want to know if I am in a position to support you all for one year if I lose? I am. There are cattle enough on the ranch to guarantee that."

"Well, while these little adventures are interesting, Mr. Farrel, the fact is I've always made it a rule not to gamble."

"Listen to the hypocrite!" his wife almost shouted. "Gambled every day of his life for twenty-five years on the New York Stock Exchange, and now he has the effrontery to make a statement like that! John Parker, roll them bones!"

"Not today," he protested. "This isn't my lucky day."

"Well, it's mine," the good soul retorted. "Miguel — you'll pardon my calling you by your first name: Miguel, but since I was bound to do so sooner or later, we'll start now—Miguel, I'm in charge of the domestic affairs of the Parker family, and I've never known time when this poor tired old business man didn't honor my debts. Roll 'em, Mike, and test your luck."

"Mother!" Kay murmured reproachfully.

"Nonsense, dear! Miguel is the first natural gentleman, the first *regular* young man I've met in years. I'm for him, and I want him to know it. Are you for me, Miguel?"

"All the way!" Don Mike cried happily.

"There!" the curious woman declared triumphantly.

"I knew we were going to be good friends. What do I see before me? As I live, a pair of box cars."

"Mother, where *did* you learn such slang?" her daughter pleaded.

"From the men your non-gambling father used to bring home to play poker and shoot craps," she almost shouted. "Well, let us see if I can roll two sixes and tie the score. I can! What's more, I do! Miguel, are these dice college-bred? Ah! Old Lady Parker rolls wretched little pair of bull's-eyes!"

Don Miguel took the dice and rolled—a pair of deuces.

"I'm going to make big money operating a boardinghouse," be informed the lady.

" 'Landlord, fill the flowing bowl until it doth flow over,' " she sang gaily. "John, you owe Miguel twelve thousand dollars, payable at the rate of one thousand dollars a month for twelve months. Have your lawyer in El Toro draw the lease this afternoon."

Parker glanced at her with a broad hint of belligerence in his keen gray eyes.

"My dear," he rasped, "I wish you would take me seriously once in a while. For twenty-five years I've tried to keep step with you, and I've failed. One of these bright days I'm going to strike."

"I recall three occasions when you went on strike, John, and refused to accept my orders," the mischievous woman retorted sweetly. "At the conclusion of the strike, you couldn't go back to work. Miguel, three separate times that man has declined to cease money-making long enough to play, although I begged him with tears in my eyes. And I'm not the crying kind, either. And every time he disobeyed, he blew up. Miguel, he came home to me as hysterical as a high

156

school girl, wept on my shoulder, said he'd kill himself if he couldn't get more sleep, and then surrendered and permitted me to take him away for six months. Strange to relate, his business got along very nicely without him. Am I not right, Kay?"

"You are, mother dear. Dad reminds me of a horse at a livery stable fire. You rescue him from the flames, but the instant you let go his halter-shank, he dashes into the burning barn." She winked ever so slightly at Farrel. "Thanks to you, Don Mike," she assured him, "father's claws are clipped for one year; thanks to you again, we now have a nice, quiet place to incarcerate him."

Farrel could see that John Parker, while outwardly appearing to enjoy this combined attack against him, was secretly furious. And Don Mike knew why. His pride as a business man was being cruelly lacerated; he had foolishly crawled out on the end of a limb, and now there was a probability, although a remote one, that Miguel Farrel would saw off the limb before he could crawl back.

"Perhaps, Mr. Farrel," he replied, with a heroic attempt at jocularity, "you will understand now that it was not altogether a cold hard heart that prompted me to decline your request for a renewal of the mortgage this morning. I couldn't afford to. I had agreed to gamble one million dollars that you were thoroughly and effectually dead—I couldn't see one chance in a million where this ranch would get away from me."

"Well, do not permit yourself to become downhearted, Mr. Parker," Don Mike assured him whimsically. "I cannot see one chance in a million where you are going to lose it."

"Thank you for the heartening effect of those words, Mr. Farrel."

157

"I think I understand the reason underlying all this speed, Mr. Parker. You and Okada feared that next year the people of this state will so amend their faulty anti-alien land law of 1913 that it will be impossible for any Oriental to own or lease California land then. So you proceeded with your improvements during the redemption period, confident that the ranch would never be redeemed, in order that you might be free to deal with Okada before the new law went into effect. Okada would not deal with you until he was assured the water could be gotten on the land."

"Pa's thrown out at first base!" Mrs. Parker shrilled. "Poor old pa!"

Don Mike's somber black eyes flashed with mirth.

"I understand now why you leased the hacienda and why that twelve-thousand dollar board bill hurt," he murmured. He turned to Kay and her mother. "Why the poor unfortunate man is *forced* to remain at the Rancho Palomar in order to protect his bet." His thick black brows lifted piously. "Don't cheer, boys," he cried tragically; "the poor devil is going fast now! Is there anybody present who remembers a prayer or who can sing a hymn?"

Kay's adorable face twitched as she suppressed a chuckle at her father's expense, but now that Parker was being assailed by all three, his loyal wife decided to protect him.

"Well, Johnny's a shrewd gambler after all," she declared. "If you do not redeem the ranch, he will get odds of two and a half to one on his million dollar bet and clean up in a year. With water on the lands of the San Gregorio, Okada's people will pay five hundred dollars an acre cash for the fifty thousand acres."

"I grant you that, Mrs. Parker, but in the meantime he

158

will have increased tremendously the value of all of my land in the San Gregorio valley, and what is to prevent me, nine months from now, from floating a new loan rather handily, by reason of that increased valuation, paying off Mr. Parker's mortgage and garnering for myself that two and a half million dollars' profit you speak of?"

"I fear you will have to excuse us from relishing the prospect of that joke, Don Mike," Kay murmured.

"Work on that irrigation project will cease on Saturday evening, Mr. Farrel," Parker assured his host.

Nevertheless, Farrel observed that his manner belied his words; obviously be was ill at ease. For a moment, the glances of the two men met; swift though that visual contact was, each read in the other's glance an unfaltering decision. There would be no surrender.

The gay mood into which Mrs. Parker's humorous sallies had thrown Farrel relaxed; there came back to him the memory of some graves in the valley, and his dark, strong face was somber again. Of a sudden, despite his victory of the morning, he felt old for all his twenty-eight years—old and sad and embittered, lonely, futile and helpless.

The girl, watching him closely, saw the light die out in his face, saw the shadows come, as when a thundercloud passes between the sun and a smiling valley. His chin dropped a little on his breast, and for perhaps ten seconds he was silent; by the faraway gleam in his eyes, Kay knew he was seeing visions, and that they were not happy ones.

Instinctively her hand crept round the corner of the table and touched his arm lightly. Her action was the result of impulse; almost as soon as she had touched him, she withdrew her hand in confusion.

159

But her mother had noticed the movement, and a swift glance toward her husband drew from him the briefest of nods, the most imperceptible of shrugs.

"Come, Johnny dear," she urged, and her voice had lost its accustomed shrillness now; "let us go forth and see what has happened to the Little Old Man of the Spuds."

He followed her outside obediently, and arm in arm they walked around the patio toward the rear gate.

"Hello!" he murmured suddenly, and, with a firm hand under her chin, he tilted her handsome face upward. There were tears in her eyes. "What now?" he demanded tenderly. "How come, old girl?"

"Nothing, John. I'm just an old fool—laughing when I'm not weeping and weeping when I ought to be laughing."

XVIII

DON MIKE'S ASSUMPTION that Pablo would seek balm for his injured feelings at the expense of the potato baron was one born of a very intimate knowledge of the mental processes of Pablo and those of his breed. And Pablo, on that fateful day, did not disappoint his master's expectations. Old he was, and stiff and creaky of joint, but what he lacked in physical prowess he possessed in guile. Forbidden to follow his natural inclination, which was to stab the potato baron frequently and fatally with a businesslike dirk which was never absent from his person except when he slept, Pablo had recourse to another artifice of his peculiar calling—to wit, the rawhide riata.

As Okada emerged from the dining room into the

160

patio, Pablo entered from the rear gate, riata in hand; as the Japanese crossed the garden to his room in the opposite wing of the hacienda, Pablo made a deft little cast and dropped his loop neatly over the potato baron's body, pinioning the latter's arms securely to his sides. Keeping a stiff strain on the riata, Pablo drew his victim swiftly toward the porch, round an upright of which he had taken a hitch; in a surprisingly brief period, despite the Jap's frantic efforts to release himself, Pablo had his man lashed firmly to the porch column, whereupon he proceeded to flog his prisoner with a heavy quirt which, throughout the operation, had dangled from his left wrist. With each blow, old Pablo tossed a pleasantry at his victim, who took the dreadful scourging without an outcry, never ceasing a dogged effort to twist loose from his bonds until his straining and flinching loosed the ancient rusty nails at top and bottom of the upright, and, with a trash, the Oriental fell headlong backward on the porch, as a tree falls. Thereupon, Pablo kicked him half a dozen times for good measure, and proceeded to roll him over and over along the porch toward his room. Eventually this procedure unwound him from the riata; Pablo then removed the loop, and Okada staggered into his room and fell, half fainting, on his bed.

His honor now quite clean, Pablo departed from the patio. He had been less than five minutes on his mission of vengeance, and when John Parker and his wife came out of the dining room, the sight of the imperturbable old majordomo unconcernedly coiling his "twine" roused in them no apprehension as to the punishment that had overtaken Okada.

Having finished their luncheon—a singularly pleasant tête-à-tête—Don Mike and Kay joined Mr. and Mrs. Parker. At once Farrel's glance marked the absence of

161

the porch column.

"I declare," he announced, with mock seriousness, "a portion of my veranda has given way. I wonder if a man could have been tied do it. I heard a crash, and at the time it occurred to me that it was a heavy crash — heavier than the weight of that old porch column would produce. Mr. Parker, may I suggest that you investigate the physical condition of our Japanese friend? He is doubtless in his room."

Parker flashed his host a quick glance, almost of resentment, and went to Okada's room. When he returned, he said soberly:

"Pablo has beaten the little fellow into a pitiable condition. He tied him to that porch column and flogged him with a quirt. While I cannot defend Okada's action in releasing Loustalot, nevertheless, Mr. Farrel—" Don Mike's black eyes burned like live coals. "Nevertheless—I—well—" Parker hesitated.

Don Mike's lips were drawn a trifle in the ghost of a smile that was not good to see.

"I think, sir," he said softly, distinctly, and with chill suavity, "that Mr. Okada might be grateful for the services of the excellent Murray, if the potato baron is, as I shrewdly suspect he will be, leaving within five minutes."

"Good Heavens, man, I believe it will be an hour before he can walk!"

Farrel glanced critically at his wristwatch and seemed to ponder this.

"I fear five minutes is all I can permit, sir," he replied. "If he should be unable to walk from his room, Murray, who is the soul of thoughtfulness, will doubtless assist him to the waiting automobile."

Five minutes later, the potato baron and the potato

162

baron's suitcase were lifted into the tonneau of the car by Murray and William. From over by the blacksmith shop, Don Mike saw Parker bid his Japanese confrère adieu, and as the car dipped below the mesa, Parker came over and joined them.

"Thought you were going in to El Toro this afternoon," the young man suggested.

"I had planned to, but changed my mind after beholding that Nipponese ruin. To have driven to El Toro with him would have broken my heart."

"Never mind, pa," Mrs. Parker consoled him; "you'll have your day in court, will you not?"

"I think he's going to have several of them," Don Mike predicted maliciously, and immediately withdrew the sting from his words by placing his hand in friendly fashion on Parker's shoulder and shaking him playfully. "In the interim, however," he continued, "now that our unwelcome guests have departed and peace has been reestablished on El Palomar (for I hear Pablo whistling 'La Paloma' in the distance), what reason, if any, exists why we shouldn't start right now to get some fun out of life? I've had a wonderful forenoon at your expense, so I want you and the ladies to have a wonderful afternoon at mine." He glanced alertly from one to the other, questioningly.

"I wonder if the horses have recovered from their furious chase of this morning," Kay ventured.

"Of course. That was merely an exercise gallop. How would you all like to come for a ride with me over to the Agua Caliente basin?"

"Why the Agua Caliente basin?" Parker queried casually. "That's quite a distance from here, is it not ?"

"About seven miles—fourteen over and back. Suppose William follows with the car after his return

163

from El Toro. You can then ride back with him, and I'll bring the horses home. I realize fourteen miles is too great a distance for inexperienced riders."

"Isn't that going to considerable trouble?" Parker suggested suavely. "Suppose we ride down the valley. I prefer flat land to rolling country when I ride."

"No game down that way," Farrel explained patiently. "We'll take the hounds and put something up a tree over Caliente Basin way before we get back. Besides, I have a great curiosity to inspect the dam you're building and the artesian wells you're drilling over in that country."

"Confound you, Farrel! You realized the possibilities of that basin, then?"

"Years ago. The basin comes to a bottleneck between two high hills; all you have to do is dam that narrow gorge, and when the Rio San Gregorio is up and brimming in freshet time, you'll have a lake a hundred feet deep, a mile wide, and five miles long before you know it. Did you ever consider the possibility of leading a ditch from the lake thus formed along the shoulder of El Palomar, that forty-five-hundred-foot peak for which the ranch is named, and giving it a sixty-five percent. nine-hundred-foot drop to a snug little power station at the base of the mountain. You could develop thirty or forty thousand horsepower very easily and sell it easier; after your water had passed through the penstock and delivered its power, you could run it off through a lateral to the main ditch down the San Gregorio and sell it to your Japanese farmers for irrigation."

"By Jupiter, I believe you would have done something with this ranch if you had had the backing, Farrel!"

"Never speculated very hard on securing the backing," Don Mike admitted, with a frank grin. "We

164

always lived each day as if it were the last, you know. But over in Siberia, far removed from all my easygoing associations, both inherited and acquired, I commenced dreaming of possibilities in the Agua Caliente basin."

"Well then, since you insist, let's go over there and have your curiosity satiated," Parker agreed, with the best grace possible.

While the Parkers returned to the hacienda to change into their riding clothes, Miguel Farrel strolled over to the corral where Pablo Artelan, wearing upon his leathery countenance the closest imitation of a smile that had ever lighted that dark expanse, joined him and, with Farrel, leaned over the corral fence and gazed at the horses within. For a long time, neither spoke; then, while his glance still appraised the horses, Don Mike stiffened a thumb and drove it with considerable force into Pablo's ancient ribs. Carolina, engaged in hanging out the Parker wash in the yard of her *casa,* observed Don Mike bestow this infrequent accolade of approbation and affection, and her heart swelled with pride. Ah, yes; it was good to have the child back on the rancho again.

Carolina and Pablo had never heard that the ravens fed Elijah; they had never heard of Elijah. Nevertheless, if they had, they would not have envied him the friendship of those divinely directed birds, for the Farrels had always fed Pablo and Carolina and their numerous brood, now raised and scattered over the countryside. At sight of that prod in the ribs, Carolina dismissed forever a worry that had troubled her vaguely during the period between old Don Miguel's death and the return of young Don Miguel—the fear that a lifetime of ease and plenty had ended. Presently, she lifted a falsetto voice in a Spanish love song two centuries old.

I await the morrow, Niña mia,
    I await the morrow, all through the night, For
the entrancing music and dancing
    With thee, my songbird, my heart's delight.
Come dance, my Niña, in thy mantilla,
    Think of our love and do not say no;
Hasten then my treasure, grant me this pleasure,
    Dance then tomorrow the bolero!

Over at the corral, Pablo rolled a cigarette, lighted it, and permitted a thin film of smoke to trickle through his nostrils. He, too, was content.

"Carolina," he remarked presently, in English, "is happy to beat hell."

"I haven't any right to be, but, for some unknown reason, I'm feeling gay myself," his master replied.

He started toward the harness room to get the saddle for Panchito, and Pablo lingered a moment at the fence, gazing after him curiously. Could it be possible that Don Miguel José Maria Federico Noriaga Farrel had, while sojourning in the cold land of the bewhiskered men, lost a modicum of that particularity with women which had formerly distinguished him in the eyes of his humble retainers?

"Damn my soul eef I don't know sometheeng!" Pablo muttered, and followed for a saddle for the gray gelding.

XIX

WHEN THE PARKERS EMERGED FROM THE HACIENDA, they found Don Mike and Pablo holding the horses and waiting for them. Kay wore a beautifully tailored riding habit of dark unfinished material, shot with a faint

166

admixture of gray; her boots were of shining black undressed leather, and she wore a pair of little silver-mounted spurs, the sight of which caused Pablo to exchange sage winks with his master. Her white-piqué stock was fastened by an exquisite little cameo stickpin; from under the brim of a black-beaver sailor hat, set well down on her head, her wistful brown eyes looked up at Don Mike, and caught the quick glance of approval with which he appraised her, before turning to her mother.

"The black mare for you, Mrs. Parker," he suggested. "She's a regular old sweetheart and single-foots beautifully. I think you'll find that stock saddle a far more comfortable seat than the saddle Miss Kay is using."

"I know I'm not as light and graceful as I used to be, Mike," the amiable soul assured him, "but it irks me to have men notice it. You *might* have given me an opportunity to decline Kay's saddle. There is such a thing as being too thoughtful, you know."

"Mother!" Kay cried reproachfully.

Don Mike blushed, even while he smiled his pleasure at the lady's badinage. She observed this,

"You're a nice boy, Michael," she murmured, for his ear alone. "Why, you old-fashioned young rascal!"—as Don Mike stooped and held out his hand. She placed her left foot in it and was lifted lightly into the saddle. When he had adjusted the stirrups to fit her, he turned to aid Kay, only to discover that the gallant Panchito had already performed the honors for that young lady by squatting until she could reach the stirrup without difficulty.

Parker rode the gray horse, and Farrel had appropriated a pinto cow pony that Pablo used when line riding.

With the hounds questing ahead of them, the four jogged up the San Gregorio, Don Mike leading the way, with Kay riding beside him. From time to time she stole a sidelong glance at him, riding with his chin on his breast, apparently oblivious of her presence. She knew that he was not in a mood to be entertaining today, to be a carefree squire of dames; his mind was busy grappling with problems that threatened not only him but everything in life that he held to be worth while.

"Do we go through that gate?" the girl queried, pointing to a five-rail gate in a wire fence that straggled across the valleys and up the hillside.

He nodded.

"Of course you do not have to go through it," he teased her. "Panchito can go over it. Pie for him. About five feet and a half."

"Enough for all practical purposes," she replied, and touched her ridiculous little spurs to the animal's flank, took a firm grip on the reins with both hands, and sat down firmly in the saddle. "All right, boy!" she cried, and, at the invitation, Panchito pricked up his ears and broke into an easy canter, gradually increasing his speed and taking the gate apparently without effort. Don Mike watched to see the girl rise abruptly in her seat as the horse came down on the other side of the gate. But no! She was still sitting down in the saddle, her little hands resting lightly on the horse's neck; and while Farrel watched her in downright admiration and her mother sat, white and speechless on the black mare, Kay galloped ahead a hundred yards, turned, and came back over the gate again.

"Oh, isn't he a darling?" she cried. "He pulls his feet up under him like a dog, when he takes off. I want to

168

take him over a seven-foot hurdle. He can do it with yours truly up. Let's build a seven-foot hurdle tomorrow and try him out."

"Fine! We'll build it," Don Mike declared enthusiastically, and Parker, watching his wife's frightened face, threw back his head and laughed.

"You are encouraging my daughter to kill herself," the older woman charged Farrel. "Kay, you tomboy, do not jump that gate again! Suppose that horse should stumble and throw you."

"Nonsense, mother. That's mere old hopscotch for Panchito. One doesn't get a jumping jack to ride every day, and all I've ever done has been to pussyfoot through Central Park."

"Do you mean to tell me you've never taken a hurdle before?" Don Mike was scandalized. She nodded.

"She'll do," Parker assured him proudly.

Farrel confirmed this verdict with a nod and opened the gate. They rode through. Kay waited for him to close the gate. He saw that she had been captivated by Panchito, and as their glances met, his smile was a reflection of hers—a smile thoroughly and childishly happy.

"If you'd only sell him to me, Don Mike," she pleaded. "I'll give you a ruinous price for him."

"He is not for sale, Miss Kay."

"But you were going to give him away to your late battery commander!"

He held up his right hand with the red scar on the back of it, but made no further reply.

"Why will you not sell him to me?" she pleaded. "I want him so."

"I love him," he answered at that, "and I could only part with him—for love. Someday, I may give him to

169

somebody worthwhile, but for the present I think I shall be selfish and continue to own him. He's a big, powerful animal, and if he can carry weight in a long race, he's fast enough to make me some money."

"Let me ride him in the tryout," she pleaded. "I weigh just a hundred and twenty."

"Very well. Tomorrow I'll hitch up a work team and disk the heart out of our old racetrack—Oh, yes; we have such a thing"—in reply to her lifted brows. "My grandfather Mike induced my great-grandfather Noriaga to build it way back in the 'Forties. The Indians and *vaqueros* used to run scrub races in those days—in fact, it was their main pastime."

"Where is this old racetrack?"

"Down in the valley. A fringe of oaks hides it. It's grass-grown and it hasn't been used in twenty-five years, except when the Indians in this part of the country foregather in the valley occasionally and pull off some scrub races."

"How soon can we put it in commission?" she demanded eagerly.

"I'll disk it tomorrow. The ground is soft now, after this recent rain. Then I'll harrow it well and run a culti-packer over it—well, by the end of the week it ought to be a fairly fast track."

"Goody! We'll go in to El Toro tomorrow and I'll wire to San Francisco for a stopwatch. May I sprint Panchito a little across that meadow?"

"Wait a moment, Miss Kay. We shall have something to sprint after in a few minutes, I think." As the hounds gave tongue in a path of willows they had been investigating far to the right, Don Mike pulled up his horse and listened. "Hot trail," he informed her. "They'll all be babbling in a moment."

170

He was right.

"If it's a coyote, he'll sneak up the wash of the river," he informed the girl, "but if it's a cat, he'll cut through that open space to tree in the oaks beyond—Ha! There goes a mountain lion. After him!"

His alert pony went from a halt to a gallop, following a long, lithe tawny animal that loped easily into view, coming from the distant willow thicket. In an instant, Kay was beside him.

"Head him off," he commanded curtly. "This ruin of Pablo's is done in a quarter mile dash, but Panchito can outrun that cat without trying. Don't be afraid of him. They're cowardly brutes. Get between him and the oaks and turn him back to me. Ride him down! He'll dodge out of your way."

She saw that he was uncoiling his riata as he spoke, and divined his purpose, as, with a cluck and a boot to Panchito, she thundered after the big cat, her heart thumping with mingled fear and excitement. Evidently this was an old game to Panchito, however, for he pinned his ears a little and headed straight for the quarry. Seemingly he knew what was expected of him, and had a personal interest in the affair, for as he came up to the animal, he attempted to run the panther down. The animal merely snarled and gave ground, while gradually Panchito "hazed" him until the frightened creature was headed at right angles to the course he had originally pursued. And now Don Mike, urging the pinto to top speed, came racing up and cut him off.

"Catch him; catch him!" Kay screamed excitedly. "Don't let him get away!" She drove Panchito almost on top of the panther, and forced the beast to stop suddenly and dodge toward the approaching Farrel. As Panchito dashed by, Kay had a glimpse of Don Mike riding in,

171

his looped riata swinging in wide, slow concentric circles—casually, even. As she brought Panchito round on his nimble heels, she saw Don Mike rise in his stirrups and throw.

Even as the loop left his hand, he appeared to have no doubt of the outcome, for Kay saw him make a quick turn of his rope round the pommel of his saddle, whirl at a right angle, and, with a whoop of pure, unadulterated joy, go by her at top speed, dragging the panther behind him. The loop had settled over the animal's body and been drawn taut around his loins.

Suddenly the pinto came to an abrupt pause, sliding on his haunches to avoid a tiny arroyo, too wide for him to leap. The strain on the riata was thus momentarily slackened, permitting the big cat to scramble to all fours and turn to investigate this trap into which he had fallen. Instantly he charged, spitting and openmouthed, and, for some unknown reason, Farrel led the screaming fury straight toward Kay and Panchito. The cat realized this, also, for suddenly he decided that Panchito offered the best opportunity to vent his rage, and changed his course accordingly. Quick as he did so, Farrel whirled his pinto in the opposite direction, with the result that the panther left the ground with a jerk and was dragged through the air for six feet before striking heavily upon his back. He was too dazed to struggle while Farrel dragged him through the grass and halted under a lone sycamore. While the badly shaken cat was struggling to his feet and swaying drunkenly, Farrel passed the end of his riata over a limb, took a new hitch on his pommel, and ran out, drawing the screaming, clawing animal off the ground until he swung, head down, the ripping chisels on his front paws tearing the grass up in great tufts.

The pinto, a trained roping horse, stood, blown and panting, his feet braced, keeping the rope taut while Farrel dismounted and casually strolled back to the tree. He broke off a small twig and waited, while the hounds, belling lustily, came nosing across the meadow. Kay rode up, as the dogs, catching sight of the helpless cat, quickened their speed to close in; she heard Farrel shout to them and saw him lay about him with the twig, beating the eager animals back from their still dangerous prey.

Mr. and Mrs. Parker had, in the meantime, galloped up and stood by, interested spectators, while Don Mike searched round until he found a hard, thick, dry, broken limb from the sycamore.

"This certainly is my day for making money," he announced gaily. "Here's where I put thirty dollars toward that three-hundred-thousand dollar mortgage." He stepped up to the lion and stunned it with a blow over the head, after which he removed the riata from the creature's loins, slipped the noose round the cat's neck, and hoisted the unconscious brute clear of the ground.

"Now then," he announced cheerfully, "we'll just leave this fellow to contemplate the result of a life of shame. He shall hang by the neck until he is dead—dead—dead! We'll pick him up on our way back, and tonight I'll skin him. Fall in, my squad! On our way."

"Do you do that sort of thing very often, Mr. Farrel?" Parker queried.

"Life is a bit dull out here, sir. Any time the dogs put up a panther in the open, we try to rope him and have a little fun. This is the first one I have roped alone, however. I always did want to rope a panther all by myself. Ordinarily, I would not have told Miss Kay to head that cat in toward me, but, then, she didn't flunk

173

the gate back yonder, and I had a great curiosity to see if she'd flunk the cat. She didn't and"—he turned toward her with beaming, prideful eyes—"if I were out of debt, I wouldn't trade my friendship with a girl as game as you, Kay, for the entire San Gregorio valley. You're a trump."

"You're rather a Nervy Nat yourself, aren't you?" her droll mother struck in. "As a Christian martyr, you would have had the Colosseum to yourself; every tiger and lion in Rome would have taken to the tall timber when you came on."

As he rode ahead, chuckling, to join her daughter, Farrel knew that at all events he had earned the approval of the influential member of the Parker family. Mrs. Parker, on her part, was far more excited than her colloquial humor indicated.

"John," she whispered, "did you notice it?"

"Notice what?"

"I don't know why I continue to live with you— you're so dull! In his excitement, he just called her 'Kay.' Last night, when they met, she was 'Miss Parker.' At noon today, she was 'Miss Kay' and now she's plain 'Kay.' " A cloud crossed his brow, but he made no answer, so, woman-like, she pressed for one. "Suppose our daughter should fall in love with this young man?"

"That would be more embarrassing than ever, from a business point of view," he admitted, "and the Lord knows this fellow has me worried enough already. He's no mean antagonist."

"That's what the panther probably thought, John."

"His decoration, and that stunt—dazzling to the average girl," he muttered.

"In addition to his good looks, exquisite manners,

174

and, I am quite certain, very high sense of honor and lofty ideals," she supplemented.

"In that event, it is more than probable that a consideration of his desperate financial strait will preclude his indicating any lively interest in Kay." Parker glanced anxiously at his wife, as if seeking in her face confirmation of a disturbing suspicion. "At least, that would be in consonance with the high sense of honor and lofty ideals with which you credit him. However, we must remember that he has a dash of Latin blood, and my experience has been that not infrequently the Latin's high sense of honor and lofty idealism are confined to lip service only. I wonder if he'd be above using Kay as a gun to point at my head."

"I'm quite certain that he would, John. Even if he should become interested in her for her own sake, he would, of course, realize that the genuineness of his feeling would be open to suspicion by—well, most people, who comprehend his position—and I doubt very much if, under these circumstances, he will permit himself to become interested in her."

"He may not be able to help himself. Kay gets them all winging."

"Even so, he will not so far forget his ancestral pride as to admit it, or even give the slightest intimation of it."

"He *is* a prideful sort of chap. I noticed that, Still, he's not a prig."

"He has pride of race, John. Pride of ancestry, pride of tradition, pride of an ancient, undisputed leadership in his own community. He has been raised to know that he is not vulgar or stupid or plebeian; his character has been very carefully cultivated and developed."

He edged his horse close to hers.

"Look here, my dear," he queried; "what brought the

tears to your eyes at luncheon today?"

"There was a moment, John, when the shadow of a near-break came over his face. Kay and I both saw it. He looked wistful and lonely and beaten, and dropped his head like a tired horse, and her heart, her very soul, went out to him. I saw her hand go out to him, too; she touched his arm for an instant and then, realizing, she withdrew it. And then I knew!"

"Knew what?"

"That our little daughter, who has been used to queening it over every man of her acquaintance, is going to batter her heart out against the pride of Palomar."

"You mean—"

"She loves him. She doesn't know it yet, but I do. Oh, John, I'm old and wise. I know! If Miguel Farrel were of a piece with the young men she has always met, I wouldn't worry. But he's so absolutely different—so natural, so free from that atrocious habit of never being able to disassociate self from the little, graceful courtesies young men show women. He's wholesome, free from ego, from that intolerable air of proprietorship, of masculine superiority and cocksureness that seems so inseparable from the young men in, her set."

"I agree with you, my dear. Many a time I have itched to grasp the jawbone of an ass and spoil a couple of dozen of those young pups with their storybook notions of life."

"Now, that Don Mike," she continued critically, "is thoughtful of and very deferential to those to whom deference is due, which characteristic, coupled with the fact that he is, in a certain sense, a most pathetic figure at this time, is bound to make a profound impression on

176

any girl of ready sympathy. And pity is akin to love."

"I see." Parker nodded sagely. "Then you think he'll go down to defeat with his mouth shut?"

"I'm certain of it, John."

"On the other hand, if he should succeed in sending me down to defeat, thereby regaining his lost place in the sun, he might—er—"

"Let us be practical, John. Let us call a spade a spade. If he regains the Rancho Palomar, his thoughts will inevitably turn to the subject of a mistress for that old hacienda. He has pride of race, I tell you, and he would be less than human if he could contemplate himself as the last of that race.

"John, he did not capture that panther alive a few moments ago merely to be spectacular. His underlying reason was the thirty dollar bounty on the pelt and the salvation of his cattle. And he did not capture that Basque this morning and extort justice, long delayed, with any thought that by so doing he was saving his principality for a stranger. He will not fight you to a finish for that."

"What a philosopher you're getting to be, my dear!" he parried ironically. And, after a pause, "Well, I see very clearly that if your predictions come to pass, I shall be as popular in certain circles as the proverbial wet dog."

Her roguish eyes appraised him.

"Yes, John; you're totally surrounded now. I suppose, when you realize the enormity of the odds against you, you'll do the decent thing and—"

"Renew his mortgage? Not in a million years!" Parker's voice carried a strident note of finality, of purpose inflexible, and he thumped the pommel of his saddle thrice in emphasis. He was a man who, although normally kind and amiable, nevertheless reserved these qualities for use under conditions not connected with the serious business of profiting by another's loss. Quite early in life he had learned to say "No." He preferred to say it kindly and amiably, but none the less forcibly; some men had known him to say it in a manner singularly reminiscent of the low, admonitory growl of a fierce old dog.

"But, John dear, why are we accumulating all this wealth? Is not Kay our sole heir? Is not—"

"Do not threaten me with Kay," he interrupted irritably. "I play my game according to the time-honored rules of that game. I do not ask for quarters and I shall not give it. I'm going to do all in my power to acquire the Rancho Palomar under that mortgage I hold—and I hope that young man gives me a bully fight. That will make the operation all the more interesting.

"My dear, the continuous giving of one more chance to the Farrels has proved their undoing. They first mortgaged part of the ranch in 1870; when the mortgage fell due, they executed a new note plus the accrued interest and mortgaged more of the ranch. Frequently they paid the interest and twice they paid half the principal, bidding for one more chance and getting it. And all these years they have lived like feudal barons on their principal, living for today, reckless of tomorrow. Theirs has been the history of practically all of the old California families. I am convinced it would be no kindness to Don Miguel to give him another chance now; his Spanish blood would lull him to ease and forgetfulness; he would tell himself he would pay the mortgage *mañana*. By giving him another chance, I would merely remove his incentive to hustle and make good."

"But it seems so cruel, John, to take such a practical

178

view of the situation. He cannot understand your point of view and he will regard you as another Shylock."

"Doubtless," he replied; "nevertheless, if we are ever forced to regard him as a prospective son-in-law, it will be comforting to know that even if he lost, he made me extend myself. He is a man and a gentleman, and I like him. He won me in the first minute of our acquaintance. That is why I decided to stand pat and see what he would do." Parker leaned over and laid his hand on that of his wife. "I will not play the bully's part, Kate," he promised her. "If he is worth a chance he will get it, but I am not a human Christmas tree. He will have to earn it." After a silence of several seconds he added, "Please God he will whip me yet. His head is bloody but unbowed. It would be terrible to spoil him."

XX

MIGUEL FARREL PULLED UP HIS PINTO on the brow of a hill which, along the Atlantic seaboards would have received credit for being a mountain, and gazed down into the Agua Caliente basin. Half a mile to his right, the slope dipped into a little saddle and then climbed abruptly to the shoulder of El Palomar, the highest peak in San Marcos County. The saddle was less than a hundred yards wide, and through the middle of it a deep arroyo had been eroded by the Rio San Gregorio tumbling down from the hills during the rainy season. This was the only outlet to the Agua Caliente basin, and Don Mike saw at a glance that Parker's engineers had discovered this, for squarely in the outlet a dozen two horse teams were working, scraping out the foundation for the huge concrete dam for which Parker had

179

contracted. Up the side of El Palomar peak, something that resembled a great black snake had been stretched, and Farrel nodded approvingly as he observed it.

"Good idea, that, to lay a half mile of twelve-inch steel pipe up to that limestone deposit," he remarked to Parker, who had reined his horse beside Don Mike's. "Only way to run your crushed rock down to the concrete mixer at the dam site. You'll save a heap of money on delivering the rock, at any rate. Who's your contractor, Mr. Parker?"

"A man named Conway."

"Old Bill Conway, of Santa Barbara?"

"The same, I believe," Parker replied, without interest.

"Great old chap, Bill! One of my father's best friends, although he was twenty years younger than dad. He must feel at home on the Rancho Palomar."

Mrs. Parker could not refrain from asking why.

"Well, ever since Bill Conway was big enough to throw a leg over a horse and hold a gun to his shoulder, he's been shooting deer and quail and coursing coyotes on this ranch. Whenever he felt the downhill drag, he invited himself up to visit us. Hello! Why, I believe the old horse thief is down there now; at least that's his automobile. I'd know that ruin anywhere. He bought it in 1906, and swears he's going to wear it out if it takes a lifetime. Let's go down and see what they're up to there. Come on, folks!" And, without waiting to see whether or not he was followed, he urged the pinto over the crest and rode down the hillside at top speed, whooping like a wild Indian to attract the attention of Bill Conway. In a shower of weeds and gravel the pinto slid on his hind quarters down over the cut bank where the grading operations had bitten into the hillside, and landed with a

180

grunt among the teams and scrapers.

"Bill Conway! Front and center!" yelled the master of Palomar.

"Here! What's the row?" a man shouted, and, from a temporary shack office a hundred yards away, a man stepped out.

"What do you mean by cutting into my dam site without my permission?" Farrel yelled and drove straight at the contractor. "Hey, there, old settler! Mike Farrel, alive and kicking!" He left the saddle while the pinto was still at a gallop, landed on his feet in front of Bill Conway and took that astounded old disciple of dump wagon and scraper in a bearlike embrace.

"Miguel! You young scoundrel!" Conway yelled, and forthwith he beat Farrel between the shoulderblades with a horny old fist and cursed him lovingly,

"Cut out the profanity, Mr. Conway," Don Mike warned him. "Some ladies are about due on the job."

"When'd you light in the Palomar, boy? Gimme your hand. What the—say, ain't it a pity the old man couldn't have lasted until you got back? Ain't it, now, son?"

"A very great pity, Mr. Conway. I got home last night."

"Boy, I'm glad to see you. Say, you ran into surprises, didn't you?" he added, lowering his voice confidentially.

"Rather. But, then, so did the other fellow. In fact, sir, a very pleasant time was had by all. By the way, I hope you're not deluding yourself with the belief that I'm going to pay you for building this dam."

"By Judas priest," the alert old contractor roared, "you certainly do file a bill of complications! I'll have to see Parker about this right away—why, here he is now."

181

The Parkers had followed more decorously than had Farrel; nevertheless, they had arrived in more or less of a hurry. John Parker rode directly to Conway and Farrel.

"Well, Mr. Conway," he shouted pleasantly, "the lost sheep is found again."

"Whereat there is more rejoicing in San Marco County than there will be over the return of some other sheep—and a few goats—I know of. How do you do, Mr. Parker?" Conway extended his hand, and, as Kay and her mother rode up, Farrel begged their permission to present him to them. Followed the usual commonplaces of introduction, which Farrel presently interrupted.

"Well, you confounded old ditch digger! How about you?"

"Still making little rocks out of big ones, son. Say, Mr, Parker, how do we stack up on this contract, now that Little Boy Blue is back on the Palomar, blowing his horn?"

Parker strove gallantly to work up a cheerful grin.

"Oh, he's put a handful of emery dust in my bearings, confound him, Mr. Conway! It begins to look as if I had leaped before looking."

"Very reprehensible habit, Mr. Parker. Well—I'm getting so old and worthless nowadays that I make it a point to look before I leap. Mike, my son, do you happen to be underwriting this contract?"

Don Mike looked serious. He pursed his lips, arched his brows, drew some bills and small coins from his pocket, and carefully counted them.

"The liquid assets of the present owner of that dirt you're making so free with, Mr. Conway, total exactly sixty-seven dollars and nine cents. And I never thought the day would come when a pair of old-time

182

Californians like us would stoop to counting copper pennies. Before I joined the army, I used to give them away to the cholo children, and when there were no youngsters handy to give the pennies to, I used to throw them away."

"Yes," Bill Conway murmured sadly. "And I remember the roar that went up from the old-timers five years ago when the Palace Hotel in San Francisco reduced the price of three fingers of straight whiskey from twenty-five cents to fifteen. Boy, they're crowding us out."

"Who's been doing most of the crowding in San Marcos County while I've been away, Mr. Conway?" Farrel queried innocently.

"Japs, my son. Say, they're comin' in here by the shipload."

"You don't tell me! Why, two years ago there wasn't a Jap in San Marcos County with the exception of a couple of shoemakers and a window washing outfit in El Toro."

"Well, those hombres aren't mending shoes or washing windows any more, Miguel. They saved their money and now they're farming—garden truck mostly. There must he a thousand Japanese in the county now—all farmers or farm laborers. They're leasing and buying every acre of fertile land they can get hold of."

"Have they acquired much acreage?"

"Saw a piece in the El Toro *Sentinel* last week to the effect that nine thousand and twenty acres have been alienated to the Japs up to the first of the year. Nearly all the white men have left La Questa valley since the Japs discovered they could raise wonderful winter celery there."

"But where do these Japanese farmers come from,

183

Mr. Conway?" Parker inquired. "They do not come from Japan because, under the gentlemen's agreement Japan restricts emigration of her coolie classes."

"Well, now," Bill Conway began judicially. "I'll give Japan the benefit of any doubts I have as to the sincerity with which she enforces this gentlemen's agreement. The fact remains, however, that she does not restrict emigration to Mexico, and, unfortunately, we have an international boundary a couple of thousand miles long and stretching through a sparsely settled, brushy country. To guard our southern boundary in such an efficient manner that no Jap could possibly secure illegal entry to the United States via the line, we would have to have sentries scattered at hundred-yard intervals and closer than that on dark nights. The entire standing army of the United States would be required for the job. In addition to the handicap of this unprotected boundary, we have a fifteen-hundred mile coastline absolutely unguarded. Japanese fishermen bring their nationals up from the Mexican coast in their trawlers and set them ashore on the southern California coast. At certain times of the year, any landlubber can land through the surf at low tide; in fact, ownerless skiffs are picked up on the south coast beaches right regularly."

"Well, you can't blame the poor devils for wanting to come to this wonderful country, Mr. Conway. It holds for them opportunities far greater than in their own land."

"True, Mr. Parker. But their gain is our loss, and, as a matter of common sense, I fail to see why we should accord equal opportunity to an unwelcome visitor who enters our country secretly and illegally. I grant you it would prove too expensive and annoying to make a firm effort to stop this illegal immigration by preventive measures along our international boundary and coastline, but if we destroy the Jap's opportunity for profit at our expense, we will eliminate the main incentive for his secret and illegal entry, which entry is always very expensive. I believe seven hundred and fifty dollars is the market price for smuggling Japs and Chinamen into the United States of America."

"But we should take steps to discover these immigrants after they succeed in making entry—"

"Rats!" the bluff old contractor interrupted. "How are we going to do that under present conditions? The cry of the country is for economy in governmental affairs, so Congress prunes the already woefully inadequate appropriation for the Department of Labor and keeps our force of immigration inspectors down to the absolute minimum. These inspectors are always on the job; the few we have are splendid, loyal servants of the government, and they prove it by catching Japs, Chinamen, and Hindus every day in the week. But for every illegal entrant they apprehend, ten escape and are never rounded up. Confound them; they all look alike, anyhow! How are you going to distinguish one Jap from another?

"Furthermore, Mr. Parker, you must bear this fact in mind: The country at large is not interested in the problem of Oriental immigration. It hasn't thought about it; it doesn't know anything about it except what the Japs have told it, and a Jap is the greatest natural born liar and purveyor of half-truths and sugarcoated misinformation this world has known."

"Easy, old timer!" Don Mike soothed, laying his hand on Conway's shoulder. "Don't let your angry passions rise."

Conway grinned.

"I always fly into a rage when I get talking about Japs," he explained deprecatingly to the ladies. "And it's such a helpless, hopeless rage. There's no outlet for it. You see," he began all over again, "the dratted Jap propagandist is so smart—he's so cunning that he has capitalized the fact that California was the first state to protest against the Japanese invasion. He has made the entire country believe that this is a dirty little local squabble of no consequence to our country at large. He keeps the attention of forty-seven states on California while he quietly proceeds to colonize Oregon, Washington, and parts of Utah. Lately he has passed blithely over the hot, lava-strewn, and fairly non-irrigated state of Arizona to the more fertile agricultural lands of Texas. And yet a couple of hundred prize boobs in Congress talk sagely about an amicable settlement of the Jap problem in California! When they want information, they consult the Japanese ambassador!"

"But why," Kay ventured to ask, "do the Japanese not acquire agricultural lands in the Middle West? There are no restrictions in those states in the matter of outright purchases of land, and surely the soil is fertile enough to suit the most exacting Jap."

"Ah, young lady," Bill Conway boomed. "I'm glad you asked me that question. The Jap is a product of the temperate zone; he does not take kindly to extremes of heat and cold. Unlike the white man he cannot stand such extremes and function with efficiency. That's why the extreme northern part of Japan, which is very cold in winter, is so sparsely populated, although excellent agricultural land. Why freeze to death up there when, by merely following the Japan Current as it laves the west coast of North America from British Columbia down, one can, in a pinch, dispense with an overcoat in

January?"

"Enough of this anti-Japanese propaganda of yours, Señor Conway," Don Mike interrupted. "Our friends here haven't listened to anything else since I got home last night. Mr. Parker, being quite ignorant of the real issue, has, of course, fallen under the popular delusion; and I've been trying my best to lead him to the mourner's bench, to convince him that when he acquires the Rancho Palomar—which, by the way, will not be for at least a year, now that I've turned up to nullify his judgment of foreclosure—that it will be a far more patriotic action on his part, even if less profitable, to colonize the San Gregorio with white men instead of Japs. In fact, Mr. Parker, I wouldn't be surprised if you should succeed in putting through a very profitable deal with the state of California to colonize the valley with ex-soldiers."

Old Bill Conway turned upon John Parker a smoldering gaze.

"So I'm building a dam to irrigate a lot of Jap truck gardens, am I?" he rumbled.

The sly, ingenious manner in which Miguel Farrel had so innocently contrived to strew his already rough path with greater obstacles, infuriated Parker, and for an instant he lost control of himself.

"What do you care what it's for, Conway, provided you make your profit out of the contract?" he demanded brusquely.

"Ladies," the contractor replied, turning to Mrs. Parker and Kay, "I trust you will pardon me for discussing business in your presence just for a minute, Miguel, am I to understand that this ranch is still Farrel property?"

"You bet! And for a year to come."

187

"Then I gather that Mr. Parker has contracted with me to build a dam on your land and without your approval. Am I right?"

"You are, Mr. Conway. I am not even contemplating giving my approval to the removal of another scraper of dirt from that excavation."

Conway faced Parker.

"Am I to continue operations?" he demanded. "I have a cost plus fifteen percent contract with you, Mr. Parker, and if you are not going to be in position to go through with it, I want to know it now."

"In the absence of Mr. Farrel's permission, I have no alternative save to ask you to suspend operations, Mr. Conway," Parker answered bitterly. "I expect, of course, to settle with you for the abrupt cancellation of the contract, but I believe we are both reasonable men and that no difficulty will arise in that direction."

"I'm naturally disappointed, Mr. Parker. I have a good crew and I like to keep the men busy—particularly when good men are as hard to procure as they are nowadays. However, I realize your predicament, and I never was a great hand to hit a man when he was down."

"Thank you, Mr. Conway. If you will drop in at the ranch house tomorrow for dinner, we can put you up for the night, I dare say." He glanced at Farrel, who nodded. "We can then take up the matter of compensation for the cancelled contract."

"In the meantime, then, I might as well call the job off and stop the expense," Conway suggested "We'll load up the equipment and pull out in the morning."

"Why be so precipitate, Mr. Conway?" Don Mike objected, almost fiercely. "You always were the most easygoing, tenderhearted old scout imaginable, and that's why you've never been able to afford a new automobile. Now, I have a proposition to submit to you, Mr. Conway, and inasmuch as it conflicts radically with Mr. Parker's interests, I feel that common courtesy to him indicates that I should voice that proposition in his presence. With the greatest good will in life toward each other, nevertheless we are implacable opponents. Mr. Parker has graciously spread, face up on the table for my inspection, an extremely hard hand to beat; so now it's quite in order for me to spring my little joker and try to take the odd trick. Mr. Conway, I want you to do something for me. Not for my sake or the sake of my dead father, who was a good friend of yours, but for the sake of this state where we were both born and which we love because it is symbolical of the United States. I want you to stand pat and refuse to cancel this contract. Insist on going through with it and make Mr. Parker pay for it. He can afford it, and he is good for it. He will not repudiate a promise to pay while he has money in bank or securities to hypothecate. He is absolutely responsible financially. He owns a controlling interest in the First National Bank of El Toro, and he has a three-hundred-thousand dollar equity in this ranch in the shape of a first mortgage ripe for foreclosure—you can levy on those assets if he declines to go through with the contract. Force him to go through; force him, old friend of my father and mine and enemy of all Japanese! For God's sake, stand by me! I'm desperate, Mr. Conway—"

"Call me 'Bill,' son," Conway interrupted gently.

"You know what the Farrels have been up against always, Bill," Don Mike pleaded. "That easygoing Spanish blood! But, Bill, I'm a throwback. By God, I am! Give me this chance—this God-given chance—and the fifty percent Celtic strain in me and the twenty-five percent Gaelic that came with my Galvez blood will save the San Gregorio to white men! Give me the water, Bill; give me the water that will make my valley bloom in the August heat, and then, with the tremendous increase in the value of the land, I'll find somebody, some place, who will trust me for three hundred thousand paltry dollars to give this man and save my ranch. This is a white man's country, and John Parker is striving, for a handful of silver, to betray us and make it a yellow paradise."

His voice broke under the stress of his emotion; he gulped and the tears welled to his eyes.

"Oh, Bill, for God's sake don't fail me!" he begged. "You're a Californian! You've seen the first Japs come! Only fifteen years ago, they were such a rare sight the little boys used to chase them and throw rocks at them just to see them run in terror. But the little boys do not throw rocks at them now, and they no longer run. They have the courage of numbers and the prompt and forceful backing of a powerful fraternity across the Pacific. You've seen them spread gradually over the land—why, Bill, just think of the San Gregorio five years hence—the San Gregorio where you and I have hunted quail since I was ten years old. You gave me my first shot-gun —"

"Sonny," said old Bill Conway gently, passing his arm across Farrel's shoulders, "I wish to goodness you'd shut up! I haven't got three hundred thousand dollars, nor a tenth of it. If I had it I'd give it to you now and save argument. But I'll tell you what I have got, son, and that's a sense of humor. It's kept me poor all my life, but if you think it will make you rich you're welcome to it." He looked up, and his glance met Kay's.

"This chap's a limited edition," he informed her gravely. "After the Lord printed one volume, he destroyed the plates. Mr. Parker, sir—" He stepped up to John Parker and smote the latter lightly on the breast—"Tag; you're it!" he announced pleasantly. "I'll cancel this contract when you hand me a certified check for twenty-four billion, nine-hundred and eighty-two million, four hundred and seventeen thousand, six hundred and one dollars, nine cents, and two mills."

"Conway," Parker answered him quietly, "I like your sense of humor, even if it does hurt. However, you force me to fight the devil with fire. Still, for the sake of the amenities, we should always make formal declaration of war before beginning hostilities."

"And that's a trick you didn't learn in Japan," the old contractor reminded him.

"So I hereby declare war. I'm a past master at holding hard to whatever I do not wish the other fellow to take away from me, so build your dam and be damned to you. Of course, if you complete your contract eventually, you will force me to pay you for it, but in the interim you will have had to use clam shells and woodpecker heads for money. I know I can stave off settlement of your judgment for a year; after that, should I acquire title to the Rancho Palomar, I will settle with you promptly."

"And if you shouldn't acquire title, I shall look to my young friend, Don Miguel Farrel, for reimbursement. While at present the future may look as black to Mike as the Earl of Hell's riding-boots, his credit is good with me. Is this new law you've promulgated retroactive?"

"What do you mean?"

"You'll settle with me for all work performed up to the moment of this break in diplomatic relations, won't you?"

"That's quite fair, Conway. I'll do that." Despite the chagrin of having to wage for the nonce a losing battle, Parker laughed heartily and with genuine sincerity. Don Mike joined with him and the charged atmosphere cleared instantly.

"Bill Conway, you're twenty-four carat all through." Farrel laid a hand affectionately on his father's old friend. "Be sure to come down to the hacienda tomorrow night and get your check. We dine at six-thirty."

"As is?" Conway demanded, surveying his rusty old business suit and hard, soiled hands.

" 'As is,' Bill."

"Fine! Well, we've come to a complete understanding without falling out over it, haven't we?" he demanded of Kay and her mother. "With malice toward none and justice toward all—or words to that effect. Eh?"

"Oh, get back into your office, Conway, and cast up the account against me. Figure a full day for the men and the mules, although our break came at half-past three. I'm a contrary man, but I'm not small. Come on, Mr. Farrel, let's go home," Parker suggested.

"Little birds in their nest should agree," old Conway warned, as, with a sweep of his battered old hat to the ladies, he turned to reenter his office. With a nod of farewell, John Parker and his wife started riding down the draw, while Farrel turned to unloosen his saddle girth and adjust the heavy stock saddle on the pinto's back. While he was thus engaged, Kay rode up to the door of Conway's rough little office, bent down from, Panchito, and peered in.

"Bill Conway!" she called softly.

Bill Conway came to the door.

"What's the big idea, Miss Parker?"

The girl glanced around and saw that Don Mike was busy with the latigo, so she leaned down, drew her arm around the astounded Conway's neck, and implanted on his ruddy, bristly cheek a kiss as soft—so Bill Conway afterward described it—as goose-hair.

"You build that dam," she whispered, blushing furiously, "and see to it that it's a good dam and will hold water for years. I'm the reserve in this battle— understand? When you need money, see me, but, oh, please do not tell Don Mike about it. I'd die of shame."

She whirled Panchito and galloped down the draw, with Miguel Farrel loping along behind her, while, from the door of his shack of an office, old Bill Conway looked after them and thoughtfully rubbed a certain spot on his cheek. Long after the young folks had disappeared round the base of El Palomar, he continued to gaze. Eventually he was brought out of his reverie when a cur dog belonging to one of the teamsters on the grading gang thrust a cold muzzle into his hand.

"Pure," murmured Mr. Conway, softly, "this isn't a half-bad old world, even if a fellow does grow old, and finds himself hairless and childless and half broke and shackled to the worst automobile in the world, bar none. And do you know why it isn't such a rotten world as some folks claim? No? Well, I'll tell you, purp. It's because it keeps a movin'. And do you know what keeps it a movin'? Purp, it's love!"

XXI

AT THE BASE OF EL PALOMAR, Farrel and his party were met by the Parker chauffeur with the car. Pablo had guided him out and was lounging importantly in the seat beside William.

"Don Nicolás Sandoval came to the hacienda an hour ago, Don Miguel," he reported. "He brought with him three others; all have gone forth to take possession of Loustalot's sheep."

Farrel nodded and dismounted to assist Mrs. Parker as the latter came down from her horse, somewhat stiffly. When he turned to perform a similar office for her daughter, however, the girl smilingly shook her head.

"I shipped for the cruise, Don Mike," she assured him. "May I ride home with you? Remember, you've got to pick up your rope and that panther's pelt." Her adorable face flushed faintly as her gaze sought her mother's. "I have never seen a panther undressed," she protested.

"Well," her amiable mother replied, with her customary hearty manner, "far be it from me to deprive you of that interesting sight. Take good care of her, Miguel. I hold you responsible for her."

"You are very kind to trust me so."

Both Parker and his wife noted that his words were not mere polite patter. Farrel's gravely courteous bearing, his respectful bow to Mrs. Parker and the solemnity with which be spoke impressed them with the conviction that this curious human study in light and shadow regarded their approval as an honor, not a

194

privilege.

"I shall take very good care of Miss Kay," he supplemented. "We shall be home for dinner."

He mounted the gray gelding, leaving Pablo to follow with the black mare and the pinto, while he and Kay cantered down the wide white wash of the Rio San Gregorio.

From their semi-concealment among the young willow growth, scrub cattle gazed at them or fled, with tails aloft, for more distant thickets; cottontail rabbits and an occasional jackrabbit, venturing forth as the shadows grew long in the valley, flashed through the low sage and weeds; from the purpling hillsides cock quails called cheerily to their families to come right home. The air was still and cool, heavy with the perfume of sage, blackberry briars, *yerba santa,* an occasional bay tree and the pungent odor of moist earth and decaying vegetation. There had fallen upon the land that atmosphere of serenity, of peace, that is the peculiar property of California's foothill valleys in the late afternoon; the world seemed very distant and not at all desirable, and to Kay there came a sudden, keen realization of how this man beside her must love this darkling valley with the hills above presenting their flower-clad breasts to the long spears of light from the dying day . . .

Don Mike had caught the spirit of the little choristers of his hidden valley, she heard him singing softly in rather a pleasing baritone voice:

> Pienso en ti, Teresita mia,
> Cuando la luna alumbra la tierra
> He sentido el fuego de tus ojos,
> He sentido las penas del amor.

"What does it mean?" she demanded, imperiously.

"Oh, it's a very ordinary little sentiment, Miss Ray. The Spanish cavalier, having settled himself under his lady's window, thrums a preliminary chord or two, just to let her and the family know he's not working on the sly; then he says in effect: 'I think of thee, my little Tessie, when the moonlight is shining on the world; your bright eyes have me going for fair, kid, and due to a queer pain in my interior, I know I'm in love.' "

"You outrageous Celt!"

He chuckled. "A Spaniard takes his love very seriously. He's got to be sad and despairing about it, even when he knows very well the girl is saying to herself: 'For heaven's sake, when will this windy bird get down to brass tacks and pop the question?' He droops like a stale eschscholtzia, only, unlike that flower he hasn't sense enough to shut up for the night!"

Her beaming face turned toward him was ample reward for his casual display of Celtic wit, his knowledge of botany. And suddenly she saw his first real smile—a flash of beautiful white teeth and a wrinkling of the skin around the merry eyes. It came and went like a flicker of lightning; the somber man was an insouciant lad again.

A quarter of a mile across the valley they found the torn and mutilated carcass of a heifer, with a day-old calf grieving beside her.

"This is the work of our defunct friend, the panther," Farrell explained. "He had made his kill on this little heifer and eaten heartily. It occurred to me while we were chasing him that he was logey. Well—when Mike's away the cats will play."

He reached down, grasped the calf by the forelegs

and drew the forlorn little animal up before him on the saddle. As it stretched out quietly across his thighs, following a halfhearted struggle to escape, Ray saw Don Mike give the orphan his left index finger to suck.

"Not much sustenance in it, is there, old timer?" he addressed the calf. "Coyotes would have had you tonight if I hadn't passed by."

"What a tiny calf," Kay observed, riding close to pat the sleek head.

"He's scrubby and interbred; his mother bore him before she had her own growth and a hundred generations of him got the same poor start in life. You've seen people like this little runt. He really isn't worth carrying home, but—"

It occurred to her that his silence was eloquent of the inherent generosity of the man, even as his poetic outburst of a few minutes before had been eloquent of the minstrel in him. She rode in silence, regarding him critically from time to time, and when they came to the tree where the panther hung he gave her the calf to hold while he deftly skinned the dead marauder, tied the pelt behind his saddle, relieved her of the calf and jogged away toward home.

"Well," he demanded, presently, "you do not think any the less of me for what I did to your father this afternoon, do you?"

"Of course not. Nobody likes a mollycoddle," she retorted.

"A battle of finances between your father and me will not be a very desperate one. A gnat attacking a tiger. I shall scarcely interest him. I am predestined to defeat."

"But with Mr. Conway's aid—"

"Bill's aid will not amount to very much. He was always a splendid engineer and an honest builder, but a

197

poor business man. He might be able to maintain work on the dam for awhile, but in the end lack of adequate finances would defeat us. And I have no right to ask Bill to sacrifice the profit on this job which your father is willing to pay him, in return for a cancellation of the contract; I have no right to ask or expect Bill Conway to risk a penniless old age for me. You see, I attacked him at his weakest point—his heart. It was selfish of me."

She could not combat this argument, so she said nothing and for a quarter of a mile her companion rode with his chin on his breast, in silence. What a man of moods he was, she reflected.

"You despair of being able to pay my father the mortgage and regain your ranch?" she asked, at length.

He nodded.

"But you'll fight to win—and fight to the finish, will you not?" she persisted.

He glanced at her sharply. "That is my natural inclination, Miss Kay—when I permit sentiment to rule me. But when I apply the principles of sound horse sense—when I view the approach of the conflict as a military man would view it, I am forced to the conviction that in this case discretion is the better part of valor. Battles are never won by valorous fools who get themselves killed in a spectacular manner."

"I see. You plan to attempt the sale of your equity in the ranch before my father can finally foreclose on you."

"No, that would be the least profitable course to pursue. A hundred-thousand-acre ranch is not sold in a hurry unless offered at a tremendous sacrifice. Even then it is of slow sale. For the following reasons: Within a few years, what with the rapid growth of population in this state and the attrition of alien farmers on our agricultural lands, this wonderful valley land of the Rancho Palomar will cease to be assessed as grazing land. It is agricultural land and as a matter of equity it ought to pay taxes to the state on that basis. And it will. I do not know—I have never heard of—a cattleman with a million dollars cash on hand, and if I could find such a cattleman who was looking for a hundred thousand acre ranch he would not want half of it to be agricultural land and be forced to bankrupt himself paying taxes on it as such."

"I think I understand. The ranch must be sold to some person or company who will purchase it with the idea of selling half of the ranch as grazing land and the valley of the San Gregorio as agricultural land."

"Quite so. I would have to interest a subdivision expert whose specialty is the sale of small farms, on time payments. Well, no business man ever contemplates the purchase, at a top price, of property that is to be sold on mortgage foreclosure; and I think he would be an optimist, indeed, who would bid against your father."

"Of course," he continued, patiently, "when the ranch is sold at auction to satisfy the mortgage your father will bid it in at the amount of the mortgage. It is improbable that he will have to pay more."

"Am I to understand then, Don Mike, that for approximately three hundred thousand dollars he will be enabled, under this atrocious code of business morals, to acquire a property worth at least a million dollars?"

"Such is the law—a law as old as the world itself."

"Why, then, the whole thing is absurdly simple, Don Mike. All you have to do is to get a friend to bid against my father and run the price up on him to something like a halfway decent sum. In that way you should manage to save a portion of your equity."

He bent upon her a benign and almost paternal glance. "You're tremendously sweet to put that flea in my ear, Kay. It's a wonderful prescription, but it lacks one small ingredient—the wealthy, courageous and self-sacrificing friend who will consent to run the sandy on your astute parent, as a favor to me."

She gave him a tender, prescient little smile—the smile of one who sees beyond a veil objects not visible to the eyes of other mortals.

"Well, even if he is my dear father he ought to be nice about it and see to it that you receive a fair price for your equity." She clenched her little fist. "Why, Don Mike, that's just like killing the wounded."

"My dear girl, I do not blame your father at all. What claim have I on his sympathy or his purse? I'm a stranger to him. One has to be a sport in such matters and take the blow with a smile."

"I don't care. It's all wrong," she replied with spirit. "And I'm going to tell my father so."

"Oh, I've thought up a plan for escaping with a profit," he assured her, lightly. "it will leave you folks in undisputed possession of the house and the ranch, leave Bill Conway free to proceed with his valuable contract and leave me free to mount Panchito and fare forth to other and more virgin fields—I trust. All of this within a period of forty-eight hours."

Was it fancy, or had her face really blanched a little?

"Why—why, Don Mike! How extraordinary!"

"On the contrary, quite ordinary. It's absurdly simple. I need some getaway money. I ought to have it—and I'm going to get it by the oldest known method—extortion through intimidation. Your father is a smart man and he will see the force of my argument."

"He's a very stubborn man and doesn't bluff worth a cent," she warned him and added: "Particularly when he doesn't like one or when he is angry. And whatever you do, do not threaten him. If you threaten him, instantly he will be consumed with curiosity to see you make good."

"I shall not threaten him. I shall merely talk business to him. That's a language he understands."

"How much money do you expect to realize?"

"About half a million dollars."

"In return for what?"

"A quit claim deed to the Rancho Palomar. He can have a title in fee simple to the ranch by noon tomorrow and thus be spared the necessity for a new suit to foreclose that accursed mortgage and the concomitant wait of one year before taking possession. He will then be free to continue his well drilling and dam building in Caliente Basin; he can immediately resume his negotiations with Okada for the purchase of the entire valley and will be enabled, in all probability, to close the deal at a splendid profit. Then he can proceed to erect his hydroelectric plant and sell it for another million dollars' profit to one of the parent power companies throughout the state; when that has been disposed of he can lease or sell the range land to André Loustalot and finally he can retire with the prospect of unceasing dividends from the profits of his irrigation company. Within two years he will have a profit of at least two million dollars, net, but this will not be possible until he has first disposed of me at a total disposing price of five hundred thousand dollars."

"Please explain that."

"As I think I have remarked in your presence once before, there is extreme probability that the State of California will have passed additional anti-Jap legislation, designed to tighten the present law and eliminate the legal loopholes whereby alien Japanese continue to acquire land despite the existing law. If I stand pat no Jap can set foot in the San Gregorio valley for at least one year from date and by that time this legislation may be in force, in which event the Jap deal will be killed forever. Also, there is always the off chance that I may manage, mysteriously, to redeem the property in the interim. It would be worth a quarter of a million dollars to your father this minute if he could insure himself against redemption of the mortgage; and it would be worth an additional quarter of a million dollars to him if he were free to do business with Okada tomorrow morning. Okada is a surefire prospect. He will pay cash for the entire valley if I permit the deal to go through now. If, however, through my stubbornness, your father loses out with Okada, it will be a year hence before he can even recommence work on his irrigation system and another year before he will have it completed. Many things may occur during those two years—the principal danger to be apprehended being the sudden collapse of inflated wartime values, with resultant money panics, forced liquidation and the destruction of public confidence in land investments. The worry and exasperation I can hand your respected parent must be as seriously considered as the impending tremendous loss of profit."

"I believe you are a very shrewd young man, Don Mike," the girl answered, sadly. "I think your plan will be much more likely to produce half a million dollars of what you call 'getaway money' than my suggestion that a friend run up the price on father at the sale. But how do you know Okada will pay cash?"

"I do not know. But if your father's attorneys are

Californians they will warn him to play safe when dealing with a Jap."

"But is it not possible that Okada may not have sufficient money to operate on the excessive scale you outline?"

"Not a chance. He is not buying for himself; he is the representative of the Japanese Association of California."

"Well, Don Miguel Farrel," the girl declared, as he ceased speaking, "I have only known you twenty-four hours, but in that time I have heard you do a deal of talking on the Japanese question in California. And now you have proved a terrible disappointment to me."

"In what way?" he demanded, and pulled his horse up abruptly. He was vaguely distressed at her blunt statement, apprehensive as to the reason for her flushed face and flashing eye, the slightly strident note in her voice.

"I have regarded you as a true blue American—a super-patriot. And now you calmly plan to betray your state to the enemy for the paltry sum of half a million dollars!"

He stared at her, a variety of emotions in his glance. "Well," he replied, presently, "I suppose I shall deserve that, if I succeed with my plan. However, as a traitor, I'm not even a runner-up with your father. He's going to get a couple of million dollars as the price of his shame! And he doesn't even need the money. On the other hand, I am a desperate, mighty unhappy ex-soldier experiencing all of the delights of a bankrupt, with the exception of an introduction to the referee in bankruptcy. I'm whipped. Who cares what becomes of me? Not a soul on earth except Pablo and Carolina and they, poor creatures, are dependent upon me. Why should I sacrifice my last chance for happiness in a vain effort to stem a yellow tide that cannot be stemmed? Why do you taunt me with my aversion to sacrifice for my country—I who have sacrificed two years of my life and some of my blood and much of my happiness?"

Suddenly she put her little gauntleted hand up to her face and commenced to weep. "Oh, Don Mike, please forgive me! I'm sorry. I—I—have no right to demand such a sacrifice, but oh, I thought—perhaps—you were different from all the others—that you'd be a true—-knight and die—sword in—hand—oh, dear, I'm such a—little ninny—"

He bit his lower lip but could not quite conceal a smile.

"You mean you didn't think I was a quitter!" His voice was grim and crisp. "Well, in the dirty battle for bread and butter there are no decorations for gallantry in action; in that conflict I do not have to live up to the one that Congress gave me. And why shouldn't I quit? I come from a long line of combination fighter quitters. We were never afraid of hardship or physical pain, danger or death, but—we couldn't face conditions; we balked and quit in the face of circumstance; we retired always before the economic onslaught of the Anglo-Saxon."

"Ah, but you're Anglo-Saxon," she sobbed. "You belong to the race that doesn't quit—that somehow muddles through."

"If I but possessed blue eyes and flaxen hair—if I but possessed the guerdon of a noble lady's love—I might not have disappointed you, Kay. I might still have been a true knight and died sword in hand. Unfortunately, however, I possess sufficient Latin blood to make me a little bit lazy—to counsel quitting while the quitting is

204

good."

"I'm terribly disappointed," she protested. "Terribly."

"So am I. I'm ashamed of myself, but—a contrite heart is not hockable at the only pawnshop in El Toro. Buck up, Miss Parker!"

"You have called me Kay three times this afternoon, Miguel—"

He rode close to her, reached over and gently drew one little hand from her crimson face. "You're a dear girl, Kay," he murmured, huskily. "Please cease weeping. You haven't insulted me or even remotely hurt my little feelings. God bless your sweet soul! If you'll only stop crying, I'll give you Panchito. He's yours from this minute. Saddle and bridle, too. Take him. Do what you please with him, but for heaven's sake don't let your good mother think we've been quarreling—and on the very second day of our acquaintance."

She dashed the tears away and beamed up at him. "You give Panchito to me! You don't mean it!"

"I do. I told you I might give him away to somebody worthwhile."

"You haven't known me long enough to give me valuable presents, Miguel," she demurred. "You're a dear to want to give him to me and I'm positively mad to own him, but Mother and Dad might think—well, that is, they might not understand. Of course we understand perfectly, but—well—you understand, don't you, Miguel?"

"I understand that I cannot afford to have your father suspect that I am unmindful of—certain conditions," he answered her, and flushed with embarrassment. "If you do not want Panchito as a gift I shall not insist—"

"I think it would be a good idea for you to permit Dad to buy him for me. He's worth every cent of five thousand dollars—"

"I'll never sell him. I told you this afternoon I love him. I never sell a horse or a dog that I love or that loves me. I shall have to take him back, Kay—for the present."

"I think that would be the better way, Miguel." She bent upon him an inscrutable smile but in the depths of her brown eyes he thought he detected laughter.

"You'll buck up now?" he pleaded.

"I'm already bucked up."

As they rode up to the great barn, Kay dismounted, "Leave the old trifle at the door, Kay," Farrel told her. "Pablo will get him home. Excuse me, please, while I take this calf over to Carolina. She'll make a man out of him. She's a wonder at inducing little mavericks like this fellow to drink milk from a bucket."

He jogged away, while Panchito, satisfied that he had performed throughout the day like a perfect gentleman, bent his head and rubbed his forehead against Kay's cheek, seeking some evidence of growing popularity with the girl. To his profound satisfaction she scratched him under the jawbone and murmured audibly:

"Never mind, old dear. Some day you'll be my Panchito. He loves you and didn't he say he could only give you away for love?"

XXII

DINNER THAT NIGHT WAS SINGULARLY FREE from conversation. Nobody present felt inclined to be chatty. John Parker was wondering what Miguel Farrel's next move would be, and was formulating means to checkmate it; Kay, knowing what Don Mike's next move would be and knowing further that she was about to checkmate it, was silent through a sense of guilt; Mrs. Parker's eight miles in the saddle that afternoon had fatigued her to the point of dissipating her buoyant spirits, and Farrel had fallen into a mood of deep abstraction.

"Are we to listen to naught but the champing of food?" Mrs. Parker inquired presently.

"Hello!" her husband declared. "So you've come up for air, eh, Katie?"

"Oh, I'm feeling far from chatty, John. But the silence is oppressive. Miguel, are you plotting against the whites?"

He looked up with a smiling nod. "I'm making big medicine, Mrs. Parker. So big, in fact," he continued, as he folded his napkin and thrust it carefully into the ring, "that I am going to ask your permission to withdraw. I have been very remiss in my social duties. I have been home twenty-four hours and I have passed the Mission de la Madre Dolorosa three times, yet I have not been inside to pay my respects to my old friends there. I shall be in disgrace if I fail to call this evening for Father Dominic's blessing. They'll be wondering why I neglect them."

"How do you know they know you're home?" Parker demanded, suspiciously. He was wondering if Don Miguel's excuse to leave the table might have some connection with Bill Conway and the impending imbroglio.

"Brother Flavio told me so tonight. As we rode down the valley he was ringing the Angelus; and after the Angelus he played on the chimes, 'I'm Nearer Home Today.' May I be excused, Mrs. Parker?"

"By all means, Michael."

"Thank you." He included them all in a courteous nod of farewell. They heard the patio gate close behind him.

"I wish I dared follow him," Parker observed. "I wonder if he really is going down to the Mission. I think I'll make certain."

He left the room, went out to the patio gate, opened it slightly and peered out. His host's tall form, indistinct in the moonlight, was disappearing toward the palm-lined avenue, so Parker, satisfied that Don Mike had embarked upon the three mile walk to the Mission, returned to the dining room.

"Well, Mr. Sherlock Holmes?" Kay queried.

"I think he's headed for the Mission, after all, Kay."

"I never doubted it."

"Why?"

"Because he wouldn't tell a trifling lie to deceive when when there was no necessity for deceiving. His plans are fully matured and he will not act until morning. In that three mile walk to the Mission he will perfect the details of his plan of attack."

"Then he is planning?—but you said his plans are fully matured. How do you know, Kay?"

"He told me all about them as we were riding in this evening." Both Parker and his wife raised interrogatory eyebrows. "Indeed!" Mrs. Parker murmured. "So he's honoring you with his confidences already?"

The girl ignored her mother's bantering tones. "No, he didn't tell me in confidence. In fact, his contemplated procedure is so normal and free from guile that he feels there is no necessity for secrecy. I suppose he feels that it would be foolish to conceal the trap after the mouse has been caught in it."

"Well, little daughter, I haven't been caught—yet. And I'm not a mouse, but considerable of an old fox.

What's he up to?"

"He's going to sell you his equity in the ranch."

Her father stared hard at her, a puzzled little smile beginning to break over his handsome face.

"That sounds interesting," he replied, dryly. "What am I going to pay for it?"

"Half a million dollars."

"Nonsense."

"Perhaps. But you'll have to admit that his reasoning is not so preposterous as you think." And she went on to explain to Parker every angle of the situation as Don Mike viewed it.

Both Parker and his wife listened attentively. "Well, John," the good soul demanded, when her daughter had finished speaking: "What's wrong with that prescription?"

"By George, that young man has a head on his shoulders. His reasoning is absolutely flawless. However, I am not going to pay him any half-million dollars. I might, in a pinch, consider paying him half that, but—"

"Would a quitclaim deed be worth half a million to you, Dad?"

"As a matter of cold business, it would. Are you quite certain he was serious?"

"Oh, quite serious."

"He's a disappointment, Kay. I had hoped he would prove to be a worthwhile opponent, for certainly he is a most likable young man. However—" He smothered a yawn with his hand, selected a cigar from his case, carefully cut off the end and lighted it. "Poor devil," he murmured, presently, and rose, remarking that he might as well take a turn or two around the farmyard as a first aid to digestion.

Once outside, he walked to the edge of the mesa and gazed down the moonlit San Gregorio. Half a mile away he saw a moving black spot on the white ribbon of road. "Confound you," he murmured, "you're going to get some of my tail feathers, but not quite the handful you anticipate. You cannot stand the acid test, Don Mike, and I'm glad to know that."

XXIII

AS FARREL APPROACHED the Mission de la Madre Dolorosa, a man in the rusty brown habit of a Franciscan friar rose from a bench just outside the entrance to the Mission garden.

"My son," he said, in calm, paternal accents and speaking in Spanish, "I knew you would come to see your old friends when you had laid aside the burdens of the day. I have waited here to be first to greet you; for you I am guilty of the sin of selfishness."

"Padre Dominic!" Don Mike grasped the outstretched hand and wrung it heartily. "Old friend Old Saint! Not since my confirmation have I asked for your blessing," and with the words be bent his head while the old friar, making the sign of the cross, asked the blessing of God upon the last of the Farrels.

Don Mike drew his old friend down to the seat the latter had just vacated. "We will talk here for awhile, Father," he suggested. "I expect the arrival of a friend in an automobile and I would not be in the garden when he passes. Later I will visit with the others. Good Father Dominic, does God still bless you with excellent health?"

"He does, Miguel, but the devil afflicts me with

210

rheumatism."

"You haven't changed a bit, Father Dominic."

"Mummies do not change, my son. I have accomplished ninety-two years of my life; long ago I used up all possibilities for change, even for the worse. It is good to have you home, Miguel. Pablo brought us the news early this morning. We wondered why you did not look in upon us as you passed last night."

"I looked in at my father's grave. I was in no mood for meeting those who had loved him."

For perhaps half an hour they conversed; then the peace of the valley was broken by the rattling and labored puffing of an asthmatic automobile.

Father Dominic rose and peered around the corner. "Yonder comes one who practices the great virtue of economy," he announced, "for he is running without lights. Doubtless he deems the moonlight sufficient."

Farrel stepped out into the road and held up his arm as a signal for the motorist to halt. Old Bill Conway swung his prehistoric automobile off the road and pulled up before the Mission, his carbon-heated motor continuing to fire spasmodically even after be had turned off the ignition.

"Hello, Miguel," he called, cheerily. "What are you doing here, son?"

"Calling on my spiritual adviser and waiting for you, Bill."

"Howdy, Father Dominic." Conway leaped out and gave his hand to the old friar. "Miguel, how did you know I was coming?"

"This is the only road out of Agua Caliente basin—and I know you! You'd give your head for a football to anybody you love, but the man who takes anything away from you will have to get up early in the

211

morning."

"Go to the head of the class, boy. You're right. I figured Parker would be getting up rather early tomorrow morning and dusting into El Toro to clear for action, so I thought I'd come in tonight. I'm going to rout out an attorney the minute I get to town, have him draw up a complaint in my suit for damages against Parker for violation of contract, file the complaint the instant the county clerk's office opens in the morning and then attach his account in the El Toro bank."

"You might attach his stock in that institution while you're at it, Bill. However, I wouldn't stoop so low as to attach his two automobiles. The Parkers are guests of mine and I wouldn't inconvenience the ladies for anything."

"By the Holy Poker! Have they got *two* automobiles?" There was a hint of apprehension in old Conway's voice.

"*Si, señor.* A touring car and a limousine."

"Oh, lord! I'm mighty glad you told me, Miguel. I only stole the spark plugs from that eight cylinder touring car. Lucky thing the hounds know me. They like to et me up at first."

Farrel sat down on the filthy running board of Bill Conway's car and laughed softly. "Oh, Bill, you're immense! So that's why you're running without lights! You concluded that even if he did get up early in the morning you couldn't afford to permit him to reach El Toro before the courthouse opened for business."

"A wise man counteth his chickens before they are hatched, Miguel. Where does Parker keep the limousine?"

"Bill, I cannot tell you that. These people are my guests."

212

"Oh, very well. Now that I know it's there I'll find it, What did you want to see me about, boy?"

"I've been thinking of our conversation of this afternoon, Bill, and as a result I'm panicky. I haven't any right to drag you into trouble or ask you to share my woes. I've thought it over and I think I shall play safe. Parker will get the ranch in the long run, but if I give him a quitclaim deed now I think he will give me at least a quarter of a million dollars. It'll be worth that to him to be free to proceed with his plans."

"Yes, I can understand that, Miguel, and probably, from a business standpoint, your decision does credit to your common sense. But how about this Jap colony?"

"Bill, can two lone, poverty-stricken Californians hope to alter the immigration laws of the entire United States? Can we hope to keep the present Japanese population of California confined to existing areas?"

"No, I suppose not."

"I had a wild hope this afternoon—guess I was a bit theatrical—but it was a hope based on selfishness. I'm only twenty-eight years old, Bill, but you are nearly sixty. I'm too young to sacrifice my old friends, so I've waited here to tell you that you are released from your promise to support me. Settle with Parker and pull out in peace."

Conway pondered. "Wel-l-l-l," he concluded, finally, "perhaps you're right, son. Nevertheless, I'm going to enter suit and attach. Foolish to hunt big game with an empty gun, Miguel. Parker spoke of an amicable settlement, but as Napoleon remarked, 'God is on the side of the strongest battalions,' and an *amicable* settlement is much more amicably obtained, when a forced settlement is inevitable." And the cunning old rascal winked solemnly.

213

Farrel stood up. "Well, that's all I wanted to see you about, Bill. That, and to say 'thank you' until you are better paid."

"Well, I'm on my way, Miguel." The old contractor shook hands with Father Dominic and Farrel, cranked his car, turned it and headed back up the San Gregorio, while Father Dominic guided Don Mike into the Mission refectory, where Father Andréas and the lay brothers sat around the dinner table, discussing a black scale which had lately appeared on their olive trees.

At the entrance to the palm avenue, Bill Conway stopped his car and proceeded afoot to the Farrel hacienda, which he approached cautiously from the rear, through the oaks. A slight breeze was blowing down the valley, so Conway maneuvered until a short quick bark from one of Farrel's hounds informed him that his scent had been borne to the kennel and recognized as that of a friend. Confident now that he would not be discovered by the inmates of the hacienda, Bill Conway proceeded boldly to the barn. Just inside the main building which, in more prosperous times on El Palomar, had been used for storing hay, the touring car stood. Conway fumbled along the instrument board and discovered the switch key still in the lock, so he turned on the headlights and discovered the limousine thirty feet away in the rear of the barn. Ten minutes later, with the spark plugs from both cars carefully secreted under a pile of split stove wood in the yard, he departed as silently as he had come.

About nine o'clock Don Mike left the Mission and walked home. On the hills to the north he caught the glare of a campfire against the silvery sky; wherefore he knew that Don Nicolás Sandoval and his deputies were guarding the Loustalot sheep.

At ten o'clock he entered the patio. In a wicker *chaise-longue* John Parker lounged on the porch outside his room; Farrel caught the scent of his cigar on the warm, semi-tropical night, saw the red end of it gleaming like a demon's eye.

"Hello, Mr. Farrel," Parker greeted him. "Won't you sit down and smoke a cigar with me before turning in?"

"Thank you. I shall be happy to." He crossed the garden to his guest, sat down beside him and gratefully accepted the fragrant cigar Parker handed him. A moment later Kay joined them.

"Wonderful night," Parker remarked. "Mrs. P. retired early, but Kay and I sat up chatting and enjoying the peaceful loveliness of this old garden. A sleepless mocking bird and a sleepy little thrush gave a concert in the sweet-lime tree; a couple of green frogs in the fountain rendered a bass duet; Kay thought that if we remained very quiet the spirits of some lovers of the 'splendid idle forties' might appear in your garden."

The mood of the night was still upon the girl. In the momentary silence that followed she commenced singing softly:

> I saw an old-fashioned missus,
> Taking old-fashioned kisses,
> In an old-fashioned garden,
> From an old-fashioned beau.

Don Mike slid off the porch and went to his own room, returning presently with a guitar. "I've been wanting to play a little," be confessed as he tuned the neglected instrument, "but it seemed sort of sacrilegious—after coming home and finding my father gone and the ranch about to go. However—why sip

215

sorrow with a long spoon? What's that ballad about the old-fashioned garden, Miss Kay? I like it. If you'll hum it a few times—"

Ten minutes later he knew the simple little song and was singing it with her. Mrs. Parker, in dressing gown, slippers and boudoir cap, despairing of sleep until all of the members of her family had first preceded her to bed, came out and joined them; presently they were all singing happily together, while Don Mike played or faked an accompaniment.

At eleven o'clock Farrel gave a final vigorous strum to the guitar and stood up to say good night.

"Shall we sing again tomorrow night, Don Mike?" Kay demanded, eagerly.

Farrel's glance rested solemnly upon her father's face. "Well, if we all feel happy tomorrow night I see no objection," he answered. "I fear for your father, Miss Kay. Have you told him of my plans for depleting his worldly wealth?"

She flushed a little and answered in the affirmative.

"How does the idea strike you, Mr. Parker?"

John Parker grinned—the superior grin of one who knows his superior strength. "Like a great many principles that are excellent in theory, your plan will not work in practice."

"No?"

"No."

For the second time that day Kay saw Don Mike's face light up with that insouciant boyish smile.

Then he skipped blithely across the garden thrumming the guitar and singing:

Mine eyes have seen the glory of the
coming of the Lord!

216

At seven o'clock next morning, while Miguel Farrel was shaving, John Parker came to his door, knocked, and without further ado came into the room.

"Farrel," he began, briskly, "I do not relish your way of doing business. Where are the spark plugs of my two cars?"

"My dear man, I haven't taken them, so why do you ask me? I am not flattered at your blunt hint that I would so far forget my position as host as to steal the spark plugs from my guest's automobiles."

"I beg your pardon. Somebody took them and naturally I jumped to the conclusion that you were the guilty party."

Don Mike shaved in silence.

"Do you know who removed those spark plugs, Mr. Farrel ?"

"Yes, sir, I do."

"Who did it?"

"Bill Conway. He came by last night and concluded it would be better to make quite certain that you remained away from El Toro until about nine-thirty o'clock this morning. It was entirely Bill's idea. I did not suggest it to him, directly or indirectly. He's old enough to roll his own hoop. He had a complaint in action drawn up against you last night; it will be filed at nine o'clock this morning and immediately thereafter your bank account and your stock in the First National Bank of El Toro will be attached. Of course you will file a bond to lift the attachment, but Bill will have your assets where he can levy on them when he gets round to collecting on the judgment which he will secure against you unless you proceed with the contract for that dam."

"And this is Conway's work entirely?"

217

"Yes, sir."

"It's clever work. I'm sorry it wasn't yours. May I have the loan of a saddle horse—Panchito or the gray?"

"Not to ride either of them, breakfastless, twenty-one miles to El Toro in two hours. They can do it, but not under an impost of a hundred and ninety pounds. You might ruin both of them—" he scraped his chin, smiling blandly—"and I know you'd about ruin yourself, sir. The saddle had commenced to get very sore before you had completed eight miles yesterday."

"Then I'm out of luck, I dare say."

"Strikes me that way, Mr. Parker."

"Very well. You force me to talk business. What will that quitclaim deed cost me?"

"Six hundred thousand dollars. I've raised the ante since last night."

"I'll not pay it."

"What will you pay?"

"About fifty percent of it."

"I might consider less than my first figure and more than your last. Make me a firm offer—in writing—and I'll give you a firm answer the instant you hand me the document. I'm a poor bargainer. Haggling irritates me—so I never haggle. And I don't care a tinker's hoot whether you buy me off or not. After nine o'clock this morning you will have lost the opportunity, because I give you my word of honor, I shall decline even to receive an offer."

He reached over on his bureau and retrieved therefrom a sheet of paper. "Here is the form I desire your offer to take, sir," he continued, affably, and handed the paper to Parker. "Please rewrite it in ink, fill in the amount of your offer and sign it. You have until nine o'clock, remember. At nine-one you will be too

218

late."

Despite his deep annoyance, Parker favored him with a sardonic grin. "You're a good bluffer, Farrel."

Don Mike turned from the mirror and regarded his guest very solemnly. "How do you know?" he queried, mildly. "You've never seen me bluff. I've seen a few inquests held in this country over some men who bluffed in an emergency. We're no longer wild and woolly out here, but when we pull, we shoot. Remember that, sir."

Parker felt himself abashed in the presence of this cool young man, for nothing is so disconcerting as a defeated enemy who refuses to acknowledge defeat. It occurred to Parker in that moment that there was nothing extraordinary in Farrel's action; for consideration of the sweetness of life cannot be presumed to arouse a great deal of interest in one who knows he will be murdered if he does not commit suicide.

John Parker tucked the paper in his pocket and thoughtfully left the room. "The boy distrusts me," he soliloquized, "afraid I'll go back on any promise I make him, so he demands my offer in writing. Some more of his notions of business, Spanish style. Stilted and unnecessary. How like all of his kind he is! Ponderous in minor affairs, casual in major matters of business."

An hour later he came up to Don Mike, chatting with Kay and Mrs. Parker on the porch, and thrust an envelope into Farrel's hand.

"Here is my offer—in writing."

"Thank you, sir." Don Mike thrust the envelope unopened into the breast pocket of his coat and from the side pocket of the same garment drew another envelope. "Here is my answer—in writing."

219

Parker stared at him in frank amazement and admiration; Kay's glance, as it roved from her father to Don Mike and back again, was sad and troubled.

"Then you've reopened negotiations, father," she demanded, accusingly.

He nodded. "Our host has a persuasive way about him, Kay," he supplemented. "He insisted so on my making him an offer that finally I consented."

"And now," Farrel assured her, "negotiations are about to be closed."

"Absolutely?"

"Absolutely. Never to be reopened, Miss Kay."

Parker opened his envelope and read. His face was without emotion. "That answer is entirely satisfactory to me, Mr. Farrel," he said, presently, and passed the paper to his daughter. She read:

> I was tempted last night. You should have closed then. I have changed my mind. Your offer—whatever it may be—is declined.

"I also approve," Kay murmured, and in the swift glance she exchanged with Don Miguel he read something that caused his heart to beat happily. Mrs. Parker took the paper from her daughter's hand and read it also.

"Very well, Ajax. I think we all think a great deal more of you for defying the lightning," was her sole comment.

Despite his calm, John Parker was irritated to the point of fury. He felt that he bad been imposed upon by Don Mike; his great god, business, had been scandalously flouted.

"I am at a loss to understand, Mr. Farrel," he said,

coldly, "why you have subjected me to the incivility of requesting from me an offer in writing and then refusing to read it when I comply with your request. Why subject me to that annoyance when you knew you intended to refuse any offer I might make you? I do not relish your flippancy at my expense, sir."

"Do you not think, sir, that I can afford a modicum of flippancy when I pay such a fearfully high price for it?" Don Mike countered smilingly. "I'll bet a new hat my pleasantry cost me not less than four hundred thousand dollars. I think I'll make certain," and he opened Parker's envelope and read what was contained therein. "Hum-m! Three hundred and twenty-five thousand?"

Parker extended his hand. "I would be obliged to you for the return of that letter," he began, but paused, confused, at Farrel's cheerful, mocking grin.

"All's fair in love and war," he quoted, gaily. "I wanted a document to prove to some banker or pawnbroker that I have an equity in this ranch and it is worth three hundred and twenty-five thousand dollars, in the opinion of the astute financier who holds a first mortgage on it. Really, I think I'd be foolish to give away this evidence," and he tucked it carefully back in his pocket.

"I wonder," Kay spoke up demurely, "which ancestor from which side of the family tree put that idea in his head, father?"

Don Mike pretended not to have heard her. He turned kindly to John Parker and laid a friendly hand upon the latter's arm.

"I think Bill Conway will drift by about ten o'clock or ten-thirty, Mr. Parker. I know he will not cause you anymore inconvenience than he finds absolutely necessary, sir. He's tricky, but he isn't mean."

Parker did not reply. He did not know whether to laugh or fly into a rage, to offer Don Mike his hand or his fist. The latter must have guessed Parker's feelings, for he favored his guests with a Latin shrug and a deprecatory little smile, begged to be excused and departed for the barn. A quarter of an hour later Kay saw him and Pablo ride out of the yard and over the hills toward the west; she observed that Farrel was riding his father's horse, wherefore she knew that he had left Panchito behind for her.

Farrel found Don Nicolás Sandoval, the sheriff, by riding straight to a column of smoke he saw rising from a grove of oaks on a flat hilltop.

"What do you mean by camping out here, Don Nicolás?" Farrel demanded as he rode up. "Since when has it become the fashion to await a formal invitation to the hospitality of the Rancho Palomar?"

"I started to ride down to the hacienda at sunset last night," Don Nicolás replied, "but a man on foot and carrying a rifle and a blanket came over the hills to the south. I watched him through my binoculars. He came down into the wash of the San Gregorio—and I did not see him come out. So I knew he was camped for the night in the willow thickets of the river bed; that he was a stranger in the country, else he would have gone up to your hacienda for the night; that his visit spelled danger to you, else why did he carry a rifle?

"I went supperless, watching from the hillside to see if this stranger would light a fire in the valley."

"He did not?" Farrel queried.

"Had he made a campfire, my boy, I would have accorded myself the pleasure of an informal visit, incidentally ascertaining who he was and what he wanted. I am very suspicious of strangers who make

222

cold camps in the San Gregorio. At daylight this morning I rode down the wash and searched for his camp. I found where he had slept in the grass—also this," and he drew from his pocket a single rifle cartridge. "Thirty-two-forty caliber, Miguel," he continued, "with a soft-nose bullet. I do not know of one in this county who shoots such a heavy rifle. In the old days we used the .44 caliber, but nowadays, we prefer nothing heavier than a .30 and many use a .25 caliber for deer."

Farrel drew a 6 millimeter Mannlicher carbine from the gun scabbard on his saddle, dropped five shells into the magazine, looked at his sights and thrust the weapon back into its receptacle. "I think I ought to have some more life insurance," he murmured, complacently. "By the way, Don Nicolás, about how many sheep have I attached?"

"Loustalot's foreman says nine thousand in round numbers."

"Where is the sheep camp?"

"Over yonder." Don Nicolás waved a careless hand toward the west. "I saw their campfire last night."

"I'm going over to give them the rush."

"By all means, Miguel. If you run those Basques off the ranch I will be able to return to town and leave my deputies in charge of these sheep. Keep your eyes open, Miguel. *Adios, muchacho!*"

Farrel jogged away with Pablo at his heels. Half an hour later he had located the sheep camp and ridden to it to accost the four bewhiskered Basque shepherds who, surrounded by their dogs, sullenly watched his approach.

"Who is the foreman?" Don Mike demanded in English as he rode.

"I am, you — — —," one of the Basques replied, briskly. "I don't have for ask who are you. I know."

"Mebbeso some day, you forget," Pablo cried. "I will give you something for make you remember, pig." The old majordomo was riding the black mare. A touch of the spur, a bound, and she was beside Loustalot's foreman, with Pablo cutting the fellow furiously over the head and face with his heavy quirt. The other three sheepmen ran for the tent, but Don Mike spurred the gray in between them and their objective, at the same time drawing his carbine.

There was no further argument. The sheepherders' effects were soon transferred to the backs of three burros and, driving the little animals ahead of them, the Basques moved out. Farrel and Don Nicolás followed them to the boundaries of the ranch and shooed them out through a break in the fence.

"Regarding that stranger who camped last night in the valley, Don Miguel. Would it not be well to look into his case?"

Don Mike nodded. "We will ride up the valley. Pablo, as if we seek cattle; if we find this fellow we will ask him to explain."

"That is well," the old Indian agreed, and dropped back to his respectful position in his master's rear. As they topped the ridge that formed the northern buttress of the San Gregorio, Pablo rode to the left and started down the hill through a draw covered with a thick growth of laurel, purple lilac, a few madone trees and an occasional oak,. He knew that a big, five point buck had its habitat here and it was Pablo's desire to jump this buck out and thus afford his master a glimpse of the trophy that awaited him later in the year.

From the valley below a rifle cracked. Pablo slid out

of his saddle with the ease of a youth and lay flat on the ground beside the trail. But no bullet whined up the draw or struck near him, wherefore he knew that he was not the object of an attack; yet there was wild pounding of his heart when the rifle spoke again and again.

The thud of hoofs smote his ear sharply, so close was he to the ground. Slowly Pablo raised his head. Over the hog's back which separated the draw in which Pablo lay concealed from the draw down which Don Miguel had ridden, the gray horse came galloping—riderless—and Pablo saw the stock of the rifle projecting from the scabbard. The runaway plunged into the draw some fifteen yards in front of Pablo, found a cow trail leading down it and disappeared into the valley.

Pablo's heart swelled with agony. "It has happened!" he murmured. "Ah, Mother of God! It has happened!"

Two more shots in rapid succession sounded from the valley. "He makes certain of his kill," thought Pablo. After a while he addressed the off front foot of the black mare. "I will do likewise."

He started crawling on his belly up out of the draw to the crest of the hog's back. He had an impression, mounting almost to a certainty, that the assassin in the valley had not seen him riding down the draw, otherwise he would not have opened fire on Don Miguel. He would have bided his time and chosen an occasion when there would be no witnesses.

For an hour he waited, watching, grieving, weeping a little. From the draw where Don Miguel lay no sound came forth. Pablo tried hard to erase from his mind a vision of what he would find when, his primal duty of vengeance, swift and complete, accomplished, he should go down into that draw. His tear dimmed, bloodshot eyes searched the valley—ah, what was that?

A cow, a deer or a man? Surely something had moved in the brush at the edge of the river wash.

Pablo rubbed the moisture from his eyes and looked again. A man was crossing the wash on foot and he carried a rifle. A few feet out in the wash he paused, irresolute, turned back, and knelt in the sand.

"Oh, blessed Mother of God!" Pablo almost sobbed, joyously. "I will burn six candles in thy honor and keep flowers on thy altar at the Mission for a year!"

Again the man stood up and started across the wash. He no longer had his rifle. "It is as I thought," Pablo soliloquized. "He has buried the rifle in the sand."

Pablo watched the man start resolutely across the three mile stretch of flat ground between the river and the hills to the south. Don Nicolás Sandoval had remarked that the stranger had come in over the hills to the south. Very well! Believing himself undetected, he would depart in the same direction. The Rancho Palomar stretched ten miles to the south and it would be a strange coincidence if, in that stretch of rolling, brushy country, a human being should cross his path.

The majordomo quickly crawled back into the draw where the black mare patiently awaited him. Leading her, he started cautiously down, taking advantage of every tuft of cover until, arrived at the foot of the draw, he discovered that some oaks effectually screened his quarry from sight. Reasoning quite correctly that the same oaks as effectually screened him from his quarry, Pablo mounted and galloped straight across country for his man.

He rode easily, for he was saving the mare's speed for a purpose. The fugitive, casting a guilty look to the rear, saw him coming and paused, irresolute, but observing no evidences of precipitate haste, continued his retreat, which (Pablo observed, grimly) was casual now, as if he desired to avert suspicion.

Pablo pulled the mare down to a trot, to a walk. He could afford to take his time and it was not part of his plan to bungle his work by undue haste. The fugitive was crossing through a patch of lilac and Pablo desired to overhaul him in a wide open space beyond, so he urged the mare to a trot again and jogged by on a parallel course, a hundred yards distant.

"Buena dias, señor," he called, affably, and waved his hand at the stranger, who waved back.

On went the old majordomo, across the clear space and into the oaks beyond. The fugitive, his suspicions now completely lulled, followed and when he was quite in the center of this chosen ground, Pablo emerged from the shelter of the oaks and bore down upon him. The mare was at a fast lope and Pablo's rawhide riata was uncoiled now; the loop swung in slow, fateful circles—

There could be no mistaking his purpose. With a cry that was curiously animal-like, the man ran for the nearest brush. Twenty feet from him, Pablo made his cast and shrieked exultantly as the loop settled over his prey. A jerk and it was fast around the fellow's midriff; a half hitch around the pommel, a touch of a huge Mexican spur to the flank of the fleet little black thoroughbred and Pablo Artelan was headed for home! He picked his way carefully in order that he might not snag in the bushes that which he dragged behind him, and he leaned forward in the saddle to equalize the weight of the THING that bumped and leaped and slid along the ground behind him. There had been screams at first, mingled with Pablo's exultant shouts of victory, but by the time the river was reached there was no sound but a scraping, slithering one—the sound of the vengeance of Pablo Artelan.

When he reached the wagon road he brought the mare to a walk. He did not look back, for he knew his power; the scraping, slithering sound was music to his ears; it was all the assurance he desired. As calmly as, during the spring roundup, be dragged a calf up to the branding fire, he dragged his victim up into the front yard of the Rancho Palomar and paused before the patio gate.

"Ho! Señor Parker!" he shouted. "Come forth. I have something for the *señor*. Queeck, *Señor!*"

The gate opened and John Parker stepped out. "Hello, Pablo! What's all the row about?"

Pablo turned in his saddle and pointed "*Mira!* Look!" he croaked.

"Good God!" Parker cried. "What is that?"

"Once he use' for be one Jap. One good friend of you, I theenk, Señor Parker. He like for save you much trouble, I theenk, so he keel my Don Mike—an' for that I have—ah, but you see! An' now, señor, eet is all right for take the Rancho Palomar! Take eet, take eet! Ees nobody for care now—nobody! Eef eet don' be for you daughter I don't let you have eet. No, sir, I keel it you so queeck—but my Don Mike hes never forget hes one great *caballero*—so Pablo Artelan mus' not forget, too—you sleep in theese hacienda, you eat the food—ah, señor, I am so 'shame' for you—and my Don Mike—hees dead—hees dead—"

He slid suddenly off the black mare and lay unconscious in the dust beside her.

XXIV

ONCE AGAIN A TRAGIC SCENE HAD BEEN ENACTED under the shade of the catalpa tree before the Farrel hacienda. The shock of a terrible, unexpected trend of events heralded by the arrival of Pablo Artelan and his victim had, seemingly, paralyzed John Parker mentally and physically. He felt again a curious cold, weak, empty feeling in his breast. It was the concomitant of defeat; he had felt it twice before when he had been overwhelmed and mangled by the wolves of Wall Street.

He was almost nauseated. Not at sight of the dusty, bloody, shapeless bundle that lay at the end of Pablo's riata, but with the realization that, indirectly, he had been responsible for all of this.

Pablo's shrill, agonized denunciation had fallen upon deaf ears, once the old majordomo had conveyed to Parker the information of Don Mike's death.

"The rope—take it off!" he protested to the unconscious Pablo. "It's cutting him in two. He looks like a link of sausage! Ugh! A Jap! Horrible! I'm smeared—I can't explain—nobody in this country will believe me—Pablo will kill me—"

He sat down on the bench under the catalpa tree, covered his face with his hands and closed his eyes. When he ventured again to look up, he observed that Pablo, in falling from his horse, had caught one huge Mexican spur on the cantle of his saddle and was suspended by the heel, grotesquely, like a dead fowl. The black mare, a trained roping horse, stood patiently, her feet braced a little, still keeping a strain on the riata.

229

Parker roused himself. With his pocket knife he cut the spur strap, eased the majordomo to the ground, carried him to the bench and stretched him out thereon. Then, grasping the mare by the bridle, he led her around the adobe wall; he shuddered inwardly as he heard the steady, slithering sound behind her.

"Got to get that Thing out of the way," he mumbled. The great barn door was open; from within he could hear his chauffeur whistling. So he urged the mare to a trot and got past the barn without having been observed. An ancient straw stack stood in the rear of the barn and in the shadow of this he halted, removed the riata from the pommel, dragged the body close to the stack, and with a pitchfork he hastily covered it with old, weather-beaten straw. All of this he accomplished without any purpose more definite than a great desire to hide from his wife and from his daughter this offense which Pablo had thrust upon him.

He led the black mare into the barn and tied her. Then he returned to Pablo.

The old Indian was sitting up. At sight of Parker he commenced to curse bitterly, in Spanish and English, this invader who had brought woe upon the house of Farrel. But John Parker was a white man.

"Shut up, you saddle-colored old idol," he roared, and shook Pablo until the latter's teeth rattled together. "If the mischief is done it can't be helped—and it was none of my making. Pull yourself together and tell me where this killing occurred. We've got to get Don Miguel's body."

For answer Pablo snarled and tried to stab him, so Parker, recalling a fragment of the athletic lore of his youth, got a wristlock on the old man and took the dirk away from him. "Now then," he commanded, as he bumped Pablo's head against the adobe wall, "you behave yourself and help me find Don Miguel and bring him in."

Pablo's fury suddenly left him; again he was the servant, respectful, deferential to his master's guest. "Forgive me, *señor*," he muttered, "I have been crazy in the head."

"Not so crazy that you didn't do a good job on that Jap murderer. Come now, old chap. Buck up! We can't go after him in my automobile. Have you some sort of wagon?"

"Si, señor."

"Then come inside a moment. We both need a drink. We're shaking like a pair of dotards."

He picked up Pablo's dirk and give it back to the old man. Pablo acknowledged this courtesy with a bow and followed to Parker's room, where the latter poured two glasses of whiskey. Silently they drank.

"Gracias, señor. I go hitch up one team," Pablo promised, and disappeared at once.

For about ten minutes Parker remained in his room, thinking. His wife and Kay had started, afoot, to visit the Mission shortly after Don Mike and Pablo had left the ranch that morning, and for this Parker was duly grateful to Providence. He shuddered to think what the effect upon them would have been had they been present when Pablo made his spectacular entrance; he rejoiced at an opportunity to get himself in hand against the return of Kay and her mother to the ranch house.

"That wretched Okada!" he groaned. "He concluded that the simplest and easiest way to an immediate consummation of our interrupted deal would be the removal of young Farrel. So he hired one of his countrymen to do the job, believing or at least hoping,

231

that suspicion would naturally be aroused against that Basque, Loustalot, who is known to have an old feud with the Farrels. Kate is right. I've trained with white men all my life; the moment I started to train with pigmented mongrels and Orientals I had to do with a new psychology, with mongrelized moral codes—ah, God, that splendid, manly fellow killed by the insatiable lust of an alien race for this land of his they covet! God forgive me! And poor Kay—"

He was near to tears now; fearful that he might be caught in a moment of weakness, he fled to the barn and helped Pablo hitch a team of draft horses to an old spring wagon. Pablo's customary taciturnity and primitive stoicism had again descended upon him like a protecting garment; his madness bad passed and he moved around the team briskly and efficiently. Parker climbed to the seat beside him as Pablo gathered up the reins and started out of the farmyard at a fast trot.

Ten minutes later they paused at the mouth of the draw down which Farrel had been riding when fired upon. Pablo turned the team, tied them to an oak tree and started up the draw at a swift dog trot, with Parker at his heels.

Jammed rather tightly in a narrow little dry watercourse that ran through the center of the draw they found the body of Don Mike. He was lying face downward; Parker saw that flies already rosetted a wound thick with blood clots on top of his head.

"Poor, poor boy," Parker cried agonizedly.

Pablo straddled the little watercourse, got a grip around his master's body and lifted it out to Parker, who received it and laid the limp form out on the grass. While he stood looking down at Don Mike's white, relaxed face, Pablo knelt, made the sign of the cross and commenced to pray for the peaceful repose of his master's soul. It was a long prayer; Parker, waiting patiently for him to finish, did not know that Pablo recited the litany for the dying.

"Come, Pablo, my good fellow, you've prayed enough," he suggested presently. "Help me carry Don Miguel down to the wagon—*Pablo, he's alive!*"

"Hah!" Pablo's exclamation was a sort of surprised bleat. "*Madre de Cristo!* Look to me, Don Miguel. Ah, little dam' fool, you make believe to die, no?" he charged hysterically.

Don Mike's black eyes opened slightly and his slack lower jaw tightened in a ghastly little grimace. The transported Pablo seized him and shook him furiously, meanwhile deluging Don Mike with a stream of affectionate profanity that fell from his lips like a benediction.

"Listen," Don Mike murmured presently. "Pablo's new litany."

"Rascal! Little, wicked heretic! Blood of the devil! Speak, Don Miguel."

"Shut up! Took your—time—getting me—out—confounded ditch—damned—lazy—beggar—"

Pablo leaped to his feet, his dusky face radiant. "You hear!" he yelled. "Señor Parker, you hear those boy give to me hell like old times, no?"

"You ran—you *colorado maduro* good-for-nothing —left me stuck in—ditch—let bushwhacker—get away —fix you for this, Pablo."

Pablo's eyes popped in ecstasy. He grinned like a gargoyle. "You hear those boy, *señor?*" he reiterated happily. "I tell you those boy he like ol' Pablo. The night he come back he rub my head; yesterday he poke the rib of me with the thumb—now pretty soon he say

233

sometheeng, I bet you."

"Shut up, I tell you." Don Mike's voice, though very faint, was petulant. "You're a total idiot. Find my horse—get rifle—trail that man—who shot me—get him—damn your prayers—get him—"

"Ah, Don Miguel," Pablo assured him in Spanish, in tones that were prideful beyond measure, "that unfortunate fellow has been shaking hands with the devil for the last forty-five minutes."

Don Mike opened his eyes widely. He was rapidly regaining his full consciousness. "Your work, Pablo?"

"Mine—with the help of God, as your illustrious grandfather, the first Don Miguel, would have said. But you are pleased to doubt me so I shall show you the carcass of the animal. I roped him and dragged him for two miles behind the black mare."

Don Mike smiled and closed his eyes. "I will go home," he said presently, and Pablo and Parker lifted him between them and carried him down to the waiting wagon. Half an hour later he was stretched on his bed at the hacienda, while Carolina washed his head with a solution of warm water and lysol. John Parker, rejoiced beyond measure, stood beside him and watched this operation with an alert and sympathetic eye.

"That doesn't look like a bullet wound," he declared, after an examination of the rent in Don Mike's scalp. "Resembles the wound made by what reporters always refer to as 'some blunt instrument.' The scalp is split but the flesh around the wound is swollen as from a blow. You have a nice lump on your head, Farrel."

"Aches terribly," Don Mike murmured. "I had dismounted to tighten my cinch; going downhill the saddle had slid up on my horse's withers. I was tucking in the latigo. When I woke up I was lying on my face, wedged tightly in that little dry ditch; I was ill and dazed and too weak to pull myself out; I was lying with my head downhill and I suppose I lost consciousness again, after awhile. Pablo!"

"*Si, señor.*"

"You caught the man who shot me. What did you do with him?"

"Oh, those fellow plenty good and dead, Don Miguel."

"He dragged the body home at the end of his rope," Parker explained. "He thought you had been done for and he must have gone war mad. I covered the body of the Jap with straw from that stack out by the barn."

"Jap, eh?" Don Mike smiled. Then, after a long silence. "I suppose, Mr. Parker, you understand now—"

"Yes, yes, Farrel. Please do not rub it in."

"Okada wants the San Gregorio rather badly, doesn't he? Couldn't wait. The enactment of that anti-alien land bill that will come up in the legislature next year—do Mrs. Parker and your daughter know about this attempt to assassinate me?"

"No."

"They must not know. Plant that Jap somewhere and do it quickly. Confound you, Pablo, you should have known better than to drag your kill home, like an old she-cat bringing in a gopher. As for my head—well, I was thrown from my horse and struck on a sharp rock. The ladies would be frightened and worried if they thought somebody was gunning for me. When Bill Conway shows up with your spark plugs I'd be obliged, Mr. Parker, if you'd run me in to El Toro. I'll have to have my head tailored a trifle, I think."

With a weak wave of his hand he dismissed everybody, so. Parker and Pablo adjourned to the stables

235

to talk over the events of the morning. Standing patiently at the corral gate they found the gray horse, waiting to be unsaddled—a favor which Pablo proceeded at once to extend.

"Mira!" he called suddenly and directed Parker's attention to the pommel of Don Mike's fancy saddle. The rawhide covering on the shank of the pommel had been torn and scored and the steel beneath lay exposed. "You see?" Pablo queried. "You understan', *señor?*"

"No, I must confess I do not, Pablo."

"Don Miguel is standing beside thees horse. He makes tighter the saddle; he is tying those latigo and he have the head bent leetle bit while he pull those latigo through the ring. Bang! Those Jap shoot at Don Miguel. He miss, but the bullet she hit thees pommel, she go flat against the steel, she bounce off and hit Don Miguel on top the head. The force for keel heem is use' up when the bullet hit thees pommel, but still those bullet got plenty force for knock Don Miguel seelly, no?"

"Spent ball, eh? I think you're right, Pablo."

Pablo relapsed into one of his infrequent Gringo solecisms. "You bet you my life you know eet," he said.

John Parker took a hundred dollar bill from his pocket. "Pablo," he said with genuine feeling, "you're a splendid fellow. I know you don't like me, but perhaps that is because you do not know me very well. Don Miguel knows I had nothing to do with this attempt to kill him, and if Don Miguel bears me no ill-will, I'm sure you should not. I wish you would accept this hundred dollar bill, Pablo?"

Pablo eyed the bill askance. "What for?" he demanded.

"For the way you handled that murdering Jap. Pablo, that was a bully job of work. Please accept this bill. If I

236

didn't like you I would not offer it to you."

"Well, I guess Carolina mebbeso she can use eet. But first I ask Don Miguel if eet is all right for me take eet." He departed for the house to return presently with an anticipatory smile on his dusky countenance. "Don Miguel say to me, *señor:* 'Pablo, any people she's stay my house he's do what she please.' *Gracias,* Señor Parker." And he pouched the bill. "*Mille gracias, señor.*"

"Pray, do not mention it, Pablo."

"All right," Pablo agreed. "Eef you don't like eet, well, I don' tell somebody!"

XXV

BILL CONWAY DRIVING UP THE SAN GREGORIO in his prehistoric automobile, overtook Kay and her mother walking home from the Mission, and drove them the remainder of the distance back to the hacienda. Arrived here, old Conway resurrected the stolen spark plugs and returned them to Parker's chauffeur, after which he invited himself to luncheon. Apparently his raid of the night previous rested lightly on his conscience, and Parker's failure to quarrel with him lifted him immediately out of any fogs of apprehension that may have clouded his sunny soul.

"Hello, Conway," Parker greeted him, as the old contractor came into the dining room and hung his battered old hat on a wall peg. "Did you bring back my spark plugs?"

"Did better'n that," Conway retorted. "The porcelain on one plug was cracked and sooner or later you were bound to have trouble with it. So I bought you a new one."

"Do any good for yourself in El Toro this morning?"

"Nope. Managed to put over a couple of deals that will help the boy out a little, though. Attached your bank account and your bank stock. I would have plastered your two automobiles, but that tenderhearted Miguel declared that was carrying a grudge too far. By the way, where is our genial young host?"

"Horse bucked him off this morning. He lit on a rock and ripped a furrow in his sinful young head. So he's sleeping off a headache."

"Oh, is he badly hurt?" Kay cried anxiously.

"Not fatally," Parker replied with a faintly knowing smile. "But he's weak and dizzy and he's lost a lot of blood; every time he winks for the next month his head will ache, however."

"Which horse policed him?" Bill Conway queried casually.

"The gray one—his father's old horse."

"Hum-m-m!" murmured Conway and pursued the subject no further, nor did he evince the slightest interest in the answers which Parker framed glibly to meet the insistent demand for information from his wife and daughter. The meal concluded, he excused himself and sought Pablo, of whom he demanded and received a meticulous account of the "accident" to Miguel Farrel. For Bill Conway knew that the gray horse never bucked and that Miguel Farrel was a hard man to throw.

"Guess I'll have to sit in at this game," he decided, and forthwith climbed into his rattletrap automobile and returned to El Toro.

During the drive in he surrendered his mind to a contemplation of all of the aspects of the case, and arrived at the following conclusions:

238

Item. Don Nicolás Sandoval had seen the assassin walking in from the south about sunset the day previous. If the fellow had walked all the way across country from La Questa valley he must have started about two P. M.

Item. The Potato Baron had left the Farrel hacienda about one o'clock the same day and had, doubtless, arrived in El Toro about two o'clock. Evidently he had communicated with the man from La Questa valley (assuming that Don Miguel's assailant had come from there) by telephone from El Toro.

Arrived in El Toro, Bill Conway drove to the sheriff's office. Don Nicolás Sandoval had returned an hour previous from the Rancho Palomar and to him Conway related the events of the morning. "Now, Nick," he concluded, "you drift over to the telephone office and in your official capacity cast your eye over the record of long distance telephone calls yesterday afternoon and question the girl on duty."

"Bueno!" murmured Don Nicolás and proceeded at once to the telephone office. Ten minutes later he returned.

"Okada talked to one Kano Ugichi, of La Questa, at 2:08 yesterday afternoon," he reported.

"Considerable water will run under the bridges before Kano Ugichi returns to the bosom of his family," Conway murmured sympathetically. "He's so badly spoiled, Nick, we've decided to call him a total loss and not put up any headstone to his memory. It is Farrel's wish that the matter be forgotten by everybody concerned."

"I have already forgotten it, my friend," the urbane Don Nicolás replied graciously, and Bill Conway departed forthwith for the Hotel de Las Rosas.

"Got a Jap name of Okada stopping here?" he

239

demanded, and was informed that Mr. Okada occupied room 17, but that he was ill and could not be seen.

"He'll see me," quoth Bill Conway, and clumped up the stairs. He rapped peremptorily on the door of room 17, then tried the knob. The door opened and the old contractor stepped into the room to find the Potato Baron sitting up in bed, staring at him. Uttering no word, Bill Conway strode to the bed, seized the Japanese by the throat and commenced to choke him with neatness and dispatch. When the man's face was turning purple and his eyes rolling wildly, Conway released his death grip and his victim fell back on the mattress, whereupon Bill Conway sat down on the edge of the bed and watched life surge back into the little brown man.

"If you let one little peep out of you, Okada," he threatened—and snarled ferociously.

"Please, please," Okada pleaded. "I no unnerstan'. 'Scuse, please. You make one big mistake, yes, I zink so."

"I do, indeed. I permit you to live, which I wouldn't do if I knew where to hide your body. Listen to me, Okada. You sent a countryman of yours from the La Questa valley over to the Rancho Palomar to kill Don Miguel Farrel. I have the man's name, I know the hour you telephoned to him, I know exactly what you said to him and how much you paid him to do the job. Well, this friend of yours overplayed his hand; he didn't succeed in killing Farrel, but he did succeed in getting himself captured."

He paused, with fine dramatic instinct, to watch the effect of this broadside. A faint nervous twitch of the chin and the eyelids—then absolute immobility. The Potato Baron had assumed the "poker face" of all

240

Orientals—wherefore Bill Conway knew the man was on his guard and would admit nothing. So he decided not to make any effort to elicit information, but to proceed on the theory that everything was known to him.

"Naturally," he continued, "that man Pablo has ways and means of making even a stubborn Jap tell everything he knows. Now listen, O child of Nippon, to the white man's words of wisdom. You're going to depart from El Toro in a general northerly direction and you're going to do it immediately if not sooner. And you're never coming back. The day you do, that day you land in the local calaboose with a charge of conspiracy to commit murder lodged against you. We have the witnesses to prove our case and any time you're tried by a San Marcos County jury before a San Marcos County judge you'll rot in San Quentin for life. And further: If Miguel Farrel should, within the next two years, die out of his own bed and with his boots on, you will be killed on general principles, whether you're guilty or not. Do I make myself clear or must I illustrate the point with motion pictures?"

"Yes, sir. 'Scuse, please. Yes, sir, I zink I go very quick, sir."

"Three cheers! The sooner the quicker—the next train, let us say. I'll be at the station to see you off."

He was as good as his word. The Potato Baron, mounting painfully the steps of the observation car, made hasty appraisal of the station platform and observed Bill Conway swinging his old legs from his perch on an express truck. He favored Okada with a very deliberate nod and a sweeping, semi-military salute of farewell.

When the train pulled out, the old contractor slid off

241

the express truck and waddled over to his automobile, "Well, Liz," he addressed that interesting relic, "I'll bet a red apple I've put the fear of Buddha in that Jap's soul. He won't try any more tricks in San Marcos County. He certainly did assimilate my advice and drag it out of town *muy pronto*. Well, Liz, as the feller says: 'The wicked flee when no man pursueth and a troubled conscience addeth speed to the hind legs.' "

As be was driving out of town to the place of his labors at Agua Caliente basin, he passed the Parker limousine driving in. Between John Parker's wife and John Parker's daughter, Don Miguel José Farrel sat with white face and closed eyes. In the seat beside his chauffeur John Parker sat, half turned and gazing at Don Miguel with troubled eyes.

"That girl's sweeter than a royal flush," Bill Conway murmured. "I wonder if she's good for a fifty thousand dollar touch to pay my cement bill pending the day I squeeze it out of her father? Got to have cement to build a dam—got to have cash to get cement—got to have a dam to save the Rancho Palomar—got to have the Rancho Palomar before we can pull off a wedding—got to pull off a wedding in order to be happy—got to be happy or we all go to hell together . . . Well . . . I'm going down to Miguel's place to dinner tonight. I'll ask her."

The entire Parker family was present when the doctor in El Toro washed and disinfected Farrel's wound and, at the suggestion of Kay, made an X-ray photograph of his head. The plate, when developed, showed a small fracture, the contemplation of which aroused considerable interest in all present, with the exception of the patient. Don Mike was still dizzy; because his vision was impaired he kept his eyes closed; he heard a

242

humming noise as if a lethargic bumble bee had taken up his residence inside the Farrel ears. Kay, observing him closely, realized that he was very weak, that only by the exercise of a very strong will had he succeeded in sitting up during the journey in from the ranch. His brow was cold and wet with perspiration, his breathing shallow; his dark, tanned face was now a greenish gray.

The girl saw a shadow of deep apprehension settle over her father's face as the doctor pointed to the fracture. "Any danger?" she heard him whisper.

The doctor shook his head. "Nothing to worry about. An operation will not be necessary. But he's had a narrow squeak. With whom has he been fighting?"

"Thrown from his horse and struck his head on a rock," Parker replied glibly.

Kay saw the doctor's eyebrows lift slightly. "Did he tell you that was what happened?"

Parker hesitated a moment and nodded an affirmative.

"Wound's too clean for that story to impress me," the doctor whispered. "Not a speck of foreign matter in it. Moreover, the wound is almost on top of his head. Now, if he had been thrown from a horse and had struck on top of his head on a rock with sufficient force to lacerate his scalp and produce a minor fracture, he would, undoubtedly, have crushed his skull more thoroughly or broken his neck. Also, his face would have been marred more or less! And if that isn't good reasoning, I might add that Miguel Farrel is one of the two or three men in this world who have ridden Cyclone, the most famous outlaw horse in America."

Parker shrugged and, by displaying no interest in the doctor's deductions, brought the conversation to a close.

That the return trip to the ranch, in Don Mike's present condition, was not to be thought of, was apparent from the patient's condition. He was, therefore, removed to the single small hospital which El Toro boasted, and after seeing him in charge of a nurse the Parker family returned to the ranch. Conversation languished during the trip; a disturbed conscience on the part of the father, and on the part of Kay and her mother an intuition, peculiar to their sex and aroused by the doctor's comments, that events of more than ordinary portent had occurred that day, were responsible for this.

At the ranch Parker found his attorney who had motored out from El Toro, waiting to confer with him regarding Bill Conway's adroit maneuver of the morning. Mrs. Parker busied herself with some fancy work while her daughter sought the Farrel library and pretended to read. An atmosphere of depression appeared to have settled over the rancho; Kay observed that even Pablo moved about in a furtive manner; he cleaned and oiled his rifle and tested the sights with shots at varying ranges. Carolina's face was grave and her sweet falsetto voice was not raised in song once during the afternoon.

About four o'clock when the shadows began to lengthen, Kay observed Pablo riding forth on his old pinto pony. Before him on the saddle he carried a pick and shovel and in reply to her query as to what he purposed doing, he replied that he had to clean out a spring where the cattle were accustomed to drink. So she returned to the library and Pablo repaired to a willow thicket in the sandy wash of the San Gregorio and dug a grave. That night, at twilight, while the family and servants were at dinner, Pablo dragged his problem down to this grave, with the aid of the pinto pony, and hid it forever from the sight of men. Neither directly nor indirectly was his exploit ever referred to again and no inquiry was ever instituted to fathom the mystery of the abrupt disappearance of Kano Ugichi. Indeed, the sole regret at his untimely passing was borne by Pablo, who, shrinking from the task of removing his riata from his victim (for he had a primitive man's horror of touching the dead), was forced to bury his dearest possession with the adventurer from La Questa—a circumstance which served still further to strengthen his prejudice against the Japanese race.

The following morning Pablo saddled Panchito for Kay and, at her request, followed her, in the capacity of groom, to Bill Conway's camp at Agua Caliente basin. The old schemer was standing in the door of his rough temporary office when Kay rode up; he advanced to meet her.

"Well, young lady," he greeted her, "what's on your mind this morning in addition to that sassy little hat."

"A number of things. I want to know what really happened to Mr. Farrel yesterday forenoon."

"My dear girl! Why do you consult me?"

She leaned from her horse and lowered her voice. "Because I'm your partner and between partners there should be no secrets."

"Well, we're supposed to keep it a secret, just to save you and your mother from worrying, but I'll tell you in confidence if you promise not to tell a soul I told you."

"I promise."

"Well, then, that scoundrel, Okada, sent a Jap over from La Questa valley to assassinate Miguel and clear the way for your father to acquire this ranch without further legal action and thus enable their interrupted land deal to be consummated."

"My father was not a party to that—oh, Mr. Conway, surely you do not suspect for a moment—"

"Tish! Tush! Of course not. That's why Miguel wanted it given out that his horse had policed him. Wanted to save you the resultant embarrassment."

"The poor dear! And this wretch from La Questa shot him?"

"Almost."

"What became of the assassin?"

Bill Conway pursed his tobacco-stained lips and whistled a few bars of "Listen to the Mocking Bird." Subconsciously the words of the song came to Kay's mind.

> She's sleeping in the valley,
> In the valley,
> She's sleeping in the valley,
> And the mocking bird is singing
> where she lies.

"I'm afraid I don't want to discuss that boy and his future movements, Miss Parker," he sighed presently. "I might compromise a third party. In the event of a show-down I do not wish to be forced under oath to tell what I know—or suspect. However, I am in a position to assure you that Oriental activities on this ranch have absolutely ceased. Mr. Okada has been solemnly assured that, in dealing with certain white men, they will insist upon an eye for an optic and a tusk for a tooth; he knows that if he starts anything further he will go straight to that undiscovered country where the woodbine twineth and the whangdoodle mourneth for its mate."

"What has become of Okada?"

"He has dragged it out of here—drifted and went hence—for keeps."

"Are you quite sure?"

"Cross my heart and hope to die." With an unclean thumb Mr. Conway drew a large X on the geometrical center of his ample circumference. "When you've been in the contracting business as long as I have, Miss Parker," he continued sagely, "you'll learn never to leave important details to a straw boss. Attend to 'em yourself—and get your regular ration of sleep. That's my motto."

She beamed gratefully upon him. "Need any money, Bill, old timer?" she flashed at him suddenly, with delightful camaraderie.

"There should be no secrets between partners. I do."

"Quanto?"

"Cinquenta mille pesos oro, señorita."

"Help!"

"Fifty thousand bucks, iron men, simoleons, smackers, dollars—"

She reached down and removed a fountain pen from his upper vest pocket. Then she drew a check book and, crooking her knee over Panchito's neck and using that knee for a desk, she wrote him a check on a New York bank for fifty thousand dollars.

"See here," Bill Conway demanded, as she handed him the check, "how much of a roll you got, young woman?"

"About two hundred thousand in cash and half a million in Liberty bonds. When I was about five years old my uncle died and left me his estate, worth about a hundred thousand. It has grown under my father's management. He invested heavily in Steel Common, at the outbreak of the war, and sold at the top of the market just before the armistice was signed."

"Well," Conway sighed, "there is a little justice in the

247

world, after all. Here at last, is one instance where the right person to handle money gets her hands on a sizable wad of it. But what I want to know, my dear young lady, is this: Why purchase philanthropy in fifty thousand dollar installments? If you want to set that boy's mind at ease, loan him three hundred thousand dollars to take up the mortgage your father holds on his ranch; then take a new mortgage in your own name to secure the loan. If you're bound to save him in the long run, why keep the poor devil in suspense?"

She made a little moue of distaste. "I loathe business. The loaning of money on security—the taking advantage of another's distress. Mr. Bill, it never made a hit with me. I'm doing this merely because I realize that my father's course, while strictly legal, is not kind. I refuse to permit him to do that sort of thing to a Medal of Honor man." He noticed a pretty flush mount to her lovely cheeks. "It isn't sporty, Mr. Bill Conway. However, it isn't nice to tell one's otherwise lovable father that he's a poor sport and a Shylock, is it? I cannot deliberately pick a fight with my father by interfering in his business affairs, can I? Also, it seems to me that Don Mike Farrel's pride is too high to permit of his acceptance of a woman's pity. I do not wish him to be under obligation to me. He might misconstrue my motive—oh, you understand, don't you? I'm sure I'm in an extremely delicate position."

He nodded sagely. "Nevertheless," he pursued, "he *will* be under obligation to you."

"He will never know it. I depend upon you to keep my secret. He will think himself under obligation to you—and you're such an old and dear friend. Men accept obligations from each other and think nothing of it. By the way, I hold you responsible for the return of that fifty thousand dollars, not Don Mike Farrel. You are underwriting his battle with my father, are you not?"

"Yes, I am," he retorted briskly, "and I've got more conceit than a barber's cat for daring to do it. Wait a minute and I'll give you my promissory note. I'm paying seven percent for bank accommodations lately. That rate of interest suit you?"

She nodded and followed him to his office, where he laboriously wrote and signed a promissory note in her favor. Pablo, remaining politely out of sound of their conversation, wondered vaguely what they were up to.

"Don Mike has told us something of the indolent, easygoing natures of his people," Kay continued, as she tucked the note in her coat pocket. "I have wondered if, should he succeed in saving his ranch without too great an expenditure of effort, he would continue to cast off the spell of 'the splendid, idle forties' and take his place in a world of alert creators and producers. Do you not think, Mr. Bill, that he will be the gainer through my policy of keeping him in ignorance of my part in the re-financing of his affairs—if he dare not be certain of victory up to the last moment? Of course it would be perfectly splendid if he could somehow manage to work out his own salvation, but of course, if he is unable to do that his friends must do it for him. I think it would be perfectly disgraceful to permit a Medal of Honor man to be ruined, don't you, Mr. Bill?"

"Say, how long have you known this fellow Miguel?"

"Seventy-two hours, more or less."

He considered. "Your father's nerve has been pretty badly shaken by the Jap's attempt to kill Miguel. He feels about that pretty much as a dog does when he's caught sucking eggs. Why not work on your father now while he's in an anti-Jap mood? You might catch him on the rebound, so to speak. Take him over to La Questa valley some day this week and show him a little Japan; show him what the San Gregorio will look like within five years if he persists. Gosh, woman, you have some influence with him haven't you?"

"Very little in business affairs, I fear."

"Well, you work on him, anyhow, and maybe he'll get religion and renew Miguel's mortgage. Argue that point about giving a Medal of Honor man another chance."

The girl shook her head. "It would be useless," she assured him. "He has a curious business code and will not abandon it. He will only quote some platitude about mixing sentiment and business."

"Then I suppose the battle will have to go the full twenty rounds. Well, Miss Parker, we're willing. We've already drawn first blood and with your secret help we ought to about chew the tail off your old man."

"Cheerio." She held out her dainty little gloved hand to him. "See me when you need more money, Mr. Bill. And remember! If you tell on me I'll never, never forgive you."

He bent over her hand and kissed it. His caress was partly reverence, partly a habit of courtliness surviving from a day that is done in California, for under that shabby old tweed suit there beat the gallant heart of a true cavalier.

When Miss Parker had ridden away with Pablo at her heels, Bill Conway unburdened himself of a slightly ribald little chanson entitled: "What Makes the Wild Cat Wild?" In the constant repetition of this query it appeared that the old Californian sought the answer to a riddle not even remotely connected with the mystifying savagery of non-domestic felines.

250

Suddenly he slapped his thigh. "Got it," he informed the payroll he had been trying to add for half an hour. "Got it! She does love him. Her explanation of her action is good but not good enough for me. Medal of Honor man! Rats. She could loan him the money to pay her father, on condition that her father should never know the source of the aid, but if they reduced their association to a business basis he would have to decide between the ranch and her. She knows how he loves this seat of his ancestors—she fears for the decision. And if he decided for the ranch there would be no reasonable excuse for the Parker family to stick around, would there? There would not. So he is not to be lost sight of for a year. Yes, of course that's it. Methinks the lady did protest too much. God bless her. I wonder what he thinks of her. One can never tell. It might be just her luck to fail to make a hit with him. Oh, Lord, if that happened I'd shoot him. I would for a fact. Guess I'll drop in at the ranch some day next week and pump the young idiot . . . No, I'll not. My business is building dams and bridges and concrete highways . . . well, I might take a chance and sound him out . . . still, what thanks would I get . . . no, I'll be shot if I will . . . oh, to the devil with thanks. If he don't like it he can lump it . . .

> What makes the wild cat wild, boys,
> Oh, what makes the wild cat wild?"

XXVI

IT WAS FULLY TWO WEEKS before Miguel returned to the ranch from the little hospital at El Toro. During that period the willows had already started to sprout on the last abiding place of Kano Ugichi, the pain had left the Farrel head and the Farrel attorney had had André Loustalot up in the Superior Court, where he had won a drawn verdict. The cash in bank was proved to have been deposited there by Loustalot personally; it had been subject to his personal check and was accordingly adjudged to be his personal property and ordered turned over to Miguel Farrel in partial liquidation of the ancient judgment which Farrel held against the Basque. A preponderance of testimony, however (Don Nicolás Sandoval swore it was all perjured and paid for) indicated that but one quarter of the sheep found on the Rancho Palomar belonged to Loustalot, the remainder being owned by his foreman and employees. To Farrel, therefore, these sheep were awarded, and in some occult manner Don Nicolás Sandoval selected them from the flock; then, acting under instructions from Farrel, he sold the sheep back to Loustalot at something like a dollar a head under the market value and leased to the amazed Basque for one year the grazing privilege on the Rancho Palomar. In return for the signing of this lease and the payment of the lease money in advance, Farrel executed to Loustalot a satisfaction in full of the unpaid portion of the judgment. "For," as the sheriff remarked to Farrel, "while you hold the balance of that judgment over this fellow's head your own head is in danger. It is best to conciliate him, for you will never again have an

252

opportunity to levy against his assets."

"I think you're right, Don Nicolás," Farrell agreed. "I can never feel wholly safe until I strike a truce with that man. Tell him I'll give him back his eight thousand dollar automobile if he will agree on his own behalf and that of his employees, agents and friends, not to bushwhack me or any person connected with me."

"I have already made him a tentative offer to that effect, my boy, and, now that the first flush of his rage is over, he is a coyote lacking the courage to kill. He will agree to your proposal, and I shall take occasion to warn him that if he should ever break his word while I am living, I shall consider, in view of the fact that I am the mediator in this matter, that he has broken faith with me, and I shall act accordingly."

The arrangement with Loustalot was therefore made, and immediately upon his return to the ranch Farrel, knowing that the sheep would spoil his range for the few hundred head of cattle that still remained of the thousands that once had roamed El Palomar, rounded up these cattle and sold them. And it was in the performance of this duty that he discovered during the roundup, on the trail leading from the hacienda to Agua Caliente basin, a rectangular piece of paper. It lay, somewhat weather-stained, face up beside the trail, and because it resembled a check, he leaned easily from his horse and picked it up. To his amazement he discovered it to be a promissory note, in the sum of fifty thousand dollars, in favor of Kay Parker and signed by William D. Conway.

Pablo was beating the thickets in the river bottom searching out some spring calves he knew were lurking there, when his master reined up beside him.

"Pablo," he demanded, "has Señor Conway been to

253

the ranch during my absence?"

"No, Don Miguel, he has not."

"Has Señorita Parker ridden Panchito over to Señor Conway's camp at Agua Caliente basin?"

"Yes, Don Miguel. I rode behind her, in case of accident."

"What day was that?"

Pablo considered. "The day after you were shot, Don Miguel."

"Did you see Señorita Parker give Señor Conway a writing?"

"I did, truly. She wrote from a small leathern book and tore out the page whereon she wrote. In return Señor Conway made a writing and this he gave to Señorita Parker who accepted it.

"Thank you, Pablo. That is all I desired to know." And he was away again, swinging his lariat and whooping joyously at the cattle. Pablo watched narrowly.

"Now whatever this mystery may be," he soliloquized, "the news I gave Don Miguel has certainly not displeased him. Ah, he is a sharp one, that boy. He learns everything and without effort, yet for all he knows he talks but little. Can it be that he has the gift of second sight? I wonder!"

XXVII

KAY PARKER WAS SEATED ON THE BENCH under the catalpa tree when Miguel Farrel rode up the palm-lined avenue to the hacienda that night; his face, as he dismounted before her, conveyed instantly to the girl the impression that he was in a more cheerful and contented

254

mood than she had observed since that day she had first met him in uniform.

She smiled a welcome. He swept off his hat and favored her with a bow which appeared to Kay to be slightly more ceremonious than usual.

"Your horse is tired," she remarked. "Are you?"

" 'Something accomplished, something done, has earned a night's repose,' " he quoted cheerfully. "Rather a hard task to comb this ranch for a few hundred head of cattle when the number of one's riders is limited, but we have gotten the herd corraled at the old racetrack." He unbuckled his old leathern chaps, and stepped out of them, threw them across the saddle and with a slap sent his horse away to the barn.

"You're feeling quite yourself again?" she hazarded hopefully.

"My foolish head doesn't bother me," he replied smilingly, "but my equally foolish heart—" he heaved a gusty Castilian sigh and tried to appear forlorn. "Filled with mixed metaphors," he added. "May I sit here with you?"

She made room for him beside her on the bench. He seated himself, leaned back against the bole of the catalpa tree and stretched his legs, cramped from a long day in the saddle. The indolent gaze of his black eyes roved over her approvingly before shifting to the shadowy beauty of the valley and the orange-hued sky beyond, and a silence fell between them.

"I was thinking today," the girl said presently, "that you've been so busy since your return you haven't had time to call on any of your old friends."

"That is true, Miss Parker."

"You *have* called me Kay," she reminded him, "Wherefore this sudden formality, Don Mike?"

"My name is Miguel. You're right, Kay. Fortunately, all of my friends called on me when I was in the hospital, and at that time I took pains to remind them that my social activities would be limited for at least a year."

"Two of your friends called on mother and me today, Miguel."

"Anita Sepulvida and her mother?"

"Yes. She's adorable."

"They visited me in hospital. Very old friends—very dear friends. I asked them to call on you and your mother. I wanted you to know Anita."

"She's the most beautiful and charming girl I have ever met."

"She *is* beautiful and charming. Her family, like mine, had become more or less decayed about the time I enlisted, but fortunately her mother had a quarter section of land down in Ventura County and when a wildcat oil operator on adjacent land brought in a splendid well, Señora Sepulvida was enabled to dispose of her land at a thousand dollars an acre and a royalty of one-eighth on all of the oil produced. The first well drilled was a success and in a few years the Sepulvida family will be far wealthier than it ever was. Meanwhile their ranch here has been saved from loss by foreclosure. Old Don Juan, Anita's father, is dead."

"Anita is the only child, is she not?"

He nodded. "Ma Sepulvida is a lady of the old school," he continued. "Very dignified, very proud of her distinguished descent—"

"And very fond of you," Kay interrupted.

"Always was, Kay. She's an old peach. Came to the hospital and cried over me and wanted to loan me enough money to lift the mortgage on my ranch."

256

"Then—then—your problem is—solved," Kay found difficulty in voicing the sentence.

He nodded. She turned her face away that he might not see the pallor that overspread it. "It is a very great comfort to me," he resumed presently, "to realize that the world is not altogether barren of love and kindness."

"It must be," she murmured, her face still averted.

"It was the dearest wish of my poor father and of Anita's that the ancient friendship between the families should be cemented by a marriage between Anita and me. For me Señora Sepulvida would be a marvelous mother-in-law, because she's my kind of people and we understand each other. Really, I feel tremendously complimented because, even before the oil strike saved the family from financial ruin, Anita did not lack opportunities for many a more brilliant match."

"She's—dazzling," Kay murmured drearily. "What a brilliant wife she will be for you!"

"Anita is far too fine a woman for such a sacrifice. I've always entertained a very great affection for her and she for me. There's only one small bug in our amber."

"And that—"

"We aren't the least bit in love with each other. We're children of a later day and we object to the old-fashioned method of a marriage arranged by papa and mama. I know there must be something radically wrong with me; otherwise I never could resist Anita."

"But you are going to marry her, are you not?"

"I am not. She wouldn't marry me on a bet. And of course I didn't accept her dear old mother's offer of financial aid. Couldn't, under the circumstances, and besides, it would not be kind of me to transfer my burden to them. I much prefer to paddle my own

257

canoe."

He noticed a rush of color to the face as she turned abruptly toward him now. "What a heritage of pride you have, Miguel. But are you quite certain Anita does not love you? You should have heard all the nice things she said about you today."

"She ought to say nice things about me," he replied casually. "When she was quite a little girl she was given to understand that her ultimate mission in life was to marry me. Of course I always realized that it would not be a compliment to Anita to indicate that I was not head over heels in love with her; I merely pretended I was too bashful to mention it. Finally one day Anita suggested, as a favor to her and for the sake of my own self-respect, that I abandon the pose; with tears in her eyes she begged me to be a gallant rebel and save her from the loving solicitude of her parents to see her settled in life. At that moment I almost loved her, particularly when, having assured her of my entire willingness and ability to spoil everything, she kissed me rapturously on both cheeks and confided to me that she was secretly engaged to an engineer chap who was gophering for potash in Death Valley. The war interrupted his gophering, but Anita informs me that he found the potash, and now he can be a sport and bet his potash against Señora Sepulvida's crude oil. Fortunately, my alleged death gave Anita an opportunity to advance his claims, and he was in a fair way of becoming acceptable until my unexpected return rather greased the skids for him. Anita's mother is trying to give the poor devil the double-cross now, but I told Anita she needn't worry."

Kay's eyes danced with merriment—and relief. "But," she persisted, "you told me your problem was settled? And it isn't."

258

"It is. I'm going to sell about eighteen thousand dollars worth of cattle off this ranch, and I've leased the valley grazing privilege for one year for ten thousand dollars. My raid on Loustalot netted me sixty-seven thousand dollars, so that my total bankroll is now about ninety-five thousand dollars. At first I thought I'd let Bill Conway have most of my fortune to help him complete that dam, but I have now decided to stop work on the dam and use all of my energy and my fortune to put through such other deals as may occur to me. If I am lucky I shall emerge with sufficient funds to save the ranch. If I am unlucky, I shall lose the ranch. Therefore, the issue is decided. 'God's in his Heaven; all's right with the world.' What have you been doing all day?"

"Painting and sketching. I'll never be a worthwhile artist, but I like to paint things for myself. I've been trying to depict on canvas the San Gregorio in her new spring gown, as you phrase it. The arrival of the Sepulvida family interrupted me, and I've been sitting here since they departed. We had tea."

"Getting a trifle bored with the country, Kay? I fancy you find it lonely out here."

"It was a trifle quiet while you were in hospital. Now that you're back I suppose we can ride occasionally and visit some of the places of local interest."

"By all means. As soon as I get rid of that little bunch of cattle I'm going to give a barbecue and festival to the countryside in honor of my guests. We'll eat a half dozen fat two-year-old steers and about a thousand loaves of bread and a couple of barrels of claret and a huge mess of chili sauce. When I announce in the El Toro *Sentinel* that I'm going to give a *fiesta* and that everybody is welcome, all my friends and their friends and relatives will come and I'll he spared the trouble of

259

visiting them individually. Don Nicolás Sandoval remarked when he collected that Loustalot judgment for me that he supposed I'd do the decent thing, now that I could afford it. Mother Sepulvida suggested it and Anita seconded the motion. It will probably be the last event of its kind on such a scale ever given in California, and when it is finished it will have marked my transition from an indolent *ranchero* to some sort of commercial go-getter."

"I see. Little Mike, the Hustler."

He nodded, rose and stood before her, smiling down at her with an inscrutable little smile. "Will you motor me in to El Toro tomorrow morning?" he pleaded. "I must go there to arrange for cattle cars."

"Of course."

"Thank you, Kay. Now, if I have your permission to withdraw, I think I shall make myself presentable for dinner."

He hesitated a moment before withdrawing, however, meanwhile gazing down on her with a gaze so intent that the girl flushed a little. Suddenly his hand darted out and he had her adorable little chin clasped between his brown thumb and forefinger, shaking it with little shakes of mock ferocity. He seemed about to deliver some important announcement—impassioned, even, but to her huge disgust he smothered the impulse, jerked his hand away as if he had scorched his fingers, and blushed guiltily. "Oh, I'm a sky-blue idiot," he half growled and left her abruptly.

A snort—to a hunter it would have been vaguely reminiscent of that of an old buck deer suddenly disturbed in a thicket—caused her to look up. At the corner of the wall Pablo Artelan stood, staring at her with alert interest; his posture was one of a man

260

suddenly galvanized into immobility. Kay blushed, but instantly decided to appear nonchalant.

"Good evening, Pablo," she greeted the majordomo. "How do you feel after your long, hard day on the range?"

"*Gracias*, mees. Myself, I feel pretty good. When my boss hees happy—well—Pablo Artelan hees happy just the same."

The girl noted his emphasis. "That's very nice of you, Pablo, I'm sure. Have you any idea," she continued with bland innocence, "why Don Miguel is so happy this evening?"

Pablo leaned against the adobe wall, thoughtfully drew forth tobacco bag and brown cigarette paper and, while shaking his head and appearing to ponder Kay's question, rolled a cigarette and lighted it. "We-l-l, *señorita*," he began presently, "I theenk first mebbeso eet ees because Don Miguel find heem one leetle piece paper on the trail. I am see him peeck those paper up and look at heem for long time before he ride to me and ask me many question about the *señorita* and Señor Beel Conway those day we ride to Agua Caliente. He say to me: 'Pablo, you see Señor Beel Conway give to the *señorita* a writing?' '*Si, señor.*' 'You see Señorita Parker give to Señor Beel Conway a writing?' '*Si, señor.*' Then Don Miguel hee's don' say sometheeng more, but just shake hees *cabeza* like thees," and Pablo gave an imitation of a muchly puzzled man wagging his head to stimulate a flow of ideas.

A faintness seized the girl. "Didn't he say—*anything*?" she demanded sharply.

"Oh, well, yes, he say sometheeng. He say: 'Well, I'bedam!' Then that leetle smile he don' have for long time come back to Don Miguel's face and hee's happy like one baby. I don' un'erstand those boy ontil I see

261

thees business"—Pablo wiggled his tobacco-stained thumb and forefinger—"then I know sometheeng! For long time those boy hee's pretty parteecular. Even those so beautiful *señorita*, 'Nita Sepulvida, she don' rope those boy like you rope it, *señorita*." And with the license of an old and trusted servant, the sage of Palomar favored her with a knowing wink.

"He knows—he knows!" the girl thought. "What must he think of me! Oh, dear, oh, dear! if he mentions the subject to me I shall die." Tears of mortification were in her eyes as she turned angrily upon the amazed Pablo. "You—you—old sky-blue idiot!" she charged and fled to her room.

XXVIII

KAY'S FIRST COHERENT THOUGHT was to claim the privilege of her sex—a headache—and refrain from joining Don Mike and her parents at dinner. Upon consideration, however, she decided that since she would have to face the issue sooner or later, she might as well be brave and not try to evade it. For she knew now the fate of the promissory note Bill Conway had given her and which she had thrust into the pocket of her riding coat. It had worked out of her pocket and dropped beside the trail to Agua Caliente Basin, and fate had ordained that it should be found by the one person in the world not entitled to that privilege. Kay would have given fifty thousand dollars for some miraculous philter which, administered surreptitiously to Miguel Farrel, would cause him to forget what the girl now realized he knew of her secret negotiations with Bill Conway for the salvation of the ranch. Nevertheless,

262

despite her overwhelming embarrassment and distress, the question occurred to her again and again: What would Don Miguel Farrel do about it? She hadn't the slightest doubt but that his tremendous pride would lead him to reject her aid and comfort, but how was he to accomplish this delicate procedure? The situation was fraught with as much awkwardness and embarrassment for him as for her.

She was late in joining the others at table. To her great relief, after rising politely at her entrance and favoring her with an impersonal smile, Farrel sat down and continued to discuss with John Parker and his wife the great natural resources of Siberia and the designs of the Japanese empire upon that territory. About the time the black coffee made its appearance, Kay's harassed soul had found sanctuary in the discussion of a topic which she knew would be of interest —one in which she felt she could join exuberantly.

"Do tell father and mother of your plans for a *fiesta,* Miguel," she pleaded presently.

"A *fiesta,* eh?" Mrs. Parker was instantly interested. "Miguel, that is, indeed, a bright thought. I volunteer as a patroness here and now. John, you can be a judge of the course, or something. Miguel, what is the occasion of your *fiesta?*"

"At a period in the world's history, Mrs. Parker, when butter is a dollar a pound and blue denim overalls sell freely for three dollars a pair, I think we ought to do something to dissipate the general gloom. I want to celebrate my return to civil life, and my more recent return from the grave. Also, I would just as well indicate to the county at large that, outside of business hours, we constitute a very happy little family here; so if you all please, I shall announce a *fiesta* in honor of the Parker family."

"It will last all day and night and we are to have a Wild West show," Kay added eagerly.

"Where will it be held, Miguel?"

"Down at our old abandoned racetrack, about a mile from here."

Mrs. Parker nodded approval. "John, you old dud," she decided, "you always liked horse races and athletics. You're stuck for some prizes."

Her indulgent husband good-naturedly agreed, and at Kay's suggestion, Carolina brought a pencil and a large writing tablet, whereupon the girl constituted herself secretary of the carnival committee and wrote the program, as arranged by Don Mike and her father. She thrilled when Farrel announced a race of six furlongs for ladies' saddle horses, to be ridden by their owners.

"You ought to win that with Panchito," he suggested to Kay.

Kay's heart beat happily. In Farrel's suggestion that she ride Panchito in this race she decided that here was evidence that her host did not contemplate any action that would tend to render the ranch untenable for her prior to the *fiesta*; indeed, there was nothing in his speech or bearing that indicated the slightest mental perturbation now that he had discovered the compact existing between her and Bill Conway. Perhaps his pride was not so high as she had rated it; what if her action had been secretly pleasing to him?

Somehow, Kay found this latter thought disturbing and distasteful. It was long past midnight before she could dismiss the enigma from her thoughts and fall asleep.

It was later than that, however, before Don Miguel José Federico Noriaga Farrel dismissed her from his

264

thoughts and succumbed to the arms of Morpheus. For quite a while after retiring to his room he sat on the edge of the bed, rubbing his toes with one hand and holding Bill Conway's promissory note before him with the other.

"That girl and her mother are my secret allies," he soliloquized. "Bless their dear kind hearts. Kay has confided in Conway and for reasons best known to himself he has secretly accepted of her aid. Now I wonder," he continued, "what the devil actuates her to double-cross her own father in favor of a stranger?"

He tucked the note back in his pocket, removed a sock and rubbed the other foot thoughtfully. "Well, whatever happens," he decided eventually, "I've got to keep my secret to myself, while at the same time effactually preventing this young lady from advancing Bill Conway any further funds for my relief. I cannot afford her pity or her charity; I can accept her sympathy, but not her aid. Conway cannot have so soon spent much of the money he borrowed from her, and if I insist on the cessation of operations in the Basin he'll promptly give her back her fifty thousand dollars in order to save the interest charges; in the meantime I shall mail Kay the note in a plain white envelope, with the address typewritten, so she will never know where it came from, for of course she'll have to hand Bill back his canceled note when he pays it."

He blew out the light and retired, not to sleep, but to revolve plan after plan for the salvation of the ranch. To float a new loan from any source in San Marcos County he dismissed for the hundredth time as a proposition too nebulous for consideration. His only hope of a bank loan lay in an attempt to interest outside bankers to a point where they would consent to have the property appraised. Perhaps the letter from Parker which he held would constitute evidence to cautious capitalists of the sufficiency of the security for the loan. It was for that purpose that he had cunningly inveigled Parker into making him that offer to clear out and leave him a fair field and no litigation. However, Don Mike knew that between bankers there exists a certain mutual dependence, a certain cohesiveness that makes for mutual protection. If, for instance (he told himself), he should apply to a San Francisco bank for a loan on the ranch, the bank, prior to wasting either time or mental energy on his application, would first ascertain from sources other than him, whether it was remotely worth while considering the loan up to a point of sending a representative down to appraise the land. Their first move, therefore, would be to write their correspondent in El Toro—John Parker's bank, the First National—for information regarding the Farrel family, the ranch, and the history of the mortgage. Don Mike was not such an optimist as to believe that the report of Parker's bank would be such as to encourage the outside bank to proceed further in the deal.

He was also aware that the loan would not be attractive to commercial banks, who are forced, in self-protection, to loan their money on liquid assets. He must therefore turn to the savings banks and trust companies. But here again he faced an *impasse.* Such institutions loan money for the purpose of securing interest on it; the last thing they wish to do is to be forced, in the protection of the loan, to foreclose a mortgage. Hence, should they entertain the slightest doubt of his inability to repay the mortgage; should they be forced to consider the probability of foreclosure eventually, he knew they would not consider the loan. Don Mike was bitterly aware of the fact that the history of his family had been one of waste, extravagance, carelessness and inefficiency. In order to place the ranch on a paying basis and take up John Parker's mortgage, therefore, he would have to have a new loan of not less than half a million dollars, and at six percent, the lowest rate of interest he could hope to obtain, his annual interest charge would be thirty thousand dollars. Naturally he would be expected to repay the loan gradually—say at the rate of fifty thousand dollars a year. By running ten thousand head of cattle on the Palomar he knew he could meet his payments of interest and principal without lessening his working capital, but he could not do it by attempting to raise scrub beef cattle. He would gradually produce a herd of purebred Herefords, but in the meantime he would have to buy "feeders," grow them out on the Palomar range and sell them at a profit. During the present high price of beef cattle, he dared not gamble on borrowed capital, else with a slump in prices he might be destroyed. It would be a year or two, at least, before he might accept that risk; indeed, the knowledge of this condition had induced him to lease the San Gregorio for one year to the Basque sheep man, André Loustalot. If, in the interim, he should succeed in saving the ranch, he knew that a rest of one year would enable the range to recover from the damage inflicted upon it by the sheep.

In his desolation there came to him presently a wave of the strong religious faith that was his sole unencumbered heritage. Once again he was a trustful little boy. He slid out of the great bed of his ancestors and knelt on the old rag mat beside it; he poured out an appeal for help from One who, he had been told—who, he truly believed—marked the sparrow's fall. Don Mike was far from being the orthodox person one ordinarily visualizes in a Spanish-Irish Catholic, but he was deeply religious, his religious impulse taking quite naturally a much more practical form and one most pleasing to himself and his neighbors, in that it impelled him to be brave and kind and hopeful, a gentleman in all that the word implies. He valued far more than he did the promise of a mansion in the skies a certain tranquillity of spirit which comes of conscious virtue.

When he rose from his knees he had a feeling that God had not lost track of him and that, despite a long list of debit entries, a celestial accountant had, at some period in Don Mike's life, posted a considerable sum to his credit in the Book of Things. "That credit may just balance the account," he reflected, "although it is quite probable I am still working in the red ink. Well—I've asked Him for the privilege of overdrawing my account . . . we shall see what we shall see."

At daylight he awakened suddenly and found himself quite mysteriously the possessor of a trend of reasoning that automatically forced him to sit up in bed,

Fifteen minutes later, mounted on Panchito, he was cantering up the San Gregorio, and just as the cook at Bill Conway's camp at Agua Caliente Basin came to the door of the mess hall and yelled: "Come an' git it or I'll throw it out," Panchito slid down the gravel cut bank into camp.

"Where is Mr. Conway?" he demanded of the cook.

The latter jerked a greasy thumb toward the interior of the mess hall, so, leaving Panchito "tied to the breeze," Don Mike dismounted and entered.

"Hello there young feller," Bill Conway roared at him.

"Top o' the morning to you, old dirt digger," Farrel

268

replied. "Please deal me a hand of your ham and eggs, sunny side up. How be ye, Willum?"

"R'arin' to go," Conway assured him.

"All right. Pack up and go today. You're through on this job."

"Why?"

"I've changed my mind about fighting Parker on this dam deal—and no profanity intended."

"But—but—"

"But me no buts, even if you are the goat. You're through. I forbid the bans. The eggs, man! I'm famished. The midnight ride of Paul Revere was a mere exercise gallop, because he started shortly after supper, but the morning ride of Mike Farrel has been done on fresh air."

"You're a lunatic. If you knew what I know, Miguel—"

"Hush! I want to ascertain what you know. Bet you a dollar!" He slammed a dollar down on the table and held his palm over it.

Bill Conway produced a dollar and likewise covered it. "Very well, son," he replied. "I'll see your dollar. What's the nature of the bet?"

"I'm betting a dollar you didn't draw the plans for this dam."

Bill Conway flipped his dollar over to his guest.

"I'm betting two dollars!"

Conway took two silver dollars from his vest pocket and laid them on the table. "And the bet?" he queried.

"I'm betting two dollars the plans were drawn by an engineer in Los Angeles."

"Some days I can't lay up a cent," the old conractor complained, and parted with his two dollars,

"I'm betting four dollars!" Farrel challenged.

269

"See your four dollars," Conway retorted and covered the bet.

"I'm betting that those plans were drawn by the engineer of the South Coast Power Corporation."

"Death loves a shining mark, Michael, my boy. Hand over that four dollars."

Farrel produced a five dollar bill. "I'm betting five dollars," be challenged again.

"Not with me, son. You're too good. I suppose your next bet will be that the plans were drawn by the engineer of the Central California Power Company."

"Were they?"

"Yes."

"Got a set of the plans with his name on them?"

"You bet."

"I want them."

"They're yours, provided you tell your Uncle Bill the Big Idea."

Don Mike flipped some pepper and salt on his eggs and while doing so proceeded to elucidate.

"If I had two projects in mind—one for irrigation and one for power, I would not, of course, unless I happened to be a public service corporation engaged in producing and selling electric power, consider for a moment wasting my time monkeying with the hydroelectric buzz saw. Indeed, I would have to sell it, for with the juice developed here I could not hope to compete in a limited field with the established power companies. I would proceed to negotiate the sale of this by-product to the highest bidder. Bill, do you know that I've seen enough flood water running down the San Gregorio every winter to have furnished, if it could have been stored in Agua Caliente Basin, sufficient water to irrigate the San Gregorio Valley for five years?"

"I know it, Miguel."

"All a power company requires is the assurance that the dam you are building will impound in the Agua Caliente Basin during an ordinarily wet winter, sufficient runoff water to insure them against a shortage during the summer. After the water has passed over their wheels they're through with it and it can be used for irrigation, can it not?"

"Yes, of course, although you'd have to have a greater volume of water than the amount coming through the power company's penstocks. But that's easily arranged. Two ditches, Miguel!"

"If the engineer of the Central California Power Company had not examined the possibilities here and approved of them, it is reasonable to suppose that he would not have drawn the plans and Parker would not have engaged you to build the dam."

"You're on the target, son. Go on."

"Then Parker must have entered into an agreement to sell, and the Central California Power Company must have agreed to buy, if and when Parker could secure legal title to the Rancho Palomar, a certain number of miner's inches of water daily, in perpetuity, together with certain lands for a power station and a perpetual right of way for their power lines over the lands of this ranch."

"Well, son, that's what I would have done in a similar situation. Nothing to be made by letting that hydro-electric opportunity lie fallow. No profit in wasting kilowatts, Miguel. We haven't got a third of the power necessary for the proper development of this state."

"In the absence of conclusive proof to the contrary Bill, I am convinced that John Parker did enter into such a contract. Naturally, until he should secure the title to

271

the ranch, the railroad commission, which regulates all public service corporations in this state, would not grant the power company permission to gamble on the truth of an official report that I had been killed in Siberia."

"Your reasoning is sound. Now eat, and after breakfast I'll tell you things. Your visit and your eager inquiries have started a train of thought in my thick head."

Don Mike obeyed, and while he devoted himself to his breakfast, old Bill Conway amused himself rolling pellets out of bread and flipping them at a knothole in the rough wall of the mess hall.

"You've been pretty well troubled, haven't you son?" he remarked paternally when Don Mike, having completed his meal, sat back and commenced rolling a cigarette.

"*Si*. Got your train of thought ditched, Bill?"

"I have. Assuming that Parker has made a deal with the Central California Power Company, what I want to know is: Why did he do it?"

"I've just told you why he did it."

"You've just told me why he would make a deal with *a* power company, but you haven't explained why he should make a deal with this *particular* power company."

"I cannot answer that question. Bill."

" 'Nor can I. But there's a reason—perhaps two reasons. Territorially, this power site is the natural property of but two power corporations—the Central California and the South Coast. The South Coast is the second largest corporation of its kind in the state; the Central California is the fifth. Why go gunning for a dickey bird when you can tie up to an eagle?"

They were both silent, pondering the question. Then

said Bill Conway, "Well, son, if I had as much curiosity regarding the reason for this situation as you have, I'd most certainly spend some money to find out."

"I have the money and I am prepared to spend it, How would you start, Bill?"

"Well, I'd buy a couple of shares of stock in the Central California Power Company as a starter. Then I would descend upon the main office of the company, exhibit my stock and claim my stockholder's right to look over the list of stockholders and bondholders of record; also, the board of directors and the minutes of the previous meetings. You may not find John Parker's name listed either as stockholder, bondholder or director, but you might find the First National Bank of El Toro, represented by the cashier or the first vice-president of that institution. Also, if I were you, I'd just naturally hop the rattler for San Francisco, hire myself to some stockbroker's office to buy this stock, and while buying it look over the daily reports of the stock market for the past few years and see if the figures suggested anything to me."

"Anything else?"

"Thus endeth the first lesson, Miguel. At that it's only a vague suspicion. Get out of my way, boy. I'm going out to build a dam and you're not ready to stop me—yet."

"Bill, I'm serious about this. I want you to cease operations."

Bill Conway turned upon him almost angrily. "What for?" he demanded.

"I own the Rancho Palomar. I forbid it. I have a good and sufficient reason."

"But, son, I can finance the confounded dam. I have it financed already."

"So have I—if I cared to accept favors."

Bill Conway approached and took his young friend by each shoulder. "Son," he pleaded, "please let me build this dam. I was never so plumb interested in any job before. I'll take a chance. I know what I'm going to do and how I'm going to do it, and you aren't going to be obligated the least little bit. Isn't John Parker stuck for it all, in the long run? Why, I've got that *hombre* by the short hair."

"I know, but long before you can collect from him you'll be financially embarrassed."

"Don't worry. I've been a miser all my life and I've got a lot of money hid out. Please, son, quit interfering with me. You asked me to help you out, I accepted and I'm going to go through until stopped by legal procedure. And if you have the law on me I'll never speak to you again."

"Your attitude doesn't fit in with my plans, Bill Conway."

"Yours don't fit in with mine. Besides, I'm older than you and if there was one thing your father taught you it was respect for your elders. Two heads are better than one. You crack right along and try to save your ranch in your way and I'll crack right along and try to save it my way. You pay your way and I'll pay mine. That's fair, isn't it?"

"Yes, but—"

"Fiddlesticks; on your way. You're wasting your breath arguing with me."

Don Mike knew it. "Well, let me have a set of the plans," he concluded sulkily.

Bill Conway handed him out a roll of blueprints and Farrel mounted Panchito and returned to the hacienda. The blueprints he hid in the barn before presenting

274

himself at the house. He knew his absence from the breakfast-table would not be commented upon, because for a week, during the round-up of the cattle, he and Pablo and the latter's male relatives who helped in the riding, had left the hacienda at daylight after partaking of a four o'clock breakfast.

XXIX

WE'VE BEEN WAITING FOR YOU, Miguel, to motor with us to El Toro," Kay greeted him as he entered the patio.

"So sorry to have delayed you, Kay. I'm ready to start now, if you are."

"Father and mother are coming also. Where have you been? I asked Pablo, but he didn't know."

"I've been over to Bill Conway's camp to tell him to quit work on that dam."

The girl paled slightly and a look of apprehension crept into her eyes. "And—and—he's—ceasing operations?" she almost quavered.

"He is not. He defied me, confound him, and in the end I had to let him have his way."

El Mono, the butler, interrupted them by appearing on the porch to announce that William waited in the car without. Mrs. Parker presently appeared followed by her husband, and the four entered the waiting car. Don Mike, satisfied that his old riding breeches and coat were clean and presentable, had not bothered to change his clothes, an evidence of the democracy of his *ranchero* caste, which was not lost upon his guests.

"I know another route to El Toro," he confided to the Parkers as the car sped down the valley. "It's about twelve miles out of our way, but it is an inspiring drive.

275

The road runs along the side of the high hills, with a parallel range of mountains to the east and the low foothills and flat farming lands sloping gradually west to the Pacific Ocean. At one point we can look down into La Questa Valley and it's beautiful."

"Let us try that route, by all means," John Parker suggested. "I have been curious to see La Questa Valley and observe the agricultural methods of the Japanese farmers there."

"I am desirous of seeing it again for the same reason, sir," Farrel replied. "Five years ago there wasn't a Jap in that valley and now I understand it is a little Japan."

"I understand," Kay struck in demurely, "that La Questa Valley suffered a slight loss in population a few weeks ago."

Both Farrel and her father favored her with brief, sharp, suspicious glances. "Who was telling you?" the latter demanded.

"Señor Bill Conway."

"He ought to know better than to discuss the Japanese problem with you," Farrel complained, and her father nodded vigorous assent. Kay tilted her adorable nose at them.

"How delightful to have one's intelligence underrated by mere men," she retorted.

"Did Bill Conway indicate the direction of the tide of emigration from La Questa?" Farrel asked craftily, still unwilling to admit anything. The girl smiled at him, then leaning closer she crooned for his ear alone:

> He's sleeping in the valley,
> The valley,
> The valley,
> He's sleeping in the valley,

276

And the mocking bird is singing
where he lies.

"Are you glad?" he blurted eagerly. She nodded and thrilled as she noted the smug little smile of approval and complete understanding that crept over his dark face like the shadow of clouds in the San Gregorio. Mrs. Parker was riding in the front seat with the chauffeur and Kay sat between her father and Don Mike in the tonneau. His hand dropped carelessly on her lap now, as he made a pretense of pulling the auto robe up around her; with quick stealth he caught her little finger and pressed it hurriedly, then dropped it as if the contact had burned him; whereat the girl realized that he was a man of few words, but—

"Dear old idiot," she thought. "If he ever falls in love he'll pay his court like a schoolboy."

"By the way, sir," Farrel spoke suddenly, turning to John Parker, "I would like very much to have your advice in the matter of an investment. I will have about ninety thousand dollars on hand as soon as I sell these cattle I've rounded up, and until I can add to this sum sufficient to lift the mortgage you hold, it scarcely seems prudent to permit my funds to repose in the First National Bank of El Toro without drawing interest."

"We'll give you two and one-half percent, on the account, Farrel."

"Not enough, I want it to earn six or seven percent and it occurred to me that I might invest it in some good securities which I could dispose of at a moment's notice, whenever I needed the money. The possibility of a profit on the deal has even occurred to me."

Parker smiled humorously. "And you come to me for advice? Why, boy, I'm your financial enemy."

277

"My dear Mr. Parker, I am unalterably opposed to you on the Japanese colonization scheme and I shall do my best to rob you of the profit you plan to make at my expense, but personally I find you a singularly agreeable man. I know you will never resign a business advantage, but, on the other hand, I think that if I ask you for advice as to a profitable investment for my pitiful little fortune, you will not be base enough to advise me to my financial detriment. I trust you. Am I not banking with your bank?"

"Thank you, Farrel, for that vote of confidence. You possess a truly sporting attitude in business affairs and I like you for it; I like any man who can take his beating and smile. Yes, I am willing to advise an investment. I know of a dozen splendid securities that I can conscientiously recommend as a safe investment, although, in the event of the inevitable settlement that must follow the war and our national orgy of extravagance and high prices, I advise you frankly to wait awhile before taking on any securities. You cannot afford to absorb the inevitable shrinkage in the values of all commodities when the showdown comes. However, there is a new issue of South Coast Power Company first mortgage bonds that can be bought now to yield eight percent and I should be very much inclined to take a chance on them, Farrel. The debentures of the power corporations in this state are about the best I know of."

"I think you are quite right, sir," Farrel agreed. "Eventually the South Coast Company is bound to divide with the Pacific Company control of the power business of the state. I dare say that in the fullness of time the South Coast people will arrange a merger with the Central California Power Company."

"Perhaps. The Central California Company is under

financed and not particularly well managed, Farrel. I think it is, potentially, an excellent property, but its bonds have been rather depressed for a long time."

Farrel nodded his understanding. "Thank you for your advice, sir. When I am ready will your bank be good enough to arrange the purchase of the South Coast bonds for me?"

"Certainly. Happy to oblige you, Farrel. But do not be in too great a hurry. You may lose more in the shrinkages of values if you buy now than you would make in interest."

"I shall be guided by your advice, sir. You are very kind."

"By the way," Parker continued, with a deprecatory smile, "I haven't entered suit against you in the matter of that foreclosure. I didn't desire to annoy you while you were in hospital and you've been busy on the range ever since. When can I induce you to submit to a process server?"

"This afternoon will suit me, Mr. Parker."

"I'll gladly wait awhile longer, if you can give me any tangible assurance of your ability to meet the mortgage."

"I cannot do that today, sir, although I may be able to do so if you will defer action for three days."

Parker nodded and the conversation languished. The car had climbed out of the San Gregorio and was mounting swiftly along the route to La Questa, affording to the Parkers a panorama of mountain, hill, valley and sea so startling in its vastness and its rugged beauty that Don Mike realized his guests had been silenced as much by awe as by their desire to avoid a painful and unprofitable conversation.

Suddenly they swung wide around a turn and saw,

279

two thousand feet below them, La Questa Valley. The chauffeur parked the car on the outside of the turn to give his passengers a long, unobstructed view.

"Looks like a green checkerboard with tiny squares," Parker remarked presently.

"Little Japanese farms."

"There must be a thousand of them, Farrel."

"That means not less than five thousand Japanese, Mr. Parker. It means that literally a slice of Japan has been transplanted in La Questa Valley, perhaps the fairest and most fruitful valley in the fairest and most fruitful state in the fairest and most fruitful country God ever made. And it is lost to white men!"

"Serves them right. Why didn't they retain their lands?"

"Why doesn't water run up hill? A few Japs came in and leased or bought lands long before we Californians suspected a 'yellow peril.' They paid good prices to inefficient white farmers who were glad to get out at a price in excess of what any white man could afford to pay. After we passed our land law in 1913, white men continued to buy the lands for a corporation owned by Japanese with white dummy directors, or a majority of the stock of the corporation ostensibly owned by white men. Thousands of patriotic Californians have sold their farms to Japanese without knowing it. The law provides that a Japanese cannot lease land longer than three years, so when their leases expire they conform to our foolish law by merely shifting the tenants from one farm to another. Eventually so many Japs settled in the valley that the white farmers, unable to secure white labor, unable to trust Japanese labor, unable to endure Japanese neighbors or to enter into Japanese social life weary of paying taxes to support schools for the

280

education of Japanese children, weary of daily contact with irritable, unreliable and unassimilable aliens, sold or leased their farms in order to escape into a white neighborhood. I presume, Mr. Parker, that nobody can realize the impossibility of withstanding this yellow flood except those who have been overwhelmed by it. We humanitarians of a later day gaze with gentle sympathy upon the spectacle of a noble and primeval race like the Iroquois tribe of Indians dying before the advance of our Anglo-Saxon civilization, but with characteristic Anglo-Saxon inconsistency and stupidity we are quite loth to feel sorry for ourselves, doomed to death before the advance of a Mongolian civilization unless we put a stop to it—forcibly and immediately!"

"Let us go down and see for ourselves," Mrs. Parker suggested.

Having reached the floor of the valley, at Farrel's suggestion they drove up one side of it and down the other. Motor truck after motor truck, laden with crated vegetables, passed them on the road, each truck driven by a Japanese, some of them wearing the peculiar bamboo hats of the Japanese coolie class.

The valley was given over to vegetable farming and the fields were dotted with men, women and children, squatting on their heels between the rows or bending over them in an attitude which they seemed able to maintain indefinitely, but which would have broken the hack of a white man.

"I know a white apologist for the Japanese who in a million pamphlets and from a thousand rostrums has cried that it is false that Japanese women labor in the fields," Farrel told his guests. "You have seen a thousand of them laboring in this valley. Hundreds of them carry babies on their backs or set them to sleep on

281

a gunnysack between the rows of vegetables. There is a sixteen-year-old girl struggling with a one-horse cultivator, while her sisters and her mother hold up their end with five male Japs in the gentle art of hoeing potatoes."

"They live in wretched little houses," Kay ventured to remark.

"Anything that will shelter a horse or a chicken is a palace to a Jap, Kay. The furnishings of their houses are few and crude. They rise in the morning, eat, labor, eat, and retire to sleep against another day of toil. They are all growing rich in this valley, but have you seen one of these aliens building a decent home, or laying out a flower garden? Do you see anything inspiring or elevating to our nation due to the influence of such a race?"

"Yonder is a schoolhouse," Mrs. Parker suggested "Let us visit it."

"The American flag floats over that little red schoolhouse, at any rate," Parker defended.

William halted the car in the schoolhouse yard and Farrel got out and walked to the schoolhouse door. An American schoolteacher, a girl of perhaps twenty, came to the door and met him with an inquiring look. "May we come in?" Farrel pleaded. "I have some Eastern people with me and I wanted to show them the sort of Americans you are hired to teach."

She smiled ruefully. "I am just about to let them out for recess," she replied. "Your friends may remain in their car and draw their own conclusions."

"Thank you." Don Mike returned to the car, "They're coming out for recess," he confided. "Future American citizens and citizenesses. Count 'em."

Thirty-two little Japanese boys and girls, three

Mexican or Indian children and four of undoubted white parentage trooped out into the yard and gathered around the car, gazing curiously. The schoolteacher bade them run away and play and, in her rôle of hostess, approached the car. "I am Miss Owens," she announced, "and I teach this school because I have to earn a living. It is scarcely a task over which once can enthuse, although I must admit that Japanese children are not unintelligent and their parents dress them nicely and keep them clean."

"I suppose, Miss Owens," Farrel prompted her, having introduced himself and the Parkers, "that you have to contend with the native Japanese schools."

She pointed to a brown house half a mile away. Over it flew the flag of Japan. "They learn ancestor worship and how to kowtow to the Emperor's picture down there, after they have attended school here," she volunteered. "Poor little tots! Their heads must ache with the amount of instruction they receive. After they have learned here that Columbus discovered America on October 12th, 1492, they proceed to that Japanese school and are taught that the Mikado is a divinity and a direct descendant of the Sun God. And I suppose, also, they are taught that it is a fine, clean, manly thing to pack little, green, or decayed strawberries at the bottom of a crate with nice big ones on top—in defiance of a state law. Our weights and measures law and a few others are very onerous to our people in La Questa."

"Do you mean to tell me, Miss Owens," Parker asked, "that you despair of educating these little Japanese children to be useful American citizens?"

"I do. The Buddhist school over yonder is teaching them to be Japanese citizens; under Japanese law all Japanese remain Japanese citizens at heart, even if they

283

do occasionally vote here. The discipline of my school is very lax," she continued. "It would be, of course, in view of the total lack of parental support. In that other school, however, the discipline is excellent."

She continued to discourse with them, giving them an intimate picture of life in this little Japan and interesting revelations upon the point of view, family life and business ethics of the parents of her pupils, until it was time to "take up" school again, when she reluctantly returned to her poorly paid and unappreciated efforts.

"Well, of course, these people are impossible socially," John Parker admitted magnanimously, "but they do know how to make things grow. They are not afraid of hard work. Perhaps that is why they have supplanted the white farmers."

"Indeed they do know how, Mr. Parker. And they can produce good crops more cheaply than a white farmer. A Japanese with a wife and two fairly well grown daughters saves the wages of three hired men. Thus he is enabled to work his ground more thoroughly. When he leases land he tries to acquire rich land, which he robs of its fertility in three years and then passes on to renew the outrage elsewhere. Where he owns land, however, he increases fertility by proper fertilization."

"So you do not believe it possible for a white man to compete economically with these people, Farrel?"

"Would you, if you were a white farmer, care to compete with the Japanese farmers of this valley? Would you care to live in a rough board shack, subsist largely on rice, labor from daylight to dark and force your wife and daughter to labor with you in the fields? Would you care to live in a kennel and never read a book or take an interest in public affairs or thrill at a sunset or consider that you really ought to contribute a

284

dollar toward starving childhood in Europe? Would you?"

"You paint a sorry picture, Farrel." Parker was evasive.

"I paint what I see before me," he answered doggedly. "This—in five years. And if this be progress as we view progress—if this be desirable industrial or agricultural evolution, then I'm out of tune with my world and my times, and as soon as I am certain of it I'll blow my brains out."

Parker chuckled at this outburst and Kay prodded him with her elbow—a warning prod. The conversation languished immediately. Don Mike sat staring out upon the little green farms and the little brown men and women who toiled on them.

"Angry, Don Mike?" the girl asked presently. He bent upon her a glance of infinite sadness.

"No, my dear girl, just feeling a little depressed. It's hard for a man who loves his country so well that he would gladly die a thousand dreadful deaths for it, to have to fight the disloyal thought that perhaps, after all, it isn't really worth fighting for and dying for. If we only had the courage and the foresight and the firmness of the Australians and New Zealanders! Why, Kay, those sane people will not even permit an Indian prince—a British subject, forsooth—to enter their country except under bond and then for six months only. When the six months have expired—*heraus mit em!* You couldn't find a Jap in Australia, with a search warrant. But do you hear any Japanese threats of war against Australia for this alleged insult to her national honor? You do not. They save that bunkum for pussy-footing, peace-loving, backward-looking, dollar-worshiping Americans. As a nation we do not wish to

285

be awakened from our complacency, and the old theory that a prophet is without honor in his own country is a true one. So perhaps it would be well if we discuss something else —luncheon, for instance. Attention! Silence in the ranks! Here we are at the Hotel De Las Rosas."

Having dined his guests, Farrel excused himself, strolled over to the railroad station and arranged with the agent for cattle cars to be spotted in on the siding close to town three days later. From the station he repaired to the office of his father's old attorney, where he was closeted some fifteen minutes, after which he returned to his guests, awaiting his return on the wide hotel veranda.

"Have you completed your business?" Parker inquired.

"Yes, sir, I have. I have also completed some of yours. Coming away from the office of my attorney, I noticed the office of your attorney right across the hall, so I dropped in and accepted service of the complaint in action for the foreclosure of your confounded old mortgage. This time your suit is going to stick! Furthermore, as I jogged down Main Street, I met Judge Morton, of the Superior Court, and made him promise that if the suit should be filed this afternoon he would take it up on his calendar tomorrow morning and render a judgment in your favor."

"By George," Parker declared, apparently puzzled, "one gathers the impression that you relish parting with your patrimony when you actually speed the date of departure."

Mrs. Parker took Don Mike by the lapel of his coat. "You have a secret," she charged.

He shook his head.

"You have," Kay challenged. "The intuition of two women cannot be gainsaid."

Farrel took each lady by the arm and with high, mincing steps, simulating the utmost caution in his advance, he led them a little way down the veranda out of hearing of the husband and father.

"It isn't a secret," he whispered, "because a secret is something which one has a strong desire to conceal. However, I do not in the least mind telling you the cause of the O-be-joyful look that has aroused your curiosity. Please lower your heads and incline your best ears toward me . . . There! I rejoice because I have the shaggy old wolf of Wall Street, more familiarly known as John Parker, beaten at his favorite indoor sport of high and lofty finance. 'Tis sad, but true. The old boy's a gone fawn. *Le roi est mort! vive le roi!*"

Kay's eyes danced. "Really, Miguel?"

"Not really or actually, Kay, but—er—morally certain."

"Oh!" There was disappointment in her voice. Her mother was looking at Don Mike sharply, shrewdly, but she said nothing, and Farrel had a feeling that his big moment had fallen rather flat.

"How soon will John be called upon to bow his head and take the blow?" Mrs. Parker finally asked. "Much as I sympathize with you, Miguel, I dislike the thought of John hanging in suspense, as it were."

"Oh, I haven't quite made up my mind," he replied. "I could do it within three days, I think, but why rush the execution? Three months hence will be ample time. You see," he confided, "I like you all so well that I plan to delay action for six months or a year, unless of course, you are anxious for an excuse to leave the ranch sooner. If you really want to go as soon as possible, of course

287

I'll get busy and cook Señor Parker's goose, but—"

"You're incorrigible!" the lady declared. "Procrastinate, by all means. It would be very lonely for you without us, I'm sure."

"Indeed, it would be. That portion of me which is Irish would picture my old hacienda alive at night with ghosts and banshees."

Mrs. Parker was looking at him thoughtfully: seemingly she was not listening. What she really was doing was saying to herself: "What marvelous teeth he has and what an altogether *debonair*, captivating young rascal he is, to be sure! I cannot understand why he doesn't melt John's business heart. Can it be that under that gay, smiling, lovable surface John sees something he doesn't quite like? I wonder."

As they entered the waiting automobile and started for home, Farrel, who occupied the front seat with the chauffeur, turned and faced the Parkers. "From this day forward," he promised them, "we are all going to devote ourselves to the serious task of enjoying life to the utmost. For my part, I am not going to talk business or Japanese immigration any more. Are you all grateful?"

"We are," they cried in unison.

He thanked them with his mirthful eyes, faced around in his seat and, staring straight ahead, was soon lost in day dreams. John Parker and his wife exchanged glances, then both looked at their daughter, seated between them. She, too, was building castles in Spain!

When they alighted from the car before the hacienda, Mrs. Parker lingered until the patio gate had closed on her daughter and Farrel; then she drew her husband down beside her on the bench under the catalpa tree.

"John, Miguel Farrel says he has you beaten."

"I hope so, dear," he replied feelingly. "I know of but

one way out for that young man, and if he has discovered it so readily I'd be a poor sport indeed not to enjoy his victory."

"You never really meant to take his ranch away from him, did You, John ?"

"I did, Kate. I do. If I win, my victory will prove to my entire satisfaction that Don Miguel José Federico Noriaga Farrel is a throwback to the *Mañana* family and in that event, my dear, we will not want him in ours. We ought to improve our bloodlines, not deteriorate them."

"Yet you would have sold this valley to that creature Okada."

"Farrel has convinced me of my error there. I have been anti-Jap since the day Farrel was thrown from his horse and almost killed—by a Jap."

"I'm sure Kay is in love with him, John."

"Propinquity," he grunted.

"Fiddlesticks! The man is perfectly charming."

"Perhaps. We'll decide that point later. Do you think Farrel is interested in Kay?"

"I do not know, John," his better half declared hopelessly. "If he is, he possesses the ability to conceal it admirably."

"I'll bet he's a good poker player. He has you guessing, old girl, and the man who does that is a *rara avis*. However, Katie dear, if I were you I wouldn't worry about this—er—affair."

"John, I can't help it. Naturally, I'm curious to know the thoughts in the back of that boy's head, but when he turns that smiling innocent face toward me, all I can see is old-fashioned deference and amiability and courtesy. I watch him when he's talking to Kay —when he cannot possibly know I am snooping, and still, except for that frank friendliness, his face is as communicative as this

289

old adobe wall. A few days ago he rode in from the range with a great cluster of wild tiger lilies—and he presented them to me. Any other young man would have presented them to my daughter."

"I give it up, Kate, and suggest that we turn this mystery over to Father Time. He'll solve it."

"But I don't want Kay to fall in love with Don Mike if he isn't going to fall in love with her," she protested, in her earnestness raising her voice, as was frequently her habit.

The patio gate latch clicked and Pablo Artelan stood in the aperture.

"Señora," he said gravely. "Ef I am you I don' worry very much about those boy. Before hee's pretty parteecular. All those hightone' *señorita* in El Toro she give eet the sweet look to Don Miguel, jus' the same like thees—" Here Pablo relaxed his old body, permitted his head to loll sideways and his lower jaw to hang slackly, the while his bloodshot eyes gazed amorously into the branches of the catalpa tree. "But those boy he don' pay some attention. Hee's give beeg smile to thees *señorita,* beeg smile to thees one, beeg smile to that one, beeg smile for all the mama, but for the *querida* I tell to you Don Miguel hee's pretty parteecular. I theenk to myself—Carolina, too—'Look here, Pablo. What he ees the matter weeth those boy? I theenk mebbeso those boy she's goin' be old bach. What's the matter here? When I am twenty-eight *años* my oldes' boy already hee's bust one bronco'." Here Pablo paused to scratch his head. "But now, " he resumed, "by the blood of those devil I know sometheeng!"

"What do you know, you squidgy-nosed old idol, you?" Parker demanded, with difficulty repressing his
290

laughter.

"I am ol'man," Pablo answered with just the correct shade of deprecation, "but long time ago I have feel like my *corazon*—my heart—goin' make barbecue in my belly. I am in love. I know. Nobody can fool me. An' those boy, Don Miguel, I tell you, *señor,* hee's crazy for love weeth the Señorita Kay."

Parker crooked his finger, and in obedience to the summons Pablo approached the bench.

"How do you know all this, Pablo?"

Let us here pause and consider. In the summer of 1769 a dashing, carefree Catalonian soldier in the company of Don Gaspar de Portola, while swashbuckling his way around the lonely shores of San Diego Bay, had encountered a comely young squaw. *Mira, señores!* Of the blood that flowed in the veins of Pablo Artelan, thirty-one-thirty-seconds was Indian, but the other one-thirty-second was composed of equal parts of Latin romance and conceit.

Pablo's great moment had arrived. Lowly peon that he was, he knew himself at this moment to be a most important personage; death would have been preferable to the weakness of having failed to take advantage of it.

"Why I know, Señor Parker?" Pablo laughed briefly, lightly, mirthlessly, his cacchination carefully designed to convey the impression that he considered the question extremely superfluous. With exasperating deliberation he drew forth his little bag of tobacco and a brown cigarette paper; he smiled as he dusted into the cigarette paper the requisite amount of tobacco. With one hand he rolled the cigarette; while wetting the flap with his garrulous tongue, he gazed out upon the San Gregorio as one who looks beyond a lifted veil.

He answered his own question. "Well, *señor*—and

you, *señora!* I tell you. *Por nada*—forgeeve; please, I speak the Spanish—for notheeng, those boy he poke weeth hee's thumb the rib of me."

"No?" cried John Parker, feigning profound amazement.

"*Es verdad.* Eet ees true, *señor.* Those boy hee's happy, no? Eh?"

"Apparently."

"You bet you my life. Well, las' night those boy hee's peench weeth his thumb an' theese fingair—what you suppose?"

"I give it up, Pablo."

Pablo wiped away with a saddle-colored paw a benignant and paternal smile. He wagged his head and scuffed his heel in the dirt. He feasted his soul on the sensation that was his.

"Those boy hee's peench—" a dramatic pause. Then: "Eef you tell to Don Miguel those things I tol' you—*Santa Marias*—Hees cut my throat."

"We will respect your confidence, Pablo," Mrs. Parker hastened to assure the traitor.

"All right. Then I tol' to you what those boy peench —weeth hees thumb an' thees fingair. *Mira.* Like thees."

"Cut out the pantomime and disgorge the information, for the love of heaven," Parker pleaded.

"He peench"—Pablo's voice rose to a pseudo-feminine screech—"the cheek of"—he whirled upon Mrs. Parker and transfixed her with a tobacco-stained index finger—"Señorita Parker, so help me, by Jimmy, eef I tell you some lies I hope I die pretty queeck."

Both the Parkers stared at the old man blankly, He continued:

"He peench—queeck—like that. He don' know hee's

goin' for peench—hees all time queeck like that—he don' theenk. But after those boy hee's peench the cheen of those girl, hee's got red in the face like blackbird's weeng. 'Oh,' he say, 'I am sky blue eedete—ot,' an' he run away queeck before he forget heemself an' peench those girl some more."

John Parker turned gravely to his wife. "Old hon," he murmured softly, "Don Mike Farrel is a pinch bug. He pinched Kay's chin during a mental lapse; then he remembered he was still under my thumb and he cursed himself for a sky blue idiot."

"Oh, John, dear, I'm so glad." There were tears in Mrs. Parker's eyes. "Aren't you, John?"

"No, I'm not," he replied savagely. "I think it's an outrage and I'd speak to Farrel about it if it were not apparent nobody realizes more keenly than does he the utter impossibility of permitting his fancy to wander in that direction."

"John Parker, you're a hard-hearted man," she cried, and left him in high dudgeon, to disappear into the garden. As the gate closed behind her, John Parker drew forth his pocket book and abstracted from it a hundred dollar bill, which he handed to Pablo Artelan.

"We have had our little differences, Pablo," he informed that astounded individual, "but we're gradually corking around toward a true spirit of brotherly love. In the language of the classic, Pablo, I'm here to tell the cockeyed world that you're one good Indian."

Pablo swept his old *sombrero* to the ground. *"Gracias, señor, mille gracias,"* he murmured, and shuffled away with his prize.

Verily, the ways of this Gringo were many and mysterious. Today one hated him; tomorrow—

"There is no doubt about it," Pablo soliloquized, "it *is* better to be the head of a mouse than the tail of of a lion!"

XXX

THE FOLLOWING DAY Don Mike, Pablo and the latter's male relatives, who had so mysteriously appeared on the premises, were early ahorse, driving to El Toro the three hundred-odd head of cattle of all ages and sizes rounded up on the Palomar. The cattle were corraled at a ranch halfway to El Toro the first night, and there watered and fed; the following night they were in the cattle pens at El Toro, and the following day Farrel loaded them aboard the cars and shipped them out to Los Angeles, accompanying the shipment personally. Two days later he was back on the ranch, and the Parkers noticed that his exuberant spirits had not in the least subsided.

"I'd give a ripe peach to know what that fellow is up to," John Parker complained. "Confidentially, I've had him shadowed from the moment he arrived in Los Angeles until the moment he returned to El Toro and started back for the ranch. He has conferred with nobody except the stockyard people. Nevertheless, he has a hen on."

"Yes, and that hen will hatch a young bald-headed eagle to scratch your eyes out," his daughter reminded him, whereat he chuckled.

"Old Bill Conway's drilling away at his dam site," he volunteered presently, "and his suit against me for damages, due to breach of contract, is set for trial so far down Judge Morton's calendar that the old judge will have to use a telescope to find it. However, I shouldn't

294

charge the judge with a lack of interest in my affairs, for he has rendered a judgment in my favor in the matter of that mortgage foreclosure and announced from the bench that if this judgment doesn't stick he'll throw the case out of court the next time it is presented for trial. I wonder what Farrel's next move will be?"

"I heard him announce that he was going to get ready for the *fiesta,*" Kay replied.

For two weeks he was busy harrowing, disking and rolling the old racetrack; he repainted the weatherbeaten poles and reshingled the judge's stand; he repaired the fence and installed an Australian starting gate, dug a pit for the barbecue and brought forth, repaired and set up under the oaks close to the racetracks, thirty long wooden tables at which, in an elder and more romantic day, the entire countryside, as guests of the Farrels and Noriagas, had gathered to feast. Farrel worked hard and saw but little of his guests, except at mealtimes; he retired somewhat early each night and, insofar as his guests could note, he presented a most commendable example of a young man whose sole interest in life lay in his work.

"When do you plan to give your *fiesta,* Miguel?" Kay inquired one evening as they sat, according to custom, on the veranda.

"In about a month," he replied. "I've got to fatten my steers and harden them on a special diet before we barbecue them. Don Nicolás Sandoval will have charge of the feast, and if I furnished him with thin, tough range steers, he'd charge me with modernism and disown me. Old Bill Conway never would forget it. He'd nag me to my grave."

"When do we give Panchito his tryout, Don Mike?"

"The track is ready for it now, Kay, and Pablo tells

me Panchito's half brother is now a most dutiful member of society and can get there in a hurry when he's sent for. But he's only a half thoroughbred. Shall we start training tomorrow?"

"Oh, goody. By all means."

The long and patient methods of education to which a green racehorse is subjected were unknown on the Rancho Palomar. Panchito was a trained saddle animal, wise, sensible, courageous and with a prodigious faith that his rider would get him safely out of any jam into which they might blunder together. The starting gate bothered him at first, but after half a dozen trials, he realized that the web, flying upward, had no power to hurt him and was, moreover, the signal for a short, jolly contest of speed with his fellows of the rancho. Before the week was out he was "breaking" from the barrier with speed and serenity born of the knowledge that this was exactly what was expected of him; whereupon the other horses that Don Mike used to simulate a field of competitors, took heart of hope at Panchito's complacency and broke rather well with him.

Those were long, lazy days on the Palomar. June had cast its withering smile upon the San Gregorio and the green hills had turned to a parched brown. Grasshoppers whirred everywhere; squirrels whistled; occasional little dust devils whirled up the now thoroughly dry riverbed and the atmosphere was redolent of the aroma of dust and tarweed. Pablo and his dusky relatives, now considerably augmented (albeit Don Mike had issued no invitation to partake of his hospitality), trained colts as roping horses or played Mexican monte in the shade of the help's quarters. Occasionally they roused themselves long enough to justify their inroads upon Don Mike's groceries by harvesting a forty acre field of alfalfa and irrigating it for another crop, for which purpose a well had been sunk in the bed of the dry San Gregorio.

The wasted energies of these peons finally commenced to irritate John Parker.

"How long are you going to tolerate the presence of this healthy lot of *cholo* loafers and grafters, Farrel?" he demanded one day. "Have you any idea of what it is costing you to support that gang?"

"Yes," Farrel replied. "About ten dollars a day."

"You cannot afford that expense."

"I know it. But then, they're the local color, they've always been and they will continue to be while I have title to this ranch. Why, their hearts would be broken if I refused them permission to nestle under the cloak of my philanthropy, and he is a poor sort of white man who will disappoint a poor devil of a *cholo.*"

"You're absolutely incomprehensible," Parker declared.

Farrel laughed. "You're not," he replied. "Know anything about a stopwatch?"

"I know *all* about one."

"Well, your daughter has sent to San Francisco for the best stopwatch money can buy, and it's here, I've had my father's old stopwatch cleaned and regulated. Panchito's on edge and we're going to give him a half mile tryout tomorrow, so I want two stopwatches on him. Will you oblige, sir?"

Parker willingly consented, and the following morning Farrel and his guests repaired to the racetrack. Kay, mounted on Panchito in racing gear, was, by courtesy, given a position next to the rail. Eighty pounds of dark meat, answering to the name of Allesandro Trujillo and claiming Pablo Artelan as his grandfather, drew next position on Peep-sight, as Farrel had christened Panchito's half brother, while three other half-grown *cholo* youths, gathered at random here and there, faced the barrier on the black mare, the old gray roping horse and a strange horse belonging to one of the volunteer jockeys.

There was considerable backing, filling and some bucking at the barrier, and Pablo and two of his relatives, acting as starters, were kept busy straightening out the field. Finally, with a shrill yip, Pablo released the web and the flighty young Peep-sight was away in front, with the black mare's nose at his saddlegirth and the field spread out behind him, with Panchito absolutely last.

At the quarter pole Kay had worked her mount easily up through the ruck to contend with Peep-sight. The half-thoroughbred was three years old and his muscles had been hardened by many a wild scramble up and down the hills of El Palomar; he was game, he was willing, and for half a mile he was marvelously fast, as Farrel had discovered early in the tryouts. Indeed, as a "quarter horse" Farrel knew that few horses might beat the comparatively green Peep-sight and he had been indiscreet enough to make that statement in the presence of youthful Allesandro Trujillo, thereby filling that young hopeful with a tremendous ambition to race the famed Panchito into submission for the mere sport of a race.

In a word, Allesandro's Indian blood was up. If there was anything he loved, it was a horse-race for money, chalk, marbles or fun. Therefore when a quick glance over his shoulder showed Panchito's blazed face at Peep-sight's rump, Allesandro clucked to his mount, gathered the reins a trifle tighter and dug his dirty bare heels into Peep-sight's ribs, for he was riding bareback, as an Indian should. Peep-sight responded to the invitation with such alacrity that almost instantly he had opened a gap of two full lengths between himself and Kay on Panchito.

Farrel and Parker, holding their stopwatches, watched the race from the judge's stand.

"By Jove, that Peep-sight *is* a streak," Parker declared admiringly. "He can beat Panchito at that distance, even at proportionate weights and with an even break at the start."

Farrel nodded, his father's old racing glass fixed on Allesandro and Kay. The girl had "gathered" her mount; she was leaning low on his powerful neck and Farrel knew that she was talking to him, riding him out as he had never been ridden before. And he was responding. Foot by foot he closed the distance that Peep-sight had opened up, but within a hundred yards of the finish Allesandro again called upon his mount for some more of the same, and the gallant Peep-sight flattened himself perceptibly and held his own; nor could Panchito's greatest efforts gain upon the flying half-breed a single inch.

"Bully for the Indian kid," Parker yelled. "Man, man, that's a horse race."

"They'll never stop at the half mile pole," Farrel laughed. "That race will be won by Panchito when Panchito wins it. Ah, I told you so."

"Well, Peep-sight wins at the half by one open length —and the *cholo* boy is using a switch on him!"

"He's through. Panchito is gaining on him. He'll pass him at the three-quarter pole."

"Right-o, Farrel. Panchito wins by half a length at the three-quarter pole—"

"I wish Kay would pull him up," Farrel complained. "He's gone too far already and there she is still heading for home like the devil beating tanbark . . . well, if she breaks him down she's going to be out the grandest saddle animal in the state of California. That's all I have to say . . . Kay, Kay, girl, what's the matter with you? Pull him up . . . by the blood of the devil, she can't pull him up. She's broken a rein and he's making a run of it on his own."

"Man, look at that horse go."

"Man, look at him come!"

Panchito had swung into the homestretch, his white face and white front legs rising and falling with the strong, steady rhythm of the horse whose stout heart refuses to acknowledge defeat, the horse who still has something left for a supreme effort at the finish.

"There is a true racehorse," Parker cried exultantly. "I once won a ten-thousand dollar purse with a dog that wasn't fit to appear on the same track with that Panchito."

The big chestnut thudded by below them, stretched to the limit of his endurance, passed what would have been the finish had the race been a mile and a sixteenth, and galloped up the track with the broken bridle rein dangling. He slowed down as he came to the other horses in the race, now jogging back to the judge' stand, and one of the *cholo* youths spurred alongside of him, caught the dangling rein and led him back to the judge's stand.

Kay's face was a little bit white as she smiled up at her father and Farrel. "The old darling ran away with me," she called.

Farrel was instantly at her side and had lifted her out of the saddle. She clung to him for the barest moment, trembling with fear and excitement, before turning to examine Panchito, from whom Pablo had already stripped the saddle. He was badly blown, as trembly as the girl herself, and dripping with sweat, but when Pablo slipped the headstall on him and commenced to walk him up and down to "cool him out," Don Mike's critical eye failed to observe any evil effects from the long and unaccustomed race.

John Parker came down out of the grand stand, his thumb still tightly pressing the stem of his stopwatch, which he thrust under Farrel's nose.

"Look, you star-spangled ignoramus, look," he yelled. "You own a horse that's fit to win the Melbourne Cup or the American Derby, and you don't know it. What do you want for him? Give you ten thousand for him this minute—and I am not so certain that race hasn't hurt him."

"Oh, I don't want to sell Panchito. I can make this ranch pay ten thousand dollars, but I cannot breed another Panchito on it."

"Farrel, if you refuse to sell me that horse I'm going to sit right down here and weep. Son, I don't know a soul on earth who can use twelve—yes, fifteen—thousand dollars handier than you can."

Don Mike smiled his lazy, tantalizing smile. "I might as well be broke as the way I am," he protested. "What's a paltry fifteen thousand dollars to a man who needs half a million? Mr. Parker, my horse is not for sale at any price."

"You mean that?"

"Absolutely."

John Parker sighed. Since that distant day when he had decided that he could afford such a luxury, his greatest delight had been in owning and "fussing" with

301

a few really great racehorses. He had owned some famous sprinters, but his knowledge of the racing game had convinced him that, could he but acquire Panchito, he would be the owner of a true king of the turf. The assurance that, with all his great wealth, this supreme delight was denied him, was a heavy blow.

Kay slipped her arm through his. "Don't cry, pa, please! We'll wait until Don Mike loses all his sheep and cow money and then we'll buy Panchito for a song."

"Oh, Kay, little girl, that horse is a peach. I think I'd give a couple of toes for the fun of getting my old trainer Dan Leighton out here, training this animal quietly up here in the valley where nobody could get a line on his performances, then shipping him east to Saratoga, where I'd put a good boy on him, stick him in rotten company and win enough races to qualify him for the biggest event of the year. And then! Oh, how I would steal the Derby from John H. Hatfield and his four-year-old wonder. I owe Hatfield a poke anyhow. We went raiding together once and the old sinner double-crossed me."

"Who is John H. Hatfield?" Don Mike queried mildly.

"Oh, he's an aged sinner down in Wall Street. He works hard to make the New Yorkers support his racing stables. Poor old John! All he has is some money and one rather good horse."

"And you wish to police this Hatfield person, sir?"

"If I could, I'd die happy, Farrel."

"Very well. Send for your old trainer, train Panchito, try him out a bit at Tia Juana, Lower California, at the meeting this winter, ship him to Saratoga and make Señor Hatfield curse the day he was born. I have a very

302

excellent reason for not selling Panchito to you, but never let it be said that I was such a poor sport I refused to loan him to you—provided, of course, Kay agrees to this course. He's her mount, you know, while she's on El Palomar."

Parker turned to his daughter. "Kay," he demanded, "do you love your poor old father?"

"Yes, I do, pa, but you can't have Panchito until you do something for me."

"Up jumped the devil! What do you want?"

"If you accept a favor from Miguel Farrel you ought to be sport enough to grant him one. If you ever expect to see Panchito in your racing colors out in front at the American Derby, Miguel must have a renewal of his mortgage."

"Oh, the devil take that mortgage. You and your mother never give me a moment's peace about it. You make me feel like a criminal; it's getting so I'll have to sit around playing mumbley-peg in order to get a thrill in my old age. You win, Kay. Farrel, I will grant you a renewal of the mortgage. I'm weary of being a Shylock."

"Thanks ever so much. I do not desire it, Mr. Parker. One of these bright days when I get around to it, and provided luck breaks my way, I'll take up that mortgage before the redemption period expires. I have resolved to live my life free from the shadow of an accursed mortgage. Let me see, now. We were talking about horse racing, were we not?"

"Miguel Farrel, you'd anger a sheep," Parker cried wrathfully, and strode away toward his automobile waiting in the infield. Kay and Don Mike watched him drive straight across the valley to the road and turn in the direction of El Toro.

"Wilder than a March hare," Don Mike commented.

"Not at all," Kay assured him. "He's merely risking his life in his haste to reach El Toro and telegraph Dan Leighton to report immediately."

XXXI

JOHN PARKER'S BOREDOM HAD BEEN CURED by a stopwatch. One week after Panchito had given evidence of his royal breeding, Parker's old trainer, Dan Leighton, arrived at the Palomar. Formerly a jockey, he was now in his fiftieth year, a wistful little man with a puckered, shrewd face, which puckered more than usual when Don Mike handed him Panchito's pedigree.

"He's a marvelous horse, Danny," Parker assured the old trainer.

"No thanks to him. He ought to be," Leighton replied. His cool glance measured Allesandro Trujillo, standing hard by. "I'll have that dusky imp for an exercise boy," he announced. "He's built like an aeroplane—all superstructure and no solids."

For a month the training of Panchito went on each morning. Pablo's grandson, under Danny Leighton's tuition, proved an excellent exercise boy. He learned to sit his horse in the approved jockey fashion; proud beyond measure at the part he was playing, he paid strict attention to Leighton's instructions and progressed admirably.

Watching the horse develop under skilled scientific training, it occurred to Don Mike each time he held his father's old stopwatch on Panchito that racehorses had, in a great measure, conduced to the ruin of the Noriagas and Farrels, and something told him that Panchito was

304

likely to prove the instrument for the utter financial extinction of the last survivor of that famous tribe. "If he continues to improve," Farrel told himself, "he's worth a bet—and a mighty heavy one. Nevertheless, Panchito's grandfather, leading his field by six open lengths in the homestretch, going strong and a surefire winner, tangled his feet, fell on his nose and cost my father a thousand steers six months before they were ready for market. I ought to leave John Parker to do all the betting on Panchito, but—well, he's a racehorse— and I'm a Farrel."

"When will Panchito be ripe to enter in a mile and a sixteenth race?" he asked Parker.

"About the middle of November. The winter meeting will be on at Tia Juana, Baja California, then, and Leighton wants to give him a few tryouts there in fast company over a much shorter course. We will win with him in a field of ordinary nags and we will be careful not to win too far or too spectacularly. We have had his registry brought up to date and of course you will be of record as his owner. In view of our plans, it would never do for Danny and me to be connected with him in any way."

Don Mike nodded and rode over to Agua Caliente Basin to visit Bill Conway. Mr. Conway was still on the job, albeit Don Mike hazarded a guess that the old schemer had spent almost two hundred thousand dollars. His dam was, as he facetiously remarked, "taking concrete shape," and he was rushing the job in order to have the structure thoroughly dry and "set" against the coming of the winter rains. To his signal relief, Farrel asked him no embarrassing questions regarding the identity of the extremely kind hearted person who was financing him; he noticed that his young friend appeared a trifle preoccupied and depressed. And well he might be. The secret knowledge that he was obligated to Kay Parker to the extent of the cost of this dam was irritating to his pride; while he felt that her loving interest and sympathy, so tremendously manifested, was in itself a debt he would always rejoice in because he never could hope to repay it, it did irk him to be placed in the position of never being able to admit his knowledge of her action. He prayed that Bill Conway would be enabled to complete the dam as per his contract; that Judge Morton would then rush to trial Conway's suit for damages against Parker for non-performance of contract; that Conway would be enabled immediately to reimburse himself through Parker's assets which he had attached, repay Kay and close the transaction.

On November fifteenth Danny Leighton announced that Panchito was "right on edge" and, with a few weeks of experience in professional company, fit to make the race of his career. The winter meeting was already on at Tia Juana and, with Farrel's consent Panchito was lovingly deposited in a well-padded crate mounted on a motor truck and transported to El Toro. Here he was loaded in an express car and, guarded by Don Mike, shipped not to Tia Juana, as Parker and his trainer both supposed he would be, but to San Diego, sixteen miles north of the international boundary—a change of plan originating with Farrel and by him kept a secret from Parker and Danny Leighton. With Panchito went an ancient Saratoga trunk, Pablo Artelan, and little Allesandro Trujillo, ragged and barefooted as usual.

Upon arriving in San Diego Don Mike unloaded Panchito at the Santa Fé depot. Gone now were the leg bandages and the beautiful blanket with which Danny Leighton had furnished Panchito at starting. These

306

things proclaimed the racehorse, and that was not part of Don Mike's plan. He led the animal to a vacant lot a few blocks from the depot and, leaving him there in charge of Pablo, went up town to the Mexican consulate and procured passports into Baja California for himself and Allesandro. From the consulate he went to a local stockyard and purchased a miserable, flea-bitten, dejected saddle mule, together with a dilapidated old stock saddle with a crupper, and a well-worn horsehair hackamore.

Returning to the depot, he procured his old Saratoga trunk from the station master and removed from it the beautiful black-leather, hand carved, silver-mounted stock saddle he had won at a *rodeo* some years previous; a pair of huge, heavy, solid silver Mexican spurs, with tan carved leather straps, and a finely plaited handmade rawhide bridle, *sans* throatlatch and browband and supporting a long, cruel, solid silver Spanish bit, with silver chain chin-strap and heavily embossed. In this gear he arrayed Panchito, and then mounted him. Allesandro mounted the flea-bitten mule, the old Saratoga trunk was turned over to Pablo, and with a fervent "*Adios,* Don Miguel. Go with God!" from the old majordomo, Don Mike and his little companion rode south through the city toward the international boundary.

They crossed at Tecarte next day and in the somnolent little border town Don Mike made sundry purchases and proceeded south on the road toward Ensenada.

Meanwhile, John Parker, his wife and daughter and Danny Leighton had motored to San Diego and taken rooms at a hotel there. Each day they attended the races at Tia Juana, and as often as they appeared there they

307

looked long and anxiously for Don Miguel José Federico Noriaga Farrel. But in vain.

Three days before Thanksgiving the entries for the Thanksgiving handicap were announced, and when Danny Leighton read them in the morning paper he at once sought his employer.

"That fellow Farrel has spoiled everything," he complained furiously. "He's entered Panchito in the Thanksgiving Handicap at a mile and a sixteenth, for a ten thousand dollar purse. There he is!"

Parker read the list and sighed. "Well, Panchito is his horse, Danny. He has a right to enter him if he pleases—hello! Katie! Kay! Here's news for you. Listen!"

He read aloud:

DON QUIXOTE AND SANCHO PANZA, JR.

ARRIVE AT TIA JUANA—THEY ENTER PANCHITO IN THE THANKSGIVING HANDICAP

By the Rail Bird

Considerable interest having developed among the followers of the sport of kings at Tia Juana racetrack anent the entry of Panchito in the Thanksgiving Handicap, and the dope books yielding nothing, your correspondent hied him to the office of the secretary of the Lower California Jockey Club; whereupon he was regaled with the following extraordinary tale:

Two days ago a Mexican rode into Tia Juana from the south. He was riding Panchito and his outfit was the last word in Mexican magnificence. His saddle had cost him not a *real* less than five hundred dollars gold; his silver spurs could have been pawned in any Tia Juana loan office for twenty-five dollars and many a longing glance was cast on a magnificent bridle that would have cost any bricklayer a month's pay. Panchito, a splendid big chestnut with two white stockings and a blazed face, was gray with sweat and alkali dust and shod like a plow horse. He wore cactus burrs in his tail and mane and had evidently traveled far.

His rider claimed to have been on the road a week, and his soiled clothing and unshaven face gave ample testimony of that fact. He was arrayed in the traditional costume of the Mexican ranchero of means and spoke nothing but Spanish, despite which handicap the racing secretary gleaned that his name was Don Miguel José Maria Federico Noriaga Farrelle. Following Don Miguel came Sancho Panza, Junior, a stringy Indian youth of fourteen summers, mounted on an ancient flea-bitten mule. The food and clothing of these two adventurers were carried behind them on their saddles.

An interpreter informed the secretary that Don Miguel was desirous of entering his horse, Panchito, in the Thanksgiving Handicap. The horse's registration papers being in order, the entry was accepted, Don Quixote and Sancho Panza, Junior, were each given a badge, and a stall was assigned to Panchito. At the same time Don Quixote made application for an apprentice license for young Sancho Panza, who answers to the name of Allesandro Trujillo, when the *enchiladas* are ready.

Panchito, it appears, is a five-year-old, bred by Michael J. Farrel, whose post-office address is El Toro, San Marcos County, California. He is bred in the purple, being a descendant of Duke of Norfolk and, according to his present owner, Don Quixote, he can run circles around an antelope and has proved it in a number of scrub races at various *fiestas* and celebrations. According to Don Quixote, his horse has never hitherto appeared on a public racetrack. Panchito knows far more about herding and roping steers than he does about professional racing, and enters the list with no preparation other than the daily exercise afforded in bearing his owner under a forty-pound stock saddle and scrambling through the cactus after longhorns. Evidently Don Quixote knows it all. He brushed aside with characteristic Castilian grace some well-meant advice tendered him by his countrymen, who have accumulated much racing wisdom since the bangtails have come to Tia Juana. He spent the entire day yesterday telling everybody who understands Spanish what a speed marvel is his Panchito, while Sancho Panza, Junior, galloped Panchito gently around the track and warmed him in a few quarter mile sprints. It was observed that the cactus burrs were still decorating Panchito's tail and mane.

Don Quixote is a dead game Mexican sport, however. He has a roll that would choke a hippopotamus and appears willing to bet them as high as a hound's back.

Figure it out for yourself. You pays your

money and you takes your choice. Bobby Wilson, the handicapper, says Don Quixote smokes *marijuana*, but the *jefe politico* says he knows it's the fermented juice of the century plant. However, Bobby is taking no chances as the wise ones will note when they check the weights. Panchito, being a powerful horse and (according to Don Quixote) absolutely unbeatable, faces the barrier with an impost of 118 pounds, not counting his shoes, cactus burrs and stable accumulations.

Watch for Sancho Panza, Junior. He rides barefooted in a two-piece uniform, to wit, one "nigger" shirt and a pair of blue bib overalls, and *Viva* Panchito. *Viva* Don Quixote. *Ditto* Sancho Panza, Junior.

John Parker finished reading and his glance sought Leighton's. "Danny," he informed the trainer in a low voice, "here is what I call a dirty, low, Irish trick. I suppose he's been making a night bird out of Panchito, but you can bet your last nickel he isn't neglecting him when they're alone in the barn together. He gets a grooming then; he gets well fed and well rubbed and the cactus burrs and the stable accumulations are only scenery when Panchito's on parade. He removed the racing plates you put on Panchito and substituted heavy work shoes, but—Panchito will go to the post with racing plates. I think we had better put a bet down on him."

"I wouldn't bet tin money on him," Danny Leighton warned. "He can outrun anything in that field, even if he has broken training a little, but those wise little jockeys on the other horses will never let him win. They'll pocket him and keep him there."

"They'll not!" Kay's voice rose sharply. "Panchito will be off first, no matter what position he draws, and Don Mike's orders to Allesandro will be to keep him in front. But you are not to bet on him, father."

"Why not? Of course I shall bet on him."

"You know very well, Dad, that there are no bookmakers of Tia Juana to make the odds. The Paris Mutuel system obtains here and the public makes the odds. Consequently the more money bet on Panchito the lower will be his price. I'm certain Don Mike will bet every dollar he has in the world on Panchito, but he will bet it, through trusted agents, in poolrooms all over the country. The closing price here should be such that the poolrooms should pay Don Mike not less than fifteen to one."

"So you've been his confidante, have you?" Parker scrutinized his daughter quizzically.

"He had to take somebody into his confidence in order to have his plans protected," she confessed blushingly.

"Quite so! Somebody with a deal of influence," Mrs. Parker interjected. "John, this is simply delicious. That rascal of a Don Miguel has reverted to type. He has put aside his Celtic and Gaelic blood and turned Mexican. He tells people the truth about his horse and a reporter with a sense of humor has advertised these truths by writing a funny story about him and Panchito and the Indian imp."

"They'll have him up in the judge's stand for an explanation five minutes after the race is won," Danny Leighton declared. "Panchito will be under suspicion of being a ringer and the payment of bets will be held up ."

"In which case, dad," Kay reminded him demurely,

312

"you and Mr. Leighton will be furnished with an excellent opportunity to prove yourselves heroes. Both of you will go to the judge's stand immediately and vouch for Don Mike and Panchito. If you do not I shall—and I fancy John Parker's daughter's testimony will be given some consideration, Mr. John Parker being very well known to every racing judge in America."

"There are days," murmured John Parker sadly, "when I find it impossible to lay up a cent. I have nurtured a serpent in my bosom."

"Tush! There are no snakes in Ireland," his humorous wife reminded him. "What if Don Mike has hoisted you on your own petard? Few men have done as much," and she pinched his arm lovingly.

XXXII

FOUR DAYS BEFORE THANKSGIVING Brother Anthony returned from El Toro with Father Dominic's little automobile purring as it had not purred for many a day, for expert mechanics had given the little car a thorough overhauling and equipped it with new tires and brake lining at the expense of Miguel Farrel. Father Dominic looked the rejuvenated ruin over with prideful eyes and his saintly old face puckered in a smile.

"Brother Anthony," he declared to that mildly crack-brained person, "that little conveyance has been responsible for many a furious exhibition of temper on your part. But God is good. He will forgive you, and has He not proved it by moving our dear Don Mike to save you from the plague of repairing it for many months to come?"

Brother Anthony, whose sense of humor, had he ever

313

possessed one, had long since been ruined in his battles with Father Dominic's automobile, raised a dour face.

"Speaking of Don Miguel, I am informed that our young Don Miguel has gone to Baja California, there to race Panchito publicly for a purse of ten thousand dollars gold. I would, Father Dominic, that I might see that race."

Father Dominic laid his hand on poor Brother Anthony's shoulder. "Because you have suffered for righteousness' sake, Brother Anthony, your wish shall be granted. Tomorrow you shall drive Pablo and Carolina and me to Tia Juana in Baja California to see Panchito race on the afternoon of Thanksgiving Day. We will attend mass in San Diego in the morning and pray for victory for him and his glorious young master."

Big tears stood in Brother Anthony's eyes. At last! At last! Poor Brother Anthony was a human being, albeit his reason tottered on its throne at certain times of the moon. He did love racehorses and horseraces, and for a quarter of a century he had been trying to forget them in the peace and quiet of the garden of the Mission de la Madre Dolorosa.

"Our Don Mike has made this possible?" he quavered.

Father Dominic nodded.

"God will pay him," murmured Brother Anthony, and hastened away to the chapel to remind the Almighty of the debt.

Against the journey to Baja California, Carolina had baked a tremendous pot of brown beans and fried a hundred tortillas. Pablo had added some twenty pounds of jerked meat and chili peppers, a tarpaulin Don Mike had formerly used when camping, and a roll of bedding; and when Brother Anthony called for them at daylight the following morning, both were up and arrayed in their Sunday clothes and gayest colors. In an empty tobacco sack, worn like an amulet around her fat neck and resting on her bosom, Carolina carried some twenty-eight dollars earned as a laundress to Kay and her mother; while in the pocket of Pablo's new corduroy breeches reposed the two hundred dollar bills given him by the altogether inexplicable Señor Parker. Knowing Brother Anthony to be absolutely penniless (for he had taken the vow of poverty) Pablo suffered keenly in the realization that Panchito, the pride of El Palomar, was to run in the greatest horse race known to man, with not a *centavo* of Brother Anthony's money bet on the result. Pablo knew better than to take Father Dominic into his confidence when the latter joined them at the Mission, but by the time they had reached El Toro, he had solved the riddle. He changed one of his hundred dollar bills, made up a little roll of ten two dollar bills and slipped it in the pocket of the brown habit where he knew Brother Anthony kept his cigarette papers and tobacco.

At Ventura, when they stopped at a garage to take on oil and gasoline, Brother Anthony showed Pablo the roll of bills, amounting to twenty dollars, and ascribed his possession of them to nothing more nor less than a divine miracle. Pablo agreed with him. He also noticed that for reasons best known to himself, Brother Anthony made no mention of this miracle to his superior, Father Dominic.

At about two o'clock on Thanksgiving Day the pilgrims from the San Gregorio sputtered up to the entrance of the Lower California Jockey Club at Tia Juana, parked, and approached the entrance. They were hesitant, awed by the scenes around them. Father Dominic's rusty brown habit and his shovel hat

315

constituted a novel sight in these worldly precincts, and the old Fedora hat worn by Brother Anthony was the subject of many a sly nudge and smile. Pablo and Carolina, being typical of the country, passed unnoticed.

Father Dominic had approached the gateman and in his gentle old voice had inquired the price of admittance. It was two dollars and fifty cents! Scandalous! He was about to beat the gatekeeper down; surely the management had special rates for prelates—

A hand fell on his shoulder and Don Miguel José Maria Federico Noriaga Farrel was gazing down at him with beaming eyes.

"Perhaps, Father Dominic," he suggested in Spanish and employing the old-fashioned courtly tone of the *haciendado*, "you will permit me the great honor of entertaining you." And he dropped a ten dollar bill in the cash box and ushered the four *San Gregoriaños* through the turnstile.

"My son, my son," murmured Father Dominic. "What means this unaccustomed dress? One would think you dwelt in the City of Mexico. You are unshaven—you resemble a loafer in *cantinas*. That *sombrero* is, perhaps, fit for a bandit like Pancho Villa, but, my son, you are an American gentleman. Your beloved grandfather and your equally beloved father never assumed the dress of our people—"

"Hush! I'm a wild and woolly Mexican sport for a day, *padre.* Say nothing and bid the others be silent and make no comment. Come with me to the grandstand, all of you, and look at the races. Panchito will not appear until the fifth race."

Father Dominic bent upon Brother Anthony a glance which had the effect of propelling the brother out of earshot, whereupon the old friar took his young friend by the arm and lifted his seamed, sweet old face toward him with all the *insouciance* of a child.

"Miguel," he whispered, "I'm in the throes of temptation. I told you of the thousand dollars which the Señora Parker, in a moment of that great-heartedness which distinguishes her (what a triumph, could I but baptize her in our faith!) forced Señor Parker to present to me. I contemplate using it toward the needed repairs to the roof of our Mission. These repairs will cost at least three thousand dollars, and the devil has whispered to me—"

"Say no more about it, but bet the money," said Miguel. "Be a sport, Father Dominic, for the opportunity will never occur again. Before the sun shall set this day, your one thousand will have grown to ten. Even if Panchito should lose, I will guarantee you the return of your money."

Father Dominic trembled. "Ah, my son, I feel like a little old devil," he quavered, but—he protested no more. When Don Mike settled him in a seat in the grandstand, Father Dominic whispered wistfully, "God will not hold this worldliness against me, Miguel. I feel I am here on His business, for is not Panchito running for a new roof for our beloved Mission? I will pray for victory."

"Now you are demonstrating your sound common sense," Don Mike assured him. His right hand closed over the roll of bills Father Dominic surreptitiously slipped him. Scarcely had he transferred the Restoration Fund to his trousers' pocket when Brother Anthony nudged him and slipped a tiny roll into Don Miguel's left hand, accompanying the secret transfer with a wink that was almost a sermon.

"What news, Don Miguel?" Pablo ventured presently.

"We will win, Pablo."

"*Valgame dios!* I will wager my fortune on Panchito. Here it is, Don Miguel—one hundred and eighty dollars. I know not the ways of these Gringo races, but if the stakeholder be an honest man and known personally to you, I will be your debtor forever if you will graciously consent to attend to this detail for me."

"With pleasure, Pablo."

Carolina drew her soiled little tobacco bag from her bosom, bit the string in two and handed bag and contents to her master, who nodded and thrust it in his pocket.

Two tiers up and directly in back of Don Miguel and his guests, two men glanced meaningly at each other.

"Did you twig that?" one of them whispered. "That crazy Greaser is a local favorite, wherever he comes from. Those two monks and that *cholo* and his squaw are giving him every dollar they possess to bet on this quarter horse entered in a long race, and I'll bet five thousand dollars he'll drop it into that machine, little realizing that every dollar he bets on his horse here will depress the odds proportionately."

"It's a shame, Joe, to see all that good money dropping into the maw of those Paris Mutuel sharks. Joe, we ought to be kicked if we allow it."

"Can you speak Spanish?"

"Not a word."

"Well, let's get an interpreter. That Tia Juana policeman yonder will do."

"All right. I'll split the pot with you, old timer."

Directly after the first race a Mexican policeman touched Farrel on the arm. "Your pardon, *señor*," he murmured politely, "but two American gentlemen have asked me to convey to you a message of importance.

318

Will the *señor* be good enough to step down to the betting ring with me?"

"With the utmost delight," Don Miguel replied in his mother tongue and followed the policeman, who explained as they proceeded toward the betting ring the nature of the message.

"These two gentlemen," he exclaimed, "are bookmakers. While bookmakers who lay their own odds are not permitted to operate openly and with the approval of the track authorities, there are a number of such operating quietly here. One may trust them implicitly. They always pay their losses—what you call true blue sports. They have much money and it is their business in life to take bets. These two gentlemen are convinced that your horse, Panchito, cannot possibly win this race and they are prepared to offer you odds of ten to one for as much money as the *señor* cares to bet. They will not move from your side until the race is run and the bet decided. The odds they offer you are greater than you can secure playing your money in the Mutuel."

Don Mike halted in his tracks. "I have heard of such men. I observed the two who talked with you and the *jefe politico* assured me yesterday that they are reliable gentlemen. I am prepared to trust them. Why not? Should they attempt to escape with my money when Panchito wins—as win he will—I would quickly stop those fine fellows." He tapped his left side under the arm-pit, and while the policeman was too lazy and indifferent to feel this spot himself, he assumed that a pistol nestled there.

"I will myself guard your bet," he promised.

They had reached the two bookmakers and the policeman promptly communicated to them Don Mike's ultimatum. The pair exchanged glances.

"If we don't take this lunatic's money," one of them suggested presently, "some other brave man will. I'm game."

"It's a shame to take it, but—business is business," his companion laughed. Then to the policeman: "How much is our high-toned Mexican friend betting and what odds does he expect?"

The policeman put the question. The high-toned Mexican gentleman bowed elaborately and shrugged deprecatingly. Such a little bet! Truly, he was ashamed, but the market for steers down south had been none too good lately, and as for hides, one could not give them away. The American gentlemen would think him a very poor gambler, indeed, but twelve hundred and twenty-eight dollars was his limit, at odds of ten to one. If they did not care to trifle with such a paltry bet, he could not blame them, but—

"Holy Mackerel. Ten to one. Joe, this is like shooting fish on a hillside. I'll take half of it."

"I'll take what's left."

They used their cards to register the bet and handed the memorandum to Don Mike, who showed his magnificent white teeth in his most engaging smile, bowed, and insisted upon shaking hands with them both, after which the quartet sauntered back to the grandstand and sat down among the old shepherd and his flock.

As the bugle called out the horses for the handicap, father Dominic ceased praying and craned forward. There were ten horses in the race, and the old priest's faded eyes popped with wonder and delight as the sleek, beautiful thoroughbreds pranced out of the paddock and passed in single file in front of the grandstand The fifth horse in the parade was Panchito—and somebody had cleaned him up, for his satiny skin glowed in the semi-tropical sun. All the other horses in the race had ribbons interlaced in their manes and tails but Panchito was barren of adornment.

"Well, Don Quixote has had him groomed and they've combed the cactus burrs out of his mane and tail, at any rate. He'd be a beautiful animal if he was dolled up like the others," the bookmaker, Joe, declared.

"Got racing plates on today, and that *cholo* kid sits him like he intended to ride him," his companion added. "Joe, I have a suspicion that nag is a ringer. *He looks like a champion.*"

"If he wins we'll *know* he's a ringer," Joe replied complacently. "We'll register a protest at once. Of course, the horse is royally bred, but he hasn't been trained, he's never been on a track before and even if he has speed, both early and late, he'll probably be left at the post. He's carrying one hundred and eighteen pounds and a green *cholo* kid has the leg up. No chance, I tell you. Forget it."

Don Mike, returning from the paddock after saddling Panchito and giving Allesandro his final instructions, sat majestically in his seat, but Father Dominic, Brother Anthony, Pablo and Carolina paid vociferous tribute to their favorite and the little lad who rode him. Allesandro's swarthy hands and face were sharply outlined against a plain white jockey suit; somebody had loaned him a pair of riding boots and a cap of red, white and blue silk. This much had Don Mike sacrificed for convention, but not the willow switch. Allesandro waved it at his master and his grandparents as he filed past.

Pablo stood up and roared in English: "*Kai!* Allesandro! Eef you don' win those race you gran'father hee's goin' cut you throat sure. I look to you all the

321

time, *muchacho*. You keep the mind on the bus-i-ness. You hear, Allesandro *mio?*"

Allesandro nodded, the crowd laughed and the horse went to the post. They were at the post a minute, but got away to a perfect start.

"Sancho Panza leads on Panchito!" the bookmaker, Joe, declared as the field swept past the grandstand. He was following the flying horses through his racing glasses. "Quarter horse," he informed his companion. "Beat the gate like a shot out of a gun. King Agrippa, the favorite, second by two lengths, Sir Galahad third. At the quarter! Panchito leads by half a length, Sir Galahad second, King Agrippa third! At the half! Sir Galahad first, Panchito second, King Agrippa third! At the three-quarter pole! King Agrippa first, Panchito second, Polly P. third. Galahad's out of it. Polly P's making her spurt, but she can't last. Into the stretch with Panchito on the rail and coming like he'd been sent for and delayed. Oh, Lord, Jim, that's a horse—and we thought he was a goat! Look at him come! He's an open length in front of Agrippa and the *cholo* hasn't used his willow switch. Jim, we're sent to the cleaner's—"

It was a Mexican racetrack, but the audience was American and it is the habit of Americans to cheer a winner, regardless of how they have bet their money. A great sigh went up from the big holiday crowd. Then, "Panchito! Come on, you Panchito! Come on, Agrippa! Ride him, boy, ride him!" A long, hoarse howl that carried with it the hint of sobs.

At the paddock the gallant King Agrippa gave of the last and the best that was in him and closed the gap in a dozen furious jumps until, as the field swept past the grandstand, Panchito and King Agrippa were for a few seconds on such even terms that a sudden hush fell on

322

the race-mad crowd. Would this be a dead heat? Would this unknown Panchito, fresh from the cattle ranges, divide first money with the favorite?"

The silence was broken by a terrible cry from Pablo Artelan.

"Allesandro! I cut your throat!"

Whether Allesandro heard the warning or whether he had decided that affairs had assumed a dangerous pass, matters not. He rose a trifle in his saddle, leaned far out on Panchito's withers and delivered himself of a tribal yell. It was a cry meant for Panchito, and evidently Panchito understood, for he responded with the only answer a gallant racehorse has for such occasions. A hundred feet from the wire King Agrippa's wide-flung nostrils were at Panchito's saddle girth; under the stimulus of a rain of blows he closed the gap again, only to drop back and finish with daylight showing between his head and Panchito's flowing tail.

Father Dominic stood gazing down the track. He was trembling violently. Brother Anthony turned lackluster eyes toward Farrel.

"You win, Brother Anthony," Don Mike said quietly.

"How good is God," murmured Brother Anthony. "He has granted me a joy altogether beyond my deserts. And the joy is sufficient. The money will buy a few shingles for our roof." He slumped down in his seat and wiped away great tears.

Pablo waited not for congratulations or exultations, but scrambled down through the grandstand to the railing, climbed over it and dropped down into the track, along which he jogged until he met Allesandro galloping slowly back with Panchito. "Little treasure of the world," he cried to the boy, "I am happy that I do not have to cut your throat," and he lifted Allesandro out of the saddle and pressed him to his heart. That was the faint strain of Catalonian blood in Pablo.

Up in the grandstand Carolina, in her great excitement, forgot that she was Farrel's cook. When he was a baby she had nursed him and she loved him for that. So she waddled down to him with beaming eyes—and he patted her cheek.

"Father Dominic," Don Mike called to the old friar, "your Mission Restoration Fund has been increased ten thousand dollars."

"So?" the gentle old man echoed. "Behold, Miguel, the goodness of God. He willed that Panchito should save for you from the heathen one little portion of our dear land; He was pleased to answer my prayers of fifty years that I be permitted to live until I had restored the Mission of our Mother of Sorrows." He closed his eyes. "So many long years the priest," he murmured, "so many long years! And I am base enough to be happy in worldly pleasures. I am still a little old devil."

Don Mike turned to the stunned bookmakers. "For some reason best known to yourselves," he addressed them in English, bowing graciously, "you two gentlemen have seen fit to do business with me through this excellent representative of the civil authority of Tia Juana. We will dispense with his services, if you have no objection. Here, my good fellow," he added, and handed the policeman a ten dollar bill.

"You're not a Mexican. You're an American," the bookmaker Joe cried accusingly, "although you bragged like a Mexican."

"Quite right. I never claimed to be a Mexican, however. I heard about this Thanksgiving Handicap, and it seemed such a splendid opportunity to pick up a few thousand dollars that I entered my horse. I have

324

complied with all the rules. This race was open to four-year-olds and up, regardless of whether they had been entered in a race previously or had won or lost a race. Panchito's registration will bear investigation; so will his history. My jockey rode under an apprentice license. May I trouble you for a settlement, gentlemen ?"

"But your horse is registered under a Mexican's name, as owner."

"My name is Miguel José Maria Federico Noriaga Farrel."

"We'll see the judges first, Señor Farrel."

"By all means."

"You bet we will. The judges smell a rat, already. The winning numbers haven't been posted yet."

As Don Mike and his retinue passed the Parker box, John Parker and Danny Leighton fell in behind them and followed to the judges' stand. Five minutes later the anxious crowd saw Panchito's number go up as the winner. Don Mike's frank explanation that he had deceived nobody, but had, by refraining from doing things in the usual manner, induced the public to deceive itself and refrain from betting on Panchito, could not be gainsaid—particularly when an inspection of the records at the betting ring proved that not a dollar had been wagered on Panchito.

"You played the books throughout the country, Mr. Farrel?" one of the judges asked.

Don Mike smiled knowingly. "I admit nothing," he replied.

The testimony of Parker and Danny Leighton was scarcely needed to convince the judges that nothing illegal had been perpetrated. When Don Mike had collected his share of the purse and the bookmakers, convinced that they had been out-generaled and not

325

swindled, had issued checks for their losses and departed, smiling, John Parker drew Farrel aside.

"Son," he demanded, " did you spoil the Egyptians and put over a Roman holiday?"

Again Don Mike smiled his enigmatic smile. "Well," he admitted, "I'm ready to do a little mortgage lifting."

"I congratulate you with all my heart. For heaven's sake, take up your mortgage immediately. I do not wish to acquire your ranch—that way. I have never wished to, but if that droll scoundrel, Bill Conway, hadn't managed to dig up unlimited backing to build that dam despite me, and if Panchito hadn't cinched your case for you today, I would have had no mercy on you. But I'm glad you won. You have a head and you use it; you possess the power of decision, of initiative, you're a sporting, kindly young gentleman and I count it a privilege to have known you." He thrust out his hand and Don Mike shook it heartily.

"Of course, sir," he told Parker, "King Agrippa is a good horse, but nobody would ever think of entering him in a real classic. I told Allesandro to be careful not to beat him too far. The time was nothing remarkable and I do not think I have spoiled your opportunity for winning with him in the Derby."

"I noticed that. Thank you. And you'll loan him to me to beat that old scoundrel I told you about?"

"You'll have to arrange that matter with your daughter, sir. I have raced my first and my last race for anything save the sport of a horse-race, and I am now about to present Panchito to Miss Kay."

"Present him? Why, you star-spangled idiot, I offered you fifteen thousand dollars for him and you knew then I would have gone to fifty thousand."

Don Mike laid a patronizing hand on John Parker's

shoulder. "Old settler, you're buying Panchito and you're paying a heavier price than you realize, only, like the overcoat in the traveling salesman's expense account, the item isn't apparent. I'm going to sell you a dam, the entire Agua Caliente Basin and watershed riparian rights, a site for a power station and a right of way for power transmission lines over my ranch. In return, you're going to agree to furnish me with sufficient water from your dam, in perpetuity, to irrigate every acre of the San Gregorio Valley."

John Parker could only stare, amazed. "On one condition, Miguel," he replied presently. "Not an acre of the farm lands of the San Gregorio shall ever be sold, without a *proviso* in the deed that it shall never be sold or leased to any alien ineligible to citizenship."

"Oh, ho! So you've got religion, eh?"

"I have. Pablo dragged it into the yard last spring at the end of his riata, and it lies buried in the San Gregorio. That makes the San Gregorio consecrated ground. I always had an idea I was a pretty fair American, but I dare say there's room for improvement. What do you want for that power property?"

"I haven't the least idea. We'll get together with experts some day and arrive at an equitable price.

"Thank you son. I'll not argue with you. You've given me a first-class thrashing and the man who can do that is quite a fellow. Nevertheless, I cannot see now where I erred in playing the game. Mind telling me, boy?"

"Not at all. It occurred to me—assistance by Bill Conway—that this property must be of vital interest to two power companies, the Central California Power Company and the South Coast Power Corporation. Two hypotheses presented themselves for consideration.

327

First, if you were developing the property personally, you had no intention of operating it yourself. You intended to sell it. Second, you were not developing it personally, but as the agent of one of the two power companies I mentioned. I decided that the latter was the best hypothesis upon which to proceed. You are a multi-millionaire trained in the fine art of juggling corporations. In all probability you approached my father with an offer to buy the ranch and he declined. He was old and he was sentimental, and he loved me and would not sell me out of my birthright. You *had* to have that ranch, and since you couldn't buy it you decided to acquire it by foreclosure. To do that, however, you had to acquire the mortgage, and in order to acquire the mortgage you had to acquire a controlling interest in the capital stock of the First National Bank of El Toro. You didn't seem to fit into the small town banking business; a bank with a million dollars capital is small change to you."

"Proceed. You're on the target, son, and something tells me you're going to score a bull's-eye in a minute."

"When you had acquired the mortgage following such patient steps, my father checkmated you by making and recording a deed of gift of the ranch to me, subject of course to the encumbrance. The wartime moratorium, which protected men in the military or naval service from civil actions, forced you to sit tight and play a waiting game. Then I was reported killed in action. My poor father was in a quandary. As he viewed it, the ranch now belonged to my estate, and I had died intestate. Probate proceedings dragging over a couple of years were now necessary, and a large inheritance tax would have been assessed against the estate. My father broke under the blow and you took possession. Then I

328

returned—and you know the rest.

"I knew you were powerful enough to block any kind of a banking loan I might try to secure and I was desperate until Bill Conway managed to arrange for his financing. Then, of course, I realized my power. With the dam completed before the redemption period should expire, I had something definite and tangible to offer the competitor of the power company in which you might be interested. I was morally certain I could save my ranch, so I disabused my mind of worry."

"Your logical conclusions do credit to your intelligence, Miguel. Proceed."

"I purchased, through my attorney, a fat little block of stock in each company. That gave me *entrée* to the company books and records. I couldn't pick up your trail with the first company investigated—the Central California—but before my attorney could proceed to Los Angeles and investigate the list of stockholders and directors of the South Coast Power Corporation, a stranger appeared at my attorney's office and proceeded to make overtures for the purchase of the Agua Caliente property on behalf of an unknown client. That man was in conference with my attorney the day we all motored to El Toro via La Questa Valley, and the instant I poked my nose inside the door my attorney advised me—in Spanish,—which is really the mother tongue of El Toro—to trail his visitor. Out in the hall I met my dear friend, Don Nicolás Sandoval, the sheriff of San Marcos County, and delegated the job to him. Don Nicolás trailed this stranger to the First National Bank of El Toro and observed him in conference with the vice-president; from the First National Bank of El Toro Don Nicolás shadowed his man to the office of the president of the South Coast Power Corporation, in Los Angeles.

"We immediately opened negotiations with the Central California Power Company and were received with open arms. But, strange to relate, we heard no more from the South Coast Power Corporation. Very strange, indeed, in view of the fact that my attorney had assured their representative of my very great desire to discuss the deal if and when an offer should be made me."

John Parker was smiling broadly. "Hot, red hot, son," he assured Farrel. "Good nose for a long, cold trail."

"I decided to smoke you out, so arbitrarily I terminated negotiations with the Central California Power Company. It required all of my own courage and some of Bill Conway's to do it, but—we did it. Within three days our Los Angeles friend again arrived in El Toro and submitted an offer higher than the one made us by the Central California Power Company. So then I decided to shadow you, the president of the South Coast Power Corporation, and the president of the Central California Power Company. On the fifteenth day of October, at eight o'clock, P.M., all three of you met in the office of your attorney in El Toro, and when this was reported to me, I sat down and did some thinking, with the following result:

"The backing so mysteriously given Bill Conway had you worried. You abandoned all thought of securing the ranch by foreclosure, and my careless, carefree, indifferent attitude confirmed you in this. Who, but one quite certain of his position, would waste his time watching a racehorse trained? I knew then that news of my overtures to the Central California people were immediately reported to the South Coast people. Evidently you had a spy on the Central California payroll, or else you and your associates controlled both

330

companies. This last hypothesis seemed reasonable, in view of the South Coast Power Corporation's indifference when it seemed that I might do business with the Central California people, and the sudden revival of the South Coast interest when it appeared that negotiations with the Central people were terminated. But after that meeting on the fifteenth of October, my attorney couldn't get a rise out of either corporation, so I concluded that one had swallowed the other, or you had agreed to form a separate corporation to develop and handle the Agua Caliente plant, if and when, no matter how, the ranch should come into your possession I was so certain you and your fellow conspirators had concluded to stand pat and await events that I haven't been sleeping very well ever since, although not once did I abandon my confident pose.

"My position was very trying. Even with the dam completed, your power in financial circles might be such that you could block a new loan or a sale of the property, although the completion of the dam would add a value of millions to the property and make it a very attractive investment to a great many people. I felt that I could save myself if I had time, but I might not have time before the redemption period should expire. I'd have to lift that mortgage before I could smoke you three foxes out of your hole and force you to reopen negotiations. Well, the only chance I had for accomplishing that was a long one—Panchito, backed by every dollar I could spare, in the Thanksgiving Handicap. I took that chance. I won. Tag! You're It."

"Yes, you've won, Miguel. Personally, it hurt me cruelly to do the things I did, but I was irrevocably tied up with the others. I hoped—I almost prayed—that the unknown who was financing Bill Conway, in order to

331

render your property valuable and of quick sale, to save your equity, might also give you a loan and enable you to eliminate me. Then my companions in iniquity would be forced to abandon their waiting game and deal with you. You are right, Miguel. That waiting game might have been fatal to you."

"It *would* have been fatal to me, sir."

"Wouldn't Conway's friend come to your rescue?"

"I am not informed as to the financial resources of Bill Conway's friend and, officially, I am not supposed to be aware of that person's identity. Conway refused to inform me. I feel assured, however, that if it were at all possible for this person to save me, I would have been saved. However, even to save my ranch, I could not afford to suggest or request such action."

"Why?"

"Matter of pride. It would have meant the violation of my code in such matters."

"Ah, I apprehend. A woman, eh? That dashing Sepulvida girl?"

"Her mother would have saved me—for old sake's sake, but—I would have been expected to secure her investment with collateral in the shape of a six dollar wedding ring."

"So the old lady wanted you for a son-in-law, eh? Smart woman. She has a long, sagacious nose. So she proceeded, unknown to you, to finance old Conway, eh?"

"No, she did not. Another lady did."

"What a devil you are with the women! Marvelous — for one who doesn't pay the slightest attention to any of them. May I ask if you are going to—ah—marry the other lady?"

"Well, it would never have occurred to me to propose

332

to her before Panchito reached the wire first, but now that I am my own man again and able to match her, dollar for dollar, it may be that I shall consider an alliance, provided the lady is gracious enough to regard me with favor."

"I wish you luck," John Parker replied coldly. "Let us join the ladies."

Three days later, in El Toro, Don Mike and his attorney met in conference with John Parker and his associates in the office of the latter's attorney and completed the sale of the Agua Caliente property to a corporation formed by a merger of the Central California Power Company and the South Coast Power Corporation. A release of mortgage was handed Miguel Farrel as part payment, the remainder being in bonds of the South Coast Power Corporation, to the extent of two million dollars. In return, Farrel delivered a deed to the Agua Caliente property and right of way and a dismissal, by Bill Conway, of his suit for damages against John Parker, in return for which John Parker presented Farrel an agreement to reimburse Bill Conway of all moneys expended by him and permit him to complete the original contract for the dam.

"Well, that straightens out our muchly involved affairs," John Parker declared. "Farrel, you've gotten back your ranch, with the exception of the Agua Caliente Basin, which wasn't worth a hoot to you anyway, you have two million dollars in good sound bonds and all the money you won on Panchito. By the way. if I may be pardoned for my curiosity, how much money did you actually win that day?"

Don Mike smiled, reread his release of mortgage, gathered up his bundle of bonds, backed to the door, opened it and stood there, paused for flight.

333

"Gentlemen," he declared, "I give you my word of honor—no, I'll give you a Spaniard's oath—I swear, by the virtue of my dead mother and the honor of my dead father, I did not bet one single *centavo* on Panchito for myself, although I did negotiate bets for Brother Anthony, Father Dominic, and my servants, Pablo and Carolina. Racing horses and betting on horse racing has proved very disastrous to the Noriaga-Farrel tribe, and the habit ceased with the last survivor of our dynasty. I'm not such a fool, Señor Parker, as to risk my pride and my position and my sole hope of a poor but respectable future by betting the pitiful remnant of my fortune on a horse-race. No, sir, not if Panchito had been entered against a field of mules *Adios, señores!*"

"In the poetical language of your wily Latin ancestors," John Parker yelled after him, "*Adios!* Go with God!" He turned to his amazed associates. "How would you old penny pinchers and porch climbers like to have a broth of a boy like that fellow for a son-in-law?" he demanded.

"Alas! My only daughter has already made me a grandfather," sighed the president of the Central California Power Company.

"Let's make him president of the merger," the president of the South Coast Power Corporation suggested. "He ought to make good. He held us up with a gun that wasn't loaded. Whew-w-w! Boys! Whatever happens, let us keep this a secret, Parker."

"Secret your grandmother! I'm going to tell the world. We deserve it. Moreover, that fine lad is going to marry my daughter; she's the genius who double-crossed her own father and got behind Bill Conway. God bless her. God bless him. Nobody can throttle my pride in that boy and his achievements. You two tried to mangle him and you forced me to play your game. While he was earning the medal of honor from Congress, I sat around planning to parcel out his ranch to a passel of Japs. I'll never be done with hating myself."

That night at the *hacienda,* Don Mike, taking advantage of Kay's momentary absence, drew Mr. and Mrs. Parker aside.

"I have the honor to ask you both for permission to seek your daughter's hand in marriage," he announced with that charming, old-fashioned Castilian courtliness which never failed to impress Mrs. Parker. Without an instant's hesitation she lifted her handsome face and kissed him.

"I move we make it unanimous," Parker suggested, and gripped Don Mike's hand.

"Fine," Don Mike cried happily. He was no longer the least bit Castilian; he was all Gaelic-American. "Please clear out and let me have air," he pleaded, and fled from the room. In the garden he met Kay, and without an instant's hesitation took her by the arm and led her over to the sweet lime tree.

"Kay," he began, "on such a moonlit night as this, on this same spot, my father asked my mother to marry him. Kay, dear, I love you. I always shall. I have never been in love before and I shall never be in love again. There's just enough Celt in me to make me a one girl man, and since that day on the train when you cut my roast beef because my hand was crippled, you've been the one girl in the world for me. Until today, however, I did not have the right to tell you this and to ask you, as I now do, if you love me enough to marry me; if you think you could manage to live with me here most of the time—after I've restored the old place somewhat. Will

335

you marry me, Kay—ah, you will, you will!"

She was in his arms, her flower face upturned to his for his first kiss.

They were married in the quaint, old-world chapel of the now restored Mission de la Madre Dolorosa by Father Dominic, and in accordance with ancient custom, revived for the last time, the master of Palomar gave his long delayed *fiesta* and barbecue, and the rich and the poor, honest men and wastrels, the *gente* and the *peons* of San Marcos County came to dance at his wedding.

Their wedding night Don Mike and his bride spent, unattended save for Pablo and Carolina, in the home of his ancestors. It was still daylight when they found themselves speeding the last departing wedding guest; hand in hand they seated themselves on the old bench under the catalpa tree and gazed down into the valley. There fell between them the old sweet silence that comes when hearts are too filled with happiness to find expression is words. From the Mission de la Madre Dolorosa there floated up to them the mellow music of the Angelus; the hills far to the west were still alight on their crests, although the shadows were long in the valley, and Don Mike, gazing down on his kingdom regained, felt his heart filled to overflowing.

His wife interrupted his meditations. He was to learn later that this is a habit of all wives.

"Miguel, dear, what are you thinking about?"

"I cannot take time to tell you now, Kay, because my thoughts, if transmuted into print, would fill a book. Mostly, however, I have been thinking how happy and fortunate I am, and how much I love you and that— yonder. And when I look at it I am reminded that but for you it would not be mine. Mine? I loathe the word. From this day forward—ours! I have had the ranch homesteaded, little wife. It belongs to us both now. I owed you so much that I could never repay in cash— and I couldn't speak about it until I had the right—and now that Bill Conway has taken up all of his promissory notes to you, and his suit against your father has been dismissed and we've all smoked the pipe of peace, I've come to the conclusion that I cannot keep a secret any longer. Oh, my dear, my dear, you loved we so you wouldn't let them hurt me, would you?"

She was holding his hand in both of hers and she bent now and kissed the old red scar in the old tender, adoring way; but said nothing. So he was moved to query:

"And you, little wife—what are you thinking of now?"

"I was thinking, my husband, of the words of Ruth: 'Entreat me not to leave thee, and to return from following after thee: for whither thou goest I will go; and where thou lodgest I will lodge; thy people shall be my people and thy God my God. Where thou diest will I die, and there will I be buried; the Lord do so to me, and more also, if aught but death part thee and me.'"

We hope that you enjoyed reading this
Sagebrush Large Print Western.
If you would like to read more Sagebrush titles,
ask your librarian or contact the Publishers:

Isis Publishing Ltd
7 Centremead
Osney Mead
Oxford
OX2 0ES
UK
+44 (0)1865 250333